Ghosts of Manila

GHOSTS

of

MANILA

James Hamilton-Paterson

FARRAR STRAUS GIROUX

NEW YORK

Library of Congress Cataloging-in-Publication Data
Hamilton-Paterson, James.
Ghosts of Manila / James Hamilton-Paterson. — 1st American ed.
    p.   cm.
1. Manila (Philippines)—Social life and customs—Fiction.
2. City and town life—Philippines—Manila—Fiction.   3. Violence—
Philippines—Manila—Fiction.   I. Title.
PR6058.A5543G54   1994
823'.914—dc20   94-14360

My thanks to Jun Bautista, Jim Gomez, Sen. Ernesto Herrera, Gene T. Javier, Frank Sionil José, Lynda T. Jumilla, Sen. Orlando Mercado, Elmer Mesina, Wilfredo P. Ronquillo and Armand C. Sebastian, as to all my friends in Caganhao. Especial gratitude is due Policarpio R. Mabilangan for his insights into aspects of Manila police work and, above all, to Tony Bergonia for patience and help during long sessions after-hours in 'Remember When'. It is a pleasure to acknowledge the tenacity and courage he and his press colleagues share.

I must stress that the characters in this book are entirely fictitious and that they, like the 'Philippine Heritage Museum' and its director, bear no relation to existing people or institutions.

J. H-P.

'Like other exotic disorders, amok does not require a unitary disorder to explain it. Its sudden pathognomonic onset is usually due to the fact that previous symptoms of distress have gone unnoticed, rather than to their sudden appearance.'

Lee Sechrest
(in Caudill & Lin [eds.],
Mental Health Research in Asia and the Pacific, 1969)

'The researches of many commentators have already thrown much darkness on this subject, and it is probable that, if they continue, we shall soon know nothing at all about it.'

Mark Twain

As we sweep out of night above certain tropic cities our gummy eyes take in the pinchbeck Manhattan of a new commercial centre, the crowded low-rise blocks slashed by grey arteries of highway thickening with morning's commuters, the brown photo-chemical bruise already rising among the layered airs and wisps of dawn. The hour is unreal, the place not obviously either destination or stopover. As the aircraft's PA system bings and bongs with needless advice and expressions of sycophantic goodwill, there come glimpses of ponds and fields dotted among the sprawl below. They are the last vestiges of a rural canker the city is slow to purge from its body, being indolent in its own massive inertia. By the time we have reached the ground and sunk back in a taxi we have forgotten these green and ochre patches. The view is once again of grimy streets full of the fluffy braying of exhausts, of shacks and shops and construction sites knitted together by overhead skeins of cable. It conforms all too neatly with the memory of previous visits and is easily dismissed as part of the necessary gauntlet to be run before the hotel, the cold shower, the bed can be reached. We never remember that behind these very streets – beyond where the side roads fray into muddy alleys and lead, in turn, along pathways of improvised duckboards through the perpetual slime of squatter areas – must lie those realms neither precisely fields nor waste lots which from the air looked briefly like implausible flecks of true countryside. On the ground they hide themselves with the stealth of cemeteries.

Such places are only ever flown over, never visited. They comprise a no-man's-land of a stuff which has especially low visibility, like the abandoned triangles between motorway junctions and flyovers everywhere, now lying beneath the elevated levels on which life takes place. Thus in broad daylight entire terrains can sink from view. Yet if the traveller to that distant city were to brave the directionless tangle of slums on foot, to persevere across rickety bridges over noxious black estuaries and along unpromising stretches strewn with the rusting chassis of dumped vehicles, he might win through into this hidden land. It exists as much in acoustic as in territorial terms, a demarcation of comparative quiet between the tumult of the city and the airport's intermittent thunder. Chickens are audible as they scratch the earth and comment on their findings. Ducks paddle in a plot of freshly irrigated taro plants. Beneath a mango tree, which would have been old before the first aircraft ever flew, a water buffalo is tethered, licking the flies from its nose with glutinous tongue. Far away between the white toadstools of water towers and the backs of hoardings an occasional high slab of primary colour moves across the horizon like the sail of a barge along an unseen canal. It is the tail fin of an airliner turning at the end of a runway or rumbling around the perimeter. Parching breaths of kerosene blow over the land.

Jet fuel is not the only thing to be smelt. Somewhere a sour heap of rubbish is always smouldering: melted plastic, scorched eggshells, singed leaves; while the various sheds dotted here and there are like as not the centres of cottage industries, each with its pungency. In one of them car batteries are being dismantled and the recoverable parts put into heaps outside. There is a hillock of plastic casings, a mound of electrodes, boxes of old terminals and other scraps of lead, some of which are presently being rendered down in a trypot over a butane stove. For many yards around the soil is bleached and bare, steeped in sulphuric acid. Some way off a man in a conical straw hat is spreading pig dung over his smallholding. His hut is in the shape of a parallelogram, leaning away from the airport as if it regularly took the blast of jet engines. This seems implausible; but just now a vast Boeing on its final approach is sagging overhead, lights blazing in broad day, so low the lines of rivets are visible, the entire monster ragged with extended flaps and dangling undercarriage doors and air brakes. Although it passes less than three hundred feet above the hut it leaves no appreciable wake, just the familiar smell of burning Jet A-1 and sonic vibrations which shake the air and batter the earth. It is sheer din, then, which causes the farmer's hut to lean. He himself never glances up but forks and throws, forks and throws the reeking nuggets.

Still nearer the airport, in a belt of tall reeds or perhaps sugar cane, there is a building rather larger than a family garage: a workshop solidly built of concrete blocks with a tin roof. Sometimes an appetising aroma of cooking drifts from it. Certainly the place is seldom without a few scavenging dogs skulking in and out of the reeds and sniffing the wind with fanatic glare. We would not be surprised to find a van drawn up outside with a sign in Chinese on it which mentioned *siopao* or *dimsum*, something containing little porky *bonnes-bouches*, at any rate. There is in fact a van drawn up but it belongs to the police on one of their regular visits. At the instant when the distant Boeing touches its wheels to the rubber-streaked runway two men are carrying a yellow bundle from the van into the workshop. Almost at once they re-emerge with a folded ochre tarpaulin, climb into the van and bump away along a track leading off through the screen of reeds towards a barbed-wire enclosure containing arrays of identically-angled lights to guide incoming pilots. Dwindling, the van skirts this and vanishes in the direction of the airport highway, on a raised section of which the coloured wink of traffic can be seen.

Behind the closed doors of the workshop a radio is playing Madonna's 'La Isla Bonita' and four Chinese are busy. They wear cotton singlets, shorts and rubber sandals, for despite twin extractor fans the air is hot and steamy. They also have on long aprons of clear plastic as well as surgeons' gloves. There has been some debate between them as to whether they ought to be wearing full protective clothing including masks, for wild rumours have reached them of AIDS, described variously as being harder to catch than TB or else of the toxicity of plutonium, such that a single atom of infection within a hundred yards infallibly homes in and condemns one to death. But then, it's a foreigner's disease and the body the police have just brought in is unmistakably that of a local, a young man probably in his early twenties with a wisp of moustache. He has two stab wounds, one in his chest and one in his back. Quick, in any case: heart, lungs and liver. Where he came from, who he was, nobody in the shed knows or wants to know. The chances are (for it is a fresh corpse) he is one of the police's own victims, street trash efficiently killed with an eye for a sale since apart from the two wounds the scrawny body is unmarked – unless one counts the gang logo tattooed on one buttock.

In the early days of this cottage industry the bodies had tended to be unidentified remains washed up on the foreshore or found ripely rotting, stuffed inside drainpipes or into barrels, still with their hands securely bound amid the bloat. Missing limbs, bones shattered by gunfire or bent by malnutrition had made the men's task harder. They would disassemble such skeletons entirely and put the bones into labelled polythene ice-cream containers. These were referred to as 'spare parts' which might later be useful for 'mix-'n'-match'. The men wore gauze masks soaked in cheap cologne which, even with lysol and alum crystals crunching underfoot, did little to sweeten the task. They were carried through more by things such as Madonna and gallows humour. Had they been apprentices thirty years younger they would have held maggot races in their lunch breaks. The irony was that now they had their business well established and could afford to deal almost exclusively with fresh bodies in reasonable condition, the end of the trade was in sight. The good old honest materials would no longer do, apparently. Everything nowadays was a substitute, a fake, phony. Plastic was on – and in the case of dentures, between – everybody's lips. Plastic was replacing cash. Plastic was replacing bone.

The building is divided into four areas corresponding to the stages of production, each jocularly named as if in a workshop specialising in the restoration of old vehicles. There are, in turn, 'the body shop', 'steam clean' and 'blow dry', 'rebuild' and 'the paint shop'. (It is in 'rebuild' that the skills of 'mix-'n'-match' have sometimes to be deployed. For instance, with the rise of Japanese gangs in the city Yakuza members turn up now and then with their left-hand wing mirrors missing: the top joint of the little finger. These have to be replaced from spare parts.) A long copper cauldron, much discoloured and holding 100 gallons, is held in a steel cradle above three gas burners. It is covered by a sheet of tin and, with steam escaping at the edges, looks like a monster fish kettle. One of the men goes over and with tongs lifts a corner of the tin. The water is bubbling fiercely so he turns down the gas to an economical simmer. The cauldron has been so long in use the steam smells of corrupt broth which mixes unhappily with the carbolic reek of lysol from the body shop. Two of the men now take down butcher's knives from a magnetic rack. As they do so another airliner passes low overhead, drowning the radio and rattling the roof. They pay no attention but quickly cross themselves in a perfunctory gesture which, apart from a crucifix on one wall with the legend 'Bless This House', is their only sign of superstition. All four Chinese are, as a matter of fact, Catholics. One takes the upper half of the body, the other the lower. Deftly they remove the arms and legs. Leaving the trunk lying on the stainless steel table with the gutters they transfer the limbs to polythene cutting blocks where they swiftly flense as much muscle and flesh as they can without nicking the bone. The meat goes into an orange plastic bin. They are intent as they work, their faces closed as against thought or smells. Neither face is harsh. Each might in time fall into the same deeply etched lines of their older companions to form expressions that only the most sentimental Westerner might have the confidence to call sorrowful. Soon one man takes the limbs, now ragged pink-and-white branches, still articulated, and drops them into the cauldron, turning up the gas. The head is meanwhile being dissected away from the top cervical vertebra. In this way the spine can be processed intact, leaving the discs of cartilage in place so that later they can be sterilised and dried out to the colour and consistency of hide dog chews. Nowadays, of course, in keeping with the general plastification of life, the discs can be replaced with silicone inserts, but the men prefer to work in the way they always have. They are none of them young and, watching them, one would think that in their deft, efficient manner they are craftsmen.

With the head off, one of the Chinese can easily work up from under the chin, removing tongue and palate. Then he slits from the back of the neck up through the middle of the scalp and down the forehead to the bridge of the nose. Changing to a smaller knife he separates the scalp from the skull, rumpling each half down in a rough roll of skin and hair. The victim's eyes are semi-closed, dry eyeballs gleaming dully between his lids. With his hair – which he must have had cut only a few days ago, his last-ever haircut – in a ruff about his ears and with his white peeled dome rising through it, this boy suddenly starts to look mutilated whereas before he looked like a body being dismembered. These, then, are the lips (now being sliced away from the

5

gums) his mother suckled, she who just might still have young children somewhere; these the cheeks she powdered against heat rash; this the face (now removed in two halves and dropped into the orange bin) of her son, her child, hope for the future, despair of the present. This face is dumped that was uniquely his own, the one which only yesterday afternoon friends and enemies still recognised in the street, which lovers had gazed at and fallen asleep by. Left are snarling teeth, popping eyes and, incongruously, a broad nose intact between them. A minute later it and the eyes have gone too and the pulpy mansion of his mind is being extracted through the hole in the base of his skull with a long-handled scoop. This is the technique pioneered by the ancient Egyptians, except that they more often removed the brain through the nose as one of those useless bits of stuffing which it was advisable to replace with sawdust and pieces of rag to prevent putrefaction. This present victim's head is likewise swiftly emptied. Grudges, memories, his mother's expression on his elementary school Graduation Day, the smell of copra drying one September morning in a province far away, the sound of Madonna herself – all these meld into a scrambled whitish heap. The empty skull is placed in a wooden box and rinsed out with short bursts from a high pressure water jet. Then it joins the limbs and torso in the cauldron. Another Boeing is homing in overhead. Businessmen reset their watches a hundred and eighty feet above the orange bin among whose contents is a wispy moustache. The roof stops rattling, a lid is put on the bin, the copper bubbles and the men sluice down the body shop. It has taken them twenty-seven minutes. Extractor fans whir and outside amongst the scrub the curs lift their noses.

If the victim's dismembering was efficient, his rebuilding is expert. After many hours' boiling the bones, all marrow leached out, leave 'steam clean' for 'blow dry': a large cabinet artfully constructed from the heating element and fans of a commercial tumble drier. They are then spread out on a table and inspected for adhering gristle, shreds of cartilage and the like. Again they are brought to the boil in a pickling solution containing formaldehyde and left to steep and cool for twenty-four hours. During this time the bactericide penetrates areas of finely divided bone such as the sinuses in the skull. The next day the bones will be redried before the young man's dismantled chassis is laid out on the long table in 'rebuild' and painstakingly fitted with a graded assortment of ready-made loops of brass wire. These are inserted in holes drilled with a small HobbyKraft air drill and fixed with clear Araldite epoxy resin. Phalange by phalange, metatarsal by metatarsal, the skeleton comes together. A larger brass ring is let into the top of the skull. The final stage will be in two days' time, when after passing once more through 'blow dry' it is hung in the 'paint shop' cabinet and sprayed with clear lacquer. Special orders sometimes require the ribs to be numbered in indian ink before being varnished. Usually the skeleton emerges unmarked, gleaming white, the loyal framework of a man who, four days ago, still walked the city's streets, cracking jokes and making mistakes like getting into police patrol cars. So, *ecce homo*: one export-quality skeleton for the use of medical departments, museums and ghoulish students thousands of miles away from his native land.

The four men form a specialist business somewhere between a cottage industry and a small firm, and as such are a legally constituted trading entity. They have various certificates and inspectorate slips to prove it, and by and large they abide by the rules. One of these forbids the sale of 'waste matter' for any purpose whatsoever, including fertiliser and animal feed. Every day the orange bin is trundled on a handcart to a fenced-off pit among the reeds and emptied together with the broth from the cauldron (which is, however, sieved first for stray teeth and bullets and the bones of the middle ear). Then a layer of quicklime is added, together with a covering of soil. To one of the fence posts a crucifix is tied. No-one besides the men ever comes near. Only the dogs approach, slinking and cringing and trembling with hunger at the scent in the air. The reeds whisper in the light, kerosene-laden breeze. Overhead the bleary travellers glance down and glimpse some peasants, perhaps, clinging nobly to their smallholding on the fringes of the city, still carrying on the timeless rituals of seed-time and harvest. Then the memory vanishes as the wheels thud onto the runway, sporadic applause breaks out from the rear of the economy section and the passengers' adrenaline count soars steeply with the anxiety of arrival.

Soon the young man's bones join those of a dozen others, including two children, already hanging in polythene garment bags on a rail in the stockroom. The buyer, another Chinese, will collect them all in a day or two but his visits are becoming less frequent even though the

7

price for the genuine article has been rising slightly as the market dries up. Rarity value, the men suppose. According to their information many developed countries have stopped importing real skeletons and have gone over to plastic. Or it may be that nations like India, which used to supply the majority of the British market until the mid-Eighties, have instead banned the export of their own ex-citizens. From now on illegal emigrants should be flesh and blood. Perhaps after all it is an uneasy business, smacking too much of Burke and Hare and unquiet graves.

Swabbing down and sweeping up to the sound of jet aircraft and pop songs the Chinese use a lot of water which runs away under the doors. The dogs wait for the lysol-flavoured runnels, fighting over nearly invisible strands of jelly. A skilled profession is winding down. Two of the men, who in evening light look almost elderly, might well retire. The other two – they are all distantly related to each other by blood or pacts – might stay on in business to fill special orders. One never knows where demand might come from. Only last month a trainee Buddhist arrived with the wrapped body of his master whose last wish had been that his bones might be used for his neophytes' meditation. Plastic might constitute a *memento mori* but was hardly as talismanic as the very bones of the teacher. Everyone thought this perfectly proper, including the police who saw no reason to interfere with religious wishes. They had taken their cut and gone their way. That had been good work: the two in the body shop had forgotten to cross themselves and had whistled while they worked. Some jobs just felt right.

2

WHO COULD remember 199-? Presidential shenanigans, monarchies on the blink. Growing populations of the homeless and workless swirling ever higher as if to swamp the classical columns of the nation states' capitols, a demotic pollution eating away at the very marble of the seats of government. Wars, famines, fresh prodigies of international terrorism. The usual furniture of world events, in short, being moved about the same old room, while from outside came the rumblings of the familiar volcano or earthquake or disastrous typhoon. All this in that same year plus, of course, a spectacular outbreak of vampirism in a Manila squatter area. That, too, was a recurrent story, certainly no more mythic than wheat futures.

It was the year in which John Prideaux submitted an unconventional text as his dissertation, having concluded there was no other way of writing it. If it posed as a fictional account it would at least have an edge of readability over the more familiar slabs of word-processorese which passed as anthropology. After all, fact, like justice, was negotiable. People sometimes said that a weakness of much modern fiction was that it tried too hard to be documentary rather than 'imaginative'; that it aspired to be journalism decked out with a few subjective ruffs and bows. Prideaux maintained that much journalism was vitiated by a pretence of objectivity. The average TV documentary, for example, had come to feel like pure fiction. Its language and conventions and formulae were all stock, by now so familiar that it dropped unremarked down the general well of

9

entertainment, at par with the news and re-runs of *The Flintstones*. Famine victims tottered and wept just as predictably as prime ministers emerged from shiny limousines smirking or careworn. *C'était leur métier.* (His views on the subject of newzak were all too familiar to members of the university's Faculty of Media Studies.)

He knew that an unconventional thesis ought as far as possible to be dressed up to resemble the regular article. Yet he soon found even this minimal disguise hard to achieve. It was usual at the outset to state the subject, after which the preferred method was to append the standard authorities and explain how one had managed to uncover, by sheer cleverness and originality, a loophole in their research or a weak point in the argument that fatally dated their work. Prideaux's problem was that, faced with the eventual pile of his own typescript, he no longer knew what the subject was. It was therefore impossible to follow with the customary abstract: the pithy couple of sentences in bold print which summarised the whole thing. 'Displaced Oklahoma dirt farmers enter the non-lucrative mid-1930s California citrus industry', he had once seen somebody précis *The Grapes of Wrath*. How could even the laziest academic think this was a useful exercise? Proper fieldwork could hardly be boiled down without gross distortion or banality any more than literature could.

He had also to confront the issue of his own middle-age, since he discovered it had a bearing on such matters. Maybe the typical anthropology student in their early twenties might have picked the sort of subject that could easily be summarised, which lacked resonance. But a mature student in his forties looked at a different world through different eyes. Who with daughters and sons of their own at university would think *'Kinship Systems Among the Nambikwara'* a nice, neutral little topic when the very word *family* had become synonymous with private anxiety, bafflement and guilt? The years went by and interests became more compromised and intricate even as tastes grew simpler. That went for theses, too. Such considerations were ignored by the academic establishment, whose judgements and expectations were based on the energetic callowness of comparative babies.

Initially, while still casting about for a suitable subject, Prideaux had been tempted by the wholly fictitious, as anyone would be who had once admired Carlos Castaneda. He had toyed with many titles, half prepared to research and write a thesis to match any which took his fancy. *'The Tribe That Dare Not Speak Its Name'* had had real possibilities and would have been a great pleasure to write. Only the difficulty of trying to invent a plausible location for this intensely superstitious and shy people had finally dissuaded him. Given the fictive nature of even the most scientific undertaking (its inventiveness, its arbitrariness as a human endeavour carried out according to human rules), he saw how the driest doctoral essay could become a *roman à thèse*. He had not considered this when he began his research and had given little thought to how his choice of topic was bound to be related to private preoccupations and public anxieties: the high whistling noise and cracking sounds as chips flew off interior façades. Was he not like the worried scientist in a disaster movie, taking an evening stroll along the top of the dam and suddenly noticing that the white lines in the middle of the road no longer quite match up? Eventually, though, his chosen area had seemed to settle itself; at the time he never wondered why. The very idea of a 'national character' was too nebulous and reductive for serious scholarship, but one might legitimately sidle up to it by calling the subject Transcultural Psychopathology. After all, every culture had its own peculiar vulnerabilities, no less than each individual, and these might be quite revealing. Accordingly he had reviewed the literature, beginning with the mediaeval dancing manias and children's crusades, through the epidemic religious hysterias such as the 'Jumpers' and 'Barkers' in the Eastern US to the nuns in a German convent who believed themselves possessed by, or changed into, cats. He knew, too, of more specific and exotic disorders. There was *pibloktoq* in which Eskimos – mainly women – lapsed into a fit of crying and speaking in tongues before sprinting away naked across the ice. There was *latah* in Malaysia which also usually afflicted middle-aged women, a trance state featuring zombielike obedience which could be precipitated by the sound of a bicycle bell or the mere mention of a name. And there was Windigo psychosis among the Cree and Ojibwa Indians, when the sufferer became nauseated by ordinary food and could only be satisfied by cannibalism.

Lastly, there was *amok*. John Prideaux had read his van Loon, his van Wulfften-Palthe, Yap, Caudill & Lin, Hirst & Woolley and much else. To these authorities *amok* was a standardised, culturally-acceptable form of emotional release, a disorder which, though temporary, often involved indiscriminate slaughter and for that reason equally often proved terminal to the patient. But such descriptions left him feeling they had stopped short. Had their authors been uneasier, less pedestrian, might they not have perceived an emblematic dimension to *amok*? The classic summary of its three stages (a period of brooding followed by homicidal frenzy and ending in exhausted amnesia) could equally well define extended periods of military service and combat duty, for instance. Come to that, it could apply to whole lives lived under any kind of unremitting stress. Was it too fanciful to imagine an entire society composed of individuals who, without knowing it, acted out from cradle to grave the symptoms of a chronic *amok* attack, slowed down by a factor of thousands? (If any of his examiners could say an unhesitating *Yes* at this point, Prideaux recklessly felt, they should stop reading at once and turn with relief to a more regular script.)

Finally, he knew that anthropology theses should be tricked out to look and sound 'objective' in a way that aspired to the scientific. It was even rather touching. Such a thing might just be feasible in a laboratory experiment involving transgenic mice, but despite the best intentions fieldwork was still conducted by people, and people were culturally-dependent constructs. To deal with people *was* to deal with fiction. Thus he figured in his own narrative as 'Prideaux', who by telling his own tale came in the end to sound disconcertingly like a character. Wishing (before he disappeared entirely) to observe what remaining norms he could, he thought it only proper to acknowledge his *dramatis personae*, all of whom he had interviewed extensively, thanking them sincerely for their often extreme patience and help. In alphabetical order they were:

> Vic Agusan
> Ysabella Bastiaan
> Fr. Policarpio Bernabe
> Insp. Gregorio Dingca, WPDC, City of Manila
> Crispa Gapat
> Fr. Nicomedes Herrera
> 'Capt. Melchior'
> Sharon Polick

Epifania Tugos
Sen. Benigno Vicente

It was Ysabella Bastiaan who stepped into his thesis the instant she exited the portals of Ninoy Aquino International Airport, Manila. Jet-lagged and wilting in the early morning heat within yards of leaving the air-conditioned concourse, she allowed herself to be taken over by white shirts and brown arms pulling her towards one taxi or another. We note that a curious passivity can overtake people after a long flight similar to that of patients newly arrived in hospital. There is the same desire to press foolish sums into the nearest hand in the hopes of soon being left alone in a cool dark room. According to her later description Ysabella found herself in a luxury cab padded in white Naugahyde whose windscreen was partly obscured by a portrait of Jesus hanging from the rear-view mirror with a sign reading 'Bless Our Trip O Lord We Pray' and the following verselet:

> Grant me, O Lord
> A Steady hand and
> A Watchful eye
> That no-one shall be hurt
> As I pass by.

Somewhere in the general ruckus beyond the tinted windows she caught sight of a newspaper vendor. The banner headline of a popular daily read (had she been able to understand it) 'Binondo Vampire Strikes Again! 3 Sucked Dry!' Without knowing it she had just entered the past. Or maybe the future. The present definitely eluded her as the taxi dragged through the badlands of Pasay before beginning the long haul down Roxas Boulevard, Manila Bay on her left and the irregular line of seafront properties to her right: nightclubs burnt out in gang wars interspersed with high rise apartment blocks and condos.

She reached Imelda Marcos's showpiece, the Philippine Cultural Center, and was swung eastwards into the tourist belt of Ermita, here coming to a near halt. The traffic was backed up like sewage. No lights were working. At occasional crossroads a man in khaki uniform was blowing a whistle and thrashing his arms.

'Brownout,' said her driver laconically. And indeed Ysabella had been wondering at all the little generators on the pavements adding their clatter and monoxides to that of the stalled traffic. Behind these was a series of clubs and bars, some with slats of wood nailed crosswise over their doors and painted with the slogan 'Closed By Order of Mayor Lim'. The others pulsed a dismal thudding of disco music into the generators' roar. Now and then a door opened briefly. Against the interior's perpetual night-time gleamed pale limbs and teeth and pallid dresses designed to shimmer electrically in ultraviolet lighting. At eleven-thirty in the morning? she wondered. She had entered that febrile state when things could be noticed but not taken in, leaving at their back a vague disquiet as of something fatally wrongheaded, of an intolerable future being presaged when the remainder of the planet would also be locked into slow-motion anarchy and din and the disruption of appropriate appetites.

Her hotel came into view trailing a thick diesel plume from its own generators, a blocky white cruise liner bound for nowhere. By the time she checked in, the glacial aircon calm of the hotel lobby was no antidote to her forebodings. Peace and private space were expensive commodities in rationed supply. The polished marble and uniformed bellhops gave off something precarious which mixed uneasily with the vanilla ghost of hot waffles seeping from an invisible coffee room. The corners of her eyes constantly picked up a tremble in the lights, the flicker of emergency power supply. Cycles per second. The concealed fluorescent tubes in the Hitachi lift buzzed faintly. Her curtained room felt rubberised in its insulation. Floor, walls and ceiling gave back not the slightest echo. Dead space for the dead tired. The bellhop turned the air-conditioner on and left her standing in an icy blast of mildew, yeasts and fungi. By parting the curtains Ysabella could see derelict rooftops and a traffic-locked street which the tinted glass turned wan mauve. From an inch away the pane transmitted the midmorning heat of outside. The airline passenger's world.

3

N OT MANY MILES to the south, beyond the outskirts of Manila at a place called Muntinlupa, was the National Penitentiary. Every morning police Inspector Gregorio ('Rio') Dingca practically passed its doors as he drove his unregistered stainless steel jeep into the city from his home in San Pedro, Laguna. From this prodigious jail, as well as from the various penal colonies scattered throughout the archipelago, some 2,725 prisoners had escaped in the previous five years, leading a senator to describe the prison system recently as 'Porous. Of a porosity impossible without the active connivance of the highest officials.' Inspector Dingca seldom wondered, when he passed the compound travelling in the other direction at night, how many were still there who had been inside that morning. Sooner or later he would probably find out.

After seventeen years on the force Dingca rated himself as peaceable. If he was in favour of 'salvaging' constant offenders who were a menace to society, and drove with his Llama copy of the 1911 Model Colt .45 automatic holstered and cocked on the transmission console next to him, he was no different from most of his colleagues. 'Don't make waves and be prepared' was the advice he gave to rookies. This unexceptional precept was too banal and grandmotherly to impress the new kids, who were mostly conscious only that they presented a gleaming target as they took their freshly-bought uniform out on patrol. Either that or they were eager to latch as soon as possible onto the various scams which could bump their wages up from the beggarly to within striking distance of the poverty line. They had, after all, paid for that new uniform out of their own pocket. Indeed, they had had to buy everything they stood up in from shoes to hat; everything except their badge and gun, and most replaced the gun as soon as they could afford to. This was a Squires Bingham .38 of local manufacture, generally rated as life-threatening to all except the person being fired at.

Some of the scams were dead simple. With a bit of help you could set up a *tong* collection point and take thirty pesos off every jeepney driver who passed, all day, every day. Do that for a month or two and you were talking big money, which was why the help would need to be quite senior. It was also advisable to bring in as many people for questioning as you could, irrespective of whether they were genuine suspects. From each one could mulct some *matrikula* or 'tuition fee'. It had a certain elegance to it, getting people to pay for their own wrongful arrest. But best of all were the grander deals which needed connections and seniority to bring off successfully. Of these, one of the most popular was hiring out prisoners for the day from Muntinlupa Penitentiary and other jails. There was elegance in this, too. The rich always needed crimes committed: a bank transfer stolen, a rival permanently removed, a grievance settled, a nightclub burnt down. Who better to use than a professional already behind bars for armed robbery or murder? The perfect alibi. Seen in this light, places like Muntinlupa were simply overcrowded talent pools waiting to be tapped.

One way to work it was to bribe the warden to allow your prisoner of choice out under armed escort for a checkup in a private clinic or hospital. At a pre-arranged moment he would disappear into medical regions, leaving his guards to some uneventful hours in a waiting room doing crosswords and flirting with nurses. Meanwhile the prisoner was speeding along the highway being briefed on his mission. A typical job would be like the one some weeks ago when a businessman was assassinated with an Armalite in broad daylight in Luneta within sight of strollers and their children as well as a scattering (*mot juste*) of tourists. By *merienda* time the killer was back in his cell in Muntinlupa, alibi intact, having struck a deal whereby he would be allowed to escape within the month at no risk of being shot. Guaranteed.

If Insp. Dingca was not outraged by such things it was because there was nothing to be done about them without changing the entire system, top to bottom. As that would include himself, and as the system sometimes worked in the police's favour, he thought this unlikely and probably undesirable. *Status quo.* And yet he had to admit the *status quo ante* had once been a lot better. For the first two or three years back in the Seventies Ferdinand Marcos's Martial Law had brought some discipline at last. A few significant heads had rolled. Rackets were regularised, if not actually cleaned up. Guns had been harder to come by. 'Shabu' (or 'crack' or whatever they called it in the States) had not yet been invented. Like many other cops, journalists and savants of recent history the Inspector was sure he could date the moment when things had started to go wrong, when the welcome orderliness of Martial Law began to slump irreversibly into total corruption. This had been on November 7th 1975 when Imelda Marcos became Governor of Manila, a few months before she appointed herself to her own newly-created post of Minister for Human Settlements. Poor old Marcos. It was often the way with these men of vision, Dingca thought. They never noticed until too late what was going on right under their own noses, the slow taking-over of the reins of power by some cunning bitch. By the time he had woken up to what was happening the wretched man was too ill to do anything about it, disinclined to stray too far from all that emergency medical hardware in Malacañang Palace.

God, this traffic was awful. . . For the last two years Dingca had been assigned to the Northern Capital Command under a police reshuffle, which was less than convenient for somebody living way to the south in San Pedro, Laguna. But he'd finally paid off the mortgage and was damned if he was going to up sticks and move now. Seventeen years ago the pressure on land hadn't been so acute and his lot in new Ylang-ylang Village had been generous. Nowadays he couldn't hope to afford anything as good elsewhere, not with his own mature mango tree in the yard, to say nothing of the kids' schools and the Bowl-o-Rama lanes one block over. No, he would stay put if the commuting killed him. Besides, it would be just his luck to move north of the river and find himself posted south within a couple of months. Ahead, the Superhighway traffic crawled beneath a rug of fumes which yet allowed the early sun to splash dazzlingly off windscreens and polished aluminium. A jeepney driver in front of him revved his engine and sent a sooty blare of frustration billowing from twin tailpipes, momentarily engulfing Dingca's open-sided jeep. The Inspector cursed and punched the squawk box on the roof. A siren under the hood wailed briefly and died with throaty menace. But what the hell was this? *Woo-woo-woo.* . . The bastard was razzing him *back*! Anarchy, right? Anyone with five hundred pesos could go into a shop and buy one of those little Taiwanese gadgets. They had a selector knob and gave a choice of twenty – check it out – *twenty* different wahs and wails: ambulance, police, bing-bongs, screamers, bells, whistles, you name it. Real cops were reduced to simmering in silence in traffic jams, a cocked automatic pistol by the gearshift and the day's first sweat beginning to pool around the coccyx.

There was some scheme afoot to lessen the rush hour by making government employees clock in at seven a.m. and go home at four, while private companies couldn't open before nine. In Dingca's opinion this was simply going to prolong the nightmare instead of diluting it. Out of office hours and outside Metro Manila the expressway turned into a racetrack with buses and jeepneys cutting each other up in clouds of smoke, chunks of rubber flying off their retreads. Vehicles going in unexpected directions, too, when one thought of that tanker a while ago laden with x gallons of coconut oil which had driven all the way up from Batangas or somewhere with a stopcock open leaving a seventy-mile oil slick behind it. That had been a caper. Over sixty accidents but by some miracle only two dead. Comedy, really. Sometimes you'd think this was Africa.

Half an hour later Insp. Dingca had just crossed the Pasig River which muddily bisected the city more or less east-to-west. He wished he could call the station on his radio, tell them he'd be late, make someone jump, just order up a cup of coffee. It had taken him a long time to pry loose the money for the radio – a natty Japanese hip-pocket affair with a stubby black antenna. Loose, that is, from the usual press of school fees, phone bills, water charges and just plain living, since it was his personal property. It crackled to an invisible world of commands and messages and curt witticisms, as well as long rambling calls about girls between parvenu executives. Still, having access to that world made him feel like a proper cop. Unlike in the American serials, though, the whole thing fell apart since the station had no funds to buy its own radio and nobody there could receive him. Most police work was done by phone. How – thought the Inspector as he turned into the station compound at last – was one expected to fight crime without the most basic equipment? Even the vehicles the cops used were mostly their own private cars, with no allowance for wear-and-tear or maintenance, just some coupons for a measly ration of fuel. What were 300 litres a month? Nothing, not in this traffic. In the middle of the compound was the station's only official vehicle, an aged Tamaraw, with one wheel off. In the back were three blue oil drums which he recognised. He braked by it.

'What now?'

'Bearing, Lieutenant.' The Tamaraw driver habitually used his old rank. His various assistants looked up from where they crouched, hands black with grease. 'Overloaded, probably.' This was said without a smile but Dingca knew his sergeant. 'Deadweight.'

'Better get a tarp over them. The sun.'

'Right.'

Dingca swung away and parked by the weapons range. He thrust the holstered pistol into his waistband, pulled his shirt down over it and trotted up the steps into the station, suddenly a tall and agile man and not another beer paunch with private wheels. On the splintered desk a candle guttered. The overhead fans were still. A couple of twilight figures were slumped in the holding pen.

'How long has Cruz been working on that Tamaraw?'

'Since night shift. Before I came on.' The fat desk sergeant wore a pair of tortoiseshell framed spectacles. 'He had to go up to Kalookan to get a new bearing. Asks to remind you to indent for it and go and pay them by lunch.' He produced an invoice.

'I'm afraid his passengers will be experiencing a slight delay.'

'No complaints yet,' said the desk sergeant, whose greying hair and horn rims gave him a benign, even wise, air.

'You can't say they weren't warned,' said Dingca. 'We told them often enough we'd give them a free ride to Malabon. Generous. They just weren't allowed to quibble about when.'

'There you are,' the sergeant agreed.

'So what's on?'

'Rumoured snap CapCom inspection, but they aren't going to do it while there's a brownout and the beer's warm. Couple of drunks in the tank. One of them's a Rugby-head, too. Doesn't look good. Keeps puking.'

'Cut him loose before he dies on us, Jun. Glue and rum? Get him out.'

'He couldn't walk out of here for a pension.'

'Jhon-Jhon in yet? Get him to take the fellow home, if he's got a home. Goodwill gesture. Support your local police. We're service-oriented, not mission-oriented. . . What have I left out?'

'Sniff only the best glue. Avoid inferior brands.'

'Right. That it?'

It was mid-morning before the battered Tamaraw, wheel restored, was ready to leave. An ochre tarpaulin covered the three blue drums in the back.

'I don't want to know, Cruz, but not that Chinese pie factory this time. One of your passengers is *intsik*, isn't he?'

'Sure, Lieutenant. They're going for a vacation by the sea. Miami Beach.'

4

UP AMONG the trestle tables heaped with shards and bones the two women had slipped into competitive mode. The Californian was slightly older and of much greater professional experience, while Ysabella was just Ysabella in a deplorably oblique, British sort of way – slightly grand, it had to be said. On grounds of looks it would be a truce. Ysabella thought Sharon resembled a toothpaste advertisement, actually; a little too aggressively healthy, especially for Manila. *Overjogged* was the word that came to her. Overjogged yet voluptuous. That wasn't right.

For her part Sharon had taken several days to identify the train of thought set in motion on first meeting her new assistant. Then she had remembered a noisy scandal involving a peer's daughter which was much in the yellow press headlines some years ago during her spell in the British Museum. She could still recall an evocative phrase from the tabloids: 'Raven-haired temptress "strict at bathtime".' Evocative of what, though? It was puzzling to the point of being faintly sinister, as if the British way of washing was subject to rigid codes of behaviour and baths were in any case rationed. For much of her time in London Sharon had thought there were a good few cultural subtexts she was missing, and this was more or less exactly what she now felt about Ysabella. She wondered if it were mutual. Ysabella was holding up a skull so deformed by binding it was practically boxlike.

'Unfortunate though this poor creature's life probably was, he or she at least had the great advantage of never having to travel by air.'

'You'd prefer to have walked to Manila?'

'I'd like to have come by sea. But given that one's virtually forced to fly everywhere nowadays, tell me why anything which aims for a mass market – be it air travel or fast food or advertising – always infantilises the consumer.'

'It does?'

'You can't not have noticed, surely. Airline travel, like having babies, does something terrible to the intelligence. They both entail a public discourse of mindless twitter. Imagine – grown women and men, often extremely distinguished, paying large sums of money to sit meekly for hours under a bombardment of nannyish announcements. Complete rubbish in a mixture of gentilityspeak and Dr Johnson. Talk about quaint, always presuming the airlines want their messages understood by a polyglot audience. What do we get?' Ysabella asked her skull. 'Lavatories are never at the back. *Toilets* are, instead, *located at the rear of the passenger compartment* and even sometimes *aft*. Passengers are never asked, they are *requested*. Cigarettes are never put out, only *extinguished*. Nobody ever says "Please don't smoke" in plain English. They say "You are requested to refrain from smoking". On my flight we were "kindly requested to refrain from opening the overhead compartments without undue caution". Without undue caution? Illiterate drivel. And as for that horrid little litany they tack onto everything, "For your own comfort and convenience", as if three hundred adults hadn't yet discovered what made them comfortable. . . Tell me that's not infantile. I rest my case.' Ysabella turned the skull around so its empty-eyed gaze faced Sharon.

'I guess your jury's been out a long time on that one, Counsellor. Since maybe the Twelfth century. But I could see they were impressed by the way they kept nodding.'

Ysabella withdrew her finger from the hole in the base of the misshapen skull. 'Where was it you said this was from?'

'Iloilo. Down in the Visayas. Received wisdom says it was done for beauty but since there are no written records nobody can possibly know. That's the joy of received wisdom. How about this one?' which had been bound so as to accentuate the cranium's rearward occipital bulge, collapsing the forehead until it sloped backwards into a cylindrical extrusion like the end of a vegetable marrow. 'Skull moulding.' She handed it to Ysabella.

'No odder than body sculpture, really. You know, pumping iron. In fact, it probably did less damage to the intelligence than lifting weights does.'

'Chinese foot binding was extremely painful. Practised only on females, of course.'

Ysabella looked about her at the cavernous room. 'A lot of stuff.' They were in the Philippine Heritage Museum, which was housed in a vast capitolesque pile sometimes remembered as the Old Congress Building. The Museum straggled over two floors sandwiched between the Department of the Ombudsman downstairs and the Senate up. She had already been introduced to a grandee in the Senate lounge; had taken in the cerise carpet, the flames beneath the silver tureens on the buffet table at one end of the room, the grey hopsack sofas and settees around the walls. The people who counted wore filmy white *barong Tagalog* shirts. Now and then they were besieged by a Press contingent dressed for action: denim flak jackets, ponytails, holstered power-packs. That comfortable, oddly informal atmosphere which sizzled with power reigned a mere dozen feet overhead. The Department of Archaeology, by contrast, was gimcrack and dusty. In the hollow square of corridors beyond its door roamed crocodiles of school-children, giggling and staring blankly at the display cases past which they were shooed by harassed teachers. In the room where Ysabella worked uncatalogued artefacts were piled on splintery tables and plywood desks were squeezed between them where impoverished scholars sat with borrowed dictaphones. Now and then some fairly ordinary mass-produced Ming tradeware vanished and the Depart-ment could at last buy itself a secondhand office copier or desktop computer. The scholars deeply resented the nation's heritage having to be sold off in order that the Philippine Heritage's collection might be properly catalogued, studied and protected, but times were hard all over.

'Infantilism seems to be the flavour of the month in your current demonology?' Sharon observed.

'I learned last night that according to Mormon teaching, after his second coming Jesus Christ will designate Independence, Missouri, as the New Jerusalem. Did you know that?'

'Probably. It's the sort of thing one tends to forget, not living in Missouri.'

'That's why I wanted to tell you while I still remembered. Why there, I wonder? Maybe Joseph Smith owned real estate in town. How did he manage to second-guess the divinity's geographical preferences? Or why should he, of all people, be told in advance? These are deep waters. Infantilism? I don't know why it's suddenly got to me. A foreign city, perhaps.' Or the dark pall coming up from behind to settle around the shoulders, that gown of strangerhood from whose folds the view even of one's own culture falls apart into oddity. 'I'm noticing fast food chains, each with its cartoon grotesque outside – Ronald McDonald, Mr Jollibee and so on – and inside, too-strong lighting and bolted-down playschool furniture in horrid colours. The food's designed for children, too, because you're not expected to be able to manage anything grownup like cutlery or proper napkins. Polystyrene boxes full of buns and slime. Nursery eating. I can't imagine how such places ever caught on. I mean, the food's not even particularly cheap.'

'Staple diet of the urban poor.'

'Well, leave aside that with a bit of effort they could make themselves proper meals at half the price, why does it all have to be so babyish? Ah, bones. They're what it all comes down to.' She hefted a femur. 'Half lives. Atomic decay. Thermoluminescence. What's Ronald McDonald? Plaster and chicken wire; I don't know.' All this was watched in silence by several departmental drones as well as by the eminent author of a monograph which had stood on its head the original conclusions – or received wisdom – of the Sta. Ana burial site. Baffled, amused or disgusted as they may have been, they mainly appeared respectful. Sharon found it irritating: too patient, too indulgent by far of this peculiar and opinionated Briton.

'The Director will be back next week,' she told Ysabella. 'Then you can be properly assigned.' She had long since decided that her eccentric visitor was not really an archaeologist at all, not if one thought it a matter of temperament as much as of the intellect. Her own leanings had developed into an obsession with historic Manila, the last thousand years, a period which could be further narrowed by starting at Magellan's arrival in 1521 and ending with the razing of the city's centre in 1945 when American troops finally crushed the Japanese. Much of her own fieldwork had been done a bare half mile away in Intramuros, the old Spanish citadel. In the 1970s one of Manila's

24

worst slums had been bulldozed and there, practically in the shadow of San Agostin church, Sharon had dug down beneath the broken rum bottles and flattened pork-and-beans cans of squatterdom, past Japanese helmets and rusting bayonets, back to coins of Philip II whose name a nation had inherited. She had recognised that these holes of hers dug within the dark grey sloping walls had become a private earthworks thrown up against sundry ghosts and vampires which stalked the caverns of the Philippine Heritage Museum: chiefly, the ghost of General Yamashita and the vampires of pot-hunting. At the most she would only ever find curios: a fragment of machine gun belt, a dented powder flask, a doubloon or two, pieces of messware. These things were safe, of little monetary value. From them she could reconstruct the ebb and flow of the citadel's boundaries which did not always match the plans contained in vellum-bound archives in Madrid. That palimpsest of site over site, shifting and blurring (did the charred staves of *narra* wood at 4m 85cm corroborate the magazine fire recorded in 1688?), the verticality of her personal world, partially safeguarded her against the horizonless present. This was the cliché of scholarship, naturally. But most archaeologists had not to contend with museum authorities selling off items from its own collection to the tourist industry, nor with the hysteria of treasure hunting which surrounded any discovery or dig. At the merest hint of Japanese capital behind a construction site, island or beach resort anywhere in the provinces, the story would spread that somebody had inside information about the vast treasure looted by General Yamashita and hidden somewhere in the archipelago as he fled in 1945, hoping to retrieve it at leisure. Or a scuba diver had only to find a barnacle-encrusted dish or cannon to trigger a well-equipped assault on the site by rival gangs of looters. Conflicting claims were sometimes settled at sea or on beaches by night with brisk firefights of automatic weaponry. Far in the rear, the agents of the state came puffing along in leaky boats with rented gear, waving Ferdinand Marcos's 1974 Presidential Decree no. 374 which specifically included underwater sites in the Cultural Properties Protection and Preservation Act (1966). By the time they arrived the vampires had like as not torn the place apart and irrevocably scrambled yet another fragment of the past. Laws these people had coming out of their ears; implementation was something else.

'Properly assigned,' Ysabella was saying. 'Improperly assigned. What is it he's doing, exactly, this Director of yours?'

'Liwag? He's down in Panay, at Tugtugo. That's the galleon I was telling you about? In eighty feet of water? He said he'd be back mid-next week. Assuming there's no *bagyo*.'

'*Bagyo?*'

'Sorry, typhoon. One of the acts of God which rule life in these parts. A bad typhoon and the country falls apart for a few days into seven thousand storm-lashed islands, each fighting it out with the hatches battened down. No flights, no boats, often no radio. But it's the wrong season. He's probably haggling with the Aussies.'

'The Aussies' were a professional team of archaeological divers the Museum often employed to beef up its own over-stretched resources. Bonifacio Liwag had a real liking for fieldwork, to the extent that his desk in the office down the passage was nearly always empty. He had, Sharon had observed over the years, a real interest in Chinese ceramics and Australian divers. He was rumoured to be a member of Opus Dei, too, an organisation with a shadowy reputation for being a cross between Masonry and the Mafia. She wondered what he would make of Ysabella.

5

IT WAS NOT UNTIL late morning, after Vic Agusan had said 'John, it's a chance' for the umpteenth time, that the two watchers saw the Tamaraw van approach down the track, lurching in the potholes. They were crouched in weeds, hot and shadeless behind the burnt-out remains of a Fuso truck caught months ago in the crossfire of hardscrabble living. It was an overcast December day but the sunlight was still intense enough for objects to throw faint shadows. In front of them stretched the marshy fringes of northern Manila Bay. They were well off the map, up in the wilds of Navotas, Prideaux thought. He had become lost once Vic had turned off Honorio Lopez after crossing the estuary. Beyond the last housing project – which he noticed was called Singalong Subdivision – was a grey rim of shantytown, and beyond that these tidal flats sculpted into eccentric lots as fishpans. It was hard to see where land ended and water began. Much of Manila was low-lying and subject to floods, parts of Tondo being virtually tidal. (The highway authorities there planned roadworks around the phases of the moon.) Here, too, were clear signs of flooding. A line of salt ran at mid-door level around the rusted cab of the hulk they squatted behind. Everything was festooned with rags of plastic, tatters of bags snagged on tussocks, lengths of timber and tangles of wire. So flat was this terrain that, three miles to the south across the estuary, Smoky Mountain reared up like a volcano, flanks steaming, its fallout of effluent and litter spreading far beyond these marshes.

'There,' said Vic in triumph. 'I told you my guy was reliable. These

27

police don't even bother to hide it now. Broad daylight.' He took a reading from the light meter hanging on its cord and raised the Nikon, resting the long snout of the lens on the truck chassis. He shot the van bumping down the boggy track towards them, the windscreen's intermittent glare. 'That'll do. Right there, please. That's far enough. You might get stuck.'

As if the driver agreed, the vehicle swung to a halt a hundred yards off, angled slightly away from the watchers. Prideaux was tense with fear. He had been hoping the Tamaraw would not come so close. He wished the camera's shutter was quieter. It sounded like machine-gunning.

''Yon. . .' Vic was breathing. The doors had opened and the driver had turned his face. 'Sergeant Cruz! I love you, baby.' *Flack-flack-flack-flack-flack.*

A third man in jeans and T-shirt became visible as he stood up in the rear of the van, tugging at the yellow tarpaulin. The three blue drums emerged and gleamed dully. Cruz's assistant climbed up and helped the man tilt and roll one of the drums on its rim, at the last moment heaving it off the end so that it cleared the dangling tailgate. It fell with the weight of a dud bomb, embedding itself with a wet thud which reached the watchers a half second later. Sergeant Cruz appeared with a mallet and long chisel. The T-shirts huddled over the drum. The hammer rose and fell.

'Move your ass! C'mon, c'mon, *move.* I can't see a – 'yon! Ayos!' as Cruz straightened up. The last of the clips was whacked loose. The lid burst open and liquid gushed out. The two men upended the drum as Cruz watched. When it was empty they set it aside and the other two were dealt with in the same way. Prideaux wondered what Vic was getting. They were crouched so low the intervening tussocks hid nearly everything at ground level. He hoped he wouldn't get carried away and stand up, though Vic of all people knew the risks they were running. In a matter of minutes the drums were empty, loosely re-lidded and stowed back in the van beneath the tarpaulin. Cruz retrieved the hammer and chisel and, holding them like a picnicker collecting firewood, swung suddenly around and stared in their direction. He had put on a pair of mirrored sunglasses, megashit bent cop or maybe family man setting about a barbecue in his mail order shades. Then he gazed out to sea in the direction of Corregidor Island, preparing to bore the kids with the usual yawny stuff about General MacArthur and the Japanese. No, actually, the man was taking a leak. *Flack-flack-flack.* Blow *that* one up for the Press Club notice board. The Tamaraw slammed its doors, coughed black fumes, turned slowly so Vic got its rear plate *flack-flack* and drove off, noticeably bouncier over the bumps.

In the distance the van was lost among the shanties. Prideaux began to stand up, sweat pouring down his back. Vic pulled him down again with a suddenly thrown-out hand. He was following the van through the telephoto lens, finger off the shutter release. 'Crafty Cruz, they call him. We wait.' They remained crouched. Prideaux's knee joints burned; his feet had gone to sleep. After a long ten minutes Vic said, 'Don't move. Just turn your head. You see that heap of sand?' It was by the road, perhaps a quarter of a mile away. 'Go left to the *sari-sari* store with the white sign. The corner of the block.' A vehicle was parked in the shadow, just its nose visible and the windscreen's flat stare.

'Shit and derision.'

'Told you he was foxy. He doesn't suspect us. He's curious to know if anyone noticed enough to come trotting over for a look. I don't think they've got binoculars. I've never seen a cop with binoculars.'

Prideaux had followed Vic's instruction to wear dull colours. His army green T-shirt was black with sweat. A drip formed at the end of his nose and fell onto a slab of charred upholstery in the grass. The pain in his knees became a clock he began to watch with narrowed attention. When he next looked up the Tamaraw was gone and the world empty in a general glare.

'Okay now.' Vic stood up. 'I'll even tell you *where* they've gone. There's a Savory's on Del Rosario down in Tondo. They'll be ordering half a fried chicken each and probably drink five beers apiece. Then back to the station. Another day, another dollar.'

Prideaux was not listening to this breezy lore. The blood was getting back to feet that were stumps of cement with hot wires running through them. His knees felt arthritic. Middle age.

'So what did we see?' Vic asked. 'Could be what? Illegal dumping of toxic waste? "Fishpans seen contaminated for fifty years. Judge raps cops turned moonlighting waste disposal experts".' He had begun walking towards where the Tamaraw had unloaded, limber as a child in his trainers, pouching the big lens and fitting something shorter. 'Yeah. What they do, you see, is economise.'

They had reached the three bodies which had already started to bloat during their long hours in the drums. All had their thumbs tied behind their backs with plastic twine which ran down between the buttocks to both big toes, drawing them into a semi-squat. Their eyes were open but slitted with puffiness, their hair was beginning to dry. Vic shot them carefully, moving from face to face. 'Don't recognise any of them.' *Flack-flack-flack.* All three shirts were rucked up, revealing the scarred, scrawny torsos of marginal living. 'Get the tattoos? BCJ here, Sigue-Sigue Commando here. Jailbirds. Don't know about this one. Could be he's *kuwerna*, unmarked. He'd have had a bad time inside. No protection.'

The face of a boy, thought Prideaux, even a subnormal boy, now staring at a flattened Magnolia ice cream carton caught in the grasses as if trying to make sense of the letters on its side. Children with flying pigtails played with a beachball in fading print in a cloud of summery words: Fun! Yum! He gazed at the bare feet. Twenty-five years younger than his own, he thought, and feeling would never return to them.

'Come on, we've got enough. Someone else can find them.' They began the long walk back to where they had left the Hersheymobile a good mile and a half away. 'No expense, you see. Sometimes they don't even like to waste bullets on street trash. Those guys weren't heavies, just losers. In and out of jail and then one day, bingo, staring up at the sun in a marsh in Navotas. They do it at night, out behind the station. The cops fill the drums with water and shove their man in, which takes a few of them because even if the guy's all tied up he doesn't want to go. By the time they get the lid fixed on he's probably got an inch or two of air up under the lid, what with all the water that's slopped out. So they load them on the van upside down.'

Why was dying upside down worse? Was it worse? One of the drowned men had been grinning. ' "Where Asia wears a smile",' he said, quoting the Tourist Board slogan. His voice sounded strange to himself.

'There it is,' said Vic. He had done a journalism course at Columbia or somewhere where all the teachers must have been Vietnam vets. 'Okay, John?' He was looking up into Prideaux's face with interest as much as concern. 'Skip lunch? Pass on the fried chicken?'

It was real, all right; as if a dozen stories had been squeezed together to yield a numbing ichor filling parts of him which were not the stomach. *Freshly killed men.* Earlier in their friendship Vic had told him of being a rookie police reporter back in 1986. The Marcoses had fled ten months earlier. Tyranny was officially dead. He was newly returned from the States, confident, full of the Woodward-and-Bernstein ethic, keen to get good contacts in what in those days was still the Philippine Constabulary. One night a lieutenant he trusted had rung the office and said, 'We're having a party, police-style. We're betting you won't come.' Vic had taken the challenge in the invitation as a warning: In or Out, it's up to you now, hotshot. How could he refuse? He had sat up front in a closed van with wire mesh over the cab's rear window. 'Jail transfer,' his contact said, lighting a cigarette from the driver's. 'We get to keep the vehicle for some drinking afterwards.' Something in the air made Vic disinclined to ask which jail lay out past Quezon City towards the hills of Marikina. The van had swung into a field, the rear had been unlocked and four handcuffed prisoners in leg irons were pulled out followed by three police officers in street clothes. The scene was lit by the van's rear lights, an eerie red.

'Nice ride, fellas?' asked Vic's contact. 'Now, we're sporting guys and we've decided you've earned a chance not to go back to jail, even though you're scumbags. You see? It's the humane face of People Power. Christmas is coming, season of forgiveness, time to be with the wife and kids – or one of the wives, anyway, ha-ha. So what we thought is, you'd respond to a challenge. Specially you, Banjo.' The tail lights shone as red dots in the eyes of the stocky prisoner with the shaven skull; the face of a jovial killer. 'This is a nice big field and it's good and dark. We're going to take off your irons and you're going to run. We'll give you a count of ten. You'd better hope you'll be out of sight, 'kay?' By now Vic had caught on and was expecting some jocular pistol practice. From the van the three cops took M-16s and slapped in magazines while Vic watched his man undo first the leg irons and then the prisoners' handcuffs. He noticed how even when freed the men remained huddled together as if still bound, until the shout of 'Go!' Three took off at desperate speed in different directions. They were not allowed to get more than a dozen feet before the Armalites on full auto. blew them into darkness. Only Banjo had not run, the red sweat twinkling on his scalp. 'Maybe you got some brains after all, Banjo. Next time, huh?' Banjo was put back in irons and they all drove off again. The marksmen's excited voices could be heard from the grilled compartment behind the cab, each describing how, when, who, punctuated with high laughter. The three dead men had hijacked a bus going to Batangas and shot a passenger while Banjo had cut the driver's throat in exemplary fashion, turning the spraying man this way and that to douse any remaining sparks of resistance. Such was Vic's mentor's account as they had driven back to Q.C. Later, there had been a lot of drinking and some girls. At some point the lieutenant had carried out a bucket of deep fried chicken and a *grande* of San Miguel beer for Banjo to manage with his manacled hands. Vic had vomited a lot that night back in 1986. He was off campus for good. In the bleak blur of 4 a.m. Manila he realised he was In and not Out any more, but it no longer seemed enviable.

He recounted the episode well, something of the original horror still about his eyes. Prideaux thought he had told it to very few people. The contamination of knowledge; contagion's yearning shame. The very informality of salvaging-and-drinking sprees was chilling and opaque. Behind its inscrutable smoked lenses were rogue cops and fond fathers who might be one and the same. Without chiding Vic had made it clear from the start that what Prideaux might fancy as fieldwork ('*The Philippine Press: Freedom and Licence in a Developing Democracy*', or was it '*The Category of* Amok: *the Breaking-point and its Cultural Determinants*'?) involved real fields in Marikina, real marshes in Navotas, real lives without number lived untouched by the least hint of freedom or democracy. So get your comfortable academic ass in gear... In or Out, hotshot?

6

In AD 1100 the area now occupied by Metro Manila was low, swampy grassland full of deer. It flooded readily in the monsoon rains, during typhoons or at seasonal high tides. Shellfish were plentiful and so were mosquitoes. As in all flatlands the least undulation was pronounced; there were definite areas of rising ground amid the general marsh, even a lump or two which might qualify as hillocks. However, there was nothing high enough to obstruct an inland view of real hills – almost mountains – to the east. It was not an ideal place to live compared to the nearby foothills where fruits and timber were abundant and the terrain well suited to the indigenous people's slash-and-burn agriculture. Yet at some time in the early Twelfth century people began moving down into the marshes surrounding the bay to take advantage of trade offered by southern Chinese who sailed up in their junks bringing ceramics and cloth and metalwares. The pre-Filipinos, who had long been using their own pottery for ritual and burial purposes, must have been overwhelmed by the sophistication and beauty of the Chinese ceramics, for the archaeological record shows they began adopting them more and more extensively. The boggy settlements grouped around the Pasig's estuary cohered in time into a small port. The Tagalogs who lived there (*taga* + *ilog*, 'inhabitants of the river') had unwittingly founded Manila. Such, at least, was the received wisdom.

It was precisely the small undulations in a landscape that a modern city so effectively obscured, just as its lights did the stars at night.

Nowadays it was nearly impossible to detect amid the traffic and concrete the hillocks where deer had once raced through shining grasses. They had to be deduced by the way floodwaters ran, tumbling with them the yellow worms of noodles beside the kerb. Moreover, except from the top of the very tallest blocks downtown one could no longer see the foothills of Laguna and Marikina, not least because of the brown smog rising in the foreground like urban halitosis. Yet the bumps and lumps were still there, mainly identifiable as places which scarcely ever flooded. The great necropolitan triangle up past the San Lazaro racetrack (La Loma cemetery, the Chinese cemetery and North cemetery) was on somewhat raised terrain from where it was actually possible to look down on a few roofs. In one particular place at the foot of a cemetery wall the ground rose again, forming a small valley through which a black *estero* called the Kapilang ran in its shattered culvert. This rise of ground, whose topmost point remained for ever ill defined, was the San Clemente squatter area.

By squatter standards San Clemente was old. A whole generation had grown up not thinking of it as makeshift or temporary. Many of the lower shanties had concrete block foundations to withstand the sudden rises of the Kapilang, which acted as a storm drain in monsoon weather. This generation was now giving birth to its own children who would be even less aware that at the stroke of a pen bulldozers could raze the village without so much as a day's notice in the name of the city or of a private individual who had suddenly dusted off his title to the land. Village? But in all important ways that was what it was. Back in January 1981 the Minister for Human Settlements had hastily dressed her stage for the visit of Pope John Paul II. She had given orders for high cinderblock walls to go up along the inner angle formed by the junction of two major thoroughfares. They had been painted white, of a shade popularly referred to as 'sepulchre', against which a few remaining prewar trees offered a plausibly verdant prospect. Thus screened from sight, San Clemente effectively vanished as far as the pelt of roaring traffic was concerned. Even today's sandwiched commuters on the elevated LRT trains glimpsed little between the foliage; just another faint swelling of tin roofs among so many. Imelda Marcos's action had intensified the village effect by demarcating San Clemente's outer boundary. And not just in San Clemente, either. Even the foreign back-packers and good-timers of the tourist belt daily walked unknowingly past entire shanty villages, tucked away behind their walls, now no longer white. (And even after all Imelda's beautifying zeal, the papal visit had turned out less than a total triumph. The man had struck her as obtuse and lacking in class, breaking with the divine tradition of neutrality by making impertinent remarks about poverty, human rights and even *elections*. At least, that was how the Press had interpreted them. The whole thing had culminated in a monstrous public snub during an open air Mass when His Holiness, faced with a front row of concupiscent oligarchs with their eyes closed and their tongues out, had turned down the obvious and glamorous first choice and instead called up some scruffy unknown brat who, she hoped, had choked on the wafer.)

To strengthen the village analogy still further, many of San Clemente's inhabitants had originally come from the same area of a single province in the northern Visayas and had largely preserved their dialect, customs and outlook. If one closed one's eyes it was sometimes possible to believe oneself back in a distant barrio, for on two sides the high walls shut out much of the traffic noise and on the third lay the comparative peace of the cemeteries. The sparrows which lived among the Chinese tombs became audible between LRT trains as they flittered and scrabbled on the tin roofs. For human inhabitants, meanwhile, there were two ways in and out of San Clemente. One was across a rickety board spanning the *estero* and leading to a muddy passage between shops which faced the roaring canyon beneath the light railway. The other was a breach in the cemetery wall most frequently used by people fetching water, for the Chinese dead were well supplied, some of the mausoleums being plumbed.

'Which would you rather be, a dead Chinese or a living Filipino?' ran the joke question that was neither question nor joke and expected no answer. Insofar as there was an answer it lay on the other side of the cemetery wall in the shape of a parody suburb in miniature. Here were well-swept, empty roads with proper pavements and neat plots with patches of lawn, each with its little building. Or house. Or *palace*, even, for some were cased in polished marble. Behind their padlocked wrought iron gates a sarcophagus rested in what could only be a living room, given the mats and vases of flowers, the brooms tucked neatly behind the staircase in one corner. Stairs because there was often another room above which no doubt (according to those from over the

35

wall) contained a fax machine, a Betamax, a telephone and all the other things essential to dead Chinese businessmen. Votive lights burned in the tombs of the Catholics, otherwise in shrines containing curling photographs, old joss sticks and scraps of red tissue paper. Solidly built and mostly well maintained, these vacant houses with their water and electricity were visited on anniversary and feast days by families who parked their cars in the empty street and bore supplies of food and metal polish through the iron gates.

Not all these tombs were well looked after, just as many were not palaces. Some – especially those of such flamboyantly weird design as could only have belonged to the sort of lone eccentrics who leave no family – were in sad disrepair. They were cracked, tumbledown, overgrown. One or two were broken into and inhabited briefly by squatters until noticed and ejected by the cemetery's police detachment. Generally, the grander and newer tombs were those offering services and it was behind one of these that an illegal standpipe had been plumbed into a water main and supplied the people living on that side of San Clemente. The ordinary muser, the stroller in the cemetery (it being one of Manila's few oases of comparative calm) might wander for hours in this Lilliputian townlet without knowing of San Clemente's existence, or of its barely distinguishable neighbouring slums separated each from each by a stretch of wall, a muddy lane or a rivulet of effluent. Only, from one or other vantage point grey waves and crests and hollows could be glimpsed as the shanty roofs spread out below in a frozen sea of tin. True, children came up from these barrios to play, but they stayed close to the gaps in the wall, ready to scuttle back at the sign of a patrol by the cemetery police. This detachment was billeted in an infrequently used chapel somewhere in the middle. Their presence was assured by the city's predominantly Chinese administration, as well as by the privately donated funds of the Chinese community. They were there partly to prevent the ever-rising tide of squatters from lapping over the walls and flooding in (swirling around the classical columns, eroding the very marble!). But they were there also to stop the stealthy bands of grave robbers who might otherwise come by night and dig to their hearts' content. Never mind gold teeth: there was a brisk market in any old teeth to supply the nation's thousands of dental students, each of whom had to acquire some for practical exam projects. Many a body lay in a provincial cemetery minus lower jaw or entire skull. Much, too, might be mentioned of more occult purposes.

San Clemente, then, rose to the flanks of this cemetery from a miasmic dell of sewage to a lesser eminence, sandwiched between the living and the dead (if the mainstream of city life was represented by howling boulevards like José Abad Santos and Aurora Avenue). Upwards of two hundred families were crammed in. Inside this walled village were no streets, only trails scarcely four feet wide which twisted and dipped according to the haphazard siting of the shanties. Here, some casually abandoned planking jutted untrimmed from somebody's wall, forcing passers-by to dogleg around it. There, certain of the huts with upper storeys (houses, really) had fused together at head height and the path plunged into a slimy tunnel for yards at a stretch. In the dry season these thoroughfares set hard into the lumps and bumps left from winter's mud, peppered with embedded bottle caps, wicks of plastic and stumps of wood polished by bare feet. Tiny stores opened their shutters onto the paths, their shelves lined with staple goods, a courtesy box of matches dangling on a string for those who bought their cigarettes singly. There were always surprises. Cold drinks and ice were often on sale, arguing a refrigerator. Behind curtained doorways or up stygian staircases more like bent ladders might be veritable parlours with a bamboo settee, a colour TV, an electric fan, as well as that hallmark of the returning overseas remittance man, a suitcase-sized radio cassette player. Such things gave San Clemente an illusory aspect of permanence. One could forget that these homes were often little more than huts cobbled together from scraps, resting on bare earth which at any time might be reclaimed. Indeed, a certain patina of age hung about them and in places it would have been impossible to say for sure how old a group of shanties was. At night, especially, or during brownouts when the little stores glowed yellow with candlelight, San Clemente might have been an impoverished *souk* of great antiquity.

Epifania Tugos – or Nanang Pipa, as she was generally known – ran a sewing cooperative from her house about a third of the way up San Clemente's slope above the creek. This was perhaps a slight exaggeration since the business was really no more than a loose organisation of various families who had the requisite skill and access to a machine. It could never become a real cooperative, a legal entity with the minimum fifteen members and eligibility for bank loans, because it lacked a proper address. In all other respects, though, it was run very much as a business with outlets for its jeans, T-shirts and children's underwear in Divisoria Market as well as with regular suppliers of material. There were links, too, with Nanang Pipa's home province, where relatives of many of San Clemente's inhabitants carried on the rag trade for their local markets. The people in her group had divided up their labour. Those without machines did the cutting or took the cartons of finished clothes down to the market. At almost any time one might meet a great bundle of bright material with a pair of polished brown legs beneath it threading its way adroitly through San Clemente's mud lanes.

In the early days of this cottage industry harsh lessons had been learned by those living down near the creek. If one happened to be out at the time of a flash flood one might return to find the house partially demolished or, more likely, the ground floor room full of drowned rats and the sulphurous smell of drains, the walls black with mud up to the ceiling, the Singer sewing machine festooned with slime. The chief things the villagers feared most were floods and fire, followed by ghosts. (Much too far down their list came bulldozers.) Floods were quite bad enough, though, for those forced by lack of land to live within the danger zone. In the months of July to November someone tried to be always on hand, ready at the first sign of flooding to begin carrying everything upstairs or to safety in a house further up the hill. Often the first sign wasn't mere heavy rain but the sudden appearance of cockroaches in unusual numbers. They, too, were headed upwards, swarming in the roof. In 1989 when Munding's children were swept off by the Kapilang in spate the villagers remembered seeing two balls of beetles twirling away downstream: the children's heads alive with cockroaches. (It was either a miracle or an iron grille at the entrance to the underground sewer which had saved them. Or maybe Bats Lapad, who had actually hauled them out.)

All these matters of low-lying terrain, floods and sewing came together in the issue of the Tugos family's comfort room. Various crappers like thatched hen coops stood on stilts out over the Kapilang, which meant that in times of rising water worse things than cockroaches could appear in one's living room. The Tugos crapper was a cupboard built over a trench leading down to the stream, up and down which rats and piglets ran and grew fat. But the time had come, Nanang Pipa said, when enough was enough. She and her workers sitting jammed all over the house at their machines could no longer endure the stench. It was time for Edsel to get off his bum and dig. They would have a deep pit soakaway with a cement bowl, a proper comfort room.

'The money,' her husband groaned, meaning the effort.

'I work, I pay,' she retorted. 'You dig. Get together those layabouts you spend your time playing *pusoy* with. Judge, Billy, Petring. All that lot. Bats, too. It shouldn't take you long. *Bayanihan*, of course: they can do it for free in a spirit of neighbourliness. Starting tomorrow. We'll supply you with *merienda* and cigarettes.'

'We haven't any spades.'

'Yes, you have. When Bats left the Department of Public Works and Highways he brought some souvenirs with him. I know about six DPWH shovels, an air compressor and twenty bags of cement because the cement went into our floors, the compressor was lost at cards and Virgie told me only the other day she's sick of having those dirty spades under the bed.'

'Read all about it,' muttered Edsel in a bitter allusion to his wife's unofficial nickname 'Diyario', she being a veritable news-sheet of information about San Clemente and its folk.

'Just dig, Eddie. Please. Think how nice it'll be when it's finished and we've got a decent CR.'

And eventually the men had mustered, armed with shovels and a crowbar made from an iron fencing post. They primed themselves with strengthening tots from a bottle of San Miguel gin on whose label the Archangel, an effeminate creature in yellow Renaissance hose and slashed pantaloons, brandished his sword above a vampiric black figure with ribbed wings cowering beneath Michael's scarlet buskins on spikes of flame. Soon they were past the noisome top layer and were throwing up clods of the earth which had once nourished those far-off grasses, the long-dead deer.

7

YSABELLA HAD ABANDONED her hotel for a rented apartment on Roxas overlooking the bay. It was not cheap. It also smelt of fuel oil, which was explained by her encountering a member of the Ku Klux Klan wearing over his head a T-shirt with eye holes punched through. He was on hands and knees with a spraygun, its nozzle in the gap between the corridor's floor and wall where it roared hollowly. Oily mist hung about the passage. The maniac holes swivelled and looked up at her glisteningly as she passed, furtive and triumphant as befitted all who dealt in plague.

When she had first unpacked she spent a good deal of time faintly homesick, sitting on the bed removing labels from the clothes she had bought in a last-minute shopping spree in London's West End. This was her habit, the act without which nothing new could be worn. A small heap of names, trademarks, logos and flashes would build up beside her, victims of scissors and razor. In order to wear one's clothes as if they belonged – a prerequisite for anybody with pretensions to taste – all traces of previous affiliation had to be removed. Ysabella would marvel at people's indifference to walking around covered in slogans, signatures, bogus armorial devices or a menagerie of little crocodiles, ladybirds, pandas and turtles. 'Who wants to look as if they'd been dressed by their local airport?' she wanted to know. 'More to the point, why should I buy the clothes I want *and* be obliged to provide these shysters with free advertising?' She had spent real money on having craftsmen remove the name from the face of her Audemars

Piguet watch and make trainers in single plain colours (three black pairs, three brown). Somewhere in Belsize Park in a lock-up garage was her futuristic Japanese sports car from which she herself had removed an embarrassing name and assorted chrome letters and numerals from its rear.

The result was to give everything she wore or drove an exclusive, one-off aura. When she and Hugh had gone skiing everyone on the slopes immediately noticed her difference without as easily identifying its source. Blonde hair and striking figures were no particular rarity in Klosters; in fact they were common, and looked it. Ysabella stood out for reasons of absence, because of what she didn't have, wasn't wearing. Her absurdly expensive carbon fibre Head skis had been re-sprayed matt white, obliterating all the semiotics of skiing. Her suit was a uniform severe smoke grey. Her knitted hat was tawny, the colour of an old harrow abandoned in the corner of a field. Her exclusiveness was terrific as she sped deftly, clad in her powerful lack, among the anonymous day-glo throng. Their march was stolen. They launched counter-attacks under the 'for your own good' flag. 'Break a leg up there and you'd be only too glad to be wearing something visible to a helicopter.' 'No I shouldn't,' she retorted. 'I'd be downright ashamed.' In a closely zippered pocket she carried a large square of hideous material. 'What kind of wet goes out *dressed for rescue?* Always the safety net? A third parachute?'

But a few weeks of living by herself in Manila in something called an 'apartelle' (a word she couldn't bring herself to say) was producing its own subtle erosions, as if it had begun to unpick the nametape from the identity she treasured. There were the capering children who besieged her whenever she left the block, faces bright with snot and eyes, who she discovered were displaced victims of the Mt. Pinatubo eruption. They lived in boxes and packing cases on a scrap of wasteland behind the building, running out barefoot among the traffic temporarily halted at the lights along thundering Roxas, flitting like little ghosts with outstretched hands through the fog of exhaust fumes, begging from drivers and passengers. A part of her began to unravel slightly, leaving her both anxious and listless. It was as if a small haemorrhage had opened up which she had yet to find and staunch, a desultory tropic bleeding which did something to the will.

She was an early riser and could find nothing nearby which was open and would serve her breakfast. Dunkin' Donuts was out of the question. Instead she brought home a clutch of newspapers and made herself coffee in a kitchen which contained almost nothing except three butter knives with bamboo handles and a jar of black treacle which had been instant coffee until the humidity got to it. She would sit at a table overlooking the scatter of moored ships waiting to unload and read the Philippine English language press with diverted incredulity.

Day by day she read the papers and drank her coffee. At first the news entwined itself with the faces of friends back in England who, she thought, would particularly enjoy this irony, that outrage, those headlines. After a while, though, the stories just boiled up like a plume of oil from an abyss, spreading out into a uniform and iridescent stain, variable in local details but predictable overall. The incidents all had about them the air of having taken place at night, as if it was only the morning sun falling across the page which finally brought them to light. They covered Ysabella's news-sheets in a bright slick. A few weeks' assiduous study made of them something almost ritualistic. Yet if she thought this oily glint might be a society's recognisable features, its personality and heart remained enigmatic and concealed. Day by day policemen shot it out with each other in public, an event scarcely comprehensible to a British reader who knew that the majority of police weren't armed, or fake, or moonlighting as security guards, drug traffickers or professional kidnappers. If the papers here were to be believed, hardly a senator or member of Congress seemed not to have some taint or hidden skeleton. Suddenly, everything became interconnected. The same names kept circling like bluebottles around carrion. National heroes were accused of treason, became fugitives, lived openly in Quezon City, vanished, popped up again being invited to Malacañang Palace for talks, discussed running for the Senate next time around. Trusted generals suddenly went AWOL, turned up in Mindanao organising a blue seal cigarette smuggling racket, came back as mayor of somewhere or other, helped fix an election, were found in a supermarket freezer chest minus eyes and genitals buried beneath twenty kilos of frozen pizzas. Men who had fled with the Marcoses, accompanied by their families and as much cash as they could carry, were sniffing around for amnesty or were actually weaseling back into government. Even Imelda herself came and went, trying to buy deals for herself with the money she had stolen.

It was baffling, too labile to be grasped. The nouns Ysabella had been brought up to take for granted, which with their immutable bricklike nature went to build the administrative edifice that *was* a country, were here slippery, deformed or infinitely plastic. Everything was thrown into question, yet no question could be properly answered. A word such as 'corruption' became puny or nannyish. This was too grandly shameless a way of life to be contained – still less threatened – by invocations of morality. Yet what else was there? Here (she shook her paper in the rising sunlight) *right here* it said that the Air Force at last knew what had happened to one of its aircraft which went missing for six years. (Went missing? How did an entire aeroplane go 'missing' without talk of crashes, search parties, bad weather, grieving families and boards of inquiry?) It went missing because the colonel who used to fly it had condemned it as unfit for flying, thereby circumventing IRAN (Inspect – Repair As Necessary). He dismantled it on his own air base and sent the whole thing piece by piece, labelled as 'spare parts', to a private hangar inside Manila Domestic Airport where it was reassembled. The colonel then resprayed and used it for two years in his own transport business. (An air force colonel with a private business? Even that seemed not quite right.) After that he sold it to a company in the provinces. He had not yet been arrested because the police were still determining what charges to file.

Ysabella couldn't decide if all this was the sign of an extremely backward society which had yet to fix the essential nouns of its being so that everyone understood the same thing by *law, honesty, public service, police, elections* and so on, or whether it was actually a preview of a sophisticated futuristic state likely to hold sway everywhere sometime soon. At this distance England presented itself as an inert blob of greenish substance, quite cool and weathered like a chunk of onyx or other mineral from which the surrounding rock had been worn away by rain. On closer inspection and in a different light, however, it became very much less sharply defined, fuzzy at the edges like an aspirin dropped in water, hazy and commonplace. She resented that Manila's effect on her was to blur the fond image she had of her own country. Indeed, never before had going abroad been like this.

From afar Manila had seemed exotic, and not with the Hollywood exoticism of Bali (lithe brown folk in native costumes doing highly formalised classical dances on a beach for the massed camcorders of drunken roundeye jet-setters). Manila's aura had had something of Baudelaire's corpse-light glowing about it: existentially exotic, *morally* exotic, its legs raised by the pressure of its own putrefaction *'comme une femme lubrique'*. Yet once here she found herself being ground down by the heat, the filth, the choking traffic, the Jollibees and Pizza Huts and Dunkin' Donuts of it all. What national costume there was derived from Nineteenth century Spanish dress. What national cuisine there was merely played with Spanish and Chinese dishes. The handicrafts were not as good as those of Burma or Thailand and besides, who since the death of *chinoiserie* in Europe wanted creaky furniture made of rattan and bamboo? Or unspeakable Madonnas standing in grottoes made entirely of lacquered seashells? Nothing had prepared her for the sheer unrelieved ugliness of this city, much of which looked like a parody of the grimmer parts of Milwaukee. Yes, that was it: that the faint traces of Europe had been swamped by the worst of Pepsicolonisation.

Ysabella put down her paper, unnerved at finding herself impassioned. How could she have imagined that the archaeology here might be interesting? But she hadn't, really. She had thought it would be interesting to come here because nobody else did, a decision made as much by haughtiness as by notions of advancing her career. With her family connections and agreement to waive a year's salary it hadn't been hard to arrange. And here she was, not quite slumming deliciously in the eastwardly-turned and envious gaze of far-off friends. On the contrary, she was lost and depressed in a grimy and anarchic monster of a city. She suddenly longed for flowers. Nothing lush or gross, but celandine and periwinkle, Star of Bethlehem and speedwell, simple wayside crap crap crap – and here she hurled her newspaper at her own sentimentality like an inkwell at the devil. Celadon, yes: that ass Liwag had arrived back from Panay looking like the cat that had swallowed the cream – Australian cream, one presumed – and with cartons of Fifteenth century Chinese ware. 'Advance Happy Christmas,' he had said, handing her a barnacled object. She and Sharon had spent hours at the sinks gently removing marine encrustations. Sharon's turned out to be a fairly average little

Ming bowl. Her own was revealed as a Siamese import of much the same date, Sawankhalok or perhaps Sukhothai.

'It doesn't seem right,' she said.

'It isn't,' said Sharon cheerfully. 'But when in Rome.'

'Being Roman needn't reduce one to being a common looter.'

'So throw it back in his face. You're a woman; he won't mind.'

'But you're keeping yours.'

'Sure am. It's only mass-produced ware; the Museum's got tons of it. It adds zilch to our knowledge of Chinese ceramics, the kilns at Fu Liung, trade routes or Fifteenth century pre-Filipino taste. It's one of about half a million identical dishes. But I'm keeping it because I'm a vulgar American and I like that it's nearly six hundred years old.'

'Come to that, I'm a vulgar European with undue respect for institutions. So I'll keep it. Thanks.'

'There. See how easy it is to become Roman?'

'You've been here too long. You've become a Manileña.' And she had, Ysabella thought, thinking of the house not far from UP campus where the American and her lover had given her dinner. Or companion. At any rate there had been a double bed, but its plank base had been spread with mats, not with a mattress. And the bathroom had been a cement stall with a seatless Western-style lavatory pan and a plastic dustbin full of water in which floated a plastic scoop with a handle. Other people, too, seemed to inhabit the house. At any rate various women and girls had been involved in preparing the meal and referred to Crispa as 'Mam' while Ysabella had glimpsed a mournful boy in the yard holding a machete and the skull of a husked coconut like somebody in penitent mood after a massacre. There were two palm trees in the yard, which echoed to the trapped sound of evening commuter traffic. One could never judge the edges of things in foreign places. The demarcations of everything – of town and country, as of male and female – lay differently across the landscape. Of crime and punishment, too, come to that. Where she came from, ideas of punishment tended to blot out notions of redress. Wasn't this also true of the United States?

'Crispa's home province is Marinduque,' explained Sharon. They were eating rice and *torta* made of tiny fish fry flattened into a pancake, the black seeds of their eyes still visible. 'Here's a story. A girl from her home village goes to stay with her uncle outside Lucena City,

45

in Quezon Province. That's on the mainland opposite. He was the captain of his *barangay* there, sort of a village headman. One morning he comes into her room. It's about four-thirty and they're alone in the house since the aunt's gone off early to market, taking the servant. The uncle wakes his niece by punching her hard in the stomach so that she's winded and can't cry out. Then he rapes her. He's a man of sixty, she's a girl of fourteen. He's the village boss. He's her uncle. When he's gone away she climbs out of the window and neighbours take her to some friends who own a private clinic in town. She's bleeding badly. They find semen, do a smear, carefully list the damage, treat her and write up a report which certifies her as a rape victim. The police are called. "That's a very vague charge," says the policeman, who's not only a drinking buddy of the uncle but buys his fighting cocks and helped buy his last election, too. "A serious allegation. Better think it over." The neighbours and a percentage of the village support her to the extent that the uncle's eventually obliged to come to her with an offer of fifty thousand pesos to drop the charges. In those days that was one hell of a lot of money, I don't know – two, three thousand dollars? In a place like Marinduque someone with two or three thousand dollars was king. Hectares of coconuts, a fishing boat, a cement block house, you name it. You could run for Mayor on that. So this girl thinks of her wretched family back there and she thinks what the hell and she takes the money and goes home.'

'End of story?'

'Well, no. Beginning of a small but respectable family fortune. Lots of copra, lots of hogs, good fishing. Buy a jeep to take the produce to markets with higher prices than the local ones. Eventually buy a house and a lot near UP.'

'He was arrested, though?' Ysabella addressed this to Crispa, who smiled.

'On what charge?' she asked. 'Here there are only three or four crimes the police take seriously. Homicide, drugs, major robbery. You can expand those to include obvious things like terrorism against the state and kidnapping. Anyhow, rape's nowhere on the list because it's considered a private matter between individuals. It's up to the victim to file charges. If there's what they call an amicable settlement nobody can do anything about it. All charges dropped. Case closed. Did I do the wrong thing? I was fourteen.'

'But what *happened* to him?'

'He died a couple of years ago. Very old. A stroke, I think. We none of us went to the funeral.'

'No, I mean. . . *something* must have happened. Somebody must have done something? Sacked from his post? Spat at in the street? I don't know.'

'I believe he filed for leave of absence for two months and a deputy captain took over. It was a terrific scandal in the village, of course. He had his cronies and supporters, some of whom no doubt thought he was no end of a stud. Sixty, hey? Not bad. The majority thought he'd brought shame on the village and that he ought to resign and leave the area. But he stuck it out, sitting in his house with the shutters closed, and when nothing happened re-filed for another two months' extension of his leave of absence. Eventually it all blew over. A minor and commonplace event.'

'Don't misunderstand,' Sharon said to Ysabella when they were eating mangoes buried in chipped ice. 'People here may seem forgiving and unjudgmental to the point of moral lethargy, but they don't forget.'

'Exactly,' said Crispa. 'So wasn't I right? A vile five minutes, a miserable month, but it set us all up with capital. Surely in England they have the idea that justice involves redress as well as punishing the offender?'

'They're pretty hooked on punishment, actually. We're Protestants, you know. Forget *tout comprendre, c'est tout pardonner.* We think things like confession and forgiveness are soft and Roman.'

'But doesn't the offender compensate his victim?'

Ysabella had some vague idea that a recent British government had been keen to make criminals pay with more than their freedom. Perhaps that was drug barons, and their loot went to the government rather than to their victims? She felt whirled about by the edges of things not touching in their customary places, by shifting boundaries. 'What about impoverished rapists, then?'

'There's always natural justice. It runs riot in the provinces. People put curses on them and they get hacked to death with *bolos.* Or someone sets fire to their house with or without their children inside. . . Why this sordid topic? Sharon tells me your work is excellent.'

'That's because I've yet to do any.'

And indeed that was the problem: yet another thing whose shape was different here. When she had put archaeology into her bag in London it had been a neat package of known dimensions, of familiar colour, shape and heft. What she had taken out in Manila had become mysteriously misshapen in transit. Armed looters fought over sites. Museum directors went absent on field trips. Second-rate stuff was put on display while really interesting and valuable pieces were 're-assigned' elsewhere and became suddenly unavailable for study.

'Sharon tells me you're not married?'

'Not yet, anyway.'

All three of them would be much the same age, she thought. Small talk that ought to lead somewhere, only I'm too weary. Or too grand. Or too lazy to work up emotional ties for a year only to have to ingest them all again when I pack up, like a spider eating its own web. Conservation of energy. An elderly disdain; and yet here we are, late twenties, early thirties. Prime time. Or maybe that, too, slotted differently here. Maybe here it was already over. Hugh would have said dourly: 'Everything always is,' as part of their conspiracy of nostalgia, of *eheu fugaces* which was supposed to make sex tender so long as the talisman stood in the corner making a noise like wingèd chariots or grim reapers. Actually (she could now think, safely eight thousand miles away from him) the great drawback to sacred rites was that the more solemn and special they were, the more one's attention was distracted by the priest's crumpetlike complexion, by the embarrassing way his eyelids fluttered like those of a school chaplain feigning prayer. Hugh was doubtless another explanation for her being in Manila. A good reason for being cross with herself, if so. I only want the experience, she thought, never mind the details.

But details there were, as remorseless as an endless succession of small dishes which stubbornly refused to amount to a meal. Both her hosts were activists and let fall succulent morsels of this and that, appetisers from a banquet to which Ysabella didn't quite want an invitation. Crispa was doing research on the 'comfort women' used as slaves-cum-prostitutes in World War II, groping about in the black sack of history hoping to pluck out a few reliable names, some grey-haired survivors whom the Japanese Government might be shamed or cajoled into compensating. Sharon was lobbying her senators and diplomats to force the Philippine Government to provide adequate protection for female overseas workers presently being used as prostitutes-cum-slaves.

Ysabella was unnerved by the details, shamed by the righteousness of the girls' involvement. She was pained, too, by her own hesitancy. It was as if she had heard a shattering explosion in her childhood whose reverberations ever since were warnings against commitment to just these sorts of detail. Holes in the ground were safe: one could take refuge in them as one poked about the fragments of the buried past. Even newspaper stories lacked menace as wild fables of a land existing a little apart from the one she trod and dug, such was a stranger's queer immunity. These girls, though, lived in that other territory and gave off its details in a reek of authenticity.

Yet Ysabella had also been touched. She had left the house without feeling a burst of political solidarity with the sisterhood but liking Crispa for Sharon, whose world she now enviously saw went laterally as well as vertically. Abused overseas workers might easily be seen as having their roots in Intramuros, that colonial citadel. Her own world, on the other hand, felt ever more shapeless and hollow. It was surely without coordinates of any kind, as directionless as a view of empty ocean with dazzling chromatic glints being smacked from a coat of sulky oil.

8

FATHER HERRERA'S reputation was that of a radical without, however, his being accused of open sedition. It was difficult to imagine his fattish figure inserted into the gaunt jungle barrios of Mindanao, swapping Bible for Armalite, becoming a fully-accredited rebel priest with a price on his head and occasional *laissez-passers* to Malacañang. Prideaux had been given his name by a contact and offered him a workingman's lunch somewhere on José Abad Santos, having formed an impression of a busy and unpretentious priest disinclined to waste either time or jeepney fares going too far from his parish for a mere meal.

'The New Era,' said the voice on the telephone. 'The corner of Dumiguig.'

The New Era was, predictably, Chinese and – less predictably – new. It was full of harsh fluorescent glare. In tanks along one wall mournful eels gulped and furious crustacea attacked each other in slow motion. The tables had circular holes cut in them; underneath each a gas cylinder was connected to a ring burner. Prideaux's knees kept nudging the cylinder. 'They call this *shabu-shabu*,' said the priest delightedly. 'Not to be confused with plain *shabu*, of course, which is a drug.' What with the air conditioning and the bubbling wok between them the priest's spectacles kept misting over. Every so often he removed and polished them on the T-shirt between his breasts. This had on it a shield which to Prideaux's eye looked considerably like that of Oxford University, surrounded by comic-strip billows of steam.

Below was the legend: 'I graduated Sauna cum Laude'. 'You're an anthropologist?'

'I'm writing this thesis,' said Prideaux guardedly.

'About Filipino religion, I think Bernabe said?'

'I may have given Father Bernabe very slightly the wrong impression.'

'I imagine one often has to', said Herrera, crunchily spearing a crab from muzzle to rectum with a chopstick, 'in order to get the interview one wants.' He lifted the animal out of the wok, his eyes opaque behind twin grey panes.

'My thesis is really about the concept of *amok*. Or, perhaps, breaking points.'

'Guys going apeshit, you mean.'

'Ah. Women don't?'

Father Herrera laid down his chopsticks and took a refreshing gulp of beer. 'What a good point,' he said. 'You're implying that going to pieces is culturally determined?'

'Yes, of course. Obviously it would be pretty hard to predict the exact moment without knowing the individual, but the *ways* in which a person breaks are practically foreordained by their culture, don't you think? True *amoks* are rare in Europe, for instance. Or so they say. Anyway, if one wanted to talk about breaking points one would need to know what counted as stressful. I mean, stress in one culture might be a reassuring norm in another, mightn't it? I notice the people here seem able to tolerate a constant physical proximity which would drive the British crazy.'

'Maybe because they have to?'

'Whyever. Cultures change, too. No doubt our own merry swains used to cram together into their sod huts and couldn't have borne sleeping alone. That was then. So what's changed? Living standards, I suppose. Codes of inhibition, self control, general attitudes towards one's lot, stuff like that. Religion, too.'

'Now I see.' Herrera had also wiped his spectacles again. 'It mightn't have been easy to relay all that over the telephone via old Bernabe.'

'No. So you shouldn't feel you're here under false pretences.'

'My friend, no lunch is a false pretence. Don't you think lychees would be nice afterwards? Kumquats? Mangoes? I'm afraid my countrymen are not very religious at all. This may come as a shock.'

'It would to most travel writers, at any rate.'

'Oh, that. Well, if you will try to give thumbnail descriptions of a people you're bound to make a fool of yourself, obviously. Sure, the guidebook version says we're all deeply and fervently religious, ninety-odd percent Catholic, the only Christian country in Asia. My version is different. My version says my parishioners are about as religious as anyone anywhere living in the shadow of the West. What they are is deeply and fervently superstitious. We're Asians. China, Vietnam, Cambodia, Laos, Burma, Thailand. . . all riddled with spirits and ghosts and necromancers and soothsayers and magicians and geomancers and devils and charms and amulets and potions and curses and witchcraft and.'

'And, indeed.'

'And that's us. Do you know, I think rambutan rather than lychees? They have them sent up from Quezon or Palawan, according to season. This is Asia, this is the East. That's what people forget. Westerners are too eager to join in our own conspiracy and pretend we're practically as American as Hawaii, nearly as Spanish as the Azores. What's that cliché? Three hundred years in a monastery followed by fifty years in Hollywood. But what about ten thousand years in Asia? We simply plundered our own invaders for fresh sources of myth and superstition. That might be an interesting research project for one of you people. He could collect superstitions which probably died out in Catholic Europe a hundred years ago. They're still here in our provinces, pretty well intact, I should think. To rediscover vanished aspects of Europe you have to come all the way to the Philippines. Nicely ironic. Excellent rambutan.' The scalp of soft red prickles split between the priest's thumbnails to reveal the translucent scented brain.

'And religion?'

'Are you familiar with the concept of *balimbing*? That's what we call the star fruit, which has twelve sides. Only this morning I was hearing about a perfect *balimbing*, the eldest daughter of one of my parishioners. She was born a Catholic in the provinces. She falls in love with this boy, who is Aglipayan, our home-grown Church which broke with the Vatican early this century. So she becomes Aglipayan but then her family moves to Manila where she meets another boy whose people are Seventh Day Adventists. She becomes an Adventist while he gets engaged to someone else. Poor girl. Off she goes to Olongapo, hangs around the bars until the golden dream comes true. She meets an American sailor. Love as deep as the ocean. Together forever. He even suggests they get married here before he's posted home to San Diego. So what he's a Mormon? If he can be, so can she. Eventually she does get to the States. They have children. He beats her up. She files for divorce and falls in love with one of his friends. He's a Jehovah's Witness. No problem. . . You get the idea? That's a true story. I knew the girl. She was like any other of her age: silly, passionate, faithful, faithless. She lived in a world of *True Love Confessions* and screen romance. Perfectly normal. A nice, regular, lost kid. *Balimbing.* The only reason why she'll never be a Moslem is because she'll be too old. They like their brides very young.'

'I thought hard cases made bad law?'

'She's exceptional, I grant. But her opportunism isn't. Very well. If I dare to say, in the face of all expert assertion, that my countrymen are not essentially religious, I suppose I have to say they're deeply something else. Spiritual? Or maybe hysterical? Mightn't that have the right quasi-diagnostic ring to it to convince a man of social science like yourself?'

'I only wanted your opinion, Father,' said Prideaux. By now they were drinking green tea and from time to time he drifted away into intense little fugues of mental arithmetic, trying to prepare himself for the bill which he suspected was going to be quite a shock. 'What about crucifixions, then?'

For the first time a look of exasperation appeared on the otherwise equable face. 'It's bad enough my having to admit that the Church is losing ground to all these weird American sects without being forced to deal with a tin can mischievously tied to its tail. I often feel some of my Spanish predecessors must have been almost malevolent to allow the Christian message to become so distorted. You mean the Holy Week celebrations in places like Pampanga? The bleeding flagellants? The people dragging home-made crosses to which they are then nailed? I've seen it and it's grotesque. Nothing to do with religion, nothing at all. It's one of the sadder parts of our Hispanic legacy that we should have inherited their dark, pathological tomfooleries.'

Passion rather became him, Prideaux thought. The greedy urbanity had vanished, making his face thinner in some way, like that of a runner blown to an edge by his own swiftness. The energy of a combative intellect kicked out of its doze.

'If I could outlaw it, I would,' said Herrera. 'Do you know what having yourself crucified in public really is? Showing off. Pure, self-indulgent vanity. *Machismo.* It's a test of rival *machismos* to see who lasts the longest with the least sign of suffering. They have great local prestige, you know. They take loud public vows and build up to it for a year in advance. Everyone knows. *Next year it'll be him.* Will he go through with it? Will he chicken out? It's spectacle, a real crowd-puller. Better than television by far. One of the things that gives me hope for my people is that they stubbornly go on making jokes. They sniff out the bogus in things that pass for sacred. A few years ago one of the *penitensiyas* was called Nobo. . . you have to remember that we pronounce v's as b's. . . and he became known as Nobocaine. It was rumoured he'd injected his hands and feet. Who knows? Perhaps you should go to San Fernando and see for yourself. The atmosphere's more like a carnival than a religious ceremony. If I get angry about it it's because I can see it's a genuine expression of something I'd prefer not to be true about us. It's all show.'

'What else?'

Herrera said, as the bill arrived, 'You're not religious, I know that,' although at this very moment Prideaux, reading, inwardly uttered a sacred name. 'But I ask you, can you imagine Christ approving of such behaviour? He underwent crucifixion because he had to, in order that nobody else might have to. He was an incisive man, even quite merciless on occasion. He would say that volunteering for the same fate in the late Twentieth century was sheer useless indulgence, mere showbiz. He would ask the man if he'd do it in private, without telling anyone, without the crowds of admirers. He'd observe tartly that being crucified was easy – far easier than actually living a Christian life. It's a short cut to the stigmata, no more than that, and I'm none too happy about those, either. High time the Church came out unequivocally against these theatricals. The whole of humanity's already locked into the theatre of cruelty. The really hard thing is to learn to be kind. If you're dead to kindness, to the *poetry* of compassion, then all the Masses and Hail Marys and flagellation in the world won't save you. It's empty show. Now,' he eyed the plastic plate the waiter brought bearing a little change, '*you've* been very kind indeed. Has it been worth it?'

'Is being. But I suppose you have to get on?' The priest had eaten with haste and dexterity.

'We could certainly have some more tea. Any further pots are free. I liked your point about cultures changing. To take it at face value, I understand you're saying that a hundred, two hundred years ago Europe was the same as here, living in huts, believing in vampires and penance. You're implying that the essential difference between us is merely that of economic development. The upwardly-mobile peasant evolves into the neatly-suited banker, no longer stressed by swine fever and the weather but by exchange rates and brownouts?'

'More complicated, though.'

'Naturally. If it weren't, you'd be out of a job. . . That was a joke.'

Beyond the greenish tinted glass in the door and windows the traffic was inching past as if along a seabed. Periodically it halted. In and out of its currents moved minnowlike youths with shallow rectangular wooden boxes whose compartments held varieties of cigarettes, gum, matches, mentholated candy, a can of lighter fuel. Others dashed about with sheaves of newspapers, calling up to the jeepney passengers, thin arms locked into a muscular crook.

'You're surprised that I was vehement about such a minor thing, an annual pageant,' said Herrera. 'The point I was trying to make, try to make all the time, is that things like that are a distraction. The real issue is that the people of this country undergo crucifixion daily, nailed flat by poverty, corruption, shameless swindlers and brutal authorities. And still they make jokes. One of our senators recently called us Asia's Jews, forced to flee pogroms and vileness, going to any lengths to get away, to go abroad. Even becoming part of an exploited diaspora doesn't deter us. We still go by the thousand knowing we're going to be screwed, going illegally even if it means running and hiding from police and immigration authorities. Like the Jews we're condemned for slyness and duplicity, grudgingly praised for our skills and slave-like qualities, disliked for being truly foreign after all despite having names like Maria and Joseph. The Jews were accused of eating Christian babies; we're despised for eating dogs. But anything's worth it if only for the chance of making enough money for a proper life, enough money to send home to husbands and wives and children still caught in the trap. Should we stay where we are, be loyal to some imaginary global status quo, when everyone knows the world's just a rich man's free-for-all? But we've not yet reached that point when we all cry as one: "Enough! No more! *Never again! Next year in Manila!*" Let's hope it doesn't take the equivalent of the Holocaust. Maybe your own researches will provide us with a cool little answer to the question. What exactly does it take to make the Filipino people run *amok*?'

'That's not –'

'You were saying to yourself "Aha! A joke priest! A fat glutton who allows himself to be treated to an expensive and over-nourishing lunch while his parishioners eat boiled rice with their fingers." Of course you were and I don't condemn it. You're quite right. I am greedy. I like my food. It's a fault, undoubtedly. I used to confess it all the time. But my having yielded to your generosity has denied my parishioners nothing. Not only has it given me and my stomach great pleasure but it's providing me with an opportunity to beg you to remember only one thing. That laugh as we do, farce as it appears, what's happening in this place is deadly serious. How can you write about *amoks* without knowing how, when and why laughter suddenly stops?'

It was chastening, it was intended to be chastening. The beginning of self-righteous resentment made Prideaux guess that the priest was his junior by probably ten years. At the same time he felt justified in his increasing belief that there was a deep flaw in an academic discipline which believed it was possible to drift about the world getting to grips with the alien, erecting theories over lunch, dressing them up in scholarly rhetoric and calling them fieldwork. Did Prideaux really feel he even understood his own countrymen? They were a constant bafflement. How then could he travel eight thousand miles and presume to grasp an utterly foreign people, especially those who took shelter behind English as fluent as this priest's? What was patronage if not this? White man with tape-recorder solves kinship problem among the Fuzzies. Papuan humour cracked by Oxford don. . . He let Father Herrera ramble through a third pot of tea. The Church under threat. Condoms and Aids. Charismatics. Missionaries from Idaho and Utah wearing white short-sleeved shirts and boyish smiles and bearing a lot of nonsense about Joseph Smith into the credulous provinces. And Islam, of course. Green tea and dialectics had loosened Herrera's tongue.

'I always thought Christ was nothing like thorough enough in trying to distinguish between politics and religion. That stuff about Caesar's head on the coin was more of a wisecrack than useful, don't you think? Too evasive, too lightweight an answer. You can't just say religion's a private matter, not when you encourage the founding of a Church with revolutionary views, not when you get publicly executed for it by nervous governors. It's a messy argument. Judaism's worse: the religion *is* the people *are* the state. Islam too, but by golly they're just as hypocritical as the rest of us when they want to be. One stupid Christian missionary shoots his mouth off down in Zamboanga and the faithful put down their bottles of beer and caper about with that rabble-rousing stuff about blood and holy war. What's that got to do with spirituality?

'Down there in Mindanao they've already got their autonomous Moslem region but they still go on massacring each other. You think pork and Islam don't mix? They do in Mindanao, and a good many drink like fish, too. The mixture of alcohol and weapons there is half the problem. But that should concern nobody but them. It's a private matter. Why can't we all be humbler? Even the Prophet Mohammed made mistakes. He was admonished in the Qu'ran for paying too much attention to bigwigs and turning away from a poor blind man eager for knowledge of God. You'll find it in the *surah* called "He frowned". The Prophet's deputy, the Second Caliph, was also humbled. He admitted he was wrong for having spied on a party where he suspected they were drinking wine, for climbing up a ladder and getting over the wall into a private garden. They *were* drinking wine, but he was forced to concede it was none of his business even if he was the Second Caliph. "Which of you is without fault?" asked Christ. The same, you see. But today our great religions are perverted by egomaniacs claiming to be fundamentalists, and fundamentalists wanting to be politicians, and everyone being public busybodies at the cost of their private souls. God save us all from the zealous. Thank you for a delicious meal.'

Prideaux had the wilted sensation of a chef who from anxious curiosity has leaned too close to the oven when opening its door. Even emerging from the New Era's fragrant chill into the roaring sauna of mid-afternoon traffic came as a lesser blast.

'Give me a call,' Herrera was saying. 'The same number you used before.' He took a visiting card from his plastic wallet. It was printed in blue, overinked, slightly at an angle. 'I'll show you my parish. Next time lunch is on me. Of course you've seen squatter areas before. I imagine anthropologists are like journalists in that respect. But come anyway, if you've got time. This traffic.' He turned away with an upraised palm and was borne away on the general tide of T-shirts.

'Too old for this sort of thing,' Prideaux told himself. *Could* he be so demoralised as to have been on the point of offering the damned man a donation for his parish? He wondered how real academics managed to limit themselves to a carefully defined topic. How did you stop something unravelling at every edge? The vertiginous and disheartening pit combined with the beer he had drunk to make him fretfully hate these streets, this city. What was the point of these excoriating lectures? Stay at home. Babble of green fields.

9

BACK IN MARCH that year Insp. Dingca had attended his elder daughter's High School Graduation. His best polyester slacks were growing tighter all the time, he had noted. Must watch that. Don't want to start looking like Jun Santiago, the desk sergeant, who needed but snout and trotters. Part of the problem was having to shove a holstered pistol down his waistband. He had had a meeting first thing that morning with one of his 'assets', a transvestite informer named Babs, and had calculated things well enough to speed back to Laguna against the mid-morning traffic and sidle in at the back of the hall like a furtive schoolboy. Far away on a stage teenagers cut from sheet metal came and went, creased and ironed and shining with endeavour. Flags were saluted, anthems sung, stirring poems declaimed. Banners with golden fringes billowed gently to the delighted exhalations of hundreds of proud parents. Dingca stood and sweated and clapped with sudden force as Eunice stepped forward from the tin ranks, received her scroll with becomingly bowed head, moved away in a firestorm of flashbulbs with a demure swirl of knife-edged pleats. The collective virginity of it all was awesome and reassuring. These were good girls and boys, the hope for the future, the something or other. . . Babs had just fingered his club's owner for kidnapping children and selling them in the provinces. The proprietor was a Chinese businesswoman with close connections in the Mayor's office. It needed thought. Tangle with City Hall and the next thing you knew was you were posted to Davao or Nueva Ecija, or maybe no further than the bottom of Manila Bay.

Afterwards there was an open-air buffet on the school parade ground. The glum, brownish smell of mudwater blew in from the lake, the incense of an industry in decline since Laguna's once-flourishing fishpans were silting up or starved of oxygen or maybe just plain polluted. Dingca, who used to take a proprietorial interest in the lake he had decided to live near, was confused by the conflicting newspaper reports. Whatever they meant, Laguna de Bay had clearly become yet one more thing infected by scandal or impending disaster. For the present, the pondy smell brought an authentically rural whiff to these festivities. The capital city was spreading, true. Manila was not as far away as it had been, the cordon sanitaire of fields and creeks and paddies infiltrated now by ribbon development practically all the way from the back of the airport. But Eunice and her classmates were good girls, still thank God innocent of the tainted metropolis which yearly crept nearer. He beamed indulgently, circulating among friends and neighbours, greeting bowling cronies, Lions, Rotarians and local businessmen. They each held a plate of spaghetti in tomato sauce with sweetmeats of sticky rice, slices of white bread, and a wodge of violet gelatine all crammed together and eaten in no particular order. He came to rest beside his wife and daughters, patting little Divina on her ribboned hair.

'You cut a very distinguished figure,' he told Eunice. 'Easily the best-dressed girl of 1992' – a judicious piece of flattery since Teresita had made the clothes herself. 'I felt like a Sixth Grader.' This was true. The sight of all those seventeen-year-olds standing there with their black shoes and white ankle socks pressed together, their brown legs *sealed*, had given him an erotic jolt and he heard again an inward phrase he hadn't spoken to himself since he was thirteen: *Big Girls*. It was uneasy and enticing, so that he now over-praised his own daughter for the shocking allure of the girl who had stood two down the line, her ugly plastic ID card imaginatively concealed by a little bunch of white blossoms. 'It's a terrible burden for a father to have such a sensationally beautiful daughter.' He laid a fond fist around her shoulder, managing not to spill his glass of watery pineapple juice down her dress.

'I thought I was going to faint it was so hot up there. We were all ready to drop.'

'I know,' said her father, who hadn't noticed. 'I was sort of

60

impressed by your composure.' He saw an opening. 'Not like that poor girl standing near you. The tall one with the bunch of flowers?'

'Oh, *Patti*. Patti Gonzales. Well,' Eunice sniffed.

'I thought she looked a bit under the weather.'

'Not from the heat, I shouldn't think,' said Eunice darkly.

Dingca was about to pounce on this remark but was forestalled by the insinuating passage of his daughter's mathematics teacher, aglint with teeth and spectacles. The moment was lost, converted at once into tedious stuff about grades. His mind returned to Babs. This kidnapping young children racket was pretty small-time. Besides, it was nothing new. As long as there was a demand, kids would disappear. Babs had pointed a slender, manicured finger at Lettie Tan who owned the club he worked in on M.H. del Pilar. This was 'The Topless Pit', where the most beautiful hostesses were all male while authentic females were restricted to performing tricks like opening bottles of Coke with their vaginas, 'drinking' the contents and ejecting them in a tawny spray of froth into the delighted faces of drunken Australians. What had Iron Pussy and her colleagues to do with Dingca, whose precinct was now miles away on the other side of the Pasig? Maybe nothing. Having been posted off his old patch he was nowadays only too happy to leave the Ermita fleshpots to WPDC Station 5. None of Babs's information (*'Hot* news, Inspector. You're going to *love* this'. . . Why did Babs, of all people, call him by his correct, new, demilitarised rank?) would have registered had it not been for two recent, minor, and previously unconnected events. The first was that a woman had been arrested in Harrison Plaza shopping centre pretending to be the mother of a toddler who was trotting happily at her side, licking an ice cream. By sheer chance the real mother, who had been scanning the crowds of shoppers in panic, happened to spot her own infant even though it was now wearing a little blue cap with mouse ears. The mall's security guards had held all three, their task made no easier by the child's reluctance to show the least preference for either woman until the ice cream was gone. Then it wailed, the fake mother tried to make a run for it, was arrested and hauled away. The odd thing was that Dingca turned out to know her vaguely because she was from San Clemente and he heard of the case back at the station. The other minor event was a formal complaint lodged with his station chief by a wealthy citizen who alleged that the police were turning a blind eye to the despoliation and looting of a family cenotaph in the nearby cemetery. The wealthy citizen, who hadn't deigned to come in person but had sent a notarized letter via a young man who was either an action movie star or a goon and probably both, was Lettie Tan.

Dingca, the father not the Inspector, had for many minutes been saying 'Exactly, ma'am' and 'Nowadays you can't be too careful' to a succession of teachers wearing their best shoes. He now caught sight of Patti Gonzales a little way off and in the sudden lurch this caused him made two simultaneous discoveries. One was that she was Patti *Gonzales* as in Butz Gonzales, the owner of Bowl-o-Rama; the other was that she looked a good deal like Babs. *Babs?* That twilight creature? His asset? But yes. . . Especially the perfect teenage neck. And this realisation smeared a grotesque continuity over the whole morning, eliding the sleaze pits of Ermita with the rural innocence of San Pedro, and doing something too complicated to think about to his image of Patti. He and her father exchanged waves and began drifting in each other's direction.

'Hey, Rio.'

'How come I never knew you had a daughter? Especially one so beautiful? I thought you just had the boys.'

'She's our youngest. The scholar of the family. Thank God there's one, eh? If she gets this NCEE thing it's either the Civil Service or dentistry. Got to have someone to keep us in old age, right? No, Patti doesn't go out much. Books, books, books. Either at home in her room or in the library here. Right, Patti? Pat, come say Hi to one of Manila's Finest.'

'Finest what?' His daughter moved languidly over, the now wilting white flowers nodding tiredly over her ID as though sated and weakened by too lengthy proximity to her breasts. 'Joke only.'

'Policemen, of course,' said Butz, ignoring her last words. 'It's an expression.'

'Thank you, Daddy.' She held out a long, slender, ringless school-girl's hand. 'A great pleasure to meet you, sir.'

'This is Rio Dingca. He's a lieutenant and one of my greatest bowlers.'

'Dingca? Are you Eunice's dad, sir?'

'Yes. Indeed I am. None other. Though nowadays I'm actually an inspector.' The shy boy betrayed by his own pomposity.

'Wow. We're all envious of Eunice, you know. She's so clever. And beautiful.'

Dingca was aware, from a certain peppery scent like playground dust in the air, that he had strayed onto the outer fringes of some secret teenage battlefield. He suddenly felt protective of his own daughter. Patti's graceful neck, he now saw, had on one side the faintest blemish, a slightly darker oval patch. Only someone looking quite hard would have noticed. A fading bruise? Such as one might accidentally pick up in a library when a heavy book toppled from an upper shelf, h'm? Butz would have fallen for it. Fond dad with his attention fixed more firmly down the road at Los Baños, where he was planning to open another Bowl-o-Rama if he could arrange a little juggling with the land use of a plot on the outskirts. Dingca caught himself staring too intently at Patti, scanning her as if anxious to detect signs of coarseness from close to, little giveaways blatant only when set against his own daughter's authentic dewiness. But the faint bruise apart, there was nothing. Patti in propinquity was as monumentally perfect as Patti at a distance. *Big Girl.* Not big in the blowsy sense, and certainly not strapping. She was only slightly taller than most of her fellow students though it was exaggerated by her slender figure. No, she was a Big Girl to Dingca's little boy: the sort of girl his thirteen-year-old former self had looked up at in covert wonderment as too distant in age and beauty even to be a realistic repository for desire, for anything but the most diffuse and poignant longing. He had been obliged to turn back to girls his own age who still gulped down glasses of Sunny and went about with the ghost of an orange moustache. Touching, but not *it.* Nor were their legs ever as good as those of the Big Girls. They still bore the circular fading scars of a hundred childhood sores, most of which had healed without trace other than a slight blotchiness here and there, deeper brown on brown. But real Big Girls' legs were unmarked, as if they had been chosen from infancy to remain immune to the frequent *bakukang* around which flies clustered and which could leave legs mottled from the knees down. And if it was true of legs, so of faces. Big Girls never had acne, either. Big Gi–

'Do you know what Eunice is planning to do, sir?'

'Oh.' Dingca shook himself back to being forty-plus. 'Do? Eunice?' To his own astonishment he realised he had no idea. He must have been consulted or told a thousand times this last year, surely? He

63

nearly said 'Dentistry' before remembering in time that this was what Butz had just said Patti was considering. He found the solution. 'I thought everything nowadays depended on the, um, NCEE?'

'Do you know if there's any truth in this rumour, sir? That they're going to do away with the NCEE? Or replace it or something? A national examination, yet none of our teachers seems to know.'

'You mean a policeman would?'

One way and another it had been a weird day with its own particular ghosts in close attendance. One of the less substantial but still pervasive of these had been Lettie Tan's. Back on duty Dingca had been duly despatched with a PO1, a rookie named Benhur Daldal, to visit the cemetery and report on the condition of the Tan cenotaph. Unsure where to look they had driven up past the barrier towards the central cluster of chapels. In one of these they found the cemetery police unit playing *pusoy*. Between them they found a Tan lot on the faded old plan. Back in the jeep they meandered through the network of miniature roads with mature trees casting their shade across the pavements. They met nobody. The plot offered one of the less pretentious tombs: a plain two-storey narrow building washed in dull yellow. Instead of iron gates it had a pair of bronze doors which were shut tight. Dingca and Daldal walked all around it, peering in through a couple of barred windows. Everything seemed secure. The bars were firm in their cement, the panes unbroken. Inside, a marble sarcophagus glimmered in semi-darkness.

'Are we looking for unlawful intruders or what, sir?' asked the rookie.

'Who knows? We just had this report which said the place had been messed about. It looks okay to me.'

'It's in a lot better condition than my place.' Daldal, Dingca knew, lived on the railway tracks over in Sampaloc in a house to whose rear wall a squatter's shack clung like a barnacle, splashed whenever a train rumbled through the puddles into which the lines had sunk. 'Imagine all this just for a *dedbol*.'

'We can't see anything wrong, agreed? Woman needs her head examined.'

'You don't think,' the rookie said tentatively once they were back in the jeep with José Mari Chan singing "Beautiful Girl", 'there might be more than one Tan tomb?'

64

'No relation, you mean?'

'It's a common name.'

Back to the map. After reorienting themselves they drove down towards the gate and branched off parallel to the boundary. The road ahead curved gently around to the right, following the perimeter.

'*Susmaryosep.*' They both saw it simultaneously: a sort of miniature Moorish villa in white with turrets. Over the door, which was bound in polished brass straps like a family Bible, incised golden letters said TAN. Around the entire building ran portcullis-style iron railings, points uppermost, painted black. Evidently the place was comparatively new.

'If you saw that over in Dasmariñas Village you'd think it belonged to a presidential aide.'

'A small one, though.'

They climbed out once more and reconnoitred. From the front the place looked pretty much as the builders must recently have left it. Round the back it presented a different aspect. Several of the iron railings were missing. The white walls were covered in graffiti. From here the land sloped sharply down to the perimeter wall thirty feet away. Above this, as well as through a narrow gap, the tin roofs and hunched lean-to architecture of San Clemente were visible. In the middle of a pool of mud studded with ad hoc stepping stones (concrete blocks wrenched from the wall, the curved spine of a palm frond, a wooden plank) and littered with empty shampoo sachets, a rusty gooseneck of piping emerged. From it water dribbled and fed the surrounding swamp.

'Now I see what she's complaining about,' said Dingca. A child with a plastic bucket appeared in the gap in the wall, took a nonchalant step into the cemetery, caught sight of the two men and froze. 'Come here, boy,' called Dingca. The child fled, bucket banging hollowly. 'I wonder how long this has been going on?'

'Probably you only need to read the Tans' water meter to get a pretty good idea,' said Daldal shrewdly.

'If you're not careful you'll turn into a detective instead of a policeman.' Dingca squeezed in through the broken ironwork and inched along the gap between it and the mausoleum's wall. 'But if you look a bit closer you'll see they aren't paying. The water company is.' A pipe emerged from the ground, turned at right angles, passed

65

through a meter and entered the white wall. It was still possible to see where the trench had been cut, leading diagonally back towards the barrio and the illegal standpipe.

'Neat job, huh?'

'No,' said Dingca, 'a lash-up. See how the ground here's soggy, just beneath the meter? They cut into it one night, put in a T, couldn't borrow a proper pipe threader and wrench so just bound the joint with rubber. It's leaking steadily. More to the point, having done that and filled in the trench, why didn't they go the whole hog and run the pipe right down into San Clemente instead of stopping halfway?'

'Lack of pipe,' hazarded the rookie.

'More than likely. I wonder if that damp's getting inside? We'll have to induce Madam Tan to open up before we can make a full and proper report on damage. I'd be curious to see inside a place like this, wouldn't you?'

'Not really,' confessed Benhur. 'I don't mind morgues but I'm not too good in cemeteries. They say the Chinese dead have special spirit guards to protect them. Not like ours.'

Dingca had also heard this, otherwise he would have rejected it as a superstitious invention. 'Well anyway,' he said, 'we've got what we need. Damage to water main; damage to railings; damage to rear wall, to wit, graffiti. Gang stuff mostly, it looks like. Let's see. Oh, this'll do.' He took out a ballpoint and copied down one of the evidential phrases. ' "Wake up, Cory! The Chinese dead have roofs over their heads, your people have none!" The revolutionary lost command of San Clemente, no doubt. Come on.'

All that had been eight months ago. Within a week or two the railings had been repaired, the graffiti painted out, the MWSS had grubbed up the illegal spur. The Tans had increased their contribution to the cemetery police and arranged for one of them to be beaten up in order to encourage his comrades. The officers now made nightly visits to the tomb before settling down to their *pusoy*, reading horror comics and otherwise waiting for serious grave-robbers to strike. Lettie Tan had never allowed Rio Dingca inside to inspect for damage.

A week after her arrest the woman who had tried to abduct the child in Harrison Plaza had sworn she was unconnected to any kidnapping ring, had merely been 'freelancing' and yielded to spur-of-the-moment temptation. Bail had been posted at five thousand pesos, an absurd sum the poor woman couldn't possibly have afforded in a lifetime. The poor woman promptly paid it and vanished. Or someone paid it for her and vanished her. The main point was that the case fell through its own bottom like ice cream through a soggy cone, leaving any possible Tan connection unresolved. Then in early June Babs had been found rolled up in a mat in San Andres. His perfect teenage throat (he was actually twenty-eight, Dingca discovered) had been cut from earring to earring. His cock had also been cut off and stuffed up his own rectum. Dingca hoped very much this had happened after death but gloomily doubted it.

Poor Babs. Nowadays when he thought of him Dingca was unable to work the trick in reverse, go from the transvestite's face to that of Patti Gonzales, regenerate any of the connections that had worked once and once only for a single day in March. To tell the truth, he hadn't given another thought to Butz's daughter from that moment to this; whereas he often found himself seeing Babs passing fleetingly through the faces of perfect strangers imperfectly glimpsed, as if his asset were still hovering forlornly in limbic form, despairingly trying on body after body to find the one into which he could slip back. 'Too kind, Inspector. Fried chicken would be just the thing. A girl's got to keep her strength up if she's expected to talk as well as everything else. Now, stumped, are we? We're in need of a little tip from the twilight zone, h'm?' Dingca had in fact hardly ever seen Babs in full drag. Whenever they met on anonymous ground somewhere like Quiapo he was a rather ordinary looking young man in denim and T-shirt, not even effeminate. The policeman had tried to see in the face hungrily tearing at a chicken leg across the narrow formica tabletop the exquisite feminine lines and planes which emerged after dark in 'The Topless Pit' and which had more than once (Babs claimed) caused tourists to come to blows with each other in their attempts to carry him off to the Hilton, if not absolutely to paradise itself. It caused Dingca an additional pang that Babs had met his death in working costume. In some sense it was a beautiful young woman who had died so horribly that night. He had seen assets come and go for a variety of reasons, only a few of them terminal, but none of them affected him as Babs had. Somewhere caught up in it all, or hanging about it like a poignant scent, was an aching sense of waste. Now and again it came to him, the feeling of an unguessable substance unravelling – inside or out he couldn't tell – as if certain faces or certain presences held things together but that when they were gone a dissolution set in which could catch him sitting in front of a lone bottle of beer in a bar when he might have been driving home to San Pedro, Laguna.

Well. His old station, Station 5, had got nowhere on Babs and now never would. Tourist Belt entertainers were always turning up dead. It was a high risk profession. Impotent as he was to express any proper emotion for an informer he'd hardly known (but whom he now wished he had), Rio Dingca opted for loyalty of a sort. At least he could take seriously whatever Babs had been trying to tell him. But his last information had been vague and had already come to nothing. A finger pointed at Lettie Tan, that was all. Of course she was bent. A wealthy family who owned all sorts of things besides a night club in Ermita: how could she not be? But faint as the links were, they touched him in one way or another by connecting with San Clemente. He'd tried a friend in Station 5 for anything recent on 'The Topless Pit' and its proprietress and had come up with a sheaf of technical infringements, short cuts, bribes and a scandalous piece of conveyancing. The most one could shake out of all that would be the odd henchman, some goons, and more than a few fellow-policemen. There was no sense in even thinking of going after one of the Tans because there was no earthly way you could get anything to stick. And if you did by some miracle make a case and live to file charges and see it presented, the likelihood of a Tan seeing the inside of a jail cell even for ten minutes was too remote to bother with. And if they *did*, you'd have a lot more to worry about because your own troubles would only just have begun, and wouldn't be over until you were too.

IO

PRIDEAUX HAD ALWAYS thought the notion of Press responsibility was another of those self-negating phrases like 'Merry Christmas' or 'native delicacies'. Since meeting Vic Agusan, however, he had begun to reconsider. The need to sell newspapers did indeed result in some pretty inventive journalism now and then, but in a land already inured to grotesque scandal there was really no way of outdoing the stories which had been proved to the hilt and even turned out to understate the truth. In a sense that *was* the scandal; and those papers which took risks by publishing unconfirmed gossip or which linked already tainted public figures with – for a change – a scam of which they were quaintly innocent were not, he now thought, irresponsible within the larger context. After all, if the great and the good turned out to have been unjustly maligned they could always sue, as Cory Aquino had Luis Beltran and his publisher when he described her as trying to take cover under her bed during a coup attempt. After a duly solemn visit by the jurors to the Presidential residence on Arlegui St. the court had accepted that this was an impossibility since there was a clearance of only a few centimetres between the bed and the floor. Beltran's claim that he had merely been employing a figure of speech, such as any writer might, was of no avail. The accusation of cowardice had stung the President and now she was going to sting in return, to the tune of two million pesos.

Well, there could be no gospel version of anarchy. Coming from a country where the police were public servants whose remit was to preserve public order, Prideaux could only admire journalists like Vic Agusan as day in and day out they presented the ironic and entirely proper spectacle of the public trying to keep the police in order.

Below the surface the joke stopped abruptly. The roll of journalists who had vanished or been found dead was lengthy: over thirty in only the last five years. MIAs and KIAs, as he thought of them, for his sojourn in Manila was doing odd things to Prideaux's sense of the past.

Some time after turning forty he had begun to see his private history in a new way. Unsatisfactory now was the conventional list of milestones which anybody might tot up; less interesting, too, the inexorabilia of psychoanalytic theory. Quite the contrary: it seemed to him the things which had affected his life most radically had been *absences* rather than actual events. His recent lack of a wife, even of a companion, echoed through his days with far greater resonance than would a plausible (but always hypothetical) account of why. Why did one lack things? Why did one lack money, for example? There was no end to the answers, no combination of which had a fraction of the explicatory power over a life as did penury itself. Or aloneness. Which law of chance said it was inevitable that by the age of forty one would have met a suitable mate? Or did this mean most people became flexible as time ran out, willing to make strange compromises while still pretending to an ideal partner? In any case that was certainly one of Prideaux's absences. But lately he had become convinced that the most formative absence of his entire life was missing Vietnam.

When he was seventeen Prideaux was a bright English public schoolboy who had already won himself a place at Cambridge. Instead of leaving school at once and filling in the intervening year profitably he had elected to stay on and safely bask in the pleasures of status. It was an error of vanity, one he thought he deserved by way of reward for having overcome years of being dismissed by peers and teachers alike for a certain angularity of mind, a waywardness which occasionally bordered on the mildly outré. This, in that last mandarinesque year of his schooldays, he expressed with perfect conventionality by espousing (in a school whose last collective political thought of the faintest radicalism had coincided with the Repeal of the Corn Laws) a brand of Socialism a little to the left of the Labour Party. The stuffier teachers dutifully pretended to be provoked by this and Prideaux spent much time haranguing serious bespectacled boys in his study over large and fragrant teas of buttered toast, Battenburg cake and Earl Grey. Revolution was quite often mentioned by this young exquisite, now a weird combination of mandarin and firebrand.

If he achieved little in these long wasted months, this odious young man began at last to be aware of events outside Britain. He was conscious that US troops were being sent to South Vietnam in increasing numbers. In his first term at university came the battle of Ia Drang Valley. It was November 1965. The war had not yet become a great issue in the British press and the sketchy television news coverage must have made a particular impression on him, like the first time a musical infant hears somebody sing or play a note on a piano. Suddenly, everything conspired at once to make the growing distant war embody forms of loss and longing he never knew he had. This wasn't the death of boys his own age, it was *Morte d'Arthur*. Or it was a monstrous crime committed by imperialist capitalist lackeys against defenceless peasants who only wanted to shake off the yoke of foreign oppression. Or else it represented real life in contrast to the anaemic dreamworld in which he found himself boredly cloistered. Whatever else, it was a golden time for deeds of valour and comradeship. It was a nexus of principled opposition, of marching and speechifying and delivering exhilarating denunciations of Stone Age dons in tweed jackets. Girls could be met at parties and bedded within the hour just on the strength of shared opinions about Vietnam. On the basis of a beard, loons and a peace button total strangers could meet and exchange a vague simulacrum of the complex hand choreography of 'daps' with which black GIs were greeting each other in Vietnam. Solidarity was all. Ritually-slapped palms echoed around the world wherever the right-thinking met.

Prideaux graduated in 1968, the year of the Tet Offensive, that resounding tactical surprise whose psychological effects on America so completely outweighed the military defeat the NVA supposedly suffered. The war was lost; the war went on. Prideaux hung fire. He was not an American, he told himself and others, and he certainly wouldn't help them if he were. Yet where else was there to be at that moment? He indulged in journalism, flew to Stockholm and interviewed some draft-dodgers. His great coup was to unearth a deserter from the US Marines now living under the name of his new Swedish wife. Time passed, carrying Prideaux with it. By now he was a war groupie: Ruff-Puffs, klicks, Spooky. Even as he opposed it the war engulfed him. K-bar, A Shau, Bouncing Betty, Ben Tre. . . *Ben Tre.* . . *destroy it to save it.* By now, too, enough time had gone by for the early years to be casting a rotten, nostalgic glow. Marble Mountain, M-14s, hot LZs. He knew he would have recognised the cool, wet earthenware smell the red laterite soil exhaled at dawn, the ubiquitous stench of barrels of burning excrement soaked in jet fuel, the taste of C-rations corned beef hash. Outstanding. Airborne all the way.

It is very strange for a young man to long for war even as he watches pictures of other young men filing out of C-130s unshaven and hollow-eyed, or choppered back to base in body bags. Stranger still if they are not his countrymen and it is not his war. What are we to think about someone who identifies with 'the allies' but sides with the enemy? Nothing much; other than to presume that such things are quite common and merely evidence of the muddle of hormones and cultural inheritance which make young men everywhere willing to fight men they don't know at the behest of men who don't know them. A conspiracy of confusion from which myths sprout like headstones. Why didn't Prideaux get closer? He could have become a war correspondent and drunk life to the lees in the foxhole of his choice. He could have become part of that non-combatant elite who combined the hardbitten knowingness of grunts with classy nonchalance: *Honkers, Saigers, Pnompers.* He could have attended briefings in JUSPAO with weary and cynical disbelief then hitched a Huey into the boonies for a taste of the real raw: fragging, Grateful Dead, Morrison, Zappa, the killing box. In 1970 he joined as script consultant a film unit off to Indochina to make documentaries and wound up writing three films. There at last he was ineffectually shot at by child soldiers rendered blind by US steel helmets which fell to midnose. He went to Saigon, walked Tu Do as if he'd known it as an old hand in some previous incarnation (it did, too, feel remarkably familiar), photographed large-scale pilfering in the overcrowded port.

But already it was lost. Men were still dying, hooches still burned, but the great withdrawal had long since started. It was lost to him. He kept hearing, 'That was way back, when? Sixty-six, I guess. Shoulda seen it. Un-fuckin'-real.' Some time ago at an unspecified but always invocable moment it had been the real war, real Vietnam. Boys had lost their lives within forty-eight hours of leaving Fort Benning. Prideaux lost his watch to a snatcher in Cholon. They made the films. One was of US troops on the ground in Cambodia's Svay Rieng province, right there in the Parrot Beak area at a moment when the American administration was swearing hand on heart that none of its troops had ever violated Cambodian neutrality. A second documentary concerned the money-changing rackets run mainly by a handful of Indian families in South Vietnam itself. Filming in the first was entirely open; the second relied on a good deal of concealed camera-work with ultrafast film so the eye could plainly catch the constant riffle of notes changing hands in dark huts, the faces of GIs freely laundering military scrip (which in theory was not legal tender off-base) into regular greenbacks. In weeks of filming, tons of money flew between brown and white fingers in a dozen currencies, some of which – Chinese, Burmese, Indian – were supposed to be worthless outside those countries. Both films were widely shown and praised and both won prizes. Prideaux's scripts were adjudged 'hard-hitting' in that way which is especially irritating to film makers who know they were unable to tell the half of it. ('It's been going on for years, for Chrissake. Only now that it's practically over can we get a watered-down version of stuff like this shown. Mustn't send Mr and Mrs Porch Swing, Idaho, into cardiac arrest'.) Not now; *then*. It was always *Then*: back then, back when the real killing was being made, was going on, when a whole culture was formed and grew out of its founders like a private club.

Almost a quarter of a century later Prideaux was still able to surprise in himself a wistful yearning for retroactive membership of that club, the vast majority of whose members had never wanted to join, whose list had long ago closed and could now only dwindle. It seemed he was nostalgic for times unshared, for comrades he never had; whereas what had happened was that he had once been twenty, and his being twenty had coincided with the great issue of the times. Recalling those times still transported him to territory rich in ghosts, echoing with dated jargon. Yet it was not always reassuring since it came with reminders of failure. Why *had* he not? Not when the time was ripe? Physical fear? Cowardice? Maybe; maybe also an instinctual sense which would always tell him that no matter what one did to seize the moment it had always already passed with a flash of wings, trailing

73

behind it a purposeful smudge as it roared towards some far-off scene of action. The sidelines, the edge of things; that seemed to be Prideaux's ordained place as the shuddering air grew still.

Documentaries, documentaries.

Three years after the fall of Saigon in 1975 Prideaux turned thirty. What his twenty-year-old self would have thought an enviable career well begun had taken on the manic inconsequentiality of all TV work. Enough of the schoolboy didact remained in him to resent finding himself part of the entertainment industry, coasting on a reputation which now appeared outdated, even fraudulent, so quickly were those intense years of confrontation and revelation being left behind. He had tried to follow the two films which made his name with one they had shot in Bangkok on the back of the other productions. This was going to be gaff-blowing of a far more emotive kind, a story he had got wind of in Saigon, the one they couldn't ignore.

It was about a racket run by an ex-Master Sergeant who had resigned the service after two tours of duty in Vietnam, having sniffed out a better line of business. This was catering for the needs of troops on R&R in Bangkok. The advantage the American had over the Thais was that he knew his countrymen better than they did and understood that a few of them – a very few – would pay well for something which went beyond the usual strip-joint menu. He had spotted in the ragged hordes of war orphans sleeping on pavements and in parks a potential source of income. He bought a van and sprayed it pink and blue: jolly pastel shades on which floated solid red and yellow balloons trailing jaunty strings. The name of the ex-Master Sergeant's company, Toytime, was stencilled in white letters on both side doors. The van would deliver to clients' apartments – even sometimes to international hotels – refugee children who had been picked up off the streets, given a bath, a square meal and clean T-shirts and knickers before being whisked off to a party. The kids couldn't believe their luck. Some hours later, in response to a phone call, the same van would call with collapsible packing cases to collect their bodies. It was a straight cash deal. Toytime delivered the goods and disposed of the evidence. Nobody complained because there was nobody to complain.

Prideaux had some good stuff, including the ex-Master Sergeant's identity and military record. He filmed the van arriving and two children about eight years old being handed over at a door by the Thai driver. He filmed the van returning and two large cartons being carried out of the house. The van doors slammed, the camera followed at a distance through a rain-spotted windscreen which melted and refracted jewels of neon streaming past on both sides. Despite being a stock piece of ciné vérité this not very brisk chase somehow managed an atmosphere which was becoming the Prideaux hallmark, that of a faint intangible sadness like the pursuit of a fading dream. The sequence ended abruptly when armed Thais in uniform surrounded the camera car at some traffic lights. Between their encroaching torsos were a couple of glimpses of the pastel van with its gay balloons vanishing down a turning beside a *klong*. Next came an abortive interview with a bland senior officer of the Thai Traffic Police whom Prideaux believed was in the ex-Master Sergeant's pay. Their conversation was intercut with shots of the same officer in plain clothes behind the counter of a shop selling pilfered US matériel. The officer was taking an order in Thai for fifty M-60 grenade launchers, two thousand grenades and forty M-16s. 'No problem,' said the English subtitles. 'What about Claymores?' The camera, which was shooting from a car parked opposite, picked up a lot of shine from the shop window, plus reflections of passers-by, and intervening traffic added to the problem. But again and again there was no doubt of the officer's identity as light caught his speaking face behind the pane. The mike was concealed on the customer's belt in a pouch for sunglasses. It crackled and rustled but the words were clear and intelligible to the Thai who later did the transcription and translation. When the camera panned back to take in the shopfront itself the name above it read 'Royal Thai Road Safety Campaign'. The implication was obvious. This Thai officer was involved in rackets. If he openly brokered stolen US military equipment why mightn't he be protecting all sorts of renegade Americans such as the managing director of Toytime? How else would he get his supplies brand new and still slippery with Cosmolene?

One of the most telling shots in this short documentary was a quick cut of an international aid agency's Bangkok Field Director who spoke a few glowing sentences about Toytime as, he believed, 'typical of the small and as yet uncoordinated efforts on the part of caring people to ease the lot of perhaps the most overlooked and defenceless casualties of this appalling war'. This showed that not only did the scrawny old fool not have the first idea what Toytime was up to but the ex- Master Sergeant's business could flourish openly with the connivance of corrupt authorities and ignorant charity directors.

'Can't touch it, John.' How many mouths had he watched frame these words as they munched in London restaurants or dribbled smoke in offices? 'I mean, Christ almighty, what a *story*. I can't wait to see the rough cut. If it was up to me, of course, it would go out prime time, triple star rating, required viewing. Move over *Panorama* and *World in Action*. But I know those guys upstairs. The bottom line is *no way*.'

After they had seen some clips from the the rough cut and the lights had come up, leaving the mouths shaken and troubled, they changed to a different tack, as if relieved at finding a rationale for turning the film down.

'*You* know it's going on and *I* know it's going on. Enough to make you puke. Those poor little. But there's no. . . actual. . . *proof*. Is there? Really, John? When it comes down to it? What you've got – and I must say I think you've done an absolutely brilliant job, Christ, some of that footage – what you've got is a certain amount of very suggestive circumstantial evidence and a certain amount of hearsay, but you've not got the clincher.'

'Like a kid actually being fucked to death or throttled till her eyes pop? You mean if I had *that* you'd go with it? Put it out and hang the consequences?'

'I didn't say that, John. I only meant we could cover ourselves. Legally, morally.'

'Supposing I tell you I've got that footage?'

The mouths always opened at this point. 'Aw, Jesus.'

'Does that mean you'll show it?'

'No, of course it bloody doesn't. Look, I understand what it's like. You've become emotionally involved in this thing and who can blame you. If it'd been me I don't think I'd ever sleep again. But you know as well as I that if you're going to do investigative documentaries you've got to show the crime being crimed. By and large. That's what was so ace about *Parrot's Beak* and *Money Men*. That's why you got the awards, John. They're absolute models of how to do it. Here's what's happening. Here's your allegation in words. Here's more visual proof. *Boom*. But in this thing you've got a crime that's far too horrible and, let's face it, too *minority* to be shown. Most viewers wouldn't even stand for it being delicately hinted at, still less our Head of Docs. Not now. Not a chance. Perhaps in twenty years. But not now. . . Have you *really* got it on film?'

Of course Prideaux didn't have it on film, but of course the entire business of legality was an irrelevance. Once out in the polished roar of Great Cumberland Place he knew in his heart this was right. Certain stories were inherently untouchable. This was 1971 and the Americans were washing their hands of Vietnam. Nobody back home in the States wanted any more painful revelations about what really had gone wrong, what really had happened. They wanted oblivion. They didn't even want to see their own boys arriving home. And England, pusillanimous little England, would go on supporting them to the bitter end, not rocking the boat. His eyes filled with tears of frustration, not unmixed with a sentimental rush on behalf of the nameless victims even then, like as not, speeding to their first and last party in new knickers and T-shirt.

So fuck TV, there was always the Press. But there wasn't, for all the same reasons. For a while it looked as though the *Sunday Times* might run it in 'Insight', backed up by carefully-chosen stills from The Film No-one Would Show. But this, too, fell through. Vietnam was either too long ago or too recent, the mouths couldn't agree on that in between their gulps of wine or instant coffee. In any case the timing was wrong. So it was even for 'Footnotes' since *Private Eye* was currently distracted by libel actions.

Prideaux didn't have Manson-style snuff action in the can, but he did have a body. A voice on the phone had woken him in the old Flower Palace in Bangkok. Sound and lighting were goofing off somewhere in town so he and Pete Rivett the cameraman dressed and got into their hired Simca.

'It's at moments like this one pauses for thought,' Prideaux said, his hand on the ignition key. Outside, Patpong's nightlife thudded and flashed. 'When gumshoes are woken amid bachelor sleaze with anonymous tip-offs of corpses, they know their first duty's to tell the cops. But they, like us, want a scoop and a headstart.'

'So let's go.'

A white tourist stood woozily on the kerb and urinated at the passing cars. Prideaux stared without seeing him.

'Okay, John,' Rivett had said, 'it's a set-up. Your caller's a cop who's sick of us interfering, right? We go out, we find the bod, and suddenly *whango*, on come the headlights. "Why you no tell us? Since when you do Thai police work? Maybe you the ones who kill." That's always possible.'

'But maybe it's also that final damning piece of evidence we need.'

'Yeah,' Pete said. 'So we risk it. We go.'

In the adrenal, neon-lit night beyond the car windows a thousand reasons for not going winked with mocking clarity. Apprehensively Prideaux had started the Simca, shamed into action as, without knowing it, men are shamed into gallantry. He, as they, retained a small rage tucked away. It knew that Pete Rivett was braver because stupider. After all, he had only come up with one possible scenario. Prideaux could think of dozens.

In the film, the sequence was climactically stark, short, gaining everything from his loss of nerve.

'A midnight caller told us where one of Toytime's victims had been dumped.'

The V/O accompanied some wild footage shot from the same car on another night. Girlie bars streamed past. Revellers lurched. Traffic melted like tears, highlights rolling off cellulose curves and stippling glass.

'If true, this was not work for a British film crew but for the Thai police. If false, the information could be a trap set for meddlesome foreigners. Given what we already knew about the involvement of at least one senior officer we dared not trust the police.'

By now the car was in open country, heading down the airport road, shot three nights later when nerves had recovered and no hue and cry had started. Oh – Prideaux told Pete – he repeated it. Twice, actually. He said the next turn after Sukvannet. There's a gas station serving the village road and the *klong* running parallel to it. Drivers stop in front, boatmen tie up behind. Burnt out a couple of months back, he said. There, right behind the facilities, you'll see.

They almost missed the garage, dark as it was, and swung off across the apron, tyres poppling on char and scraps of rusty metal. We'll have to try and get it in one pass, Prideaux said, stopping abruptly like a motorist who knows he's taken a wrong turning. If it's an ambush we want it on film. Shoot from the back seat, right hand side. According to him it's behind the truck, wherever the f–, ah, yuh.

On the film the light sidles over the oval end of a rusting petrol tanker hunkered down on its brake drums in crusted puddles of wire and carbonised rubber. The relic slides past, industrial dinosaur, all blacks and greys and curved ribs as if dug out of the La Brea tar pits. Then a blotch of white. Someone is watching, casually, sitting on the rusty springs of the driver's seat down on the ground. The camera doesn't stop but drifts past, catching the whole child, leaving the individual eye to pick for ever the detail which burns. For Prideaux the instant he saw him was no different from the thousandth time that versions of him had curled up on the cutting-room floor. It was the right leg, not broken he was sure but flopped over with a child's flexibility, the inside edge of the sneaker flat on the concrete forecourt. It was the most defenceless object he had ever seen, this thin brown leg, so assertive in its vulnerability that it obviously longed to be free of the upper half of the body which was so clearly dead. The boy's head was tilted forward so the features were foreshortened and no expression was readable. He was examining the hand lying in his lap. The other was palm up beside the seat. In the shadow cast by his own features the mouth was pouchy or swollen or protrusive. As the camera passed it took in the yellow ligature around his neck, visible from the side, a rolled bandanna or Scout scarf, it looked like.

Go go go – Prideaux said, hyperventilating, although he himself was driving, and took off like a lunatic, throwing Pete into a heap of power packs and film canisters. This would be the moment for the actinic flare of headlights, the hail of bullets.

'Our unknown informant had not lied.'

'The child's body had been left exactly where we were told.'

Head bowed, the meditative small figure went on sitting in Prideaux's mind, foot bent over, palm outflung. Was still there twenty years later although by now he had stiffened into an emblem, the *rigor vitae* having set in which afflicts those doomed to live only in survivors' minds. The little body exerted a terrific gravitational pull such that unlikely moments and extraneous topics would be dragged inwards to confront it. It was he who sat in London restaurants and offices, listening to executive mouths deny him a hearing even as they chomped and sucked and swilled. Prideaux shielded him from executive eyes, denying him to all but a couple of waverers who might finally have been convinced.

'Oh my God. Oh my God. I don't know what to say. God, John, it's. I mean. The best thing you've done. In its way. It's just gotta be shown. But it can't be. No way can we put that out.'

This went on. Then one day Prideaux showed it to a friend of Pete Rivett's, an American cameraman who had freelanced Tet and sold ABC its best footage of Hue. 'Yeah,' he said at the end, stubbing out a Camel in the armrest tray, 'can we run it again?' There were only the three of them in the viewing theatre. The second time around he said 'You didn't like Bangkok, right?' He was talking to Pete.

'I didn't like the story.'

Prideaux heard this as a betrayal. 'Who did?' he asked.

'Sure. But it shows in the camera. It's not as good as your Cambodia thing. Or the money scam. Loved that. Nobody in Nam who didn't know that was going down. Sniffing out that account, what was it called, Prysumeen? Righteous stuff. But this thing don't cut the mustard. It kinda doesn't matter in the same way.'

'Doesn't *matter*?'

'It's not news, not like the others. What you've got here's a slimeball running a business for scuzzbuckets. Could be anyone, anyplace, doing a little free enterprise on the edge of a war zone. Sure, it's gross, but it's one guy in a million catering for five guys in a million. A real pity he's American, John. Y'understand what I'm saying? "The Master Sergeant". Ex-GI. Troops on R&R. War orphans. It's all claiming to be up there with My Lai and Calley but it's not. That was about what constant fear and danger and grief can do to your average down-home cracker when he reaches breaking point in hostile territory. He goes amok, right? But your guy's an entrepreneur, not a combat victim. Sure do wish he'd been French or Australian. Or a Brit. 'n I sure wish we could say his clients were chiefly foreign correspondents and cameramen 'stead of grunts on R&R. Cos I reckon the typical GI, even if he has been in firefights in the last few months, 's no more likely to want to snuff kids in a heavy sex scene than the typical film crewman who's been *filming* those firefights. 'ts what I think.'

It was what Prideaux was thinking, too, only hadn't known until that moment when he sat in the viewing theatre with a draining sensation. The child was never to have his posthumous justice, then. Or maybe the journalist would be denied his next palm.

' 'nany case the title'd have to go. Too close to that Rod Steiger thing. *The Sergeant*. Now that. Shit, that opening sequence. That landscape. Henri Persin, beautiful camerawork. "I wanna see this place CLEAR! CLEAR! CLEAR!", the whole method bit, great movie.'

Only those with Prideaux's arrogance could have understood what it was to aim for a masterpiece each time rather than for the respectably cumulative, the solid, which builds a professional reputation. It was as if he might always have given up after three films, having tried that medium, conquered it, retired disdainfully leaving the field free once more for the less talented to plod on, slowly filling their bookshelves with bronze statuary and citations sandwiched in lucite slabs. There was no provision inside him for his own miscalculation. Outright failure could always be smudged, glossed as merely a matter of ill-informed opinion. But misjudgement, wrong reading. . . How wrongly could one read the boy on the charred seat, the lolling sneaker? His next documentary was about the popularity of bingo, a sociological sign of the times in working class Britain. It was thought amusing in a melancholy sort of way, without the expected patronage, full of striking images. Vietnam was over, so Nixon's bombing of Hanoi in that Christmas week of 1972 seemed like the gratuitous start of an entirely new war. Twenty years later strange relics still survived those times, occasionally exploding with disabling force. Among this buried ordnance was always the sight of the bleakly moated US Embassy in London's Grosvenor Square. The golden eagle still spread its wings on top. The hedges down below, once trampled into matchwood by anti-war protesters and police horses skidding on toy marbles, had long grown back. Only for a few would it forever remain Genocide Square.

Documentaries, documentaries.

Those with somewhere to go, go. Those w·∵nout do supplementary degree courses in their forties. The docur,entaries had taken him everywhere and nowhere. Maybe anthropology would be a staid enough discipline on which a wayward traveller might hone a working lifetime down into a few slender rules with which to puncture stay-at-home academics. John Prideaux, the man with the producer's ticket, was long since played out and washed up. In theory he too should have matured into a mouth, wining and dining young hopefuls who nowadays didn't even have to book a viewing theatre to get their stuff seen. They produced cassettes from every pocket like cigarette packs, fed them into players, flooded your office with instant sound and images before you could say 'Make an appointment with Jackie, 'kay?' In practice, mouths were mouths because supplicants couldn't look them in the eye; couldn't raise their own vision beyond the lips spilling smoke and phrases like 'Can't use it, I'm afraid,' or 'The idea's got legs but the film just stands still.' Or just 'Jesus, have I got problems enough with the union.' Besides, British TV documentaries had long since ossified into two or three versions of the same film, which Prideaux supposed was a slight advance on the radio documentary which existed in only one version endlessly repeated. ('Do you one in a morning, single-handed, any subject you like,' he'd once told a radio producer. 'Step one is to send down to the music library for a remotely relevant theme song. For instance, anything to do with the Bank of England, the Stock Exchange or higher finance you have to get Abba going "Money, money, money". It's compulsory. You play a wodge of that at the beginning, that's three minutes' script time saved. You go on putting musical bites in at regular intervals and the half hour's already down to twenty-two minutes. You send someone out into the street to get some vox pops, any old brainless opinions, it doesn't matter. Cut those in and you've dropped to eighteen minutes. Then you ring up one of your list of tame experts to find his viewpoint and book him. You work out what the opposite view would be and find another expert to espouse that. That's called balance. Then all you need is a third expert who can say "But as usual the truth probably lies somewhere between. Meanwhile, the City. . ." and it's a wrap. Do it in my sleep.')

Where did bitterness reside, hidden away beneath weary amiability until no single incident remained, only a no-go area like a bruise which even lovers respect? And did it not transmute private failure into a noble blur, the righteousness of far-off times? After all, John Prideaux was vaguely known – if at all – as a bleeding heart from the Vietnam Era, back around that time. Didn't he kill himself? Wait a bit, maybe that was James Mossman, someone else for whose fundamental decency the world's grief had proved too much?

82

Where, come to that, did failure itself lie except in the ghost which Prideaux knew gibbered just off-screen in all his work, the spectre of inconclusiveness? The media wanted their stories cut and dried: narratives which began in mock puzzlement or affected ignorance, proceeded with the panache of revelation and closed with hard words and cell doors. A wrong righted. Or rights exposed as wronged. But the child sitting for ever in the burnt-out garage, twenty years dead, staring at his lap as if he knew it had betrayed him, was not a matter of injustice. He was a tiny event. *That was what happened when.* When wars broke out; when monsters became organised; when Prideaux went belatedly to Indochina. Like his unshown film, the child was yet another of its maker's absences.

I I

THE DIGGING in San Clemente was progressing. The pit was now too deep for two men comfortably to work in at once so Eddie Tugos, Billy, Bats and Judge took turns with the spade while the others squatted around the edge taking nips of gin and offering advice. When they encountered a large stone or the corner of a seam of stiff clay they plugged away with one of the iron fencing posts they had stolen months earlier from the Tan mausoleum. Now and then Nanang Pipa took a few minutes away from her frenetic hemming and edging to come out and cast a foreman's eye over her workers' progress. Like many Filipinos Eddie referred to his wife – only half in jest – as *Si Kumander*. Mrs Boss now looked down towards her husband's bald spot.

'It's coming along,' she conceded. 'Slowly.'

'How much deeper do you want the damn thing, anyway? All we're digging is a hole to shit into, not a well.'

'Remember the floods, Eddie. Even up here it gets bad. You want it all backing up into the kitchen? Just a bit further.'

'You're going to have to line it,' pointed out Bats. 'Otherwise the sides'll start crumbling until one day when you're comfortably engaged the whole lot'll drop straight through with you on top.'

'Really?' said Nanang Pipa. 'Is that true, Eddie?'

'Well,' said the hole.

'Best thing's hollow blocks. You'll need about a hundred.'

'A *hundred*?' Nanang Pipa eyed the mound of spoil and tried to

84

imagine a pile of a hundred hollow blocks. It seemed to her their volume would greatly exceed that of the hole. 'And how much would that cost?'

'They're, what, about four pesos each these days.'

'Four hundred pesos just to line it?'

'Excluding a couple of bags of cement and some sand. They'll have to be properly laid and grouted. When I was in the DPWH we used to -'

'Probably about seven hundred, then. Plus what, the bowl?'

'No problem with the bowl. We can get that from the Chinese over the wall. Even their dead have bowel movements, you know. It makes you think.'

'It's still a lot of money. But if we're going to do it at all we're going to do it properly.'

'We?' queried the hole.

The sides of the pit now needed expanding to accommodate the lining of hollow blocks. Through the window Pipa covertly watched the men glumly chopping at the edges, effectively filling in again much of the depth they had already achieved. Behind her the sewing machines whirred. A boy was on his knees on the floor trying to fit a consignment of T-shirts into a cardboard carton a couple of sizes too small. Bolts of cloth lay in gaudy bolsters on every available ledge. The sewers worked without stopping, without resting. Beneath their hands the cloth flowed like sheets of factory dough, falling in flakes and roundels and tubes, ruffed and puckered and frilled, so that what emerged from the process seemed to be formed of a different substance.

Tucked away in one corner a youth was hunched over a tiny, ancient Yamato edging machine. Rey was the chop-chop boy, fitting together leftover flitches of cloth of different colours, patterns and quality and assembling the patchwork into children's T-shirts and shorts. These were the cheapest garments of all, the very end of the range, and went for only nine or ten pesos. They sold well, and not just because of the low price. The chop-chop boy was inventive, artistic even. His little T-shirts were halved and quartered in different colours, lengthwise or horizontally. Their backs might be pink, their fronts blue. Diagonal stripes met patchwork hems. Arm cuffs were variegated scraps neatly joined. Rey giggled a lot and had a flair for smutty repartee. Early that morning Nanang Pipa had given him a heap of old material she had

85

unearthed. When shaken out it had been revealed as a dozen rectangles of coarse cloth: flour sacks which had been unpicked and laundered long ago. Rey was now incorporating these wittily into the kids' clothing. The red and blue print would fade with washing, no doubt, but meanwhile it was merry to include among the other scraps of material the defunct Grains Authority's stern warning *Huwag mag-aksaya*, 'Do Not Waste'; or the printed promise 'Self Raising', strategically positioned across the front of some child's shorts.

As eyes accustomed themselves to dimmer light they would perceive that Rey was not after all the lowliest member of the co-operative. At his feet on the red floor-waxed concrete sat a ten-year-old girl with a withered leg. She was cutting into tiny rectangles the scraps which even Rey couldn't use and sewing them into patchwork mats. Sometimes she made circular potholders instead. The whole room hummed with work and proximity.

The sight and sound of the digging outside suddenly affected Nanang Pipa with a melancholy unease. It had to do with precarious-ness, a reminder that any improvement, any embellishment, any expense was in the long run wasted. This was not her land. It was her house only to the extent that she had scavenged the posts and boards of which it was built. Things were going well: out of nothing they had made work and out of work they made a living, something which eluded plenty of people in San Clemente. But where was the feeling of security this ought to be bringing? It was a dangerous illusion to think of this place as a village. In reality it was a collection of shacks on a skiddy hill. Any pretence that it had the permanence implied by words like 'village' or even 'settlement' was nothing but self-deception. Only a couple of days ago she had been down in Sta. Cruz (on Dasmariñas, to be exact) scouring Chinese hardware shops for an acetylene lamp to use during brownouts. Seeing a crowd on the bridge she had joined it. On the west side of the *estero* all the squatters between Dasmariñas and Escolta were being evicted. Their shanties, which staggered out on dogleg pilings over the miasmic water, were being demolished. The most impressive thing was the silence in which onlookers and evicted alike watched the destruction of their homes, and which cut the scene out of the surrounding city's din. As if they, too, were affected by it (for probably half of them lived in similar shacks) the gang of municipal workers were not even talking or calling out among themselves. The only sounds were the clatter of their hammers and crowbars, the groan of tin roofing, the pop and snap of boards. A rusty sheet of metal which everyone could recognise as an oil drum opened out and beaten flat slid into the treacly water and vanished. Huge belches of gas from the disturbed mud roiled up. The workers were watched by an overseer sitting atop the cab of a truck; a dozen armed police stood nearby. Meanwhile, the evicted waited in a silent line with their possessions piled around them: trussed fowls, a piglet tied to a table leg, rolled mats, the whole shabby interior of scratch living exposed to the sun and the onlookers' gaze. Why did they stand and watch? she wondered. But there again, how could they not? Someone had to bear witness, as at an execution, even though the end was foregone.

Nanang Pipa wondered if she herself could manage such stoical resignation if men with hammers methodically tore down San Clemente, *this house*, as she and her neighbours stood outside in, maybe, pouring rain, surrounded by their sewing machines and ruined stock. She supposed she would, if only because the alternative was to be shot as squatters sometimes were, the landlord settling old scores by pointing out to the police the 'ringleaders', the 'troublemakers' who would have to be eliminated if law and order were to prevail. Still, a short row of shanties in Sta. Cruz was one thing; the demolition of an entire barrio was another matter and in the past such mass evictions had caused rioting which went on for days. Even children had died as frightened and ill-trained police opened fire in panic with their M-16s.

Nanang Pipa sometimes thought she was the only one of San Clemente's residents to have these uneasy thoughts about the future. The others all seemed to live from day to day, meal to meal, drinking session to drinking session. Their each day was separate, pursed, ready to spill out its small troubles and few coins. Only for her, perhaps, did time stretch itself out into a history of difficulties like a long accountancy of debt, a future of limited but definite hope in which likely setbacks flitted along the horizon like rogue gunmen on rooftops. Whether planned by men, predestined by God or fated by nature, eligible evils went about springily on silent paws, awaiting their summons. She believed this most fervently. One could ward them off or deflect them in a variety of ways but there were no guarantees. She had once read a quotation whose cynicism had made her draw a sharp breath, so extraordinary was it to see it actually printed; but it had stuck in her mind nonetheless. It was: 'If praying did any good, they'd hire men to do it.' She remembered it because not long before she had put a personal notice in the *Philippine Daily Inquirer* at a moment when everything had fallen apart at once and she was at her wits' end. Edsel was in City Jail on suspicion of car-napping (a case of mistaken identity); their eldest daughter Gaylin had admitted she was pregnant without a plausible husband in sight; that evil harridan Ligaya Rosales had walked off with a brand new edging machine and her family pretended not to know where she was; and Pipa's eldest son Boyong was shortlisted for a job as an electrician at Plastic City, out in Valenzuela. 'Make a vow,' Doding Perez had urged her. 'Remember when Maricel was trying for that job in Saudi? She got it. And Bats was elected *tanod* in the barangay elections. It was because I took a St. Jude out. Do a St. Jude, Pipa. It always seems to work better than a Holy Spirit. Everyone I know says so.'

Privately, Pipa had been dubious about St. Jude, of whom she knew nothing except that he sounded faintly tarnished by the similarity of his name to that of Judas. Scanning the personal column in the newspaper she saw this:

> Make 3 wishes, 1 bus. & 2
> impossible. Pray 9 Hail
> Marys for 9 days & on the
> 9th day put out this ad &
> your wishes will come true.
> TY Mama Mary.

This was clear and straightforward and definitely religious, a proper novena, not like those witchcraft *gayumas* involving flies and dead meat. After some thought she decided to ask for Boyong's appointment as the business favour; she ranked the restoration of the stolen sewing machine as one of the impossibles, the other being Eddie's release from jail. She said her prayers and booked her ad. Three weeks later things were pretty much the same, except that Boyong had failed to get the job. Certainly Gaylin was still pregnant.

'What did I tell you?' said Doding. 'St. Jude.'

The other reason why Pipa had held out against St. Jude was because invoking him – or, rather, thanking him when one had received the favours – took three column inches as opposed to one.

Scanning the prayer, she found there was another quid pro quo, a promise to spread the word about him. Poor man, she thought, struck suddenly by the idea of a heavenful of saints most of whom were struggling against their own obscurity to make their powers felt and appreciated. The other thing about St. Jude was that he specified when he would answer prayers and operated a No Results – No Fee scheme, unlike Mama Mary. On the eighth day of Pipa's asking St. Jude for favours Eddie walked in, thinner and with a swollen lip, freed for lack of evidence. That same day Boyong appeared for lunch, due to start work on Monday with the electricity company Meralco. And towards sunset Gaylin, who had been unwell all day, finally confirmed that she was no longer pregnant thanks to some herbs she had bought at one of the stalls outside Quiapo Church. This was the clincher. Pipa now saw how unlikely it was that Mama Mary would ever have been sympathetic to that particular prayer. It was all too much. A few days later her heartfelt, if standard, tribute appeared in the newspaper.

O, Holy St. Jude, Apostle and Martyr, great in virtue, rich in miracle, near kinsman of Jesus Christ, faithful intercessor of all who invoke your special patronage in time of need. To you I have recoursed from the depth of my heart. And humbly beg great power to come to my assistance. Help me in my present and most urgent petition. In return, I promise to make your name known and cause you to be invoked. St. Jude pray for us & all who invoke thy aid. Pray for this nine times a day, for 9 consecutive days. On the 8th day your prayers will be answered. Please don't forget to publish this once your wish is granted.

'What did I tell you?' Doding said again, this time with the irritation of someone whose free advice has proved a little too rewarding. 'St. Jude.' Ever since, Pipa kept St. Jude in venerated reserve, not wishing to abuse his evident good nature by bothering him with trivia. Yet she remained, by unexpected whirlings-about of her intelligence like a peeled stick, highly resistant to sentimental categories. She was not after all to be patronised as a humble creature of simple faith. She was tough and difficult, a complex rational being adrift in a casual universe of monstrous flukes and chance, and simply retained blurry areas common to so many as to disgrace no-one. *If it works, do it*. St. Jude had worked.

Which was more than Eddie had, once back from jail. He appeared to think the injustice he had suffered exonerated him from all further attempts to earn a living. He had been maliciously fingered by one of the car-napping gang. *Dog*-napping, now: had it been dog-napping there would have been some justice in the charge since he occasionally went out on pooch patrol with Bats's brother Gringo, who drove a taxi. When Gringo came on shift they'd drive around likely areas looking for strays. Eddie would leap out with gloves and noose and have the beast in the back before the dog itself knew what was happening. Then out came the chloroform bottle and the rags. A decent dog would net three or four hundred on the hoof. One had made them seven-fifty: a daring daylight snatch in Makati which Eddie and Gringo still recounted over drinks. It was a monster Doberman or German Shepherd or something – the boys were none too clear about breeds – being walked at the end of a long rope by a queen in a toupée. As they drove slowly past, Eddie in the back had whipped open the door, grabbed the rope and held on as Gringo floored the accelerator. Soon they were doing a good speed, the dog bowling along behind, skittling cyclists and an ice-cream cart on bicycle wheels. The damned animal weighed a ton; Eddie had a hell of a job holding the door with one hand and hauling in with the other like some demented shark fisherman.

'Slow down, for Chrissake,' he had pleaded. His arm was popping from its socket. They rounded a corner and the dog bonged off the side of a dawdling bus. 'Slow *down*, Gringo. My goddam arm's coming off.' Unquestionably the animal was stoutly built. Even after whacking into the bus it was still more or less on its feet at a woozy canter.

Gringo trod on the brakes and the dog, now on only a foot or two of rope, crunched into the taxi's rear. Gringo began laughing crazily, his forehead resting on the steering wheel as Eddie hopped out and tried to manhandle the dazed animal into the back. There were shops here, and crowds. People collected on the pavement and watched with at-a-loss giggles as Eddie took a grip on the rope with one hand and groped for the beast's tail with the other. The tail had been docked, the stump was too short. Finally he grasped a leg instead and with a convulsive heave stuffed the animal through the door and fell on top. The crowd loved it. His T-shirt was rucked up to his armpits and he was smeared with blood. Panting amid the tangle of massive brown hocks and hams he indeed looked as if he were screwing a pony, an observation voiced loudly by a peanut boy. At that moment the queen came limping around the corner, wig askew, and let out a bleat of mixed relief and horror. Gringo pulled himself together, let in the clutch with a bang and, driving erratically through shifting lenses of tears, whizzed into a slot in the traffic. The door slammed shut. 'I think my hand's gone,' said Eddie. He had taken several turns of the rope around it. From the tightened coils a bunch of pale twigs protruded. He gingerly un-wrapped the rope and found the twigs still attached to a hand deeply indented, skinned and burnt.

'Quick, give it the chloroform,' called Gringo between hoots of laughter.

Eddie tore his attention away from his own injuries to survey those of the dog. Its eyes bulged, its purple tongue lolled. The noose around its neck had sunk deep into the fur. He managed to find the slip knot and feed rope through it. The noose eased. The dog sucked a rattling gulp of air.

'I'm very much afraid, sir,' said Eddie in his Forbes Park vet's voice, 'your dear pet will have to be put down. It is beyond repair.'

This sent Gringo off again. His driving became truly terrible and it remained a mystery to both men how they ever made it to San Andres without hitting something or being stopped. It amazed them even more once they had swung into the yard behind the restaurant and climbed weakly out. The car's nearside rear quarter was dented and all too plainly smeared with fresh blood. The chef came out to inspect the goods.

'You're sure that's a dog?' he asked, looking at the moaning brute stretched the full width of the back seat. 'Eddie-boy, you bought this off a *calesa* driver.'

'This is no nag,' Eddie told him scornfully. 'Are those nag's balls? We got it off a queen in Makati. Look at the meat on it,' he said, slapping a bloody flank. 'That's pedigree dog meat, tons of it. Actually, we've been thinking it's probably too good for your customers, seeing how they're used to the starving mongrels you normally serve. All ribs and skin. They must think they're eating stewed umbrellas.' This phrase, *adobong payong*, made Gringo lean helplessly against the taxi, head on forearm. 'You're not going to have to fatten *this* dog up for a month, no sir.'

'Has it been dead long?'

'What do you mean, dead? Can't you hear it? It's resting. We had quite a fight,' Eddie said proudly. 'It didn't want to come. All you have to do is put it out of its misery and into the pot.'

Eventually the deal was struck, the animal hauled away by two men, the rear of the taxi sluiced out and Eddie's hand bandaged. His wife had heard the tale many times. 'Your dear pet'll have to be put down' had become something of a catch-phrase, quoted whenever the story was alluded to. Nanang Pipa could indeed have seen a certain justice had her husband been jailed for dog-napping, but the joke about the car-napping rap was that Eddie couldn't drive. Even if the halfwits who arrested him hadn't known it, St. Jude had and, moving in a mysterious way, organised the release. His agent had turned out to be Insp. Dingca.

'You mean our Dingca? Rio?'

'How many other Dingcas do you know?' Eddie asked her. 'A real piece of luck. He was over at the jail looking for someone, a completely different case, and he saw me and said "Hi, Eddie. What've they got you for?" So I told him it was a mistake, especially as I can't drive, and they took me down to the yard and gave me a test. We all got into a jeep and they told me to drive to where the leader of the gang lived and just park outside the house. They'd do the rest. If I did that, they said, I'd be released on the spot. I really think they were serious. I even tried a bit but it wasn't any good and after a while they told me to get out anyway, just walk, out the gate, go. "But we've got your number, Buster", that sort of stuff. It was Dingca did that. I owe him.'

Since then Eddie hadn't worked and now owed many people besides the Inspector, mainly for gin and cigarettes. It was a mercy the sewing business was going well, Pipa thought, otherwise they'd be on their beam ends. Just then Eddie himself stuck his head through the door, leaning on the posts with muddy hands.

'God knows what you've let us in for now, woman,' he said. The sewers stopped work and looked up. 'Never can leave well alone, can you? It's always "Just a little bit deeper, Eddie", or "Another day should do it".'

'What on earth are you talking about?' asked Pipa crossly.

Something in the way his head disappeared made everyone troop outside, or at least crowd around the back door, since the hole took up most of the space between the wall of the house and that of the neighbours. Here the reeking, rubbish-strewn declivity was now interrupted by a sizeable pit whose depth was exaggerated by the heaps of soil packed down by bare feet around its edge. There was nobody in it. Nanang Pipa peered down, impressed despite herself by its neatly vertical sides and the evidence of labour. At the bottom was a small, roundish white boulder.

'Now that,' Eddie told her with truculent triumph, 'is a human skull.'

12

YSABELLA BASTIAAN'S pet senator had pressed her to meet him
again in the Senate lounge. Once more she had walked up a single
flight of gritty cement stairs from the Department of Archaeology and
emerged in the corridors of power. This time they had sat at one of the
long tables set in a hollow rectangle and a cold collation was brought.
Other senators were there, some of whom she now recognised from
her daily newspaper reading. Of these, half looked like the ex-showbiz
folk they actually were. Benigno Vicente was not one of them. He was
expansive, confident enough of her now to introduce her across the
table. With every gesture he shed a strong whiff of 'L'Egoiste'.
Ysabella was tentatively wondering whether these powerful men and
women could be subdivided into old and new money, or maybe
according to their cultural leanings. The showbiz people tended to be
home-grown in the populist manner, given to answering Channel 5
news reporters in Tagalog. The others answered more or less
automatically in English. It seemed to her that most of them looked
eastwards towards America, where they had likely been to college or
had sons and daughters with law practices there. The remaining few –
her own Senator Vicente among them – looked westwards towards
London and Paris and Rome and Madrid.

'Miss Bastiaan's father was ambassador here in 1965.'

'*Chris* Bastiaan?' A senator two down from her host leaned forward
and smiled at her across the intervening meat loaf and kiwi fruit. 'I
knew him, miss. It's an honour.' This was said with great courtesy but

as if caught on the hop, still searching for the right tone. 'I was nobody at the time, of course,' he explained to his neighbour. 'Just a lawyer. But we were introduced and we met often. We used to play golf. A most admirable man, a good friend and a true British gentleman in the old sense.' This came as a shock to Ysabella, who had never heard that her father had had the least interest in sports. 'Then that terrible incident. I believe he was the youngest ambassador ever to be appointed here. My God, it seems a long time ago, the Quirino Avenue bomb thing.'

'But of course you were at Oxford,' Vicente said to her with nifty irrelevance.

'Not at the time, Ben. I was three.'

'Ah. Obviously I meant *later*.'

Off in a corner of the room cameras flashed and whirred among the sofas in one of whose corners a tiny senator was slipping down into a crack in the upholstery like a peanut. Her face wore a look of severe intelligence.

'We worry about time-wasting,' said a lady on Ysabella's left who had not previously spoken. 'Have you attended any debates yet? Then you'll know. It's very senatorial, very slow, very by-the-book. Properly dignified. But I can tell you, Ysabella, we're on the edge of an abyss in this country. Or, to be more topical, on the edge of a volcano. "The Pinatubo premonition", one of our newspapers called it. The Americans pulled out last week. Finally we've got what we wanted. Unfortunately, total independence leaves us with no-one but ourselves to blame for whatever follows. Unless we can get peace and order we're doomed. Peace and order is number one. No peace and order means no foreign investors. No foreign investors means stagnation and increasing poverty. And poverty means corruption and break-down of peace and order. A vicious circle which we have to break before all else. And in the meantime economies which were years behind us a decade or two ago are overtaking. Taiwan, South Korea, Malaysia, Thailand, and quite soon even Indonesia. It's a disaster.'

'Too much democracy, Lee Kuan Yew said the other day.'

'All right for him. An island state the size of one of our smallest provinces with a tiny population. We've got more than seven thousand islands here.'

'One of which I own,' broke in Vicente. 'I insist that you join me and my family there for a weekend very soon. I really insist. It's quiet, simple, beautiful. No formality, no loud social whirling. Seen from the land it reminds one of Mont St. Michel, I find.'

'He's rather ghastly on the face of it,' Ysabella said to Sharon later, recounting travellers' tales from the land beyond the ceiling. They were dusting the Archaeology Department, bringing to light un-catalogued lumps of this and that.

'And underneath?'

'Probably quite nice. A Europhile. Just someone from my father's diplomatic past my mother kept in touch with. I hardly knew of his existence until this trip came up. What's his reputation?'

'He tries, at least. He works. Corrupt, sure; but no worse than some and much less than most.'

'He owns an island, he says.'

'He would. They mostly do, people like that. I should go,' said Sharon. 'It'll be a unique insight into senatorial provincial life. He's already invited you?'

They were standing at one of the trestle tables laden with dusty fragments and a stencilled notice saying 'BICOL 0881'. This, Sharon explained, referred to an excavation there in 1981, of which these specimens ought to have been listed in the August catalogue.

'A vacuum cleaner would help,' said Ysabella. 'All these whisks and brooms just shift the dust around instead of removing it. This table looks as though the ceiling had collapsed.'

'It's on the list, don't worry. Maybe you already told me and I forgot, sorry, but what was your connection with Vicente? Your father knew him?'

'Sort of. He was my father's driver.'

'Oh my.'

'Until I told my mother I was coming here he was just a man in a story, a hero for a day. He was driving my father and the First Secretary in the ambassadorial Rolls-Royce when some terrorists threw a bomb or a grenade or it hit a land mine, nobody seemed very clear. I was three at the time, back in England with my mother. The Rolls wasn't armoured. Nobody bothered much with that sort of thing then. Think of Kennedy only the year before, the President of America driving through the middle of a city in an open car. It must have been a different world. My father was hit in the head. Vicente drove like mad

96

without tyres for half a mile, saw my father on the floor in the back covered in blood and the other fellow just sitting there paralysed. It was fear or drink or something, I forget now, except that he wasn't a bit hurt. So Vicente stopped, got into the back and gave my father mouth-to-mouth until someone fetched an ambulance. It wasn't any good because he died a couple of days later but my mother never forgot what Vicente did. He was only a driver, terribly young. And I don't think anybody even *knew* about mouth-to-mouth in those days, did they?'

'My God. No wonder you have mixed feelings about things here.'

'Do I? Not really. I can barely remember him. Someone faint a long way away and a long time ago. Do you know what actually killed him? *That* I do remember. It was the glass stopper from one of the little decanters in the Rolls's cocktail cabinet. It went straight into his brain.'

'And your mother kept up with Vicente all these years?'

'I suppose she must have,' said Ysabella. 'All she said to me was, "Well, if you're going *there*, darling, you'll have to look up Daddy's old driver. He's a senator now." So I did. But I can't imagine Mummy keeping up with an embassy driver except sort of the annual Christmas card, even if he was the good Samaritan. She was a diplomatic wife.'

'And diplomatic wives didn't become friendly with drivers?' Sharon's tone was that of a New World democrat.

'Well, of course not. As for how Vicente made it from the car pool to upstairs I've no idea. Only in the Philippines would one be unsurprised.'

'Or in the United States,' said Sharon acridly.

'But I think he's probably a bore, anyway. Not because he isn't old money or anything but *because*, I don't know. A bore's manner, I suppose.'

'He's probably just nervous. You're the daughter of the man who was blown up. And you do scare people, you know.'

'*I* do? Oh nonsense, Sharon.'

But she knew it was true and didn't much care, was even secretly pleased. 'He has this pet hobby-horse, doesn't he?'

'You mean the OCWs? That's the large point in his favour. It's high time somebody in the government here took some notice of what's going on. The cynicism's unbelievable. They published some statistics the other week. Every year an average of eight hundred and nineteen Filipino overseas contract workers die of maltreatment abroad. Can you imagine? Eight *hundred* a year? It's worst in the Middle East and Africa. Between six and seven hundred thousand Filipinos work there. Crispa went to the Department of Foreign Affairs and found out that between 1987 and 1990 alone more than three thousand of them died in, quote, "mysterious circumstances", unquote. Does the government here demand stricter law enforcement in the host countries, better criminal and legal enquiries, proper explanations and indemnity for the families? It sure doesn't. Between them, the OCWs worldwide are pulling three billion pesos a year into this collapsing economy and it's not about to annoy any of the geese laying all these golden eggs. Score several belated points for your senator.'

'It certainly does seem pretty feeble,' agreed Ysabella, blithely dusting. 'Good for him, then. He said Filipinos were the Jews of Asia.'

'He often does.' But Sharon's quieter remark and her sudden abandoning of the BICOL table left her companion irritated by the passion this implied. It was all very well playing naive and righteous, but what the hell did she expect? Migrant workers were by definition exploited, always had been, always would be. Having nothing to sell but their sweat they were expendable in a buyer's market. She glanced across at Sharon's back and decided not to mention slavery in the US, or John Steinbeck, or grape-pickers, or that she had once read a book of harrowing details about Castle Garden and Ellis Island where – if she remembered aright – some three thousand potential immigrants to the US had committed suicide while in detention awaiting deportation for having various ailments imaginary or otherwise, or the wrong papers, or not enough money to bribe the officials who made fortunes out of penury and despair. Not that Britain's present-day record on immigrants was anything to write home about. She had recently read that until he was deported to Hong Kong in December 1992 the UK had an unconvicted detainee who had been held in jail for seven years, scarcely a matter for national pride.

They smouldered at each other for a day or two beneath heatless professional exchanges. It was not completely clear to either why there was this smell of burning in the air. But Ysabella's casualness, with which she might have lit an airy cigarette, had evidently ignited an obscure fuse. Not even Vicente's record on OCWs was proof against

Sharon's anger when his familiar *bon mot* recurred yet again in print. In this mood, once more was once too often.

'Listen, Ysabella, the next time you see your friend kindly tell him from me not to use that comparison ever again. It's damned inaccurate. Also damned offensive.'

'I'm not quite sure –'

'Then I'll tell you, just so's you get it straight before you pass it on to Benigno-baby. In no sense whatever are the Filipinos the Jews of Asia. The Jews, alone among humanity, have survived damn near three thousand years of nonstop persecution. The Filipinos haven't been a unified people for three hundred at the longest, most would say barely since Independence in 1946, some would claim they're not a unified people yet. What unique force kept the notion of Jewishness intact for three millennia? Scholarship. Literacy. Not even merely religion but learning, enquiry, solid and unceasing mental effort. *The text.* Banished, exiled, pogromed, scattered, they were left with nothing but the pursuit of reason, reflection, the crazed certainty that justice had to prevail eventually according to humanity's own laws which it had written but periodically pretended it hadn't. I'm not a religious Jew, I'm an atheist Jew. I'm also pretty much of a pessimist. But when I get really low I cheer myself up by remembering that, incredibly, the Jews are the living proof that the pen really *is* mightier than the sword. Constantly banned from all sorts of jobs in all sorts of societies, instead of giving up and going to seed they took refuge in simple trades by day and the intellect by night. Not even the filthiest, poorest *shtetl* in Eastern Europe ever lost its awe of learning, of argument, of cynical debate. All their ancient persecutors, where are they? Babylonians, Egyptians, Romans, Crusaders? The Spanish Inquisitors, the Tsarists, the Stalinists, the Third Reich? The best you can say is that one or two have left new inheritors of their old names, and the worst that there are always fresh candidates to step into the shoes of dead persecutors. But we Jews, we've survived and even prospered, held together by tradition, by Torah and Talmud and sheer, stubborn intellectual resourcefulness.

'So you can tell Senator Vicente that when he and his people have made that effort for three thousand years he can call them the Jews of Asia. But not until. Never until. I've been here long enough to be extremely fond of this country, and I love Crispa very much indeed.

But this place's tragedy is not that of the Jews, and it only muddles and conceals the problem to pretend it is. The real tragedy of the Philippines, and plenty of other countries as well, is precisely that it *doesn't* have three thousand years of literacy and identity to draw on as remedy. What text can unify the barely literate? What scholarship shore up those with little tradition? These last two days I've thought of nothing but this. Things I'd never organised as thoughts before, certainly not in connection with my life here. So I can thank you for that, at least indirectly. This morning I worked out something grim which I know is true: the impossibility of *being* anything without *knowing* something. Without knowledge people have no identity. I'm afraid that applies just as much to nations as to individuals.'

Sharon vanished for two days after this highly partial outburst. Ysabella thought of ringing her at home, decided against it. When she reappeared she was back to the self Ysabella believed she had first met. Together they walked to Intramuros where some students were digging at her site under the supervision of an ethnology professor from UP. It was a pleasure and relief to get back to trowels and camel hair brushes, squatting beneath the greenish heat of a canvas awning. Suddenly and with tenderness Sharon put a muddy hand on Ysabella's arm, leaving a sweaty print.

'You know I told you I was an atheist Jew? Afterwards, I remembered that joke, only it's not quite a joke. A young Jew bumps into his local rabbi and feels obliged to say, "Listen, *Rebbe*. It's time I made it clear that I'm an atheist." The rabbi looks him up and down and says in amazement, "You don't know Torah, then?" "Hardly." "Not even the Wisdom of the Fathers, *Pirke Abot*?" "That least of all." "In that case I have news for you, *boychik*," the rabbi tells him disgustedly. "You're not an atheist, you're an ignoramus." '

'But you're not an ignoramus in that sense.'

'How could I be? My parents are Orthodox. I learned what I was taught and I'm glad I did. You don't have to *believe* it. Just doing the work changes you. The joke's correct: you have to earn the right to call yourself an atheist.'

'I'll tell the senator.'

'The joke?'

'How else do I tell him he's got to earn the right to call himself a Jew?'

Under strain, these days, as seasonal clouds bottled up the heat or shed warm, unrefreshing rain tasting like perspiration. Ysabella saw the strain in Sharon, began at last to see it in the faces of people doubling up to wedge themselves on and off the ever-crowded jeepneys, in the sidewalk vendors, in the drenched boys tottering beneath smoking blocks of ice, in the fabric of the city itself as its overloaded beams and girders and transoms and bridges juddered continually. England suddenly began heaving itself up behind her conversations and reflections, unaccountably, as if its very irrelevance made it uniquely apposite. After Sharon's tirade its solid presence for Ysabella, eight thousand miles over the horizon of Manila Bay, thinned uncertainly. It, too, had little which could stand beside a literate nationhood of three thousand years. Its culture was surely too much of a class and not of a people.

Daily she read the newspapers, coming to rely on her regular dose of the baroque. Yet with each turn of the page it was as though she learned, by some insinuating alchemy, the odd news of her own country's essential frailty. Here, anarchic feudalism had been built to last; there (Quiet shires! Unarmed policemen! House of Windsor!) a papery fragility suddenly hung about things as if at any moment the patient claws of *lex talionis* might at last unsheathe themselves and rend the scenery from behind. Or again (and she thought of childhood model-making with her cousin Jeremy) a Montgolfier balloon made of tissue paper would triumphantly rise trailing fumes of methylated spirits – Technology! – and turn into a brief ball of flame before descending as flakes of ash. Such an image might pop into her mind on reading something as seemingly unrelated as a newspaper account of two Manila policemen shooting each other – one fatally – in a quarrel over a corpse each had pre-sold to a rival funeral parlour. What on earth was the connection? One more in the list of uneasy mysteries which the city posed its well-heeled visitors from orderly lands.

At 4.15 a.m. in the TriTran bus terminal at Lawton she saw a wooden board nailed to a tree, half concealed by leaves. In letters of runny paint it offered circumcision, virginity restoration, bust/nose lift and a phone number. This is dawn, she said to herself as the bus didn't start and a man lay curled up on a table beneath the tree. Be stoical. Keep silent about our fate. We have to be careful of not waking whatever sleeps inside us. Sometimes it turns over, muttering of the emptiness we have embraced. We catch a few words and grow cold, knowing that soon or late and relieved its long hibernation is over, it will awake and embrace us in turn.

13

I'VE BEEN THINKING,' said the tinny voice. 'I think we ought to have a look at these vampires. Have you seen *People's* this morning? It's their lead story for the second day running. Why don't you give it the once-over?'

'Bong, I'm up to my eyes in salvaging and I've just been landed this "Queen of *shabu*" case. A paper like ours oughtn't even to *mention* vampires, much less send a reporter.' Still less your senior crime reporter hot from the Navotas marshes, Vic hoped his tone implied.

'*People's* sent Narciso.'

'Of course they did. It's the perfect Mozzy story. Remember the election?'

'Well, by God, that sold a lot more newspapers than full-page interviews with what we called "Presidentiables". Everybody loves a vampire story.'

Vic Agusan did have to concede that when the choice was between reading a political candidate's forty-third repetition of their one speech and a ghost story, most sane people chose the latter. They certainly had back in March 1992, when in the election campaign's last couple of weeks a *manananggal* had been spotted flapping over the rooftops in Tondo. This was a peculiar and terrifying creature, half woman and half bat, which perched in the rafters of houses at night and let down a long tongue into the mouths of babies and the elderly, sucking out their livers. The Tondo *manananggal* had run for several days and totally eclipsed the serious newspapers' election coverage.

Besides, a half-woman half-bat was a cartoonist's dream. The upper half appeared most felicitously as that of Miriam Santiago Defensor, a former judge who was even then being tipped by some as the next President. That she didn't win, and later accused President Ramos of having rigged the election, was neither here nor there. What one remembered was this strange composite creature, superstition melted into political caricature, hovering above the late campaign. It was not overlooked that the Philippines' Transylvania, the home territory of such horrors, was generally believed to be Iloilo which curiously enough happened also to be the lady's own province.

'So send Bobby Aguilar.'

'Bobby's on the Padilla case. Anyway, he's strictly showbiz.'

'And I'm strictly crime, Bong.'

'The Queen of Sheba doesn't sound very criminal.'

'*Shabu*, Bong, *shabu*. "Poor man's crack", if you remember. You're acting like one of those dumb uniforms in American cop soaps whose role is to have everything spelt out to him. He represents the viewer.'

'I still think it's got a smell to it.'

Vic Agusan leaned against the wall of the *National Chronicle*'s lobby and collapsed the antenna of his cellphone. A knot of people stood at the desk waiting for IDs. The doorway behind them was a rectangle of glare. Was this self-importance, or just getting older? Until recently he had revelled in the bizarre juxtapositions of newspaper work. Days were hectically slashed with stories. Grieving relatives/Leaked exam. papers?/Floods trap tots/Binondo's oldest resident. For a moment he could imagine what it felt like to be God, privy to simultaneous lives and events unrolling and intersecting in every direction. For one or two instants, in fact, he could glimpse the whole: the connections between virtually any narratives. These brief moments of insight occurred during heavy drinking sessions in whatever was the preferred after-hours watering hole. They were usually thrown as if by a film projector onto the cracked and crusty glaze of a urinal. Pilfering on increase in North Harbor/Man eats cell-mate for Xmas dinner/Police vs. Police shootout. No problem. They simply fused together. He could see exactly how each story was so dependent on the others that it was all really a single story after all. True, in the morning the mechanics of this perception had vanished and he was left with a headache and a vague understanding that each story was equally typical of this bizarre country. (That, too, was a sign of ageing. Increasingly he was looking at his own land with the eyes of an outsider preparing to board a flight out.) The Xmas dinner story had been a lulu, come to think of it. In the early hours of Christmas morning two guards in a municipal jail out in the provinces somewhere found an inmate sitting on the floor of his cell covered in blood and eating a chunk of raw liver. Next to him was the body of the cell's other occupant whom he'd attacked and killed as he slept. The weapon, Vic remembered, had been the little tin stand for a mosquito coil. Security in the jail had to be tightened to protect the man from the irate relatives of his *noche buena* snack.

Something nowadays made Vic impatient with distraction, like a soap addict wrenched from the TV by his doorbell. It really *was* all the same story: that of a country at war with itself where eighty percent of the people were landless labourers, small farmers and workers living below the poverty line, while between eighty and ninety percent of the members of the House of Representatives and the Senate were millionaires. Virtually everything else flowed from these simple facts. It was, he considered, nothing less than the world in microcosm, the globe's huge unrest transcribed as a nation's instability. Terminal, without a doubt. The notice board in the Crime office upstairs was a mass of thumb-tacked headlines and quotations which curled and wagged like tongues in the fans' draught. Some were stories he himself had worked on; most had been culled at whim. Here were sundry gems, including the *Daily Inquirer*'s ambiguous headline about a DILG official's visit to Cotabato after some rebels there had killed eighteen people in a raid, either reading of which was equally plausible: 'Alunan urges local execs to help massacre survivors.'

'Official remedy for sexual harassment of OCWs: "Send only uglies abroad".'
'Only 1 in 4 Parañaque cops use drugs.'
'Kindergarten sex slaves. Tots test HIV positive!'
' "Only a little formalin" in Xmas apples.'
' "No-one left to kill" claims disgruntled Ranger.'
'Child workers win mercury from ball-mill effluent.'
'₱ 3 bn. of Pinatubo relief diverted to ghost projects.'

'Fake circumcision rites trick farmers into surrender.'
'Husband made pregnant by wife.'
' "Please Pray the Rosary" – Mama Mary.'

It didn't much matter to him which story was thrown into his lap. More and more Vic wanted to be left to stick with it, to unravel it past its generally familiar ingredients until something else was revealed. This was usually debt or greed. Yet surprisingly often he believed he found private truths lurking behind the political scandal: a wife's frigidity, the fear of baldness, a love rejected twenty years ago. True, salvaging didn't quite fit with this. It was a classic story for Vic Agusan, doyen of crime reporters who had once offered himself as go-between in a hostage deal and had been shot in the thigh for his pains. It didn't fit because jungle law pre-empted the luxury of private symptoms. He was homing in on Sergeant Cruz. That morning spent lying out in Navotas marshes had produced evidence on film of the man's direct involvement in dumping murder victims, an activity far enough outside a policeman's official remit as to be likely to cook Cruz's goose for him even if there was still no proof that he had also killed them. It was a solid step forward but Vic couldn't pretend there was any real urgency about the story. Policemen had been killing criminals ever since juries failed to convict, and would go on doing so. Perhaps after all vampires were light relief instead of nettling to the self-esteem.

He sighed and pulled out the antenna again. For all that he worked for a rival paper Mozzy Narciso was generally friendly and helpful. Younger and slightly in awe, might have been an explanation. Yet Mozzy was himself talented. He definitely had the demotic touch. He was an ace on rapists who terrorised squatter areas most of Vic's readers scarcely knew existed; no less ace on backstreet abortionists, fake priests soliciting funds and haunted jeepneys. Vampires were right up his street. A Naga City elementary school haunted by a dog with horns had been quintessentially a Mozzy story. Mozzy's drawback – and the real reason why Vic didn't feel daunted by the threat of his rivalry – was that his aceness extended little further than tracking down exactly the right vox pops. He knew instinctively that victims themselves were often too boring, traumatised or plain ashamed to give a good quote. You went for their mothers, their quotations shook themselves free of print and stayed in the mind. 'He had spotty balls.' 'It was sad when he left. We'd grown used to the sound of his farts.' And, of a bogus gynaecologist, 'Where he operated *was* her purse.' This was Mozzy's gift. He moved from story to story tugging out nuggets while scarcely digging at all. He was no doubt giving his readers a terrific hearsay account of vampires hovering, vampires squatting and slurping, blighted neighbours clutching crucifixes. If Vic was going to get involved in the story he was going to ask: But why *there*? Why *now*? *Cui bono*? Crime taught one nothing if not that the supernatural was just another make of gun. He pushed buttons and waited until his secretary two floors overhead came on the line.

'Cindy, I'm still in the lobby. Listen, do we have Narciso's number in the book? No, not him, he's our bent Customs man. The *People's* journalist. Mozart P. Narciso. Okay, then, just remind me of the *People's* number. I'll track him down myself.'

Standing there watching the comings and goings of dark figures outlined against the glaring screen of the main door he wondered about the Englishman, Prideaux. Would John be interested in vampires? To be truthful, Vic wasn't absolutely clear about what kind of research the man was doing. Something about breaking points. For that kind of research he needed to know about the City's police: their organisation, attitudes, scams and the rest. He had interviewed senators and doctors and priests. Vic had pushed a variety of contacts his way including a personable killer on the Presidential Anti-Crime Commission, an ex-Aquino staffer unsacked for fraud, a senior inspector in the NBI's Narcotics Division and a congresswoman of great charm and immeasurable greed. More importantly, Vic had introduced Prideaux to his own wife and family, to friends and colleagues, men and women whose humour was shot through with bleakness. All had agreed that John was a good fellow with an intelligent grasp of this and that, but were none the wiser. 'Some anthropology thesis' more or less laid to rest their mildly unsatisfied curiosity. People had their own agendas. Call him up, why not? Vampires were all part of it, too.

It was only now he realised that the reason for the lobby's shadow-play was another of Manila's power failures. The chiaroscuro of flitting denizens outlined against the daylight had suited his mood. The flitting denizens outlined against the daylight had suited his mood. The lethargy which left him slumped by the water cooler with a portable phone was probably caused by the air conditioners shutting down. He pulled himself together, tilting the instrument's keys to the light.

'Vic *Agusan*? Wow. Tell you the truth, I wasn't thinking of going back there. So what's the connection? What's the connection?'

'Mozzy, old thing, relax. I promise you, I know zilch. *I'm* ringing *you* for information. If there's a criminal link here it's not one known to me or to anybody else in this building. Just Bong, with some idea that I need light relief. Vampires are it. I promise you I'm not muscling in. If ever there was copyrighted Mozzy Narciso territory, it's vampires. Everyone knows that. What can you give me?'

'Hysteria, frankly, not a lot more. They're over in San Clemente. Do you know where that is?'

'Vaguely,' Vic said guardedly. That was Cruz's patch, oddly enough. If Mozzy found out he was already on a story involving the police in that area he'd jump to conclusions. 'Sort of up by North Cemetery somewhere?'

'That's it. Just about where you'd expect vampires to hang out, come to think of it. Do you know, that hadn't occurred to me? Thanks for the tip.'

'Pleasure, Mozzy. Is there anything else you can tell me which you didn't know?'

'Not really. It's pretty much the usual thing. Couple of local drunks sitting up late at night see this figure hovering over the barrio. After a bit it sits on a roof. The only difference is this one leers and has huge fangs. *Ningas kugon*. A grass fire, a nothing story. I went back yesterday to do a follow-up and just got the usual collection of babies that won't wake and dogs giving birth to litters of cockroaches and Bibles that glow in the dark. You know. Nobody's actually *seen* anything. My guess is it's all a plot dreamed up by some local wag who's got it in for these two stumblebums. Squatter humour. Nothing to ping off the walls about unless it goes on happening. I bet most of these things start as a joke.'

'Did the creature look like Brenda?'

'According to my drunken informant's original description it had a face like that of his own wife, whom I met afterwards. I don't know whether he knows that, but he was pretty close. Anyway, today I'm on a totally different story. At last we've got a lead on the Little League cheating case. Remember that? Our team won the world title last year in Pennsylvania before being stripped of it for cheating? Right. . . That's the one. We've just found a woman who admits her boy, who was fourteen then, took on the identity and academic records of some twelve-year-old so as to be eligible for the age limit. It's a break, Vic. Once her story comes out we're betting the other mothers'll come forward. Imagine, a whole goddam national team of ghost kids. *Little League baseball!* Is nothing sacred? Okay, I can't believe it's worth our best crime reporter's time to go vampire-hunting in San Clemente, but if you want my drunken guy's name you can have it with pleasure, Vic. Full marks to you if you can dig anything out of it other than the visions of a boozy squatter. What is it drunks see in America? Isn't it pink elephants? Our equivalent is vampires. I suppose it's all those centuries of Catholicism. Ha, yes, poor old Brenda. Do you think she'll ever get her recount?'

The presidential campaign had revealed that Miriam Santiago had an alleged history of psychiatric instability. Despite the glaring sanity evidenced by her having called a congressman 'fungus face' she herself had been given one of the nicknames cheerily bestowed on the afflicted. It happened to be Brenda (for 'bren-damage'), but might just as easily have been Rita (for 'retard'). In the circumstances Vic considered that this, in its way, was a form of voting. As a keen student of the foreign English language press he had long assumed that the choice of the name 'Andy Capp' to describe the common man's dimmest strip-cartoon exemplar was no accident. It so happened there was a Rita familiar to everyone in the *Chronicle* building who mopped and mowed harmlessly about the area, his face split by a huge grin as he begged for coins and capered a few steps. He was generally treated with cheer and kindness, given small change and applauded ironically. Several of Vic's colleagues, including his own secretary Cindy, were convinced that giving Rita a 2-peso coin brought them luck. It certainly brought Rita his survival. Vic supposed this was how it had been in Europe back in the days when idiots were considered as having been touched by God, and therefore holy. Presumably modern public health provisions and state medicine had put paid to them or kept them hidden from view, poleaxed with drugs and with their affliction given one of those names which implied that somebody somewhere knew all about it. He wondered if vampires had also disappeared from the advanced West or whether they still crouched in unexpected places under an assumed identity.

14

INSP. DINGCA was himself moving through haunted weather these days. He presumed one had first to reach a certain age to allow for a build-up of the general wastage that life offered and of which one was willy-nilly a spectator, until such time as one became a ghost for somebody else. That seemed to be the deal. Babs was now a ghost, of course. Dingca was glad he had heard nothing to suggest that the entertainer had died specifically for being an informer, that he himself was directly responsible. He was thankful too that he hadn't mired Babs still further, as so many cops did their 'kids' and 'assets' by using them to funnel back onto the street part of whatever drug hauls they confiscated and which they could spare from their own habits. Dingca had always paid Babs in cash. True, he was also funneling back money which had fallen into the police's hands by one route or another: payoffs, *tong*, recovered unmarked loot. Still, he had played Babs straight and had been left with a heavy heart but a cleanish conscience.

These days other ghosts were joining Babs's. They popped into his mind at irregular intervals, stepping out of a building as he drove past, sitting in familiar offices with unfamiliar occupants, leaning on tables in bars and restaurants. They were the unresting: those whose lives had been emptied out by injustice, casually, as one might tip up a bowl of waste water. They were forced to swill about the earth, their thin voices calling endlessly for redress. Other cops saw and heard them too, he had learned from gab-sessions with Sergeant Macawili; but old Bryan had retired last year and gone off to live with his daughter in

Malolos, Bulacan. On the one occasion Dingca and a couple of others had driven up to see him (a trip marked by a near-fatal blowout at Meycauayan) they had found him almost speechless with emphysema.

What they had in common, these ghosts, was that he still felt bad about them in some way even though it was not obviously a simple matter of his own conscience. There were plenty of episodes he regretted deeply but which were not particularly haunting. It couldn't be denied there were unpleasant things to be done in the line of duty. Yet here was a mystery. In his career he had met many killers, not all crazed and quite a few in uniform, and knew absolutely about himself that he was not one of them. He did kill, however. He had seldom had to fire his gun in self-defence, but salvage was another matter. It was not really an issue of conscience for most cops, he knew, and nor was it for himself. There were certain animals who had roamed the streets long enough, wearing their gang tattoos like medals won in a war against civilisation. Left alone, they bred. They needed steady culling. As far as Dingca was concerned it was a kind of moral affirmation in the face of bribed judges and porous jails. Salvaging was seldom done by a cop working alone unless it was an especially private matter; it reinforced a comradeship which was equally affirmative. Some cops elected simply to be Out. The ones who were In all the way usually made quicker progress up through the ranks. Offhand, Dingca could hardly recall a single individual in whose death he had participated. It was not until someone brought up a name that he was occasionally able to brush the cobwebs away from a face or a scene.

All that killing had produced only one ghost for Rio Dingca, and quite unaccountably at that. It was the ghost of an expression he had glimpsed when they had gone one night to a house in Grace Park following a tip-off. The man they were after – his name still eluded Rio – was a specialist in armed robbery who had started at the age of sixteen by throwing fuming nitric acid into the faces of late-night jeepney passengers. His first attack had blinded a woman and disfigured her sleeping children and netted him 37 pesos. From this he had graduated, via a very lucrative tourist bus heist, to the daring holdup in broad daylight of an unmarked police jeep doing an emergency security run, a strongbox delivery from bank to bank. It was an inside job. In the unmarked jeep were three policemen in street clothes, including the driver. Two were sitting with Armalites across their knees, a fatal mistake when quick action was needed, especially for the one hunched up beneath the low hood in the back. The jeep was crawling along Padre Faura towards the lights on Mabini, in the heart of the tourist belt. The streets were crowded with lunchtime pedestrians, office workers from government buildings and nurses from the General Hospital nearby. The man chose his moment with care, weaving up from behind on an aged Kawasaki 100. As the jeep drew level with the corner of Bocobo the motorcyclist came up on the inside, shot dead the policeman in the front seat and then the driver before turning to deal with the one in the back who was barely starting to react. The motorcyclist fired again and hit him in the thigh, which galvanised the policeman into bringing up the Armalite in a blind frenzy, squeezing the trigger even before he could aim, hitting the already lifeless body of his comrade in front and dissolving the jeep's windscreen into a white hail of crystals until the muzzle caught on a headrest. This time the motorcyclist shot him cleanly between the eyes. He dumped the Kawasaki on its side, ran around the jeep and hauled the driver out onto the road. So far it had all taken eight seconds and pedestrians were only just beginning to realise what was going on. As the dead driver's foot came off the clutch the jeep stalled with a bang. Coolly the man climbed in, restarted the engine, swung right and, bumping over the Kawasaki's front wheel, tore up Bocobo against the one-way traffic stream, swerving on and off the pavements, with two dead bodies and a strongbox. It had all been so cold and fast and well informed that it made the headlines of the evening papers. Next morning the heavier editorials talked about war on the streets and how the police were often a more fatal medicine than the disease they were intended to cure. Right from the start it was assumed that the robber was himself a cop, which incensed only those policemen who were sure he wasn't. Their righteous anger turned sour when it emerged that the tip-off had almost certainly come from a bank guard who was indeed a moonlighting cop.

Leaving aside the one-year-old infant hit in the head by a stray bullet, one of the dead was a colleague of Dingca's. When months later they learned the motorcyclist was to be found in southern Grace Park, four of them went there one night without it even occurring to them to pay a courtesy call on Station 2. They went in front and back, flushed out some elderly women watching Raven on TV, and found their man asleep in a curtained-off alcove. He was alone and, incredibly, unarmed. He sat up on the mat, turtle-lidded in the glow of the 20w bulb, a nineteen-year-old youth wearing a Batman T-shirt and a cotton blanket. His mouth said 'Oh', even as his brain was tearing itself free of the dream which still held his face in the slack innocence of a child. And this was the expression which was to haunt Dingca as they all shot him: the eyes turned to him in soft wonderment as if he were watching a miracle, an ordinary event which without warning had leapfrogged over credibility and was waiting on the other side for him to catch up. They had found no gun under his pillow or, indeed, anywhere in the house, but had brought one for him just in case and pressed it unfired into his dead hand. For a couple of days Rio was convinced they had killed the wrong man but then the lab reports came through: fingerprints which tallied with those on the police jeep's steering wheel and matched the ones on an empty acid bottle.

After all, then, justice had been done; but in being done had left behind this ghost, this lost soul of an expression which, like the Cheshire cat's grin, hung in the air without even much of a face to go with it and lacking any sort of name. 'We'll meet again next time around,' it said to Rio, not with the promise of vengeance but with the hopeful conviction that both would somehow have shaken themselves a little more free of sheer muddle and stupidity and waste. From it alone had sprung Rio's certainty that in shooting the expression's owner they had somehow missed the true villain who would carry on flitting before them, leaping free of each host seconds ahead of their bullets and leaving behind an innocent husk. And so the world went, trundling along on its wheels of pain, trailing behind it an exhausted wistfulness which did no good at all to ageing cops.

That was a single rare instance of a Dingca ghost which had no business to be there. A far more public ghost haunted him as well as thousands of other Manileños. It was no single figure but a composite, boiling tirelessly up from the edge of the bay whenever he drove past the Yacht Club on Roxas and saw the Cultural Center of the Philippines, showpiece of the Marcoses' New Society. That particular building merely exhaled the breath of the famous old cronies Imelda had wooed into performing, the Margot Fonteyns and Van Cliburns of the international concert hall. It was the other building tucked far away behind it on the edge of the tongue of reclaimed land where the ghosts hovered of those who had died in its construction. Dingca remembered the sequence of events indelibly since they were tangled up in his own police career.

In those days there had effectively been two national police forces. One was the Philippine Constabulary (established earlier in the century by the Americans), the other the Integrated National Police, itself an amalgam of local police forces. The PC had always been closely tied to the Army. Its use against communist guerrillas and in enforcing the 1972 Martial Law decree had left it quasi-military in terms of training and orientation. By no stretch of anyone's imagination could the PC have been described as a civilian force. From 1974 that role was filled by the INP, widely considered a poor cousin saddled with the dumb domestic cop jobs: tracing stolen vehicles, breaking dog-napping rings, directing traffic and tagging the bodies left by the PC after bank raids. It was as a humble PO2 in the INP that in the Seventies Rio Dingca had worked out of Station 5 in Ermita.

By 1975 Martial Law's promise of discipline and law enforcement was visibly crumbling beneath corruption of such size and weight it could only have proceeded at the bidding – or with the indulgence – of Malacañang Palace. Views differed as to which of the incumbent First Couple was more to blame. A bonanza of unsecured 'behest' loans to the Marcoses' business friends was awarded by order and drawn on public funds. Prestige construction projects abounded in the better-heeled areas of Manila, were completed, were burnt down for the insurance money, were restarted. Meanwhile, the ordinary policing of Ermita became a serious cop's private minefield. Merely stopping the wrong vehicle for a traffic violation might cost one's badge, investigating the legality of a night club one's life. So smile benignly at the foreign pedophiles as they waddled about town with rented children in tow. Wish other tourists luck as they gambled in illegal dens. Sell them the various substances they were looking for before someone else did. Pretend not to know that men with bulbous fraternity rings drove in from middle class suburbs to a particular bar on M.H. del Pilar in order to drink, but also at some lost point in the small hours to pay a large sum of money, troop down into a hidden basement and watch truly terrible things (In or Out?). Each day turn so many blind eyes one's head became a single cataract bestowing the same milky opacity in every direction. The frustration of it compounded by guilt at what was constantly seen but denied vision, known but withheld from knowledge, and all for the sake of a bare living wage, had made it easy for Rio and his comrades to take the law into their own hands from time to time, just as the country's rulers did lawlessness. Extra-judicial deaths were a way of fighting back. In those days by no means all the bodies lying in Rizal Park at night were fornicating or sleeping. In those days Intramuros was jammed solid with parked trucks laden with goods pilfered from the nearby Port area, some of them with corpses at the wheel. In those days Rio was a newly married man and Sita was pregnant with Eunice. It was no time to be changing his job. Be canny, he told himself. Coconut trees kept their heads by bending with the typhoon, and typhoons eventually blew themselves out. (He was, as has been observed, a man of banal precept.)

In the late Seventies Imelda Marcos, rejoicing in her role as Governor of Manila, fell ever more deeply into the grip of her 'edifice complex', the earliest symptoms of which had resulted in the Cultural Center in 1969. Eighty percent of that building's $8.5m cost had gone on kickbacks. People praised it for its architecture, her for her patriotic vision. By 1981, casting around for the international status symbols Manila might be thought to lack, she decided that Cannes had had it all its own way for too long and with far less impressive sunsets than Manila Bay's. Thus the Manila International Film Festival was hastily conceived and even more hastily born in the shape of the Film Center, designed as MIFF's screening complex. It was a rush job, like many of Imelda's grand projects. The contractors were given a bare seven months to put up from scratch a seven-storey Parthenon-style building the size of a shopping mall. The project was given top priority and Imelda's personal supervision.

It was also given the services of PO2 Gregorio Dingca, ordered to keep the narrow foreshore road clear of unnecessary traffic so that dump trucks and delivery vehicles could come and go unhindered. Lighters of especially white sand stripped from a provincial beach appeared over the horizon. Projects all over Metro Manila came to a halt as cement was diverted to the Film Center. Over 5,000 labourers worked, ate and slept on the site in the traditional way of men who have come to the capital from afar and move from site to site, steadily building themselves out of a succession of temporary homes. They built by day and they built by night under arc lamps, sleeping in shifts on sheets of cardboard as hods and hoppers manoeuvred among them.

Rio himself was on night shift when at 2:35 a.m. on November 17th 1981, a day he was not going to forget, the top storey fell through. Work had proceeded so quickly that the concrete had not been allowed sufficient time to cure before the weight of another floor was added. This, together with skimpy bracing and underpinning, provoked a domino-like collapse of much of the structure into the main viewing theatre where a hundred day-shift workers were asleep. An immense tonnage of freshly poured cement, concrete and girders slammed down, together with workmen toppled from their collapsing scaffolds. A nightmarish rescue operation then began. As news of the disaster spread locally, people gathered to help. The new floor lay like a lumpy quilt over the ones below it with a series of jagged caverns beneath. The concrete was still so wet in places that workers had become embedded in it. Men dug frantically with shovels and hands to reach those trapped, uncovering here a leg, there the back of a head. Like them, Dingca was himself daubed with cement; his holster was caked with it, his boots weighed a ton. Even twenty-four hours after the collapse they were still pulling men alive out of air pockets and stairwells.

Then came the orders from Malacañang: *Leave it. Carry on building without delay.* The rescuers decided there had been some mistake, a misunderstanding, and redoubled their efforts to claw their way through the now hardened slurry to reach their friends. It was here that, if Rio's memories remained vivid, maybe events themselves became telescoped. He remembered clearly that no ambulance was allowed through for nine hours after the accident, that a complete security blanket enveloped the site. The next day a couple of newspapers had spoken of a minor accident which had killed two workers. Otherwise, total silence. It was not ambulances that arrived but staff cars and military vehicles: MetroCom and the dreaded NISA and MISA. It never occurred to him to wonder what Military Intelligence had to do with an accident on a construction site. Everyone knew. Saloon cars with smoked windows arrived carrying aides with express orders. The building was going to be finished on time, cost what it might, and time had already been lost.

Meanwhile, workers with jackhammers were still trying to free their colleagues even as the concrete hardened around their limbs. Men died fully conscious, up to their waists in setting cement. After three days the stench of unreachable bodies was dreadful. Even so, there was still life in the very walls of the tangled canyons deep inside the building. Pneumatic drill bits pierced the concrete and released gouts of blood. But orders were given and obeyed. Bulldozers arrived and began pushing everything in a rubble of flesh and stone and metal out of the building and down to the sea where the gulls swooped and dived. Back inside, men with chainsaws went about lopping off flush the limbs and still-clothed bulges which protruded from the concrete. As a police-man, Dingca had been ordered to draw his gun and prevent further rescue work on pain of death. He and his INP colleagues stood there trembling with fatigue, their drawn weapons hanging heavy with cement by their sides. Each pretended not to notice those who silently wept. Outside, Army trucks kept drawing up with fresh PC men in military uniform who leaped out, saw only what they had been told they would see – a scene of sabotage and a communist-inspired labour dispute – and cocked their weapons. Within a week work was once again in full swing. Fresh concrete was poured over the remains; the smell grew fainter.

It never was determined how many died nor how many still lay entombed in the Film Center. There were no official figures. Those on-site who could list by name their missing friends and colleagues thought over 200, but it was anyone's guess how many of their bodies had ever been removed. For all that 7,000 labourers were still working on the day before the first Manila International Film Festival opened, the building was finished on time and Imelda, who was after all the chief exhibit, had her day. Satyajit Ray chaired the panel which awarded a Golden Eagle to 36 Chowringhee Lane. But MIFF never took off and in 1983 had to show upmarket pornography in order to break even. It was doubtful whether anyone in Cannes lost even a wink of sleep over its potential threat.

MIFF was dead but the Film Center still stood. Now and again Rio caught sight of it from one of the new flyovers on Roxas, a vast, pillared cube in the distance. For him, as for the thousands who hadn't been there that appalling week in 1981, it had gone on sending up a thick plume of ghosts which hovered over the whole spit of land. They were regularly seen and heard, and just as regularly there were attempts to exorcise them. Many times the Church had sent its shamans and, when they failed, priests from the Ifugao and Igorot hill tribes tried their own expertise. Nothing worked for long and most people believed firmly that nothing ever would as long as the building remained standing. It was now an abandoned warehouse, empty, cracked and subsiding, reeking of Babylon after a mere dozen years. No earthly power would ever make Rio set foot inside it again. He knew that as soon as he did the structure would immediately become transparent and, looking up, he would see against the fabled sunset of Manila Bay the tumbled figures of the dead sitting, lying, upside down, spreadeagled, headless, shirtless, missing a leg or a hand or half a torso, their mouths full of cement and with the early stars coming out among their bones.

Such were Dingca's ghosts. They lived on in a lesser way in the subsequent history of the police force, being reawakened each time something else happened to remind him of the essential difference between the civilian force he served and the Philippine Constabulary. They were both described as the police; but while his training at the Police Academy had been 'service oriented', in the official phrase, the PC trained with the military and were 'mission oriented'. The two forces frankly despised each other, on occasion being reduced to public firefights. Then in 1991 they were officially merged, creating the Philippine National Police. The intention was to form a truly national civilian police entirely separate from the armed forces. Dingca and his INP colleagues glumly predicted what would happen and were glumly proved right. Almost without exception the ex-PC men took over the top jobs and gave their old comrades the plum assignments while the ex-INP men carried on trying to be ordinary cops. The venerable Police Academy, which in the postwar years had turned out the spruce ranks of Manila's Finest, was abolished. In its place was the National Capital Training Command in – of all ominous places for a civilian force – Camp Crame, the Army HQ.

The unhappy amalgam which was the PNP had been given two years to shake down and to date showed not the slightest sign that it ever would. Under its provisions a policeman could now be reassigned anywhere in the country, which meant there were now Manila policemen who knew nothing about the city, while men like Rio Dingca kept their heads down for fear of being posted to some godforsaken provincial oubliette. He knew perfectly well that most of the ex-Constabulary men whose orders he now took were unqualified to be policemen, as were plenty of officers who had been recruited in the old Martial Law days and who had simply bought a fake High School education certificate in order to join the force. Nowadays one had to be a College graduate, an excellent notion fatally undercut in a force already full of men unqualified to wear any but a janitor's uniform. Demoralised by politics, Dingca and his friends were unhopeful for their future. Morale was terrible, behaviour worse. Policemen rampaged like delinquents, firing off their guns at whim, organising kidnapping syndicates, drug rings, car thefts, protection rackets, the fencing of stolen goods. Almost daily they shot each other, in and out of uniform. They held each other up, busted each other's scams to take control of them, stole each other's loot. When lumped together with the armed forces one could say, as Rio Dingca often did to Sita, that the law enforcement authorities constituted the country's single biggest source of crime.

All of a sudden, out of the blue, he had been struck by the sadness, by a furious sense of waste of which Babs was only the most poignant recent example. Not long ago he had had to deal with a halfwitted squatter who had been set up for a car-napping rap which Rio was sure he hadn't merited since he knew the policemen who were running the ring. Their usual trick was to spot a car they fancied, arrest the owner and impound the vehicle, which would then vanish without trace from police custody. He had recognised the jailed squatter and had sprung him by showing that he couldn't even drive. There was a pathos to this. It was the squatter's wife he liked, an admirable and hardworking soul from whom he regularly bought his girls' T-shirts at rock-bottom prices. Shortly after restoring her worthless husband to San Clemente Rio had bumped into the parish's rogue priest, Fr. Herrera. Generally speaking, Dingca hadn't much time for priests or, indeed, for churchgoing, which he felt was all right for women. Unlike Fr. Bernabe, the parish's other priest, Herrera was unconventional, cynical, sour and knowledgeable about the most surprising things, including fighting cocks. Rio had persuaded him without much difficulty to have a cold glass of something. At the back of his mind he had an idea that he might tentatively sound the man out on the subject of ghosts, which were beginning to disquiet him more than he liked.

With old Bryan Macawili retired from the force Rio knew nobody else he wished to confide in.

As a matter of fact there were several things he quite wanted to put to Fr. Herrera but couldn't work out how to turn them into questions. Once after seeing Babs in 'The Topless Pit' he had had the most extraordinary vision of Judgement Day while driving morosely back to San Pedro, Laguna. Summoned to appear before the Almighty and explain how she had spent her time on earth, Iron Pussy would say, 'Sir, I used to open Coke bottles with my cunt for tourists. . . er, my vagina, Sir,' while cherubim and seraphim cracked up behind discreetly held wings. Dingca further fantasised that there really was justice in heaven because God would then thunder 'BRING ME THOSE TOURISTS!' instead of dumping on poor Iron Pussy, who had only been putting to use the peculiar talent He himself had given her. Such metaphysical extravaganzas were not easily translated into questions one could pose a parish priest, Rio decided.

In the event it scarcely mattered because Fr. Herrera, by then on his third bottle of Red Horse, drifted into his own strange monologue which now and then seemed to inhabit the sort of territory Dingca found interesting.

'Listen, Lieutenant,' he said. 'The sadness and cruelty of this world are overwhelming and without remedy. They leave no survivors, of course. Folk deal with this as best they may. They have recourse to their gods and their devils; their drugs like tobacco and alcohol and money; their cynicism as much as their wishful thoughts and quiet retreats snatched between blows; their lovers and families. I say without remedy because I've come to know that's true. I've also heard it said that living well is the best revenge. For years I assumed that meant wealthy living, the so-called "good life" which I must say has always struck me as a creed of dim greed. Strangely, though, I discovered that the best revenge really *is* to be good, to be moral, to live well in that sense. What's more, I know there's no alternative. It has nothing to do with pleasing a god or satisfying a social convention. It actually is the most logical and intelligent way to live. To all those not yet old or scarred enough to recognise the truth of this it sounds like bullshit, and always will. It can't be taught, only learned.'

'And that's your remedy?'

'No, I told you, there is no remedy. It's merely the proper way for a person to live. There are no rewards and no punishments: that's the worst we have to face. People think little acts of kindness, when sown here and there like – excuse the simile – mustard seeds, will grow and spread and gradually cover the earth with a bounteous crop of, well, mustard I suppose. But it doesn't happen like that because along comes a new generation and it all has to start again from scratch. Little acts of kindness are purely local. They may not be forgotten, but then nor are slights. Neither a kindness nor a slight guarantees its own propagation. It requires too much effort to take things any further. They simply vanish, the good and the bad alike. Nothing is ever learned. Each generation just starts all over again.'

'You're a strange kind of priest, I must say.'

'Is there any other kind? What do you want, Catholic dogma? I can do that, too.'

'Then what do you tell your parishioners about condoms?'

'That I've never worn one.'

'Maybe you should,' said Dingca with leaden mischievousness.

'Maybe I should. I tell them to be sure and buy good quality if they're going to buy them at all. They know perfectly well what the Church teaches. I tell them it's up to them. Everybody has to make their own decisions. But people want to be told what to do, have you noticed? They want someone identifiable to disobey, I think. You obey gods, but men can be disobeyed.'

'I thought the man represented God? The man in the Church's pay?'

'I wouldn't presume. There's nothing in the Bible about condoms, or overpopulation, or Aids. We know nothing of Christ and his teaching except what's in the New Testament. All the rest is hearsay. Pure gossip, no matter how much it's dressed up as revelation and patristic tradition. In that sense you could say I'm a fundamentalist.' Fr. Herrera tipped his bottle until the foam in his glass rushed up to cover its mouth. Then he took off his spectacles, polished them with a paper napkin and held them at arm's length, squinting up through each lens in turn. 'As for the Church's *pay*, I'm no better paid than you are, Lieutenant. Even worse, probably. In that sense God's work is a truly lousy job.'

'With respect, Father, you sound to me like a priest who's lost his faith.'

'And am I not sitting opposite a policeman who's lost his hope?

Losing your faith is like giving up smoking, I've discovered. You suddenly realise that countless millions are getting by without it and always have done. It doesn't matter. I still wish to live my life well, and for that I need no faith at all. The discovery that wishing to live my life well means helping others to do the same is oddly strengthening and calming. Not praiseworthy; simply logical.'

The two men drank in silence for a while.

'I hate my job,' said Dingca at last. 'I know it sounds stupid and naive now, but I really did want to be one of Manila's Finest when I joined. There are good men on the force, you know. Despite everything. There are still some real policemen.'

'Of course. As opposed to the military thugs you're now having to share a bed with?'

'You've said it,' was Dingca's bitter reply. 'It's in ruins. We're all lost. Everything's topsy-turvy. You're lost, too. You called me "Lieutenant" a moment ago, but you're out of date. I haven't been a Lieutenant since 1991. When we were reorganised we were all given civilian ranks to replace our military ones. I'm actually an Inspector these days. The military thugs, as you call them, have stopped being Majors and Lieutenant-Colonels and have turned overnight into fully-fledged Chief Inspectors and Superintendents. The names change, the duties change, the crimes go on being the same. We're all ghosts of what we're supposed to be.'

'I know,' said Herrera. 'But I also know you're right about there being good men on the force. It's like the fire-fighters. Despite the scoundrels who won't tackle a blaze until they're given cash or something to eat there are always men who perform absurd acts of heroism unpaid and on an empty stomach. Of course. They're the ones who understand the logic, the intelligence of living properly. That intelligence *is* compassion. You and I are really in the same line of business, Lieu- *Inspector*. Every day we see people struggling against impossible odds to live morally and intelligently. The majority of the people in this country would give their eye teeth to be able to be clean.'

'So what do you tell them?'

'I tell them they ought to rejoice at their marvellous freedom. I tell them they're free to murder and cheat and steal if they want, and equally free not to. The choice is theirs. Within that greater freedom there are, of course, predisposing factors which make certain choices more likely or more difficult. There was a French writer called Anatole France who once remarked on the freedom shared by rich and poor alike to steal bread and sleep under bridges. That's a very Filipino thing to say, I've always thought. I suspect he was really one of our Pinoy diaspora just pretending to be French. Come to that, I believe there's a Jewish saying of more or less the same meaning. Something about counting no man honest until he's had the opportunity and the need to steal. By the same token priestly virtue's no virtue at all, is it? I'm expected to be good. I'm badly paid to be good. Just like you. Since I'm never tempted to steal it'd be grotesque to commend me for honesty. It's not the middle classes who fill the jails.'

'I sometimes think this would be a better world if they did,' said Rio Dingca, surprising himself. But he knew that what really filled the jails, like the streets themselves, was ghosts.

15

A SERIOUS DISCUSSION was taking place in the Tugos house in San Clemente. Because it was so private all the shutters had to be closed owing to there being no glass in the windows and people coming and going in the mud alley in front. This gave the place a portentous air as if it were concealing a conspiracy or the goings-on of a fanatical religious sect. Inside, all sewing had been suspended. The downstairs room was full of the co-operative's members as well as Eddie, Bats, Judge and Billy, not yet properly washed after their digging. On one of the sewing tables was a cardboard box which had held packets of Birch Tree milk and now contained something far more potent. From time to time somebody lifted the flap curiously, nervously, as if to check that the skull hadn't moved or turned into something else. Nanang Pipa was automatically acting as the meeting's chairwoman, Eddie not being one of nature's chairmen. She had just sworn everyone present to secrecy, the Bible passed around and right hands raised solemnly as in courtroom dramas on television.

'I think we've got three alternatives. We can tell the police, we can tell a priest or we can try to keep quiet about it.'

'Four,' somebody said. 'We can tell Monching.'

Monching Jandusay was the barangay captain and ought indeed to have been the first to know, to have had the entire problem dumped in his official hands, had he not been so tremendously drunk most of the time. Nowadays his capacities extended little further than being able to decide that he needed to pee. Even in this he was not infallible.

'Exactly,' said Nanang Pipa briskly. 'Three alternatives. We're lucky here. People may say he's a mad radical but Father Herrera's okay. Rio Dingca's okay, too. But the problem with telling the cops is we can't guarantee to get Rio. According to him there are 157 policemen in his station and my bet is that once some senior officer hears what we've got he'll come here himself to make sure.'

To make sure he gets the loot, everyone was thinking. For that was indeed the idea at the top of each mind. Skulls meant foul play or treasure, and treasure was the preferred option. Nobody seriously believed it was General Yamashita's, of course, and in any case the Marcoses were supposed to have found that and kept it for themselves. But the details of that treasure's burial, true or not, had acquired a mythic status to which all other buried treasure ought to conform. The essence was that you forced conscripts to dig a hole and manhandle the loot down into it. Then you made them shovel half the earth back before you shot them and buried their bodies beneath the remaining soil. To anyone weaned on this myth a skull was as good as a cross over a grave. Both were an earnest that something lay beneath.

'Maybe it's just an ordinary body,' said Judge. 'Perhaps this used to be a graveyard right here a long time ago, say in the time of the Spanish. Before the city grew and they had to build the big cemeteries over there.' He gave a backward nod towards a wall covered with a polyester tapestry of a group of dogs wearing eyeshades sitting at a table, playing cards and smoking cigars. Everyone's mental eyes flew through it and up to the great burial grounds beyond.

'I suppose so,' said Nanang Pipa dubiously. Nobody liked to feel they were living over a disused cemetery. 'In which case I suppose we ought to put it back.'

'And then shit on it?' said Bats.

'Oh my God.' The original purpose of this pit was suddenly recalled. 'Maybe the – '

At this moment there was a knock on the door and a boy of about thirteen appeared holding a knotted plastic sachet containing half a cupful of soy sauce. He was one of three children in San Clemente usually distinguished by being better dressed than the others. His jeans were of heavier quality, his shirts prettier, his trainers genuine Nike or

Converse instead of local imitations. Rich foreigners were easily seduced into shelling out for the real McCoy.

'Sorry, Nanang Pipa. Mum said to return the *toyo* she owes you.'

'We're in a *business meeting*, Danny,' Pipa said sternly. 'But thank you. And please thank her as well.'

The door closed. The interruption was a timely reminder of yet another problem, which was keeping the news of their find from the barrio's other inhabitants, at least until some plan had been agreed. Once it leaked out onto the gossip circuit anything could happen. It was not lost on those present that Danny's mother was also a member of the sewing co-operative and would shortly want to know why she had been excluded from the meeting. More rumour, more rifts, unless this was handled just right.

'What we'll do,' said Nanang Pipa, 'is keep the skull here for the moment.'

'You mean in the *house*? asked Rey the chop-chop boy with a theatrical shudder. 'Oo. I shouldn't like that. Imagine, sewing away with that horrible thing beside me.'

'It won't be beside you, it'll be up on that shelf there. And it's not a horrible thing, it's just somebody's head. Or was. In any case I'm going to put the Bible in the box with it, and a rosary. Meanwhile, the boys will go on digging –'

'We've got to get to the bottom of this,' said Bats, laughing.

'– will go on digging,' resumed Pipa in her best chairwoman's no-nonsense manner, 'until they find something else or until I say so. I want a comfort room. And just remember, we're all under sacred oath. That means not a word, not a whisper, not a hint.'

'All right,' Judge said. 'But what's this meeting been about, then? People will want to know.'

'Perfectly simple,' said Pipa. 'We've been deciding what to give Danny's mother as a birthday surprise.'

And *that*, the ability to think on her feet, was what enabled her to take charge, thought Eddie with rueful pride as he and the rest of the gang trooped out of the back door. It was people like her who sat about making decisions while the aptly-named 'sons of sweat' toiled with spades. 'Go a bit slow,' he called softly down after Bats as if wearing a shred of his wife's mantle. 'We don't want to be, er, breaking anything.' This was all said in a low voice, for only a couple of feet away was a neighbour's kitchen. There was a slimy patch beneath an overhang from which washing-up water, grains of rice and escaped noodles periodically gushed and drooled between slats.

It was good advice to little avail, for within fifteen minutes there came a hollow crunching sound and up came spadefuls of earth mixed with pale fragments.

'Is that another one?'

'No!' bellowed Bats. 'It's just an old pot.'

'Shut up, Bats, you cretin,' hissed Judge, squatting on the edge. 'And go *slow*. That old pot may be part of *it*.'

'Oh. Ah. Sorry.'

The pieces were taken inside and washed. Once they had been cleaned, an imaginative eye could see they would fit together into a little blue and white porcelain bowl, round and slightly squashed, like a sea urchin's fragile shell. By nightfall there were more bones, too: a handful of sticklike objects, some curved and some straight and all stained ochre with earth. Several were so small the co-operative began to lose heart.

'Surely you don't find chicken bones in a treasure pit?'

'Maybe they stopped for lunch.'

'Well, I say we go on a bit tomorrow.'

'I don't like it,' said Mrs Piedragoso, a timid seamstress who so far had played an entirely silent part in the developing conspiracy. 'I remember this legend we used to have in Marinduque about the guardians of treasures. My father said he'd often seen them. Chinese pirates used to come ashore and bury their treasure so they could pick it up later. What they did was they posted a spirit guardian on it to stop anyone digging it up. Only the Chinese were able to do it because they had a special knowledge. My father said he'd see the spirits at night on the beach, hovering over the sand. They had demon faces with enormous fangs and blazing eyes. Supposing there's a guardian here, too? That bowl looks Chinesey to me.'

So it did to everyone else. Despite a crisp, rational 'H'm!' from Nanang Pipa a distinct uneasiness filled the room.

That night Eddie and the boys got pretty smashed, all things considered, drinking beer mixed with gin and nibbling with a fork from a tin of liver spread. Pipa was out at Danny's mother's house, a politically motivated visit of some adroitness. From outside came sudden bursts of panting and shouts, very close, together with the scuffling of bare feet on beaten earth. A basketball now and then bounced off the wall of the house with a thud. Inside, conversation was about almost anything but the afternoon's discoveries. This was partly due to a shared feeling that it would be dishonourable to get drunk and risk being overheard, but mainly because the events were still too recent to have sunk to that deeper layer of perennial topics to which a mixture of gin and beer provided reliable access.

One inevitable subject in any company which included Bats was his brother Gringo, in whose cab Eddie had shared many an adventure involving dogs, drugs and the occasional semi-conscious tourist calling for madder wine and louder women. Gringo was never stumped for loud women or just about anything else a tourist might want, including a fully-armed, leather-creaking police motorcyclist named Hitlerito. The point about Gringo that made him crop up again and again in such conversations was his laughter, which was unreal, and his rage, which was very real indeed. In 1989 he had been working for what was thought to be one of the more honest cab companies, the Silver Taxi Service, when it became the centre of a famous labour case. Silver's management had long been collecting Social Security contributions from all its drivers until the day one man, deep in a family health crisis and needing emergency funds, went along to the Social Security office to claim help and discovered that none of his remittances had ever been paid in. Neither, on closer inspection, had anybody else's. The drivers promptly called a strike, demanding to know where all their hard-earned pay had been going, thereby crippling the Silver Taxi Service. True to type, Silver's management responded by hiring a police heavy to kill the strike leaders. He assassinated the President of the drivers' union. Not long afterwards the strike collapsed. Gringo was one of many drivers interviewed by reporters, for it became a celebrated issue of its day. From them he learned there was no serious doubt about the killer's links with Silver's management since several *Inquirer* reporters had seen them all drinking together in the Sunlight, a four-star hotel which was also Silver-owned. The killer was later reassigned as provincial police chief up in Ferdinand Marcos's old territory.

Gringo, like many of the other Silver drivers, was left with considerable undischarged fury. Not only had gross injustice been done, it had been seen to be done by anybody who could read a newspaper. Yet there was no restitution, no redress. The innocent had been robbed and cowed, the guilty free to carry on stealing and intimidating. A man had been killed, his assassin promoted. Gringo being Gringo, his anger came out as anarchy: in ever-zanier exploits which often left him hunched over his own wheel, laughing until tears came. Underneath, though, anyone could recognise that injustice piled on hardship and topped with ever more injustice bedded down into something not unlike a permanent state of pain: that pain which so many carried and which now and then could break out in a frenzy with a gun spraying bullets or a machete flailing in a last, desperate attempt to clear a path for the soul through a tangling darkness.

Gringo did not, of course, own the car he drove. It was one of a fleet of thirty called Melody Cabs owned by a Chinese and named for his wife, though as Gringo would say the only melodious thing about them was gearbox whine. Melody cabs all looked a little odd inside, but in a way only someone in the know could identify. It was like one of those visual perception tests in which an apparently random jumble of black and white blotches suddenly jells into a picture of Jesus Christ. Once having seen the figure, one went on seeing it: the picture never reverted to its former incoherence. Similarly, once having driven in a Melody taxi one knew it for ever as a chop-chop cab. Chop-chops were made up of spare parts of Japanese domestic vehicles, less duty being paid on imported parts than on fully assembled cars. Labour being so cheap they could be put together in a workshop outside Manila and still represent a saving. The only problem was comparatively minor, that the Japanese drove on the left so vehicles for their home market were all right-hand drive. This required ingenuity at the assembly stage which never completely overcame a certain oddness about the fascia, the instruments being curiously grouped.

But the cabs worked, and Gringo worked. The engine was hardly ever switched off. Just as 'bedspacers' slept in shifts in a single rented bed, so Melody drivers began their stint at the wheel in a driver's seat still damp with a colleague's sweat. He would touch the luminous crucifix which dangled beneath the 'Bless Our Trip' motto, drape a clean towel behind his neck and edge out into what seemed to be the world's biggest traffic jam. It was from Gringo's tours of duty, his *pasadas*, that the news, the gossip, the stories came to enliven and inform his brother's drinking sessions with Eddie and the others tucked away behind the walls of San Clemente. The fare who fell silent in Mandaluyong because his lady escort was sitting on his face. The off-duty policeman unconscious with drink whom his riotous colleagues handcuffed to a seatbelt bracket on the floor with his own cuffs before tossing the key out of the window ('Don't worry, he'll pay,' they said as they climbed out in Balik-Balik and disappeared.) And the Canadian nun whose luggage had exploded on the way to the airport.

That had been a near thing, actually, though hilarious retrospectively. There had been two of them sitting side by side, Sisters of the Rosy Pillar or something, chatting away as they bowled along Roxas. Suddenly there was this tremendous fizzing and popping noise and immediately afterwards a muffled *thump*. In his mirror Gringo could see white smoke jetting from every crack of the suitcase, bursting even from the keyholes of the locks. In an instant, and despite the open windows, the cab filled with choking chemical clouds. Screams and a red glow were coming from the rear as he swung across two lanes of traffic into the providentially handy entrance to Navy HQ and leaped out. The rear windows had both lost their handles and were jammed down so it was easy to get a door open, grab the suitcase and hurl it out. By now flames had melted a hole in the lid but luckily seemed not yet to have spread downwards. The blackened Sisters emerged pretty much intact except for streaming red eyes behind their rimless spectacles. They leaned on each other, coughing into handkerchiefs, and watched their luggage burn. The Navy guards deserted their posts and joined the curious onlookers straggling over from squatter shanties pitched against the sea wall.

'What the hell have you got in there?' demanded Gringo, who was nervous of fire. 'Who are you, anyway? Terrorists? NPA?'

This accusation brought a swift change in the atmosphere. The Navy men unslung their M-16s; people could be heard murmuring 'Rebel nuns' and 'Sparrow Unit', no longer merely looking at the interesting sight of two religious and a blazing suitcase but seeing disguised urban terrorists, either of whom might suddenly produce an Uzi.

'We're not terrorists,' protested one of the nuns in Tagalog. 'Absolutely not. It's an accident.'

'That's what I'd say if I were Commander Mubarak,' agreed Gringo.

'*Commander Mubarak?*' said a Navy man, noisily cocking his weapon. The crowd moved back.

'Oh, don't be so silly!' cried the other nun with equal fluency. 'Do we *look* like Commander Mubarak?'

'The Marines thought he looked like an unarmed duck farmer,' said Gringo relentlessly, 'so why not an unarmed nun? He's a master of disguise. That's what the papers say.' This was a reference to a recent news story that the leader of Mindanao's most notorious kidnap gang had been surprised asleep by soldiers and summarily shot. Pictures of a body appeared on all the front pages but doubts lingered about its true identity, an issue made still more opaque since there was scarcely a photograph of him on file with the authorities, let alone fingerprints or dental records. Nevertheless, the military maintained that identification was beyond question. Overlooking the implausibility of Mindanao's most wanted gangster sleeping unarmed and unguarded in a duck house, the military pointed out that not only was the dead man's amulet – the dried foetuses of his seven-month twins – unmistakable, but so powerful that had they allowed him to wake and set foot to ground he would immediately have become invisible. President Ramos himself had said, 'This closes another chapter.' Barely a month later an NBI report said that Commander Mubarak was alive and well and setting up operations in Manila, to few people's surprise and least of all to those who had personally known the wretched duck-raiser, now buried.

Still, Scarlet Pimpernel though the real Mubarak no doubt was, it was hard to see him lurking beneath the smoke-stained habits of either of these two foreign Sisters standing by their luggage burning itself out at the main gates of Navy HQ.

'So what did you have in there?' asked a guard. He, too, was nervous of fire ever since being caught some years ago in a blaze which had gutted much of the building he was now guarding, allegedly started during a dispute over a mess bill.

'*Watusi*,' admitted the Sister whose suitcase it was.

'*Watusi!*' echoed Gringo, by now starting to enjoy himself. 'There must have been a kilo of them.' *Watusi* were little maroon fireworks looking like fragments of dried string or Dora rat poison granules which had recently become popular among children. When struck like a match against the pavement they leaped and popped among passers-by, causing a good deal of smoke and the dance steps which may have accounted for their name. A spate of deaths over the last Christmas and New Year season had revealed that it was the red phosphorus they contained which had done no good to the toddlers who had eaten them.

'We'd never seen them before,' said the Sister. 'We thought the orphans back home would like them. We never imagined. . . Oh, oh, how dreadful.' The image had evidently struck her of what might have happened had her bag done its exploding in their aircraft's baggage hold.

'And what about my taxi?' Gringo asked tragically. He was inspecting the cab and, apart from a lingering smell and some spatter burns in the plastic roof liner, found it sadly unharmed. 'Look at these burns! Renovation of entire panel of upholstery, colour match'll never be the same, oh, five hundred at least. We'll say five hundred.'

'Five hundred *pesos*?' demanded the Sister whose luggage was now a bubbling heap of fibreglass. 'Not an earthly, young man.'

'Definitely four.'

'One, if you're lucky. On top of your already illegal fare. I notice you never started the meter. But you acted promptly and saved us all from a dangerous situation. Meanwhile, the loss is all ours, and we take full responsibility for it. Since it's no use crying over burnt baggage we may as well continue our journey. Kindly take us to the airport. Come along, Sister,' she added in English to her companion, 'otherwise we shall miss the Calgary connection. I've still got our passports and tickets, which is what counts.'

Gringo had at once recognised that these two with their Tagalog and briskness were old hands, no matter how ignorant about fireworks, and drove them on to NAIA without further demur.

'I'd have given a lot to see Sister Watusi when her luggage blew up,' said Bats, spearing the last of the liver spread with the communal fork.

'Me too,' agreed Eddie blearily. 'You can still see the mark on the concrete even after all these months. Gringo and I passed it the other day. 'Course, they were really Navy nuns.' His head kept dropping so that he found himself staring for hours at a stretch at the plastic tablecloth. This was gridded into squares, each of which contained a hideous grinning face which swam in and out of little lakes of spilled beer. A more sober man than he would have called them roses.

'Wha' you mean, Navy nuns?' asked Billy. 'Isn't such a thing. Couldn't be.'

'Everyone knows Navy nuns, you cretin. Special underwater. Top secret. They're trained in Olongapo. American training. Top secret.' He got suddenly to his feet and blundered out of the house. Outside, he peed without stopping for fully half an hour, his forehead braced against the trunk of the coconut tree which held the iron basketball ring. His eyes closed. He was perfectly happy. If only he could stop peeing.

And thus Nanang Pipa found him on her return, his trouser cuffs sodden.

'You're disgusting,' she cried. 'Night after night, you and your *barkadas*. Well, tonight you can stay out. I'm not having you in the house like that.' She disappeared and Eddie closed his eyes again in relief. In the distance he could hear the sounds of eviction, then a door slam and bolts being shot. He thought it might be better to sit down and lo! when he next opened his eyes he found himself sitting. That was all there was to it. All you had to do was think something and there you were. There Bats was too, he discovered.

'Where're the others?' he asked.

'Gone home. We've been abandoned, Eddie.'

This struck both of them as terribly sad. When next he looked up Eddie thought at first the moon had fallen but then he saw it wasn't the moon at all. Perched on the roof of his own house was an appalling face. At once he felt completely sober.

'Holy Mary,' he said. 'Bats, Bats, for God's sake, look!' He kept nudging his companion until Bats fell over sideways and then sat up crossly. 'Look, Bats, on the roof. There's a demon on my roof.'

'Oh Jesus Christ and all the Saints, you're right. I – I think I know what it is, Eddie.'

'So do I. It's the Guardian of the Treasure. The one Ming Piedragoso was telling us about. God, look at those fangs. What shall we do?'

'You must wake Nanang Pipa,' said Bats. 'She's in terrible danger. She's sleeping just underneath it. Go on, take the horn by the bulls.'

They were barely fifteen feet from the house and neither wanted to go a step closer. But they clung together and ran for the door, from where they could no longer see the apparition. They banged and shouted hard and long until at last Nanang Pipa came down, not overly welcoming until she consented to be led to the palm tree to see for herself, when she became positively insulting.

'There's absolutely nothing there! All we've got here are two layabouts drunk out of their skulls, shouting and hammering and disgracing us all. Think of the neighbours!'

But at this moment a voice in the darkness came to the men's aid. 'I saw it too,' said the woman who lived opposite. 'From the window upstairs.' She was carrying a Bible held before her as one holds up a fan or newspaper to shield one's eyes from the sun's glare. 'Those terrible teeth! Fangs, fangs they were! It's a vampire without a doubt.' And as if this word, once pronounced, had the power to bring sleepers forth from their houses rubbing their eyes, a small crowd gathered. In its hands were palm frond crosses, rosaries, crucifixes, bottles of holy water and a good few charms and amulets. They bunched together, staring at the roof of the Tugos house, shaking with fear and thrill.

16

JOHN PRIDEAUX had recently become conscious of his skull and its bumps, which seemed to be getting closer to the surface. When writing up his notes he would lean his head on one turned fist and suddenly the thumb propping his brow ridge would skid, together with a fold of flesh, over an apparently increasing lump. The Neanderthal of the future. Perhaps this same bony ball, by some absurd series of flukes and chance, might one day be exhibited by a future Richard Leakey in silver shorts who would twirl it for the 3-D cameras and pronounce it the skull of 'Mario', someone who long ago crossed this wasteland looking for water, or love, or the fruit borne on plants once known as 'trees'. In the meantime, never mind survival as a couple of skull plates; who cared about the archaeological future? On tropical mornings Prideaux thought it was enough simply to have lived beyond youth, when exclusive relationships were constantly in the air. These days nobody would ever want one with him, nor he with them. How the air cleared! How springy and untrammelled he probably felt, crossing this wasteland looking for whatever! (But how insistently the bones of his head were pushing up beneath the skinny tegument of scalp!)

Only a few days ago he'd received a letter from his daughter Ruth, at university in far-off England. They exchanged news once a month or so when each tried to convey a lively fascination with what they were doing, Prideaux without paying too much attention to whatever effects his savage low moments might produce on her. 'If you can imagine the Spanish Inquisition taking place in a Dunkin' Donuts,' he'd written soon after arriving, 'you'll have a faint idea of this country's spiritual and cultural *mise-en-scène*. For its deadly and surreal law enforcement you need to be able to visualise the Khmer Rouge in Disneyland. The economic position might be summarised as that of a banana republic which imports its bananas. The whole thing's encased in such beauty, such ruination, such brutality and affection and misery and zest as to stop the heart. The brain, though, goes wild.'

Lately her replies were betraying concern barely disguised as loving exasperation. 'What *are* you up to, Jaypee?' and 'You've been gone ages,' and 'If you knew what you were doing there you'd have done it by now.' In her last she'd come clean. 'Of course I'm worried. You're my *father*, not some boy-adventurer seeing the world,' this touching filiality swerving off in typically Ruth fashion into a denunciation of Max Bruch's G minor Violin Concerto as 'plagiaristic schlock'. 'Whole passages cribbed from Beethoven, not just B's own concerto but also the Benedictus of the *Missa Solemnis*, to say nothing of the Mendelssohn. It's really ugghily sentimental and cringeworthy and it's a set text!! I need your help with some rapierlike put-downs but you're stuck a million miles away where I think it's probably much more dangerous than you're letting on.' When he re-read this he found Ruth standing so vividly before him he at once began a letter calculated to calm both their fears. Fathers were not allowed to speak of un-certainty, still less of being lost. He spoke instead of the humour and warmth he met with constantly; of defiant high spirits; of sunsets over the city when, visibility permitting, one could look eastward past heavy bronze air and cognac clouds to mulberry-coloured mountains. Funny things, too. 'My journalist friend I've mentioned before, the admirable Vic, calls this "The Land of the Inspired Coincidence". We were driving through the tourist area called Ermita (not too many hermits there nowadays) and he pointed out all the pubs and clubs and dubious dives with their entrances nailed up and notices saying "Closed By Order of Mayor Lim". Good old Mayor Lim, is the instinctive reaction. Allow us to keep you in nails. (The impression one forms is of a purposeful and kindly gentleman twinkling away behind his spectacles, a good citizen through and through, a true *civilian* at last purging the Augean stables of sleaze.) Ah, says Vic, doing a bit of twinkling himself, this civilian of yours is actually an ex-policeman and until recently the Head of the NBI (the National Bureau of Investigation, the local FBI). Well, now, a couple of years ago there was this great scandal about the Philippine Charity Sweepstakes. All sorts of rumours were going around that the prizes were rigged, and since this was a national lottery the whole country was up in arms about it. So, late in 1991 the NBI was called in to do a thorough investigation. Lim arranged for the draw to be televised. Now everyone would be able to see for themselves there was no fix. A famously clean senator was appointed to draw the winning number. The nation held its breath. *Five million pesos!* In went the senator's hand and out came the ticket. What an amazing thing! It belonged to Lim himself! The head of the NBI clapped an incredulous palm to his forehead, beaming with surprise and pleasure. It's true, I'm an inveterate buyer of lottery tickets, I often buy whole booklets at once! But I never thought for a moment. . . ! There were calls for him to return the money but he refused, saying why should he? Hadn't everyone seen him win it honestly?

'At which point Vic referred to the Land of the Inspired Coincidence. I love it, don't you? He also said that a lot of these nailed-up clubs manage to buy their un-nailing after a week or two, and really this hasn't anything to do with a putsch on vice but with a complicated and ancient struggle for control of real estate in Ermita and Malate. Who knows? Never mind the subtext – it's the sheer spectacle which grips here.'

This was true enough. Yet the energies this shadow-play released were having uneasy effects on Prideaux which slowly amassed. His dreams, already full of loss, were increasingly of wars fought in jungle green. Sometimes in the morning, still dazed, he thought such things might not after all be entirely private but part of a contemporary disquiet, something to do with people being set more and more adrift. Maybe if one dispensed with absences and put down proper roots the sundry angers of living would earth themselves, would be grounded and bleed harmlessly away. But moving constantly about built up a static charge which declared itself in painful shocks at unexpected moments, in bluish flashes in the dark and maybe even wild acts of empty violence.

Yet of what use yearning for a native soil if that, too, was vagrant?

The harder one looked at Britain from afar the mistier it became, neither quite where it had been nor what it should be. Drifting, shallow, insecure. A culture lost to itself, no longer valid. All the same it lurked remorselessly, showing through alien landscapes as the hazy lineaments of a homeland. One couldn't help staring. He had noticed how people often looked at each other like that, too: gazing hopefully into every new face as if to catch sight of a father's ghost, a mother's shade, the precious phantom of a first and only love.

His daughter's queries about what he was doing did little to help. What on earth had made him choose such an emotional subject? Why couldn't he have selected something neutral, something noncommittal and linguistic, for example? Perhaps instead he should do a thesis on *theses*: on what made people choose the subjects they chose, driven to pick at a topic like a scab. In his last letter to her he had deliberately not recounted the rest of that conversation with Vic in the traffic-locked streets of Ermita. The afternoon's hot news item was public outrage over that morning's botched attempt to rescue a kidnap victim. She was the fifteen-year-old daughter of a wealthy Chinese mestizo family, being driven to school when the van she was in was held up by twenty armed men and she was abducted. It was six-thirty in the morning. An hour later she and four of the kidnappers were in the lead car of a five-vehicle convoy, a white Nissan Sentra, when they were in turn ambushed by plain clothes soldiers from the military's 'Hammerhead' task force backed up by North CapCom police. There, right on EDSA and Quezon Avenue amid the massed commuters at one of Metro Manila's biggest road junctions, they riddled the Sentra with bullets, killing everyone on board. Then the assorted lawmen dragged the mutilated bodies out and laid them in a row on the pavement, making no distinction between those of the kidnappers and the bloody corpse of their young victim in her school uniform. An immediate inquiry had been announced. So far nobody had yet come even close to apologising. Instead, excuses had been offered, such as that the assault team couldn't have known the girl was in the car because it had heavily tinted windows. At lunchtime a senator had said he was planning to file a bill banning all smoked glass in cars. Another excuse officially given was that the Chinese-Filipino community were no longer cooperating with the police and military to help stop the frequent kidnappings for ransom.

'Nothing to say that isn't lame,' Prideaux said. 'I mean, all those witnesses. Automatic weapons right there in public.'

'*Surely* you've got the message by now, John?' There was shortness, even impatience in Vic's voice. 'We're dealing with airhead boys brought up on a diet of Rambo films who're given lethal firepower and official protection. They know that no matter what they do, however many people they kill, they'll disappear safely behind a smokescreen of enquiries. A month later it's all forgotten because something worse has happened. A year afterwards the same people turn up again, but now they're chiefs of police in the provinces. Give you a much better example. There was a great series of pictures in the *Inquirer* eighteen months ago of a stakeout at the Civil Aeronautics Administration compound in Las Piñas. They showed a tricycle driver walking out of a garage with his hands up and being shot to death by police in front of a crowd of literally hundreds of spectators. You'd be pushed to imagine a clearer case of murder, but since then nothing. Zippo. A case hasn't even been filed before the regional trial court. A strange oversight, you may be thinking, until you dig around and listen to the gossip which explains all. Rumour says it was an episode in a protracted war between two rival police gangs involved in running drugs. In any case the victim's family sort of lost interest in pursuing the matter after what they called a "top local official" had a word with them. Two words, really: Money and Threat. Stuff someone's mouth with sufficient money and you can't hear a word they say, have you noticed? So, no case.'

'But surely you don't *need* an aggrieved party to bring a private prosecution? From what you say it was a cold-blooded act committed in front of witnesses including a photographer who has it all on film.'

'*Now* you're getting the message.'

It was the child sitting strangled in the burnt-out garage all over again: injustice so outrageous that something had to happen. Yet nothing did. People said, well, there you go, just as the Marines had said *There it is*. Who was going to risk certain death by bringing charges? But when the social contract was so flagrantly and publicly torn up by a country's authorities, what was it that made people go on perversely trying to keep their side of the bargain? Why didn't everyone break out in an orgy of killing and raping and looting? Father Herrera might come up with some absurd hypothesis about the innate good in people trying to live intelligently, he supposed. Or there again maybe the species was bright enough to perceive that its own best interests lay in order: that brigandage and piracy were dandy for the odd individual but not so good if one wanted to bring up children and take real pleasure in the rite of family shopping.

This only plunged Prideaux into a mess of private unclarity, like someone gazing into a well and seeing his own image shattered and dancing in the hail of grit he himself has dislodged. For he, too, had wanted and begot a family but, it turned out, with a secret reservation. This was that the hidden buccaneer in him might one day wake and spy the moment like a particular blue day with a scuddy wind and seize it, to vanish over the horizon full of yearnings for action and comradeship and lands of awesome difference. And that reservation, concealed equally from Jessie and himself, had at last found him out. The blue day had never quite dawned; but the flawed commitment, for so long disguised as a gentlemanly tentativeness, had at last driven Jessie out of the house and out of his life, taking with her their daughter Ruth who, Prideaux believed, was the only person he had ever truly loved. Despite their closeness and the letters they wrote each other he sometimes caught himself grieving for Ruth as if she were dead instead of reading Music at Durham University.

Looking into the well, he could acknowledge that his own wobbly outline was a consistent and accurate reflection. That final escape route, the longing for his day, was all of a piece with the ghost of inconclusiveness which had haunted his better films and given them their distinctive tone. Even after more than twenty years he still occasionally yearned to have the Bangkok film shown on television, now that the public had at last caught up with certain social realities. He no longer imagined he could thereby still right a wrong, nor even (how could he have been so sentimental?) memorialise a dead child. Quite simply, he now thought it his best work, the most characteristic, the true John Prideaux lit hectically by flickers of fear and loathing. It didn't pretend to fulfil the rituals of a documentary. There was no balanced voice in the middle, no expert on international law, no spokesman from the Thai Government, no promise of retribution, no jail door clanging shut. It was just a slash of light thrown suddenly across a dark place in a dark time. He saw its very inconclusiveness as its chief merit instead of its main drawback as claimed at the time by the timid and – yes – the jealous. Prideaux disliked the self these reflections made but knew it to be truthful. Somewhere his vanity lay unappeased, as did his regret. He was sad that he had failed as a father and a husband just as he lamented that he had failed as a potential comrade in an adventure from which he had always been absent. Now Vietnam was history and the times had turned and here he was in Manila doing a self-imposed mid-life crisis degree course which an unwelcome insight was making him question as a possibly pathetic attempt to keep Ruth company or shed unsheddable years. Still, no more relationships. That at least. The relief really did clear the air.

All the same, it was not easy to be springy and untrammelled while delving beneath the surface of this city. It slid past like the Pasig River itself, pocked and dimpled by gases released constantly from below, mantled by oil and scum and the occasional great blossom torn with swags of greenery from some upland bank. In no sense was Manila lush as Bangkok had been in the old days with its network of busy *klongs* full of boats bearing brilliant heaps of vegetables and fruit, the temples' golden stupas lying shattered in the khaki water as they passed. Manila was not like that; had never been like that, to judge from the sepia photographs of Spanish colonial days. Then Intramuros, looking gloomier and crueller than ever, had frowned out across a mercantile scene of moored barges and schooners with Conradian figures on their decks, sitting on coils of rope puffing at pipes. It was unmistakably the East, but an East long moulded by European designs. One could well believe the country's interior concealed in its creeks and jungles all manner of head-hunting tribes and despotic little sultanates. But sultans, head hunters and jungles alike were not so much exotic as anomalous, waiting only for the bullet, the Bible or the axe. Here were no tigers, no elephants, few monkey species. There was no elaborate classical music, nor sophisticated native cuisine unspoilt by foreign influence. There was no monarchy, so there was no court full of monstrous splendour and antique protocol. There was no body of classical literature stretching back to the Eighth century or even to the Eighteenth.

The country's true claim to the exotic, he had decided, lay in its public and political life, and in this it was supreme. It was high baroque in its magnificent daring. It glittered in its gamy inventiveness. And if after a while it seemed a trifle repetitious, then what pageantry didn't? The whole point about traditions and customs was that they were time-honoured and hence grandly predictable. There was something gripping about seeing a system in operation which he had only ever read about, half comprehendingly, in school history books. 'The oligarchy', 'the peasantry', 'despotism', 'feudal overlords', 'the rule of the knout', 'private armies', 'mediaeval superstitions' – here they all were, in daily action, as in a museum-land preserved as a living exhibition to remind other nations soberingly of their own pasts, or to warn them of their futures.

Mostly, though, it was the present which pressed intimately against Prideaux like an anonymous someone in a crowd whose intentions, whether erotic or larcenous, are never made clear, nor even their identity. He received a phone call from San Clemente's other priest, Father Bernabe, requesting audience, practically insisting Prideaux should see him. Why ever not? he thought, and gave his address. Father Bernabe was prompt; a short, dainty man in T-shirt and dove slacks who glanced incuriously around the rented room before extending his hand and introducing himself while saying it was very kind, very kind at such short notice. 'I didn't want you to get the wrong impression the other day.'

'From Father Herrera, you mean?'

'He's inclined to shock people and I thought that you, with all your newspaper connections he mentioned, might relay a certain *radical* note that wouldn't be fully justified or fair.'

He's scared, Prideaux thought. He's scared in case I attract attention from some military hard cases with an obsession about counter-insurgency. Duc Thanh Vinh. We've been here before, interviewing a nervous Catholic priest who fears that anything he says, even quotations from the Bible, will be ruthlessly misconstrued by each faction. He's here for damage limitation, to sweep up after a risqué acolyte has shot his mouth off.

'He talked about the Jews,' Prideaux remembered. 'And people having themselves crucified in Holy Week. And girls changing their religion with their men. Oh, and Islam and Mindanao.'

'I didn't know he had views on that?' Father Bernabe went over to the window where his fingernails flashed in the sun with lacquer, like those of many police and army officials. Mindanao was the political hot potato.

'He struck me as not being at a loss for views on anything much. A man of passion and intelligence, I thought. And appetite.'

'Look,' said Bernabe, 'I wanted you to know that Father Herrera is a wonderful man. Passion and intelligence, certainly. But he's also a remarkable priest in his unconventional way. Even if I say all the Masses in our large parish there are many people who go to him and not to me for advice. Spiritual or secular, it's all the same. They get a man completely familiar with the kind of lives our squatters have to lead. But, and this is the point,' Bernabe accepted a glass of pineapple juice, 'he is – and I know he'd forgive me for saying this – he's a man in crisis. His experiences here in Manila have been very hard, very disillusioning for a young man. He's only twenty-eight, you know, and immensely strong in his way. But no-one can go on for ever without learning to bend a little, to sway before the wind, as I'm sure you've discovered for yourself. What should we call it? The art of maturity? He told me you were rather older than he'd expected.'

Given the apparent aimlessness of my presence here, Prideaux filled in savagely. Given a cub reporter's questions and receding hair.

'He's a country man, a provincial,' Bernabe went on. 'He comes from Nueva Ecija, which is New People's Army territory. Maybe he has more of a country man's thinking patterns. A touch simplistic, shall we say? A little too straightforward over *issues* for a city as sophisticated and political as this. That's no criticism, by the way. It's an attempt to identify his difference, to see how it helps him and how it might hinder him.'

It was odd hearing a priest dissect another with a care and in a tone which was surely affectionate, yet all done for a complete stranger.

'I don't really feel you're a stranger,' Bernabe said uncannily, though perhaps it hadn't been difficult to imagine his thoughts. 'Father Herrera told me about your interest in the Filipino character, your search for breaking points. Something like that. It's very difficult to be accurate when making generalisations about a race or a nation or a culture, isn't it? Many people – but not anthropologists, I assume – think it's a complete waste of time, a red herring at best, if not downright offensive. Still, like it or not, different countries do have different flavours, different systems. Preferred crimes, one might say. The Philippines is not like the States, nor like Spain, nor like China. Nor is it like anywhere else. What can a mere priest usefully say about his own country, though?

144

'I'll try and tell you what I think,' he went on without offering any hiatus for a little speculative exchange. 'God gave all races the same range of virtues and vices, but in different proportions. Consequently, some nations appear more dignified than others, some lazier. Some are warmer and more spontaneous, others reserved and a little ungiving. Still others have a tendency to be coldly efficient about the science of life but strangely ignorant of the art of living. . .'

Prideaux watched the fingertips twinkle in the sunlight at the window and braced himself for yet another sermon. Maybe this little lacquered man with the milk chocolate sneakers would throw in his tithe about the darkness of the Spanish soul, of a culture half in love with painful death.

'We Filipinos are warm, all right,' he was saying, 'but maybe sometimes it doesn't go very far. It's in this respect that poor Father Herrera's faith has been severely tested. I'll give you an example. He had a project to install hand pumps for the people over in one of our barrios. He solicited funds from every possible source so they wouldn't have to fetch water from distant faucets and drink from unclean containers and contaminated supplies. Dysentery's a constant problem here, especially for infants. He even used his own savings for this – against my advice, I should add. That's typical Herrera: the good Filipino, principled and selfless. So the pumps are bought and he has them installed *bayanihan*. You know, that's our word for neighbourliness. Everybody helps dig the hole and lay the cement surround. The people say how grateful they are. At last they have clean water for their children, for washing up and cooking. "Fine," says Father Herrera. "In return, your only responsibility is for simple maintenance and repair. Grease the pumps every so often, replace the washers when they're worn so you don't score the stainless sleeve inside." "Well, of course," everyone says.'

Anthropologists were after all little more than academic journalists, Prideaux was thinking. Like reporters, they only ever heard opinions. They had numberless conversations with people they seldom wanted to talk to (but whom *would* they have preferred?) and had to invent a plausible summation. Both the stories and glosses were rigged so as to make sense, as though to conceal an underlying lack of narrative too fearful to be allowed. It was life as documentary. He wondered sadly if Jessie had felt that, sitting beside him on the bed or propped against the

145

cooker in the kitchen, listening to his truthfully meant account of an inner life whose desperately searched nooks failed one by one to disclose her own presence. Their marriage had at last been revealed as containing yet another of John Prideaux's absences.

'Eight months later, of course, two of the pumps are broken. They've never been greased at all. The sleeve of one is cracked and sucks air and needs welding. "Who broke it?" Father Herrera asks. Everybody disappears, like cockroaches when you turn on the light. Without a murmur they go back to drinking the same old filthy water as before, as if it's all the same to them, as though all the benefits of progress can be surrendered at any time without cost or regret. Finally some kind soul with a bit of money and effort to spare has the pumps unscrewed and mended. The next day everyone's back again without a blush, pumping water merrily and complaining about how long it took to repair them. "They're really very grateful. They're just shy," we have to explain to foreigners like yourself who until then hadn't thought of shyness as a Filipino characteristic.

'That's only one small example, naturally. Both Father Herrera and I have seen similar things a hundred times. They're very disillusioning to a youngster with faith in people's essential goodness. Somewhere there's a flaw, a failure in our national character. We're quick enough to stick our hands out with every assurance of gratitude and good faith, which I still believe are truly meant at the time, as well as to sound off about our wonderful tradition of *bayanihan* as if nobody else on earth had ever helped his neighbour. But the smile soon fades. The modest request that each should contribute a few cents to change a pump washer so everyone can drink good water again is turned down flat. "*Walang bakal*", they say. "*Wala kong pera.*" "No money." Yet they won't think twice before spending twelve pesos on a bottle of rum or even a hundred and eighty for a crate of beer, never mind that their children want clean water and rice.'

'Unhappy that I am, I cannot heave my heart into my mouth', he remembered quoting to Jessie, not from pompousness or to dignify a bitter fact with borrowed finery, but because that was exactly how it felt. His heart was not there when he needed to summon it. Professional absentee, it had gone into hiding, leaving him with nothing but an Arts education to fall back on. Now and then he thought it genuinely might be that television had glared too long and

146

too brightly into their respective careers. He'd been a star, there was no doubt. But with his disdain for the mouths sucking in meals and smoke while expelling decisions mixed with expletives, he was on the wane long before he realised it, certainly before Jessie needed to say admiring things about John Prideaux's films which suddenly had a defensive ring to them. 'Absolutely, Jess,' they'd nod. 'One of the greats. No question. We'd none of us be doing our sort of stuff now had he not shown us the way.' And there it was: 'had'/'shown'. Past tense. By their tenses shall ye know them. The Moloch of the media prepares to consume its favourite son. 'You couldn't ask for better credentials, Jess, having been John Prideaux's chief research assistant.' And the day soon came when their pay cheques matched, then hers drew ahead, until finally it was she who handled his tax affairs, paid the mortgage, arranged for builders and finally proposed moving to a house she bought. The times did not permit men to feel emasculated, but the familiar sense of missing something took him by the chest and squeezed roguishly. 'It's me again!' And, as for the first time in his career he was reduced to mail-watching, it was.

'I think this unfortunate flaw we have operates at a national level, too. Father Herrera and I have had long discussions about this and we're in agreement. The parallels are too close, too consistent to be ignored. Over the last few years we Filipinos have made a lot of public noise about our sacred sovereignty and the insult to our collective pride represented by the American bases on our soil. We cursed them even as we held out our hands for still more money. We called them imperialists and colonial remnants while we begged, borrowed and stole for the privilege of queueing at their Embassy for visas. And now they've gone, and we're on our own at last with our famous pride, and precious little to show for all that money they poured into our rulers' hands. At this very moment Olongapo City is entirely dependent for its water on the system our monstrous oppressors installed for their own naval base. And our famous pride apparently doesn't extend to offering our own citizens the slightest protection from death and exploitation abroad, or the least defence of their basic rights here at home. It's the same thing, you see. Plenty of grand talk and invocations of warm togetherness, but on the other side is a strange indifference and passiveness, even if it means putting up with atrocious conditions, with daily cruelty and injustice.'

So Prideaux had found himself more and more responsible for doing Ruth's school run, for washing and ironing, for making sure she had a proper meal when she came home. Her mother was coming home later and later, smelling of smoke and drink and words, and would scarcely pick at food before shutting herself away in her study with scripts to read and computer keys to rattle, leaving Prideaux to watch the television with the air of a pianist whose career has been cut short by a stroke and who sits anonymously in audiences with a stick parked under the seat.

'Well, such things pain us all. We can't really understand them even as we recognise that cynicism and selfishness offer a kind of protection, and that nations as well as individuals can suffer from the chronic depression which produces moral lassitude. We're all in pain over this because we all know it's wrong. It isn't how we want to be, or how we really are inside. It hits Father Herrera very hard indeed. Despite his manner he's still very much an idealist, which is to be admired since it gives us all hope. But as I said, sooner or later one has to acquire the knack of bending instead of breaking. Of being flexible without compromising oneself.'

Last of all he remembered Jessie's rages, seemingly unpredictable, when she reverted with awful poignancy to a nursery stereotype of female impotence, literally tearing her own hair and stamping her foot. After the paroxysm was over and she had slammed the door of her study, or the blare of her exhaust had died away down the street outside, he had gone around in one of those silences in which still, small voices never speak, actually sweeping some longish auburn hairs into a pan and dumping them in a plastic bin liner. Only Ruth had grown unperturbed by such scenes, appearing in the kitchen with a wan smile and 'Want some coffee, Jaypee?' while he remained at the stage she had long left behind when her small white face might be spied between banisters.

'Do you think women will ever be crucified?' he asked abruptly.

Bernabe looked at him in puzzlement and Prideaux noticed there was fluff on his cheeks near the earlobes. The man didn't shave. 'I assume you mean voluntarily?'

'Yes, you know, these Holy Week rituals. I was thinking the other day that with all this stuff about women priests and how God was just as much woman as man, women might feel they should have equal opportunities for extremism. After all, various women have identified with Christ strongly enough to develop the stigmata, so why shouldn't they be crucified for real?'

'My Church,' said Bernabe bleakly, 'puts me in no position to be jocular about women as priests, let alone a female God or a female Saviour. It all strikes me as on the very verge of blasphemy.'

'Very well. Then here's a secular question I really do need an answer to. Father Herrera ducked it. Is it open to women to go amok here, or only to men?'

'Women amoks? I believe I *have* heard of such a thing,' the priest said cautiously, 'but it must be quite rare. Women aren't supposed to be as frustrated as men, are they? They're supposed to be more easily fulfilled by bearing children and looking after the home. It's mainly men who have to contend with being unable to find work, the constant worry of bringing home money and food, the disgrace of failure. Of course, things aren't always like that. Many of the women in our barrios go out to work and a good few of their husbands sit around drinking. It's often the women who are the rice-winners, as well as doing everything else. Yet it's generally men who commit suicide and not women. So maybe one could argue that, in their way, they are the more stressed.'

'Suicide? Is that common?' Strangely, Prideaux hadn't considered it before.

'We don't like to talk about it since apart from anything else it's such a terrifying admission of failure, isn't it? Both theirs and ours. Surely we priests could have done something? Said the right word at the right time? Prayed the right prayer? But yes, Mr Prideaux, it's unfortunately not at all uncommon nowadays. We had a tragic case only last week. A young man of twenty-five, a shoe repairer, who left a heartrending and completely literate note to say he was sick of the shame his poverty brought him, that he could not even afford shoes for all his family. He left six children. He used to write poems on scraps of paper and pin them to the walls of their hut. His wife's kept them all. Other than the children they're the only things left of that man of twenty-five. An immortal soul, yes, but still gone like a shadow. It was a sin, but I can't believe the Almighty will judge him harshly. With nothing but boundless compassion, I trust.'

A week passed until a morning came when the early headlines read quixotically: '10,000 Cops Face Purge'. This figure included the immediate dismissal of 6,000, half of whom were already AWOL together with their firearms, and the rest 'ghost cops' who had left the force years ago or had never existed at all but to whose names a salary was still being paid monthly. The telephone rang.

'John, do your researches include vampires?'

'Bats?'

'No, you know – Dracula and all that good stuff. We've got one going at the moment.'

Vic Agusan's voice brought back vividly the drowned bodies hog-tied thumb and toe in Navotas marshes. Prideaux was not at all sure if the despair he felt for his own researches could survive another, extraneous angle. It was only when he became this lost that he indulged in philosophical overviews of a Carlylean nature. Maybe Vic divined this because he added:

'Light relief, John. Oughtn't an anthropologist to know about the natives' quaint superstitions? After all, the thing might turn out to be genuine.'

'In this place, Vic, nothing would surprise me any longer. But what's your interest in it? It doesn't sound to me like a police reporter's business. Or are there hidden depths?'

'I agreed to do it as a favour to an editor who thinks there may be. He's probably right. Here, there are hidden depths in everything. Trace any story back far enough and you'll uncover a crime of sorts, if not an actual corpse.'

This was vintage Agusan cynicism, even if corpses went perfectly naturally with vampires. Prideaux arranged that Vic should pick him up within the hour. He wondered if this would turn out to be a light story he could happily pass on to Ruth or whether it would have to be censored.

17

YSABELLA HAD UNDERTAKEN her dawn bus journey at her own insistence and not for lack of proffered limousines. The senator had nodded with affected admiration, remarking that she was obviously her father's daughter. In due course she found herself rattling in pre-dawn darkness south past the back of Ninoy Aquino International Airport. The highway was lined with factories bearing the neon names of domestic appliances and the sort of food that came in packets. In Alabang they stopped and vendors forced their way aboard with heavy trays of freshly cooked *hopia*, newspapers and peanuts. She bought newspapers. She was unique: as far as anyone could tell, an unescorted American girl. Even more unique than you know, she thought as she returned or deflected the smiles of surprise. Assuredly she was the only person on this bus who was off to spend the weekend with a senator.

The boy beside her, who looked as though he were heading for a provincial college with a concrete statue of its founder outside it, interpreted the captions for her. She had deliberately chosen tabloids for what looked like sensational pictures on their front pages, something with which to complement the half light and glimpses of pavement life outside. The concrete underpass pillar by which they were waiting bore tattered fragments of names in red, the torn faces of hopeful politicians. Also the stencilled injunction COUPLE FOR CHRIST. Anything was possible here, where a religious sect called Good Wisdom for All Nations was on the rampage, slashing the tyres of cars caught in traffic jams and still further immobilising the congealing city. At the pillar's foot, she now noticed, a man lay with his head on a deep cushion of carbon which had collected like a drift of snow.

The picture in one tabloid showed a barrel being winched from the mud of an *estero* somewhere in Manila, its open end jammed with suggestive contours like meat and rags mixed. 'They identified him from his watch,' her neighbour translated. The bus started again, the lights went off and they drove out of their concrete nest into early morning light which came as a surprise. Had she known to look, she could have glimpsed in the distance the arched entrance to the famously porous State Penitentiary in Muntinlupa as they passed. Instead, the boy had angled a second tabloid to the window. This photo was of the interior of a burned-out car. Half-melted strips of trim and a steering wheel reduced to a wire ring confused things until she understood what she was looking at. The driver's seat tilt mechanism had collapsed until the metalwork of its headrest lay back on the frame of the rear seat. On bars and springs, in a posture of extreme reclining comfort, was a calcined skeleton. '*Dedbol na.*' Of the dead ball in question, the student explained, nothing was left but his bones and a Rolex watch. This was one up on all those dreary golfers and opera singers and mountaineers, Ysabella thought, and idly began planning a new advertising campaign for Rolex to be shot largely in mortuaries. 'Police suspect foul play.' Outside the window the factories had long since yielded to flat fields, coconut groves and wayside shanties in front of which families were heaping their produce on mats. How wrong Philip Larkin had been. What would survive of us was not love but wristwatches.

She was dropped with curious stares at the entrance to a provincial air base. In the guardhouse the senator's name produced a smartly turned-out escort who ushered her through. On a circular plot inside the gates stood a World War II American fighter of the variety she associated with old movies about the South Pacific. She remembered these films as generally including a scene where a young smoke-stained actor jumps up with a hand cupped to his ear and shouts 'Can it, fellas! That's no Zero!' (an aero engine loud in a cloud). 'That's a Hellcat! The Hellcats are here!' Fifty years on, the aircraft stood on mushy tyres with concrete blocks under its oleo legs taking most of the weight. The plexiglas cockpit canopy was tanned to a crazed amber.

Benigno and Liezel made quite a pair as they stepped from their Mitsubishi Pajero van only a few minutes later. The senator was dressed for a country weekend in slacks and a golfing shirt; his wife looked like Imelda Marcos newly arrived from a shopping spree in Zurich. Neither carried anything. Two or three helpers or bodyguards or even slaves lugged bags and what seemed to be crates of groceries from the van to a twin-engined Cessna parked in the shade of a flamboyant. A grizzled man appeared in a pair of aviator shades and a T-shirt whose slogan read 'This time it's love. Next time it's $50'.

'Hi, Major,' Vicente called affably. 'How're they hanging?'

All part of the Great Web, Ysabella told herself. Observe. It's all going to be new. Spectate your way through this weekend. She was introduced all round by Benigno, now joined by a daughter who must have been hiding in the back of the van. 'This is Woopsy, our youngest.' Woopsy was sweetly pretty with a brace on her teeth and a dreamy manner which made her name seem born of affection and not mockery. Ysabella remembered that one of Cory Aquino's daughters was called Ballsy. Liezel offered a heavily ringed hand, a gust of 'Jicky' and an intelligent and friendly smile. 'I know all about your father's death,' she said in place of platitude, 'and we're so glad you still feel able to come here. Ben's like a schoolboy, he's so happy. You must forgive him any wild behaviour. He was genuinely devoted to your father all those years ago.'

'This is strange for me,' Ysabella told her as they walked to the little blue aircraft. 'Everyone I meet seems to have known my father better than I did.'

'Not I, I'm afraid. I never met him, alas. Quirino Avenue! Oh, it sounds like history. You know you're getting old when things which happened in your own lifetime start to be historic. Like Vietnam. That was all over before Woopsy was even born. Vietnam, Woops,' she told her daughter's alerted face. 'The war.' Her child smiled blankly.

They took off and the major flew them up into a bumpy panorama of old green volcanoes and a coastline she hadn't realised was so close. The sea was of no known colour; that of secret ink which became invisible when dried on a page, perhaps, in which it was languidly drawing and redrawing an ever-vanishing white margin around the land. The sudden exaltation of adventure seized her, dispelling all remnants of her pre-dawn vision of emptiness in the deserted Manila bus terminal. It was simply a matter of going on being twenty-nine for ever and flying around in private aircraft. Her host was skimming the day's newspapers which it had presumably been too dark to read in the van. He read with the professional politician's alert casualness. These were the heavies which her ghoulish preference had led her to miss earlier. 'Bongbong has no idea of father's wealth.' 'National Power Corp.'s Cebu thermal plant to be exorcised.' It sounded like any normal day. 'Cops among kidnappers of shot Chinese schoolgirl.'

'Bongbong?' she asked above the motors' drumming.

'Marcos's only son,' said Ben, putting down the paper. 'Ferdinand Junior.'

'I thought he was in exile, too.'

'Good Lord no. He's a Congressman. Represents Ilocos Norte, his father's old province. He used to be its Governor when FM was President. He's now pretending he has no idea about his father's assets, despite being an executor of the Marcos estate. Nobody believes him, of course. It says here that even lawyers are referring to "evasive, untruthful and inherently incredible statements under oath".' He passed the paper across.

'According to this, Bongbong's a product of Oxford and Wharton universities,' said Ysabella in surprise. 'I didn't know he'd been in England.'

'Sure he was. Some of his father's diaries are being leaked around town and from them one imagines FM was pretty relieved to get him abroad and into some serious company. He admits Imelda couldn't control him when he was a teenager and says he's warned Bongbong he'll throw his friends out of the palace if they're overstaying. Poor kid, though. How could anyone brought up like that be anything but a spoiled brat? So they packed him off to Oxford. Political science and philosophy, but he'd already learned them from his father. By the time he was appointed vice-governor of Ilocos Norte at the ripe old age of twenty-three Bongbong had had some lessons in the ways of the world. A story,' said the senator expansively. 'In the mid-Seventies, at a time when Martial Law was in full swing, his father began to be seriously worried about the company Bongbong was keeping. Druggy, hippy, middle-class wastrels. Showbiz starlets, that sort. FM was very conscious that this was his only boy and all the good-time living might turn him into a drug addict. After various stern warnings Marcos learned that Bongbong was flying off for an especially merry weekend in a private planeload of his cronies. Just as the plane was about to take off the pilot was ordered to return to the ramp. There, aides came running out to tell Bongbong there'd been an urgent message from his father recalling him briefly on a pressing family matter. His friends were to go without him; he could follow in an hour or two in another aircraft. . . Do I need to go on?'

No, actually; but he had all the same, his voice raised scratchily above the noise of his own light aircraft. The plane had gone down with the loss of everyone on board. There was great public lamentation. Marcos himself went to the airport and managed some crocodile tears. Bongbong presumably learned a lesson in the exercise of paternal and presidential authority. Staring out of the window at a nearing land mass Ysabella reflected on the importance of *bodies* in this country. To judge from press and TV pictures, funeral parlours were a social nexus. People were for ever being photographed bending over the contents of satin-padded boxes equipped with all sorts of elaborate flaps and lids. Ironies abounded. She recalled the ten-year-old boy playing in the street who suddenly fell dead at his mother's feet with a bullet in his brain. Some drunken birthday reveller had fired his gun at random to make a noise, to celebrate, to show off his new toy. According to a ballistics report it had almost certainly been a policeman. The child's family were pictured in a sorrowing group around his coffin, open down to the chest, on the rest of which they had piled his favourite playthings. Among them was a toy pistol. Guns and tears. What secret satisfaction did they bring with their dramatic rituals?

Corpses here were frequently exhumed to establish identity or to prove that justice had or hadn't been done. Bodies were exhibited on pavements where they'd been shot; in police stations to which they'd been taken; on a runway where they'd been landed on by an incoming jumbo jet (not a lot left of that one. It was claimed to have been a sleeping squatter, then a salvage victim, but on this occasion even the wristwatch was missing). The picture of the tousle-haired body variously identified as the notorious Commander Mubarak or else an unknown duck-raiser had been printed and reprinted a dozen times as the case was closed and then opened again. And chief of all, of course, were the Marcos bodies: first Ferdinand's mother and then that of the ex-President himself, which had lain for four years like a dud battery in a Hawaiian deep freezer, his veins full of icy chemicals but still managing to leak a musty political voltage. The whole thing was bizarre and seemed to belong to another era. Twenties gangsters, was that it? People called 'Lips' and 'Muggsy' lying in waxy state with satin up to their jowls to conceal the damage that meathooks, blowlamps and Thompson submachine guns had caused and which not even the best Italian morticians had been able to disguise.

The Cessna flared, crabbed sideways, straightened at the last moment, touched down faultlessly and ran up to a tiny terminal with a flagpole and a crowd of faces pressed against wire netting. The children who had chivvied the goats and dogs off the airstrip went back to playing on it. A languorous sea breeze puffed through the opened door.

'Welcome to Magubat,' said Benigno Vicente, and emerged to greet his *probinsyanos*.

Another van, a Lite Ace with tinted windows and 'Gov. Vicente' stencilled on the doors. They climbed in. 'My brother,' Ben introduced Ysabella to a hayseed version of himself. 'Doy's the Governor of this province.' Ysabella was reminded of Jimmy Carter's brother Billy, hairy-gutted beer drinker, Ghadaffi crony and general embarrassment. The van yawed over an unmade track like a speedboat trailing an ochre plume of spray which blotted out wayside huts, fences draped with washing and narrowly-missed buffalo carts. They came to a jetty. The plume overtook them and thinned out over the water. There was a smell of drying fish baskets, of ozone and iodine and ultraviolet light bouncing off the sea's live glitter. A few hundred yards away across the blue strait a green-heaped islet stood on white foundations of coral sand. A knifelike craft with bamboo outriggers took them across. The sea had the clarity of a paperweight in which rocks and corals and fish were embedded. When the engine was cut and the prow grated into the sand there was a fortuitous instant of complete stillness before anyone spoke or moved. The cove was a hundred yards wide narrowing to fifty deep, a V of rocks and trees enclosing a beach at the top of which stood a futuristic house, hexagonal, octagonal, Ysabella didn't count, with tall narrow windows in each face. So skilfully contrived was this piece of modernism that until the moment of landfall she hadn't even noticed it.

'What a beautiful place,' she said for the hundredth time in a social career which had seen many a pleasure dome, many a fake-humble country retreat, manor house, castle, penthouse overlooking a sweep of river and a Renaissance city. 'What a beautiful place,' and for the first time really meaning it, suddenly pleased that gloomy Hugh and the rest would never see it.

'Well, it's just a beach house,' Liezel said, 'but we're fond of it. The children love it here. Woopsy adores it and so does Danny. Danny's our youngest. He's at the Sorbonne right now, did Ben say? He's always writing and asking about Bantol.'

'Bantol?'

'Oh, sorry, that's the name of this island. It's the locals' name for a kind of fish which has a big head and a little tail. They say the place looks like one from the seaward side but I have to admit I can't see any resemblance.'

Come to that, Ysabella thought, it wasn't much like Mont St. Michel, either. Smiling people were hurrying down the beach to greet them and unload the provisions.

'Our caretakers,' Liezel explained. 'They live down there and keep an eye on things.'

At one end of the cove a couple of thatched huts stood on stilts among boulders above the high tide mark, sheltered by overhanging branches. Nets were hung to dry on tall bamboo frames. A smaller version of the boat they had just crossed in bobbed at anchor a few yards offshore. Panting boys in tattered T-shirts began overtaking them with crates of beer on their shoulders.

'For an English ambassador's daughter,' Liezel was saying, her intelligence apparently clouded for the first time by the concerned hostess, 'I'm afraid it's probably too simple here. We're not grand people, you know.' No; not the concerned hostess. The politician's wife. 'Ben's very much a man of the people. He isn't old money like so many senators.' Somewhere along the way – in the van, presumably – she had changed out of her high heels and into a pair of lime green trainers which went oddly with the Imelda outfit and the 'Jicky', though Ysabella supposed she would have looked a good deal odder trying to walk up a coral beach in Ferragamo shoes.

They had reached a paved area in front of the house. She could now see how artfully the site had been planned, for it extended on both sides behind rock formations which hid its true dimensions from anyone landing on the beach. Also concealed from view was an oatmeal awning in whose cool shade lay a sagging black bitch, whacked out from long years of labour down the puppy mines. There was a table made of a slab of rock and various easy chairs. On the other side, equally hidden until the approaching observer drew level, was a miniature reproduction of the house itself, in size somewhere between a hut and a pavilion, finished in the same materials and with the same care.

'Oh, what an extraordinary idea,' exclaimed Ysabella involuntarily. Outside the little house a mountainous boy sat at a table, engrossed or asleep.

'That's Herman, our eldest son,' said the senator, who had come up with them. He was now wearing a Mighty Meaties baseball cap. 'I'll introduce you. You mustn't mind him. He's rather retarded, I'm afraid. He lives here. It's the only place where he's happy.'

They walked over. If Danny was at the Sorbonne, she thought, and Herman was older he must be twenty at least. It was the face of a huge child which was turning slowly to face them like a bronze moon emerging from cloud. Round, flat, blank.

'Hello, Boyboy,' said his father, laying an affectionate arm about the great shoulders. 'Here we are again.' Herman smiled up at him uncertainly, like someone who knows he has seen a face before and then remembers where. His eyes filled with tears. Before him on the table were neat heaps of seashells, sorted neither by size nor variety but, it seemed, by colour. 'And this is Ysabella. A long, long time ago I knew her father.'

'Father,' echoed Herman. His gaze fell on his objects. A slow, pudgy paw went out and picked up a cone beautifully marked with curving lines of diminishing brown peaks like a landscape of mountains sketched by a Chinese brush. The pattern, endlessly repeated, gave off a Zennish suggestion of infinite distance. The hand came up and held it out to her.

'It's lovely, Herman,' she said.

'That's for you. He's giving it to you. Oh, wait,' Ben said sharply, taking it from his son's hand before she could. Holding the shell by the fat end he examined it. 'Still alive,' he said and gave a shout. A retainer came over at a trot. The senator held out the shell, uttered scolding phrases in a crescendo while the man, a leathery fellow in his forties with a few curling fish scales dried to his mahogany calves, looked crestfallen and went 'Opo. Opo. Yes, sir. Opo,' before taking the shell away with him. 'Bilo'll bring it back when he's cleaned it,' explained Ben soothingly to his son, 'it's all right. Then you can give it to Ysabella.' He picked out a textile cone, examined it, put it back in its pile.

'What was that about?' she asked as he turned away with another fond pat of the boy's shoulder.

'That species of shell's very dangerous. It's the only one here we have to be careful about. They're poisonous.'

'I wasn't going to eat it.'

'They're quite nice to eat. No, the point was, it was still alive. He must have found it this morning. They have a defence mechanism. They shoot out a sting like a needle from the tip of the shell. It's not like being stung by a bee. They say it's as bad as sea-snake venom. Bilo's supposed to keep a close watch on Herman's shells. It's what I pay him to do, after all. That's our problem here,' he said, and it wasn't clear whether he was referring to his island or his country. 'The watchers themselves need to be watched. Bilo and his family have lived here since before we built the house. I bought him his boat, his engine, his nets. I sent both his boys to trade college, a hundred things, plus a salary to be caretaker and Herman's guardian here. All that and *still* you can't rely one hundred percent on these people. He drinks. Which reminds me, lousy host that I am.'

Ysabella was not surprised by the big Sony colour TVs, the wet bar, the shelves of paperbacks, but by the billiard table.

'A weakness of mine,' Ben explained as he poured her a Rose's lime juice. 'I caught the British habit rather than the American. I much prefer snooker to pool. It's altogether subtler.' He was still wearing his baseball cap. 'And as you see, I'm a Mighty Meaties fan. That's Swift Hotdog's basketball team. Another weakness. I don't think the British play basketball, do they?'

'I haven't the faintest idea, I'm afraid,' said Ysabella.

'Oh. Well, anyway, this year the Meaties're going to walk all over Purefoods.' He noticed his guest's attention had wandered to the shelves. 'Ah, yet another weakness. One you'll be a good deal better informed about than I am.'

It had also been a surprise seeing the pots and bowls and plates, as well as a beautiful spotted *ching-pai* boat. Several of the ceramics were superior to those in the Philippine Heritage Museum, she noticed.

'They're from all over,' he said dismissively in answer to her question. 'Just little things I've picked up here and there. My better stuff's all in Manila, I'm afraid.'

'I think Dr Liwag would be quite jealous of one or two of these.'

'Bonnie? Not him. We're old friends. He's got stuff tucked away that makes these pieces look like Tupperware.'

'Not in the Museum, surely?'

'Oh, not in the *Museum*.'

'Is it true he's a member of Opus Dei?'

'That I wouldn't know. Where did you hear that?'

'I can't remember. Gossip.'

'Would you like a swim before lunch?'

She swam; they all swam in warm water so clear it felt vertiginously like flying. Far below, among stone exfoliations and spires, heavy fish moved. They were served lunch with chilled beer. They drowsed in darkened rooms. They swam again when the worst of the afternoon heat was past. Woopsy practised dives off a rock, slim and pale, the platinum wire glittering across her pleased smiles. Some way off, the hard walruslike folds of Herman's dark blubber sank and surfaced in the shadow cast by the island. He couldn't be induced to join his family but wallowed in silent industry among the offshore boulders in front of Bilo's huts. He seemed quite at ease in the water. Sometimes Ysabella caught the moon face turned towards her wearing a diving mask's blank glare before it sank once more. A hand with a net bag tied to the wrist would flail the surface and he would be gone.

At dusk a generator hummed somewhere on the jungled slope behind the house and fireflies drifted down to the beach. The senator wore an apron and lit the barbecue, laying beside it with a surgeon's care knives, spatulas, forks and pots of sauce with brushes in them. Soon the smoke of grilling fish rose into the night air. 'If it weren't for this place we'd die,' he said. 'Or go mad.'

'It's true,' his wife agreed. 'We're both from this province. Country folk to the bone. City life has its advantages but this is where our heart is.' She was wearing a simple gown by Armani with a single tiny gold button up on one shoulder. Across the narrow strait came the soft glow of oil lamps on the mainland.

'There's no electricity?'

'There is in the main town. It's taking its time to reach the barrios,' the senator replied. 'One of brother Doy's priorities. Along with roads, water, a hospital, the telephone and so on. I'm afraid we're still quite backward here in Magubat. For God's sake don't quote me, but as a Magubateño rather than a senator I'm sometimes not unhappy that we are. Among all the hardships there are still simple pleasures which I'm afraid are the first to be corrupted by progress, as it's called. In any case I'm sorry Doy can't be here this weekend. He's having to meet our Congressman.'

'Who is?'

'Jaime Vicente? Ah, you'd know him if you were a film fan. He used to be an action movie star. He and Lito Lapid used to sweep the box office together. Martial arts and shootouts. He's still tremendously popular and *fit*. He may be making another film this Christmas with. . . who was it with, Lee?. . . Vic Sotto or someone. Vic's one of my fellow-senators. I'll have to ask him on Tuesday.'

'Jaime's another relative, I presume?'

'Just a nephew. I apologise for the coffee in advance. I'm afraid it's only local instant.'

The big, dull question underlying everything, she thought, was how had an embassy driver reached all this? But she doubted she would be given a clear answer so after dinner asked a more minor and personally interesting one. 'Have you actually met my mother?'

The senator looked at her in surprise and sipped Cointreau. 'Well, of course I have. Has she never told you?'

'Don't be offended, Ben, but I truly can't remember. I sort of grew up knowing about you as a heroic figure somewhere at the back of our lives. I'm not sure if I ever asked or if she ever told me. Don't forget I've spent most of my life away from home, first at boarding school and then at university. We've always been independent. I mean, I do remember during term getting Mum's letters from all over the place, but there wasn't anything strange about that. A young widow of independent means who used to travel and see her diplomatic friends. I suppose I vaguely thought she stayed in embassies, but I see now she couldn't have. She'd only been an ambassador's wife, after all, not a dip. in her own right. She was always very interested – still *is* very interested – in sort of developmental things. UNICEF and Save the Children. Oxfammy stuff. I don't know. She had romantic foreign lovers, we used to imagine, me and my friends.' And then stopped herself, too late, her brain too slowed by languor and drink and tropic night air and the foolishness which tends to exempt one's interlocutor from any function other than this present conversation.

'We met several times whenever she was in this part of the world,' he said carefully. 'Which for a while was not infrequently. But I'm sad to say her travels no longer seem to bring her out East, do they? In any case she remains someone I enormously admire. I like people – women especially – who are purposeful and principled. Beauty and an independent intelligence are a powerful mixture and one I find irresistible. If I may say so, you are even more beautiful than she was twenty years ago, and she was very beautiful indeed. But in addition to her looks I can see your father's aristocratic features.'

Liezel had gone to bed some time ago. Ysabella wondered if her husband's verbal gallantry had shot its bolt or was about to become corporeal, extending a hand and obliging her to decide how avuncular it was. When nothing happened, leaving his last extravagant compliment drifting away on the warm breeze, she glanced sideways at him and saw nothing to suggest he had spoken in the last half hour. He was gazing out into the dark, his face closed, as though watching figures on a screen. There was no moon. An unnoticed overcast had been sealing off the sky. Out beyond the mainland's tip night had leaked straight down into a black sea so that she couldn't determine where the horizon was. Two small lights trembled far out, surely much too high to be fishing boats but equally too low to be stars. She felt the earth tilt backwards to reposition the sea and refloat the stars as lights.

'You'll be tired,' he said at length. 'I know I am.' He got up abruptly. 'I don't imagine you're a midnight bather, but if you are –' he touched a switch and down at a steeper angle than she would have imagined a patch of water glowed bright blue-green. Far away the generator's note dropped a quarter tone.

'What a lovely effect,' she said.

'I was afraid you might think it vulgar. I installed the lights for those of our guests who like frolicking after dark. If you remember, that spot is practically a natural pool. All we had to do was put underwater lights at strategic points. They attract certain species of fish and people like watching the night life in the corals. It's quite safe.'

'No sharks?'

'Oh, they mostly like deep water. They're way out beyond the reefs. I have Bilo keep the place clear of sea urchins and those stinging fern things. Hydroids.' He plunged the water back into invisibility. 'But I can see you're more interested in your bed so I'll wish you goodnight. We turn the generator off so I've left a flashlight in your room. You must feel absolutely free to come and go as you please. Treat this place as if it were your own. You –' he paused. 'You can't possibly know how truly pleased I am to have Chris Bastiaan's own daughter here. It feels as though an unhappy episode has at last been tied up into a happy ending. After all these years. I can hardly believe it.'

Her bedroom was above the room with the billiard table in it. The family apparently slept over on the other side of the octagon, or whatever it was. Although she knew the house to be quite small, its design and the way it was lived in made it seem palatial, full of inexplicable distances. She lay awake while one of those anarchic thoughts drifted up as from an inner conversation which had been taking place in her mind's absence. Supposing Ben and my *father* had also been lovers? No, it was ridiculous, an idle idea which cost nothing because she'd never known her father and seemed not out of place in a country where anything was possible. Yet one did have to explain why the man was still so attached to the memory of a foreign diplomat whose driver he'd been for less than a year back in 1965. How kind could her father possibly have been to a mere driver who was then –what? twenty, twenty-one? Since coming to this country she had found his somewhat null parental figure taking on the genuine mysteriousness of a ghost. The land of his death was fleshing him out.

At some point in the night she emerged from sleep like a diver surfacing, found herself beached in a room dappled by moonlight filtered through leaves and broken cloud. Not far off the sea was mulling things over with small sighs. A lizard rattled the glottal prelude to its familiar series of croaking brays. In the silence which followed she heard it echoed, far away and muffled as if beneath blankets, by inarticulate howls. Then a thudding silence fell again from which she finally relaxed back into sleep.

In the morning she found the family breakfasting on fish, rice and *bibingka*, a flat and flabby round cake of rice flour and coconut.

'Eat, eat,' cried Ben brightly, in Jewish mother mode at the head of the table. 'Try a *bibingka*. They're imported.'

'From?'

'From the other side,' he said in delight. 'Freshly made this morning. An essential ingredient in a true provincial start to the day. You taste one. They don't use baking powder and all those chemicals. They put *tuba* in instead, our palm toddy, which is full of natural yeasts.'

After breakfast she found it was still only seven o'clock on a Sunday morning. During her early swim a memory returned to her. She found Ben on the terrace reading a folder, an open attaché case beside him.

'I thought I heard a strange noise in the night. Like yowling.'

He put down the folder. 'I'm sorry you were woken. I hope you weren't frightened? It was only Herman. He sometimes has fits at night. A specialist says they're triggered by nightmares, but to tell you the truth we've rather lost confidence in specialists. We've listened to dozens of explanations in dozens of clinics. It was always an ordeal because he hates travelling. He really is only happy here.' He looked through Ysabella with a little frown obviously intended for another place and other company. 'If you make a digest of everything the experts say, if you roll together all their conflicting theories of cretinism and hyperthyroidism and Down's syndrome and autism and epilepsy and schizophrenia and I don't know what, we're left with a diagnosis which is really no more useful than that of our psychic healers who say he was possessed by a devil in infancy. We have indeed been through exorcism with him.' Again he glanced at her, this time very much in the present as if to catch an incredulous smile.

'I'm sure anyone would have done the same,' she said. 'I know I would. When sufficiently at one's wits' end one will try anything.'

'That was it,' he agreed. 'Herman was our firstborn. He was like that from the beginning. But I was poor in those days. My God, we were poor. We had *nothing*. Maybe. . . He's twenty-eight, did you know that?'

This seemed to have a significance she couldn't grasp, one which went beyond pointing out the obvious fact that his son looked like a boy half his age. 'It was years before Liezel and I had the confidence to try again. Imagine our joy when Danny was normal. And not just normal but bright. Woops, too, who may turn out even brighter than Danny.'

Slowly, she worked it out. Nothing perverse, after all; nothing sinister. Just an ordinary – though in the circumstances extraordinary – kindness.

'My father gave you money. To get treatment for him.'

'Yes,' said the senator gratefully, and picked up the folder.

It was the first time she had caught a flash of vulnerability. She left him with it and went swimming again. She was losing track of time, as she had lost the horizon the previous night. She now remembered that someone at the air force base – Ben? Liezel? – had warned her they wouldn't be returning until Monday and was that all right with her? Something about it being a government holiday or National Heroes' Day or similar caper. One of those Thirdy-Worldy affairs. She had never had the sort of job which needed to take notice of such things. Now, why had she never learned the trick of clearing her eustachian tubes? There were all sorts of things she wanted to examine underwater but her ears hurt if she went more than a couple of feet below the surface. Maybe she would do a PADI course for divers on the quiet. It would be fun to wave a certificate under Hugh's nose. This view of fish among corals was genuinely timeless. In archaeology one looked at fragments of the recent past and had to suppose almost everything. Here, one was surely seeing the identical sight of five million years ago. Such a perspective did strange things to the present. True, her father had been rich. Yet the impropriety of personal gifts of money from an ambassador to his driver was most peculiar. She lay looking wistfully through her mask at a mazy cloud of tiny blue fish hanging about a head of coral below her. They blazed in the water like fragments of congealed electricity. She didn't want to know any more about her family. It was all too long ago and had no real connection with her. Just ghosts. What was one finally to suppose, then? That the underpaid, recently married *provinciano* Benigno Vicente hadn't after all spent this majestic windfall on his damaged infant? Had instead used most of it to lay down the beginnings of his fortune, just as Sharon's friend Crispa's family had her silence-money? Turning misfortune to advantage? That the price was the hulk who now collected shells, vaguely supervised in what was described as a happy idyll in a private sanctuary?

The day passed gently, interspersed with campfire cuisine. Ysabella dipped into a paperback, into the sea, into the edge of the tangled forest beyond the generator hut before being repulsed by thorns and fear of snakes. The evening meal was lit by flashes of silent lightning which intermittently revealed outlines of sea and land and clouds slightly to one side of where they had last been. She calculated that in London people would just be leaving midday offices under a sky whose exact weather she would never know but most likely grey, sifting down a penetrating moisture. She thought of Hugh with his earnest, Buddhist fancies and family title. He seemed to belong with England in a land of fable, a land of the past which she might one day (should the whimsy of her career persist) excavate like Ur or Silbury.

That night, too, she was woken, but not by howling. This time it was a soft, stylised weeping sound, the boo-hoo of English nurseries, the *hu-hu-hu* of women in Filipino comics. For all its quietness it seemed close. Ysabella knew that whoever it was, it was none of her business. House guests, despite being told to treat the place as their own, enjoyed the luxury of being able to choose not to. But as the noise persisted and no sound of slippered feet and voices came to intervene she also knew she would never sleep for the contagion of this unknown distress. She clicked the light switch uselessly, remembered the generator, found the torch, opened her door as silently as she could. It came from downstairs, from the billiard room below. Without turning on the torch she glided halfway down the curving stairs and squatted. From between the ornate banisters she could see down into the room, which was lit by moonlight filtered through yet another layer of the trees which hemmed the rear of the house. The effect was an unearthly monochrome as of a chamber found on the bed of a forgotten sea, a cell for ever hidden from colour and sunlight. On the black baize of the table lay a large unmoving mass, face down, two paws clasped over the edge.

Ysabella had imagined that Herman was safely confined to his miniature beach house at night, which would have explained how distant his previous howling had sounded. It had somehow never occurred to her that he might have the run of the place after dark. Why not, of course. He was evidently a part of this family in ways she couldn't guess. Still, she hadn't thought it. As she watched with a voyeur's fear of discovery and greed to know, she was invaded by the scene's utter despair and felt her own eyes fill involuntarily. This was no child's crying, for all its stylisation. Its very quietness showed how far removed it was from infantile complaint or demand. She didn't believe this wordless statement of profound unhappiness was meant to be overheard. She assumed he had forgotten her temporary presence in the bedroom upstairs. An urge seized her to stand up, turn on the torch, go downstairs and put a consoling arm about those huge quaking shoulders, raise the moon face with its drool of snot from the baize, make soft verbal gestures to the top of his head. But she overcame it; a failure of heart when confronted by the impossibly complex. I am not my father, she said back in her room. Leave it be. How can a stranger intervene in misery like that, in an unknowable mind whose damage might make well-meaning itself damaging? She now thought that after all Herman had been saying something, repeating over and over again, each syllable a sob, his own nickname 'Boyboy'. She covered her head with the pillow as an empty space within her echoed, but after a long spell of no-time the heat drove her back to the surface where all was silent once again.

'I'm sorry to say we had a death last night,' said Liezel to her after breakfast, as if to explain a meal which was subdued in comparison with the previous morning's. A dreadful guilt of complicity froze Ysabella until her hostess went on: 'Our old dog. You may have seen her when we arrived on Saturday? She was terribly old. But Woopsy's a bit upset, you know how children are. I suppose we were all attached to her.'

'What about poor Herman?'

'I'm afraid Boyboy doesn't notice things like that.' She was back in her Imelda travelling outfit, except for the trainers. There was a glint of something unfathomable in her eyes and voice down there among sharp corals, dark holes and fish like chips of costume jewellery. As far as Ysabella was concerned the long weekend finished on that enigmatic note. Glancing back at Bantol as the boat took them away she was reduced to banal reflections on the small mysteries and major private griefs which haunt pleasure domes no less than parliaments. Yet the weekend itself was not quite over. The province's hayseed Governor, who had returned in the gubernatorial van to fetch brother Ben and guest, carried on a conversation with the senator in rapid Tagalog so that her attention wandered, still haunted by the dark heap on the billiard table, though at one point she heard the phrase 'Philippine Heritage Museum'. Woopsy sat in the back with an electronic Bricks Game which warbled and squeaked. She seemed wholly engrossed. Once in the air, her father turned to Ysabella and said:

'My brother was telling me about the Museum's plans to open a branch there in Magubat. About time, too.'

'I'm afraid I know nothing about this province's archaeology.'

'It's the coastal waters that are interesting. The main Spanish galleon route from Mexico passed around its tip. Just off Bantol itself, as a matter of fact. I'm certain all the reefs of that southern part are littered with wrecks. There must be a mass of stuff out there. The odd Chinese trader or pirate junk, too, one would imagine. But it's the same old story. Such richness of heritage here and such poverty in the official agencies charged with its protection. Doy and I are doing our best to make sure Magubat gets onto the agenda before unscrupulous rogues start muscling in.'

'That sounds a good idea,' she said in the way that people say things who would rather not talk, especially not above twin engines. Then, thinking she wasn't making enough effort towards a host who had been generous and nearly charming, added: 'I'm sorry, I didn't realise your interest in archaeology was so active. I was thinking of you more as a private collector. It's good to know someone in your position cares about what happens to this country's treasures. Sometimes in the Museum it's like working near the mouth of a huge funnel. We can't see it but we can feel the current as it sucks stuff in which disappears and then turns up again in auction houses in London and Paris and Rome and New York.'

'I know. It's happening everywhere. All over Indochina, especially Cambodia. Russia, too, and the former Russian republics. South America. It's global rape. Global rape,' he repeated as though it were a phrase he had already used in a speech. 'And many of these countries are signatories to the 1970 UNESCO Convention. I know.'

Ysabella allowed herself to be reassured by this. At least somebody knew. But later, having dumped her overnight bag and showered in the oil-scented Roxas apartment she remembered his own collection in the beach house on Bantol. There had been nothing among his 'little things picked up here and there' later than the Fifteenth century, nothing which would have been out of place in a Ming or even Sung Dynasty trading junk. Or, for that matter, a pre-Colonial burial site. She wondered how he'd come by them. One of the oddities of that UNESCO Convention was how few of the signatory countries had ever asked the US – the major art-importing country – to impose an import ban. Why mightn't they? Then she thought about who would be responsible for making the request for such a ban. This left her naively blazing with a sudden conviction that nothing in this country was ever quite free of stain.

18

FOR A VARIETY of reasons, a few of them as purely technical as bad phones, communication between branches of the police force was often haphazard, which was why most officers of any rank bought several newspapers daily. It was one way of keeping up with the crime scene, and by no means the least reliable. Newspapers have to be read, however; and when Rio Dingca picked up a copy of the *National Chronicle*'s evening edition he merely glanced at the headline 'Queen of Shabu Nabbed' and thought 'Which one?' before folding and stuffing it up behind the jeep's visor. He tugged pistol and holster from his waistband, checked the load, cocked it and put the safety on before laying it within easy reach in its customary place by the gearshift. Only then did he start the engine and swing the unplated vehicle out of Station 14's compound and into rush hour.

The long drag south. Smoke boiled at traffic lights as the queue panted like a gored bull, collecting strength for its charge towards the next red. As he waited he remembered the newspaper and took it down, but only had time to register that the lead article was one of Vic Agusan's. Dingca had never met the journalist but he had read dozens of the man's pieces and rated him as about the best; definitely above the level of the pack who clearly felt they had *carte blanche* to write any sort of lies and slander about the police. Neither did he launch egotistical crusades in his column to have police arrested on the spot for driving vehicles without number plates, complete with homilies about how lawlessness began in small things and the men in uniform needed to learn at the outset that they themselves were not above the law, yakety-yak. The grapevine had it that Agusan was okay, that he'd been blooded, that his sympathies were firmly with the old INP cops. He certainly seemed to have few good things to say about the military in police clothing who were now calling most of the shots. Then the bull gave another snort and wearily charged again for the lights a few hundred yards ahead and Dingca had to tuck the paper away.

It was dusk when he reached San Pedro, dark by the time he let himself through the creepered palisades of wrought iron which made of the house an airy safe. Divina was doing her piano practice on the cigarette-scorched Baldwin he'd picked up from a military neighbour who had liberated it from an officers' mess. Eunice was in her room; Teresita was cooking. Thank God for the sanity of family life. He showered, changed into shorts and slippers, found a beer in the fridge and kissed the back of Sita's neck.

'Eunice wants to be a dentist.'

'So?'

'I just thought you ought to know. It's not going to be cheap, Rio. And it takes years and years. Tuition fees, equipment. Clothes, accommodation.' Sita worked in the local Department of Health offices. Her salary was barely enough to keep them in food each month. Nevertheless she was glad of the work even though it still bothered her to come back to an empty house in the late afternoon. In her home province there was always someone around. For much of the day here one could find entire blocks of nothing but empty homes, each with its patrolling dog. It didn't feel right. Sometimes in the office she would find herself thinking of this house, locked up by day, its waxed floors silent except for the occasional clicking of Butch's nails as he wandered into the kitchen for a drink of water, the girls' rooms empty with the white grins of movie pinups above the bed, the lounge walls gleaming dully with Rio's laminated citations. And now Eunice would be going away for months at a stretch. Well, it was going to happen sooner or later.

'I thought she wanted to be a teacher?'

'Oh Dad, that was *years* ago.' Eunice had come up behind her father. 'Anyway, you probably wanted to be a fireman once. Most boys do.'

'Yes, but a *dentist*.'

'The money's terrific.'

'When you've qualified.'

'Of course when you've qualified.'

'But doesn't it take six years?'

'There's lots to learn, Dad. But after that. . .'

'Go on?'

'Er, well, I'll be able to afford to pay you back. Easily.'

'Great. And just when you've finished getting me sprung from a bankrupt's cell, up will pop Divina wanting to be a brain surgeon and back I'll go.'

'You do *exaggerate*, Dad. What's for supper?'

'Fried chicken,' Sita told her, 'in special batter. You'll be doing the batter.'

'Can't, Mum, I'm right in the middle of a dentistry book.' From her open bedroom door in the distance the sound of her radio competed with her sister's pianistic stumblings.

'You haven't actually enrolled yet?' her father asked in alarm.

'Not quite. But I've decided to get a head start.'

Dingca knew that even as Sita and he were raising objections based on money neither of them really meant money. Everything nowadays cost a fortune; one simply took for granted that one couldn't actually afford it before going right ahead and juggling around later with the payments. Things sort of got paid, somehow. No, it wasn't the money. It was the thought of Eunice having to live in Manila in order to attend dentistry school. Why couldn't she commute with him? For heaven's sake, Dad, college students don't live with their *fathers*. They share digs, dorms, whatever. They have lectures at night. They have to meet professors and so on. They aren't *prisoners*, are they? They're adults with their own social lives.

But Rio's head was full of the scumbags who terrorised girls' dormitories, of what happened to tired students waiting for buses to get home after lectures, of the thousand varieties of perdition which thronged the city's streets, eyes bloodshot and fingers shaking with drugs. He didn't want to talk about it tonight, okay? Not *tonight*, Eunice. It needed thought. Goddam it, he'd only been home ten minutes before they'd sprung it on him out of the blue. A conspiracy of women, all trying to trick him into saying Yes. . .

Not until this was all said and the fridge door had closed with a muffled sigh of finality was Rio able to take a second cold beer out to the yard. Whatever you did, whichever way you turned, they'd got you by the short and curlies – whoever 'they' currently happened to be. He retrieved the evening paper from behind the jeep's visor, moved the folding chair closer to the light and, with Butch lying at his feet, finally read Vic Agusan's 'Queen of Shabu Nabbed' story.

Some Narc boys from South CapCom had arrested her in a buy-bust operation while passing a consignment of drugs to an officer posing as a buyer. 'Posing,' said Rio out loud. 'That's a laugh.' He took a mouthful of beer and then forgot to swallow as he saw the woman's name. Lettie Tan. Agusan described her as 'the owner of several businesses including night clubs in Cavite and Ermita and a string of foreign concessions, among them Japanese and Taiwanese engineering companies. Her Ermita club, "The Topless Pit", has long been known as an alleged safe haven for certain notorious drug dealers, which argues weighty protection somewhere up the line.' The man and his paper took risks, Dingca thought approvingly, at last swallowing the warm, flat mouthful. Lettie Tan, eh? That woman again.

He sat there slowly finishing his beer, no longer hearing the familiar sounds of cooking and TV voices in the house behind him, the sudden gushes of waste water. He had been joined in his yard by Babs's ghost who materialised with a rustle in the mango tree as he stared across at it. 'Was that it?' he asked his murdered asset silently. 'Was that what you were going to tell me, only. . .?' Only what, though? Had the child-kidnapping been just a sideline, or was it after all a complete red herring with no connection to Babs's employer? But suppose Babs had known about her being a drug boss. Several possibilities followed, one being that he might have preferred not to risk talking about it. This wasn't a little light toddler-snatching. This was big time, as Dingca would have known. And as Agusan implied, it was impossible to run any sort of drugs empire without reliable and senior protection in the judiciary and the police. The trouble was – and the recollection of his own dismissiveness now caused him a jab of conscience – he had never made a secret to Babs of the fact that of all forms of criminality, drugs bored him most. There was something about the whole scene which left Rio cold, even impatiently to feel that if a lot of bored cretins wanted to stuff their veins and noses with fancy chemicals which further addled their brains, that was fine by him. Much better spend one's time going after the real scalawags who were robbing the country blind, ruining the innocent and coming up squeaky clean time after time. Besides, he couldn't really understand why anyone wouldn't prefer a decent bottle of imported Black Label.

It was ironic. Two years ago when he'd still been in Station 5 with South CapCom Dingca had barely heard of Lettie Tan. Suddenly, now that he'd been posted to North CapCom and her fetid club was no longer his problem, she was assuming the proportions of a major criminal who, thanks to poor Babs, he felt was still very much his business. It was doubly irritating that under the PNP reshuffle his old team had been broken up and there were few men left in Station 5 with whom he would choose to share confidences about Lettie Tan. Two years was a long time. New alliances formed, injudicious questions could be life threatening. Now that the Narcs had their claws in her, too, there was little to be done. He dropped the newspaper and drained his glass. He actually debated ringing up this Agusan fellow to suggest that drugs would be only one of many skeletons hidden away in Lettie's cupboard and as a journalist he would have the facilities to do some digging around her other business activities. 'A string of foreign concessions' was impossible to acquire without heavywork somewhere along the line. There had been an example only last year not five miles down the road from this very yard, when a business-woman effectively tricked 294 Laguna farmers into selling 114 hectares of agricultural land and managed to get extreme pressure applied to the Secretary of the Department of Agrarian Reform to have the land's designation converted to 'industrial and commercial use' in order to set up an industrial park. This move was strictly illegal under the terms of land reform law, as Dingca had taken the trouble to verify. No-one at the time offered any prizes for guessing where the pressure had come from which was senior enough to make the Secretary of the DAR openly flout his own laws. That had become a scandal mainly because it forced Cory Aquino, by then ex-president, to deny that Malacañang had had any knowledge of the case. This denial was somewhat weakened when a personal letter to her from the business-woman was read out at the inquiry, expressly asking her presidential help in the matter. Defrauding illiterate peasants had been the easy part, of course. Dingca now wondered what equivalent mischief Lettie Tan might be involved in, never for a moment doubting it was there somewhere, probably not even very carefully hidden, so contemptuous of the law were people like her. It was not that he carried a particular flag for illiterate peasants, but this sort of thing was happening more and more often in Laguna as land prices soared in Metro Manila and the city sent its tentacles ever further into the surrounding provinces. He hadn't moved here to the country seventeen years ago to find himself surrounded in his retirement by illegally-acquired industrial parks full of noise and trucks, with gigantic neon signs making the night sky pink and mauve as they blazed forth the rival empires of Toshiba and Samsung.

After supper he walked one block over to the Bowl-o-Rama on Ylang-ylang. He felt in need of familiar faces. The reassuring rumble and clatter greeted him as he went in and several gloved hands were raised in greeting. He strolled from lane to lane, watching and chatting, until a voice a little behind him said, 'Inspector Dingca, sir?' He turned and couldn't immediately place her, beautiful and young, until a gear engaged and the months rewound themselves and he was back at the High School Graduation, looking at lines of good-as-gold boys and girls. Especially girls. *Big Girls*.

'Patti Gonzales, isn't it?'

She gave an oddly wry smile. 'You remember me, then?'

'We police have a photographic memory for faces. I thought everyone knew that.'

This obviously disconcerted her. 'Surely only for criminals, sir?'

'I'm afraid we make no distinction, since Nature doesn't. I must say you do look a little different out of school uniform.' As if worried lest she should read disappointment in his tone he added quickly, 'So how did you finally decide?'

'On what, sir?'

'Between the Civil Service and dentistry. I think that was to be your choice, wasn't it?'

It was true, she did look different. It was only reasonable that once no longer in school uniform she would look older, but that was to reckon without other changes both subtle and less so. Subtle was the way she was holding herself. The senior demureness beside which he had felt like a Sixth Grader was now transmuted into a different sort of self-confidence. She no longer stood with her calves together, just touching, or held her hand in front of her perfect teeth when she smiled. Less subtly (though it was hard to tell in the Bowl-o-Rama's lighting) she seemed to be wearing a suggestion of make-up. Oh no, Patti, he thought, foreseeing the Hostess Look which surely awaited her unless she was scrupulously careful. He had long noticed it was nearly impossible for his countrywomen to use make-up without looking like whores. It was unfortunate but true. The least attempt to paint an unnatural red on naturally brown cheeks, for instance, at once produced a bar girl straight from Ermita or Olongapo of the sort who might totter on high heels beside a towering foreigner with a bunch of crimson claws digging into his waist or dipping into his hip pocket.

'Oh, that,' she was saying. 'I gave up that idea ages ago. I mean, who wants to stare into people's mouths all day long? And imagine, six years before you earn a *sentimo*. You'd have to be a complete Brenda. Only plodders go in for dentistry.'

'Eunice has just enrolled,' said Dingca.

'Oh.' This time a hand did fly to her mouth. 'Oh, I didn't mean. . . I only meant for me, sir. Obviously some people are completely suit –' her voice ran out as her brain finally overtook it.

In the awkward pause he said kindly, 'You're right, of course. We can't all do the same thing. So what have you chosen?'

'I –' she began diffidently, 'I'd like to join the police. It was meeting you. That's why I wanted to speak to you, sir.'

'Good God!' Rio exclaimed involuntarily. 'But you're much too beautiful,' picturing the terrifying collection of slags and tomboys which to his mind characterised the policewomen he knew. 'What sort of career's that for a nice girl? The pay's lousy. Besides, as you must be well aware, the police in this country are going through a crisis at the moment. The reorganisation isn't quite –. What I mean is, there are things still to iron out. Shakedown period. . . It's a total mess,' he conceded. 'Honestly, Patti, I wouldn't recommend your joining at the moment. At the very least not until things are clearer. Perhaps I should have a word with your father. What does he say? He's never mentioned this to me.' He glanced about him. Where was Butz?

'He supports me. Whatever help you could give, sir, I'd be so grateful.'

Was there the faintest stress on the word? She couldn't surely. . .? But in spite of himself Dingca felt the beginnings of an erection. An

176

hour later, when he had talked to her father, he unhappily knew for certain. He had learned – in strictest confidence – that the scholar of the family had unfortunately failed her National College Entrance Examination, which somewhat limited Patti's chances of a higher education. Indeed, it should have made it quite impossible, dependent on her re-sitting the exam in a year's time. And for the police nowadays a college education was mandatory, wasn't it? Dingca had assured her father this was so. But *mandatory* – and here the Bowl-o-Rama's owner made flexuous gestures in the air like someone trying to rid his fingers of dough – there's mandatory and mandatory, right? We're men of the world, Rio, you and I. You're not going to tell me hand on heart that everyone on the force with a certificate of higher education has actually *been* to college? Exactly. I've heard a figure of twenty thou. mentioned. It's only a sheet of paper, after all. A date stamp, a couple of signatures, a mere formality. Old Buddy.

As it happened, ₱ 20,000 was the going rate for getting a charge of murder (which couldn't be bailed) reduced to a charge of homicide (which could). It was also the agreed sum for rich kids to pay when they were arrested with unregistered firearms and didn't want the hassle of being charged with illegal possession. So he supposed it might buy a short cut to two or three years' study. All at once he fell prey to the same weariness which had made him invite that bleak renegade Father Herrera for drinks. It was not out of line to ask friends for favours, not according to the way things were. Yet for a strange moment Dingca had experienced it as an unthinkable liberty. It was as if he had stopped being part of an imaginary society where millions forgave their dead president for robbing the country blind because he only did it to help his own family and besides, had they been in his enviable position they would have done exactly the same. Only such a society wasn't imaginary at all, and he could feel his head nodding dumbly of its own accord to signify the negation and denial and refusal he couldn't trust himself to voice.

'The job's wearing you thin,' Sita said to him later that night.

'I know it,' he agreed. In the morning he knew it still better, for the same newspaper's early edition, no longer headlining the story, said: 'Alleged Dealer Released.' 'Lack of evidence,' went on Agusan (who must have been up all night) with a bitterness Dingca himself could taste, 'is the supposed reason behind the nearly immediate release of the woman known widely as "The Queen of Shabu". A more plausible reason, according to my informants, is thought to be the direct intervention of an unnamed police Chief Superintendent and a certain businessman with "connections at court". Had those persons failed, the so-called "Magnificent Seven" could no doubt have been relied on to come up trumps. They, of course, are the seven judges on the Makati Regional Trial Court circuit who, in the words of the same reliable source, "facilitate the settlement of criminal charges against the members of drug syndicates in return for vast sums of money". They, and many others like them, are presumably what the Presidential Anti-Crime Commission recently called "hoodlums in robes". The Filipino people may wearily note that hoodlums in robes are distinct from, but often hand-in-glove with, hoodlums in uniform. (They will also recall the PACC's description a month or two ago of "hoodlums in medical robes", which referred to those doctors who form a cadet branch of the old-established Hoodlum family.) All of which means, in short, *The Queen walks.*'

On the way to work Dingca pondered the untouchable Lettie Tan with her friends at court, and her late employee Babs. He thought about anonymous Chief Superintendents and businessmen and judges to whom the world's Babses and Dingcas were so small as to be indistinguishable. He had the fantasy – at first not overtly erotic – of being assigned to take Police Cadet Gonzales from her very first days in uniform and show her exactly where she stood, which was absolutely nowhere. Her entire career could be blighted if fate moved her to flag down the wrong third-rate little birdturd for jumping the lights on Taft. He would mould her until she was sharp enough to see how things were, and hard enough to withstand them. The purity of this pedagogical vision was spoiled as it unaccountably sideslipped into a picture of the rookie, Benhur Daldal, screwing her in the Tan mausoleum. But neither this nor the early sun bouncing off the brightly buffed metalwork of his jeep brought cheer, and an officious blast on his squawk box which sent a sagging taxi swerving for cover produced no smile. Small wonder there were so many horrendous accidents, with head-on collisions between overladen buses and jeepneys 'losing their brakes' and ploughing into crowds of school-children. People simply had no idea how to drive, none whatever, which was hardly surprising given how easy it was to get a licence.

Dingca knew people in the Department of Transportation who would issue a driver's licence to a blind man for a bottle of imported Scotch.

Only the sight of Sgt. Cruz in the Station's battered Tamaraw turning into the compound ahead of him gave Rio savage satisfaction. At least someone was doing something useful, and for quite modest sums of money. In the back of the Tamaraw a blue drum – empty, obviously, from the way it wobbled – was roped loosely upright. They parked beside each other.

'I missed a party?' asked Dingca, climbing out.

'Ronnie Guzman from Station 2 sends his best. He provided Ninja.'

'And you provided the drink? God's own water for punkface and ESQ for the boys.'

'Gin and Seven Up. I've a bit of a head. But Ninja drank the most.'

'Who was he?'

'Ninja Boy Magtibay. One of the four who raped that little student up in Greenhills or Cubao or somewhere. Dental nurse, I think. Before Christmas. They pushed a broken bottle up her and left her to bleed to death. We interviewed Ninja quite thoroughly about his friends. They're booked for the same trip sooner or later.'

'Which was where, may I ask?'

'The Chinese piemen back of the airport. I owe you a couple of hundred,' Cruz said.

We never know about blood money, Rio thought later that morning as he sat in the crime room, looking at the splintery desks and the three candles planted on them in puddles of their own wax. Brownout again. The candlelight lent the large office a quaintly ecclesiastical air despite the twenty-five-year-old city map on the wall. In one corner was a large Santo Niño in a niche made entirely of polished coconut shells. We receive payment for deeds we didn't commit, for merely being a senior officer whose attitude permits their commission, or at least doesn't stop it. Had Cruz not been such an enthusiast Station 2 would certainly have provided their own equivalent. Really, blood money was no more than part of our basic wage, truly inseparable from this job, this city, this *now* in this place. We are paid for our participation in the crime which merely living here involves.

The fat desk sergeant with the horn rims came in. 'Morning, Lieutenant. Missed you earlier.'

'Must be the brownout, Jun.' It was the sergeant's habit to slip out of the back of the station past the pens to where an enterprising squatter family had set up an impromptu commissary. Here he would slurp bowls of *lugaw* and flirt in a cumbersome way until summoned back to duty by a rookie.

'Message from the Captain. He wants you to check out a story about vampires in San Clemente.'

'*Vampires?* Get lost, Sergeant.'

'No, really. Apparently it's in *People's* for the second day running.'

'Wow. It must be true, then. And where's the Captain, may I ask?'

'He's over on Carmona. Thay had an amok down there last night. Chopped up seven. Four *dedbol* plus the amok.'

'Anyone we knew?'

'Don't think so, Lieutenant. Radio repairer or something. The usual quiet sort.'

'Mm. And I get vampires, that it?'

'Only passing on what the Captain said, Lieutenant. You're the one with the contacts in San Clem.'

This provoked a snigger or two in reference to the ancient joke about Dingca's having a second wife up there among the cemeteries who made him his clothes in return for regular megaboffing. Since this was none other than the virtuous Nanang Pipa, from whom he bought the girls' T-shirts at cost, Dingca hadn't minded the ribbing. It seemed a small price to pay.

'Okay,' he said. Any job outside would be preferable to sitting here by candlelight. 'Anyone got a *People's?*'

It was headline stuff in two-inch high red capitals, a Mozart P. Narciso special full of interviews with mothers who had found their babies unaccountably drowsy with strange marks on their necks. 'I can't wake my baby,' sobbed one housewife hysterically. 'He's been asleep now for seventeen hours. He's never done it before. To my mind he's possessed.' Another resident said that although she had the greatest respect for their parish priest, San Clemente needed the services of a specialist 'like that priest who did the Cavite dwarves.' Never one to leave his readers baffled by a reference, Mozzy had taken time out – and a box outlined in heavy black type – to remind everyone of the incident some months ago when an elementary school in Cavite had been closed for days because of a plague of black dwarves which had invaded classrooms and pulled the pupils' hair. The children described the dwarves as having black beards and being about as tall as a family-size Coke bottle. A trained exorcist had been summoned and had done a number on them and successfully sent them packing back to their underground kingdom.

On his way out and with heavy humour Dingca laid his holstered pistol on the desk.

'Shan't be needing this, Jun. But can you issue me a bottle of holy water, please?'

'Yeah, look, I'm sorry, Lieutenant. It's nothing to do with me. Captain said it's not going to look good if it's up there in the headlines and not a cop in sight. You know how these stories can attract trouble.'

'We're *service*-oriented. . .'

'. . . not *mission*-oriented. You've got it.'

But Rio Dingca picked up his gun again after all and tucked it into his waistband as he trotted down the station steps into blessed sunlight.

19

A S THE *National Chronicle*'s chief crime reporter Vic Agusan rated a car and a driver, as distinct from the limo and chauffeur enjoyed by the paper's editors. For some jobs – lurking with macro-zoom lenses as cops dumped their victims, for instance – he preferred to use his own Toyota, and it was in this that he called for Prideaux on the way to San Clemente. He referred to it fondly as 'The Hersheymobile'. Years of scalding sun and atmospheric pollutants had etched its once-glossy brown cellulose to a matt bloom. Together with the odd wisps of silver trim which still adhered, the crumpled wings and dented roof, this gave the vehicle a considerable re-semblance to a block of chocolate on which somebody had stepped.

Somewhere up José Abad Santos he glanced at a map and saw that one didn't after all drive to the area in which San Clemente must lie, there being no road, so he parked the Hersheymobile in the approach to the Chinese Cemetery. Thus it was that he and Prideaux, having consulted the guard at the barrier, walked up and along past the new Tan mausoleum ('God, look at that'), cut sharply down to a hole in the hollow-block perimeter wall and squeezed through into the village. Vic thought it pretty much what he'd expected but could see his British companion apprehensively taking in a detailed inventory of slimy pathways and the shanties' patchwork sides which came practically up to the wall.

'Hooches,' Vic heard him murmur. 'It's a ville. As in "Let's waste this ville".'

It was not hard to find Eddie Tugos. With the exception of their vampire he and Bats Lapad had temporarily become San Clemente's most famous inhabitants. The visitors were led along meandering passageways strung with washing, here and there negotiable on tiptoe across swampy tracts sown with pieces of wood, a cylindrical length of palm trunk and the bashed honeycomb of a car radiator. Curious eyes and surprised giggles followed Prideaux. Hands which might or might not have been friendly clutched at his forearms. Cries of '*Kano!*' and the running feet of children could be heard spreading through the warren of alleys. Finally they reached a tiny clearing. There, beneath a single palm tree with a basketball hoop nailed to its trunk, was a low rickety table made of packing-case slats and covered in bottles and glasses. At this, holding court, sat Eddie and Bats surrounded by assorted drunks, cronies and children.

'I have to tell you,' said Eddie with becoming frankness once introductions had been made and he had overcome his initial disappointment at finding his foreign visitor was not a member of the international press, 'that you're not the first today. No, no. Never mind, eh? Come one, come all. Do you know Mozart? What do you think of him?'

'A first-rate investigative reporter,' Vic said promptly. 'It was he who suggested I came today.'

'He's a lying hound,' said Eddie. 'Generous, though.' He tilted an empty gin bottle so that it clinked with heavy significance against its hollow companions. Vic produced some money and was about to hand it to the nearest child with orders for reinforcements when Eddie called 'Judge!' A lean man in an unravelling sombrero stepped forward, took the money and vanished. The journalist read this with amusement, making a mental note to tell the Englishman afterwards since he would probably have missed it. With his celebrity Eddie was being accorded a social status which Vic was sure he never normally enjoyed, and with it went a subtle re-ordering of his friendships. The man in the hat had briefly become an *alalay*, somewhere between a bodyguard and a gofer, as if Eddie himself were a proper little *amo* now (useless lusharooney though he clearly was. Vic had taken in the whole setup the instant he'd caught sight of the gin bottles, their labels already glowing brilliantly in the morning sunlight). '*He* hasn't been today, though.'

'Who, Mozart? No, he's on another story. So who's been this morning?'

'Oh.' Eddie looked around for Judge and found Bats instead. Bats was tilted back against the tree wearing borrowed shades, Mr Cool himself, slightly but fatally upstaged because the vampire had chosen the Tugos roof on which to perch. 'Who was here, Bats?'

'*Bandera. Abante. Tempo,*' said Bats, hardly moving his mouth.

The tabloids, thought Vic disgustedly. The real scuzz, sniffing around for the tabloid angle. What the hell was he doing here wasting time with these leaky bladders? 'Why do you say Mozart's a liar, Mr Tugos? Do you think he misrepresented something you said?'

At this moment the man in the sombrero reappeared, clutching bottles and a plastic bag of ice. Bottle caps popped and twirled in the air, were retrieved by scrambling barefoot children eager to scrape out their linings to see if they'd won a jackpot. Glancing around to make sure his guests were properly seated, the glasses and bottles correctly disposed, Eddie said with unexpected precision, 'He couldn't help misrepresenting everything I said because he didn't believe a word of it. Not one word.'

'Well, I read his two articles and they seemed pretty fair to me. Good faith, and so on. After all, it's a pretty strange story, you've got to admit. And it's not as if you took photographs of the apparition.'

'It wasn't an "apparition", it was a *manananggal*, man,' said Eddie vehemently. 'That's exactly what *he* did, this Mozart friend of yours. He didn't actually write lies because he didn't need to. What he did was. . .' Eddie thought for a moment, 'undermine my credibility. That's it! Look,' he reached down and from the ground plucked two copies of *People's*. That morning's edition had a banner in three-inch red capitals which said 'THE VAMPIRE'S EVIL SPREADS' surmounted by an outline drawing of a creature all wings and fangs hovering as if about to alight on the headline. Beneath all this was room for only a couple of inches of print. One turned the page expectantly only to find a spread of perfectly ordinary stories such as 'Teenager Mashes Girls' and 'Fake Cop Nabs Real Cop in Error!'

'Page four,' said Eddie with hurt in his voice. On page four the vampire story was taken up again in normal print. 'Here's an example,' he reached across and tapped a paragraph. ' "His wife Epifania, who runs a sewing business from her home, said her husband had been under a strain recently. There had been a lot of worry over family matters." See what I mean? How craftily it's done? His wife runs a sewing business, get it? Not him. His wife. In other words she's a hard-working, level-headed woman who can be trusted. Notice it's *her* home and not mine, which I built with these two hands,' Eddie stared rhetorically at his spread palms, 'the same hands which are digging her the precious comfort room of her dreams which is causing all this –'

'Comfort rooms, Eddie,' interrupted Bats firmly from behind his shades. 'Mr Agusan and his American guest didn't come to San Clemente to hear about toilets. They came to hear about the *manananggal* which I also saw. We were equal witnesses,' he explained to Vic and Prideaux.

'Okay, okay,' agreed Eddie, though obviously unwilling to abandon his general thesis. 'The whole point is, I'm discredited, right? You know perfectly well that when someone in a newspaper's described as having been under a strain recently it means they're either off their heads or pissed incapable. I've been under a strain for more than recently!' he suddenly yelled towards his own shut front door. 'Damn near twenty-two years! It's called marriage!' Everyone looked nervously towards the house as if expecting the door to fly open and a virago spring out with a flashing pair of cutting-out shears. When nothing happened Eddie said reasonably, 'You see my point, Mr Agusan? Nobody takes it seriously. But we saw it. We *did*. That's why we all need gin. There, look at the label. See? It's a defence against the Devil. The triumph of San Miguel.'

'So what about all this other corroborative stuff?' Vic tapped the newspaper. 'The neighbours? The glowing Bibles? The cockroaches?'

'We can't say,' said Bats. 'We didn't witness any of that. I expect it's all true. Everyone knows everyone in San Clemente. We know who the liars are. It's not surprising, though, is it? When an evil spirit that powerful materialises it has all sorts of side effects. It stands to reason.'

'That's quite right!' put in a woman from among the crowd of onlookers gathered at the foot of the tree. 'I'm Julie Orallo, the Mrs Orallo in that same newspaper. My Santo Niño fell off the wall and it's never done it before. The way that Narciso man wrote it, it was a bit of a joke. But you tell me what the chances are of my Santo Niño falling at exactly the same moment as the *manananggal* appeared. You tell me that, clever-clogs!'

'*I* didn't write that, Mrs Orallo,' said Vic mildly. 'I'm just listening.'

'And I'm just telling you. All those smarty-boots journalists from downtown, they drift up here from their aircon offices and say it's all, er, *hysteria*. But we in San Clemente, we *felt* that wave of evil. That's not hysteria. That's something you feel, isn't it?' The crowd murmured its agreement. 'And all our hair stood on end at once, didn't it? And that's something anyone with eyes can see.'

'Okay,' said Vic pacifically, 'okay. I'm keeping an open mind, remember?'

'An empty head, more like,' said a voice in the crowd. 'Joke only,' it added, and there was laughter as well as nudging and shushing.

Vic turned to Bats. 'Perhaps Mr Bats here would tell me exactly where he saw the *manananggal*.'

Prideaux had followed all this with difficulty, meanwhile, since it was in Tagalog. The general drift, though, was clear enough: an anger on the part of the locals that they weren't being taken seriously. When the impassive man in dark glasses pointed to a nearby roof Prideaux saw an expanse of rusty tin, much patched and with several bald motor tyres lying on it presumably to prevent the wind lifting the sheets. The house itself was two-storeyed and leaned in neighbourly fashion against that next door, which in turn was sandwiched into a general rookery of similar buildings both high and low. He imagined that people added another floor to their houses when they had a bit of spare cash or else some materials came their way. He could even see a couple of makeshift balconies. 'Rough, I'd guess,' Vic had said on the way over when asked what San Clemente would be like, and images of violence and desperation had come to him, as they so often did nowadays. Yet sitting in the shade of a palm tree at a table hospitably spread with refreshments he felt a peaceable, almost rural atmosphere quite different from that of the carefully contrived oases downtown. Those hotel gardens squeezed by a grid of streets, their high boundary walls painted with crude trompe l'oeil vistas of Mt. Mayon as glimpsed between jungled headlands, were nothing but tropicopolitan fakery. San Clemente, despite its own high walls, was unquestionably authentic, as elemental as befitted a lot of people living on a hillside. For there was indeed a view: a rare sense, for this city, of being positioned in a landscape. From where he was sitting he could see the upper part of the barrio rising towards where, a hundred or so metres away, the huge cemetery began. Beyond the shanty roofs were big old trees, their dark crowns dense as sponge, and between them the pale gleam of tombs. He could judge the point from which Vic and he had walked down into the barrio and now saw it was not the very top of San Clemente. They had come in about a third of the way down. The shanties stretched on in a narrowing wedge beyond to a point he could calculate by mentally prolonging the cemetery wall's diagonal. Besides the vista of trees there were other signs of rurality. Ducks paddled in the sludge between the dwellings. From a nearby gully (actually the long sewage outfall leading from behind the Tugos house down to the invisible Kapilang) came the squeal of piglets, reflected from the bleached and rotting walls of the latrines lining its far side. A scatter of hens scratched in the dust, while nearby a fighting cock was tethered by one leg on a length of nylon cord simply nailed into the baked soil. Its wattles glowed with rich blood; the sun burnished its metallic plumes until they bled gold and copper and bronze; the proud arch of its tail dribbled inky lights. It was a dazzling bird.

Just then Prideaux caught sight of a familiar figure emerging from a nearby house and turning away up the alley. At least, he was pretty sure it was familiar. He hadn't seen Fr. Herrera since their lunch together in the New Era but the plump torso and spectacles were surely unmistakable. He got abruptly to his feet with one of those all-purpose hand gestures at once indicating excuses and a short absence and, without taking his eyes off the place where he'd last seen the priest, hurried after him.

Five minutes later the Tugos front door opened and a tall, fortyish man in T-shirt and slacks came out, laughing. He paused in the sun, looking over at the table and the crowd. Eddie was just describing some details of the fangs which he'd newly recalled. Everyone's attention was on him except Vic Agusan's, distracted by this stranger's appearance. How is it one can always tell? he was asking himself as he so regularly did. They had that look about them which one couldn't quite pin down. It didn't matter what they wore or what they were doing; sooner or later that little inward voice spoke up and said 'Cop'. After all these years of talking to them, drinking with them, following and watching them, Vic always knew if the man was what he called a proper cop or merely some military no-neck pretending to be one. This man was a proper cop, the full Academy-trained article with, what? eighteen or twenty years on the clock and not enough seniority to show for it. His hair was greying, Vic noticed.

The man walked over and listened for a moment before Eddie saw him and broke off in mid-reminiscence. 'Rio!' he exclaimed, getting unsteadily to his feet. 'A drink for the Inspector, Judge,' he ordered, as to the manner born. 'I owe this man my life,' he explained to his audience. 'If it hadn't been for him I'd still be rotting in jail on a trumped-up charge.' He threw an arm around the T-shirt; the tall man smiled faintly. 'Imagine *me* being accused of car-napping! It's like accusing a eunuch of rape. I couldn't do it even if I wanted to.'

'That either,' said a voice from the crowd. 'Thanks to St. Michael.' There was laughter. 'Joke only.'

'What? What?' demanded Eddie, deftly intercepting a glass of gin and draining it at a gulp. This, together with Judge's rolled eyes and raised eyebrows, drew more laughs since the drink had been intended for the new arrival.

'San Miguel, Eddie,' explained the cop with a kindly pat on his host's shoulder. 'The patron saint of family planning.' This provoked further amusement, as did the dumb show with which he managed to accept a fresh glass which Judge had passed behind Eddie's back.

But Eddie had embarked on another reminiscence, one which required an actor's concentration. ' "Just drive," they said, "that's all you have to do. Drive to the guy's house and you go free. We'll take it from there." *Rrrrmm, rrrrmm!*' He stamped his right foot repeatedly on the ground as on an accelerator pedal. '*Rrrrmm!* Nothing. Bugger all.' He stretched both arms out, gripped an imaginary steering wheel and gave several thrusts with his pelvis as if to urge a recalcitrant vehicle into motion. He glanced over the jeep's side at the unmoving ground and shook his head in bafflement. '*Rrrrmm?*' The crowd, most of whom had seen the dramatic re-telling of Eddie's miraculous deliverance from jail many times before, were perfectly content to see it again. This was vintage Eddie, pissed by ten-thirty in the morning, the darling of the ghostbusters, the man who'd just put San Clemente on the national map. This was Eddie's day.

' "*Tanga!*" says he, all charm. "*Ay, mali!* You've got to put it in gear if you want to go anywhere, you idiot. Get on with it! Stop acting the clown or we'll throw away your key." *Rrrmm!* I'm trying, I tell him. What gear? Gear? "This stick thing," he says, jiggling the shift. Well, of course I know what a gearshift is, it's just that I've never learned to use one. I can get a noise out of a mouth organ, too, but I don't know how to play it. Still, I've seen old Gringo drive his taxi zillions of times so I stick my left foot on the clutch' (Eddie stamped the ground with his foot) 'and move the stick a bit' (he let go the wheel with his right hand and made stirring motions in the air with his fist) 'and up comes my foot and *Pak!!*' He jerked his head violently forward, at the same time bringing up the flat of one upright hand to smack his face from brow to chin, simulating sudden impact. The crowd roared. It was done with such ebullient realism they could practically see blood oozing from beneath the palm still cupped over his nose and mouth as he turned his head to look apprehensively over his shoulder at someone in the back seat. 'Sorry about that, mate. Foot slipped. I know it's your jeep but you shouldn't have parked it so close to the wall. What? No, er, just. . . Just let me take you up on one small point there about my mother, could I? She's not actually a whore, you know. She runs a biscuit shop in Buenavista, Marinduque. Arrowroot biscuits, mainly. They're quite del –. Yes, all right! I'll shut up! Just stop hitting my head, please,' and Eddie hunched it down into his shoulders, crouching to protect himself from his assailant. His audience howled. Gradually he let his shoulders relax and peeped fearfully back again. 'Well, it's your fault,' he said in a reasonable, somewhat aggrieved tone. 'I never said I could drive, did I? In fact, I distinctly said I couldn't.' He gingerly uncupped his hand and searched it anxiously for blood, dabbing tenderly at his lip. 'Was this jeep very, uh, *new* or anything? *Ow! Aruy! Aruy!!*' as fresh blows rained from behind and he fell to his knees in the dust. Several of the children nearby were practically hysterical by now and plenty of adults were wiping tears of mirth which this cathartic recital had provoked.

Eddie never quite took a performer's bow, however. Just as he was getting to his feet his rubbery face suddenly became taut and distracted as if he were listening to an urgent voice. Then he slumped forward with his head beneath the table and was violently sick. In the general lifting of feet which followed Bats introduced Vic to Inspector Dingca.

'There's a strange thing,' Rio said. 'I was thinking about you only the other day. You're the only newspaperman I've ever wanted to meet.'

'I'm flattered.'

'You should be. Most of your colleagues write such crap, especially about the police.'

'Do you live here?'

'In this area? God forbid. My home's in San Pedro, Laguna,' said Dingca proudly. 'No, this place is part of the precinct. I was sent up in case all the publicity led to outbreaks of public disorder.' He nodded towards the convulsed and moaning Eddie. 'That's about it, I reckon.'

'Which station?'

'Fourteen.'

Vic's expression didn't change but he at once registered that he was dealing with a colleague, possibly a friend, of Sgt. Cruz. 'You're not one of those lingering Lieutenants, are you?'

Rio jerked his head. 'Never was. Not at heart, anyway. Not even in the old PC days. No, I guess I'm just one of life's Inspectors, Mr Agusan. A dyed-in-the-wool civilian, that's me. Listen, are you in a real hurry?'

Vic looked at Eddie and his audience, many of whom were showing signs of wanting to sit at the table and get down to some serious drinking now that their star turn had set such a memorable example. Then he raised his eyes to the roof of Eddie's house. 'Not really,' he said. 'I don't see any supernatural action here, do you?'

'Then would you mind a short stroll? There's something I'd like to discuss.'

'With a crime reporter? Is this work?'

'It could be.'

'I've got a foreigner with me, an Englishman. I'll just leave word that we'll be back.'

Dingca led the way up through the hole in the wall and into the cemetery. He could still see the patch where the illegal standpipe had been plumbed into the Tan mausoleum's water supply. It hadn't been replaced but he saw some more iron fencing had been stolen and there were fresh graffiti painted on the walls. 'Help enrich your local police,' said one. 'Kidnap a Chinese.' Together they strolled along the perimeter road, in and out of the cool puddles of shade cast by the great trees. From here they could overlook most of San Clemente, its tangled crests of canted tin falling away towards the more regular urban skyline filling the mile and a half between them and the invisible sea. The cries of unschooled children drifted up from its enclave.

'I read your pieces in the *Chronicle* about the Queen of *shabu*,' said Dingca. 'You sounded pretty sick when they sprang her.'

'More sick than angry, I guess. It was inevitable. People like that don't stay behind bars for a night, let alone for a fifteen-to-twenty stretch. You know it's going to happen but it still gets to you each time. Well, a bit of indignation's probably good for a journalist. Sharpens up the prose.'

'You do a nice job, Mr Agusan. It makes your readers indignant, too. It's right that folks should be indignant. It's the worst thing there is, indifference.'

'It's often not indifference so much as resignation.'

Dingca was staring out to where an LRT train winked and swayed along its raised track, vanishing behind trees and buildings with its segments reappearing in gaps like a maggot threading the city's heart. 'I hate what they've done. This used to be the best police force in Asia. And now look at it. *Pulitika*,' he said in disgust. Turning abruptly towards Vic he added with a mixture of belligerence and anxiety, 'You're not quoting me on that.'

'Don't worry. On the other hand it's nice to know. Now that's out of the way, what did you bring me up here to talk about? Not vampires, surely?'

'The Queen of *shabu*.'

'Well I'm damned. I thought she was just a conversational gambit. What's your interest in the case?'

So Rio Dingca explained how Lettie Tan's club had been in his precinct before he was transferred north of the river two years ago in the PNP reshuffle. He told him about his asset in 'The Topless Pit', now dead, without mentioning Babs by name. He recounted the infant-napping attempt in Harrison Plaza by a woman who had lived right here in San Clemente (pointing a finger downhill) and who his instinct told him was connected in some way. 'I want that Tan bitch,' he concluded. 'It's personal,' because brooding had made of her an epitome, a figure who stood for all that was wrong and thumbed its nose at justice. 'I don't mean I want *my* hands on her, necessarily,' he stared at his own as if they were interesting but unfamiliar tools designed for a job that had yet to be invented. 'I just want to see her go down. Down and down and *down*. That's her,' he added, indicating a direction with a pursing of his mouth and a lift of his chin.

Their stroll had brought them around to face the brilliant white Moorish confection with its icing-sugar turrets, licorice-stick portcullis and wedding cake lettering over the doors.

'*That's* her?' said Vic in amazement. '*That* Tan? That's the Queen of *shabu*?'

'Not her in person, unfortunately. Not yet. But it will be. That's the family mausoleum. Cost a bit, wouldn't you say? To add another irony, I had to come and inspect it a few months back because the Clementeños were nicking her water. It's a pity I'm just a cop. I can't go beavering away on someone else's patch or muscle in on any story that happens to interest me. I can only deal with the cases they dump in my lap down at the *presinto*. But you're a journalist, Mr Agusan. You can go where you want, a man with your reputation. You may not always get what you want but at least you can follow your nose. Am I right?'

'A couple of days ago I'd have said you were. But today I've been told to follow an editor's nose because he sniffed vampires in the wind. He's worried about the circulation figures.'

'Yeah, well, we're none of us shitproof. What I mean is, forget the *shabu* for a bit. You're not going to get anywhere, I can tell you that for nothing. Not with the protection she's got. Makati judges? They're just fixers. They sort out the paperwork. No, you're up against someone with an office in Camp Crame or Camp Aguinaldo with his own cannons and flagpole outside. Someone who can come and go at Malacañang whenever he feels like it. The sort of guy who reads himself to sleep with the security files of senators and provincial governors, like we're told J. Edgar Hoover did. Forget all that. Lettie Tan's armour-plated on the drugs score, at least for now. But you know people like her as well as I do. *Chekwa* big wheels,' said Dingca, looking around at the Chinese cemetery and lowering his voice for the racial epithet, 'they can't just stick to one thing. Never happen. It's drilled into them: Diversify. Then if the big crash comes they've got something to fall back on. Legit. stuff. Medical equipment. Pharmaceuticals. Machine tools. Paint. Dry cleaning. Real estate. For instance, when I was still at Station Five we did a quick run-down of her interests when the club's licence came up for renewal. Just for our own interest, I mean. We did the same with several club owners. The renewal was a rubber stamp job, of course. *Pangkape*,' he rubbed his fingertips together. 'Coffee money. No problem. We didn't uncover anything sensational but we did find out that along with everything else she owns a furniture company with several tourist outlets downtown. Do you know about that one?'

'New to me. You're ahead of me here.'

'She may not still have it, of course. For all we knew it was completely legit. It was handicrafts stuff, rattan and cane. I remember the company was called "Chip 'n' Dale". I don't know why I'm telling you this. You're a journalist, you know all these things as well as I do. I just, well, I guess I really wanted to hear you weren't giving up on her.'

Vic Agusan was staring at the mausoleum. The broad brass straps on the doors gleamed like terminals designed to handle prodigious voltages as if it were a substation on an exclusive national grid. 'Yes,' he said, 'I do know all that. I wasn't going to drop her, of course, but I admit I was going to put old Lettie on the back burner for a while.' He was warming to this cop. His first impression hadn't been wrong. One of the good ones of the old school. Probably as straight as was reasonable without actually starving, but you wouldn't want to commit yourself finally without first having a quick gander at this house of his out in San Pedro, at how his wife dressed and the company his kids kept. Maybe there was a deal in the offing if it could be handled just right. No crime reporter could have too many reliable police contacts. Inspector Dingca was definitely not a Sgt. Cruz, of that he was certain, but neither would he be a rat. Yet what Dingca must know about his colleague's salvage activities could doubtless fill his *Chronicle* column for weeks. 'Do you have any leads?' he asked. 'What area were you thinking of?'

'No leads,' the policeman said. 'But if I had your time and facilities there'd be two things I'd have a go at. One you mentioned in your article: these foreign concessions she holds. Famous names, any of them?'

'Household. Japanese engines, South Korean cars, Taiwanese electronics.'

'You don't get those for coffee money, right?' said Rio. 'That takes clout. You've got to have something to offer these foreign giants, something they can't get for themselves without the inside help of a national with the right connections.'

'Land, for instance.'

'Exactly. Real estate on which to build their showrooms and service centres and factories. I've no knowledge one way or the other, but I'll bet you. This cop's nose says she's into real estate somewhere along the line, and that might be another way to nail her. People like her are arrogant. Land deals haven't got the same dramatic impact that drugs have, and they certainly don't earn you a mandatory prison term, so she won't go to such lengths to cover her tracks. The deals will be shitty enough, though. Officials fixed, secret re-zonings, ministries duped, peasants tricked and destitute. There's a way for a man of your writing skill to make that sound quite as bad as drugs. Am I right?' And if there was conviction in his voice it was because Rio was indeed convinced. He had tapped into the vehemence which sprang from all his anxiety about retirement, about maybe finding Sita and himself obliged to live out their declining years marooned on an island in the middle of an industrial park. If his hunch proved correct he'd be only too glad to have given a man like Vic Agusan a little shove along the right road. At the same time it would be an opportunity to find out about possible dirty land deals in San Pedro. 'You could start with Laguna,' he said disingenuously. 'That's rated a prime development area these days.'

When they went back down to the barrio they found no John Prideaux. No Eddie Tugos, either, come to that. His inert form had since been removed by his wife, they were told, and now lay in unconscious disgrace somewhere under the very roof his vampire had chosen as its perch. Bats had taken his place as Master of Ceremonies and Keeper of the Story, though his own version was somewhat different from Eddie's. Eddie remembered a moonlike face with fangs, whereas Bats was obsessed by a flying half-woman. A learned discussion had just broken out concerning vampires, *manananggal*, *aswang* and various other horrors. Someone with a heavy Visayan accent said everybody was wrong, they were called *wakwak*, but whatever you called them the only way to deal finally with them was to stop the flying upper half of the body joining up with its lower half before dawn. Do that and it was dead for several reasons, one being that without a stomach it couldn't digest the meal of liver and entrails it had just sucked out.

'Number one job,' said this man, looking around at the crowd of drinkers and listeners, 'number one job is to find who this person is that Eddie and Bats saw. Then when her body separates at night we can take action.' Everyone looked expectantly at Bats.

'Hell, fellas,' said Bats from behind his shades, 'it was night, okay? You can't recognise a person's face at night all the way up on the roof there.'

'But you must have formed an impression?' coaxed the expert.

Bats, who had considerably embroidered his own blurred recollections of the episode some nights ago, realised that his credibility hung on naming a name, any name. He chose the barrio's current demon, the one who'd cut off their water. 'I won't swear to it, mind,' he said.

'But? Yes?'

'But it did *faintly* remind me of that woman up there,' he nodded towards the graveyard. 'The one who had her goons chase me and Eddie that time. She sucked dry our water and she's now after our blood, that's my guess.'

'*Mrs Tan.*'

'Which makes sense,' as Vic observed to Rio, standing a little apart. 'It couldn't still be poor old Brenda Miriam, ex-Presidentiable with the happy turn of phrase. "Fungus-face" – remember that? Anyway, her airspace was different. She used to fly out of Tondo.'

'There you are. It seems we're all after the same devil, each of us for our own reasons. I expect it'll turn out to be a complete illusion,' Rio added wisely, as a man who has seen ten thousand leads drain away into sand and a career's-worth of suspects evaporate. 'You think you're wasting your time here, don't you?'

'Don't you? If it's just vampires you're talking about?'

'Oh, probably,' said Rio, to whom wasted time was part of the job. 'But there'll be something underneath it somewhere. There always is. I thought I got a whiff of it in Eddie's house earlier. I was talking to his wife – I've known her a couple of years now. She's a complete contrast. Hard worker, tough, no messing about. I thought she was uneasy today, as if she was hiding something, you know? Ah, is this your Englishman coming? So look, Vic, let's stay in touch. I'm glad we met. I can tell the wife I spent the morning with a famous journalist. She's also a fan of yours.'

Prideaux was hurrying because he had become lost and then finally delayed. He had formed the impression that San Clemente was small and compact, a thinnish triangle skewed into barely an acre or so. But as he'd hurried after Fr. Herrera's stocky figure the barrio swallowed him up so that it appeared to go on without limit in every direction he took. He felt oversized, too, squeezing through the passageways and ducking low under protruding beams and sheets of tethered plastic. The cries were soon taken up: *Kano! Kano!* The American who wasn't one, who couldn't be bothered to stop and explain yet again. 'Hey, Joe!' The GI who wasn't one, either. With great effort he caught up with the priest's scurrying form, at the moment of placing a hand on his shoulder realising it was the wrong colour T-shirt. 'Hello, my friend,' said a total stranger affably. 'Where you go?'

But Prideaux never answered. He had caught sight of another figure at the end of the alley into which he had blundered. At this point the beaten earth lane was quite straight and led gently uphill between cupboard-sized stores with their wooden shutters propped up like box lids parallel to the ground. Built to allow a shorter population to pass comfortably beneath, they came at his eye level so that he was forced to duck and crane to see clearly. The figure was standing only twenty yards away, looking back at him. Suddenly a line of sight opened up between them and their eyes met. Prideaux immediately registered dread racing into him. *The Rotting Man.* The disgust he felt was explicable enough. Even at this distance he could see the misshapen head, the features encrusted with lumps and tumours. At first he thought the man's scalp had sprouted leaf-like tags of discoloured skin, then saw he was wearing a camouflage net designed to fit over a military helmet. From beneath this olive mop of plastic tatters, a madman's laurel crown, the creature held his gaze for a long moment. The dread intensified until the man turned abruptly away, making as he did so a strange gesture at once imperious and forlorn, flinging up a stump of right hand so the fascinated watcher caught the twinkle of open sores in the brilliant light.

A boy with a sack on his head bumped Prideaux from behind, jolting him to one side and out of the clutches of the dream into which he had fallen. He became aware of pairs of eyes watching him from behind the chicken wire covering the little storefronts, peering out between the dangling strips of sachets containing detergent powder, shampoo and toothpaste. Dim hands covered shadowy mouths. Soft giggles leaked out. He turned and tried to retrace his steps, haunted by the vision of the scarecrow creature standing as though on a skyline, so powerfully had it erased the shantytown setting. Just at the instant when Fr. Herrera himself turned out of a doorway and right into his path Prideaux thought he recognised the gesture The Rotting Man had made. It was an infantryman's arm signal: *Close Up* or *Follow Me*, he couldn't quite remember.

'Ah,' Fr. Herrera greeted him. 'Yes, they said there was a foreigner here today. I knew it was you from the description. Came up with the Press, didn't you? The vampires of San Clemente exercising their fascination.'

'Never mind that. I've just seen the most extraordinary person.' Prideaux described the figure which had stood and stared at him, it seemed from nowhere earthly.

'Oh, him,' said the priest. 'Sounds like you saw poor Melchior.'

'Who is he? How on earth did he get like that?'

But Fr. Herrera's mood today was unaccommodating, as if his mind were on other things and was not to be deflected. 'Who is anyone?' he asked unhelpfully. 'How did any of us get like this? He looks like that because he's sick. Dying, no doubt. He lives rough up there in the cemeteries because he's on the run. It's his choice. He won't let anyone help him.'

'Is he mad?'

'Mad? Not a bit. Very interesting guy, you ought to meet him. Used to be in the military down south. I'm sure he could help with your researches into stress. He, too, is atoning. He, too, yearns for clean hands.'

'The man I saw was probably yearning for any hands at all.'

'The hardest thing to accept,' said Fr. Herrera, ignoring him, 'is the absence of the Day of Judgement.'

Prideaux now thought the priest himself was exhibiting signs of stress. The expansive debater of their lunch together seemed to have been replaced by someone more driven, more oracular, as though he were preoccupied with putting together a definitive sermon which had to be delivered shortly and might make or break his career. Before Prideaux could explain that he must be getting back to Vic, and ask directions, Fr. Herrera was off again.

'Only yesterday somebody told me that Judgement Day was an absurd and cruel piece of mythology. Wrong! It's not absurd at all.

People have to believe what they do has consequences, whether roasting for ever in hell or condemned to suffer a thousand more lifetimes locked into the cycle of grasping and loss which Buddhism calls the *samsara* of this earthly life.'

Passers-by were stopping to listen. Prideaux was gripped by an old, familiar rage at yet again finding himself the object of an impromptu public lecture. Was there something about his face? Some quality of laxity or undecidedness which made people feel obliged to hector him back onto the solid ground of moral debate?

'Even in a barrio like this,' Herrera indicated his parishioners, 'where you'd expect to find belief less spoiled by sophisticated cynicism, I don't find much apprehensiveness about eventually being brought to book. This has a real consequence. I don't think it makes us behave worse. As I keep saying, I tell these people they're perfectly free to murder and cheat and steal if they like, but not many take me up on my offer. No, the real consequence is we become depressed and demoralised. Each day we get wind of appalling crimes, not just in this country but all over the world. Slaughters, starvings, rapes, beatings, tortures, bombings. Huge sums of money pilfered which could have saved people's lives. Even huger sums spent on hateful and ingenious weapons. Utterly ruthless men in this or that uniform ordering whole villages to be gassed or starved out as part of some private political strategy. And we look on impotently, knowing that virtually none of them will ever be made to account for it here on earth, let alone in heaven. The suspicion gradually grows. . .'

(It does indeed, Prideaux told himself.)

'. . . that the Courts of God are also full of hoodlums in robes. Why not? Doesn't the allegedly Loving Father himself stand by as his innocent children are ground up like fish meal? A few years will pass and memory will shift, and the men who did the grinding will have changed into politicians' suits and be addressing the UN to much applause. Statesmen now. And those who ran drug cartels will have children who know very little about how the family acquired its fortune, and *their* children will know nothing. They'll be at private schools and colleges in the States and Europe. By then they'll be old money. Time, the great launderer. Why blame them? According to Horace, though innocent, they must expiate their fathers' sins; but the modern world doesn't work like that. The golden word "amnesty" is spoken and tainted money becomes instantly clean. Torturers go free. The hunt for absconding dictators is called off.

'So if I lament the loss of people's faith – and I do,' said Fr. Herrera, 'I lament the loss of Judgement Day even more. If you lose your faith in all forms of accountability, whether here or after death, the heart goes out of you. The truly good couldn't care less about being rewarded because living well is the best revenge, but they wouldn't mind seeing the truly bad paid back. Why? Not for their own self-righteous pleasure, but because if they aren't the word "justice" loses all meaning and we may as well all go back to the jungle and stop pretending to be civilised creatures with souls.'

Most of the crowd which had gathered to listen to their priest's satanic advocacy would surely have missed most of it, Prideaux thought, for his English made no concessions. The speech was aimed unequivocally at him, the foreigner in their midst (but why, though?). However, its general tenor – apparently an impassioned plea for justice – was applauded on all sides. There was even the odd fervent 'Amen!' and 'Siya nawa!', for all that their priest's brand of liberation theology sounded radical to the point where Prideaux almost expected to catch a sudden stench of brimstone or see troops burst from the shanties and arrest him. He quite wished they would; it would save him having to listen to any more diatribes. He began to move sheepishly away, a sidling which finally took him to the edge of the little throng undetected, as he thought. He was wrong.

'Think about justice, John!' the priest called after him. 'You'll see it's the only consideration. Think about justice before you write your dissertation on stress. Or was it our *dis*tress? I can't remember now.'

He found he had only to turn a single corner to glimpse the lone palm's crown among the rooftops. From there it was a short walk down to where, with relief, he could see Vic Agusan standing near the rickety table in conversation with a tough-looking middleaged man in a vaguely authoritarian pair of fawn slacks.

As they walked back to the Hersheymobile Prideaux said, 'I got trapped by a rogue priest and bawled out in public. Half this barrio now thinks I'm a criminal.'

'That's unusual,' said Vic, who was thinking about his new alliance with Inspector Dingca.

'Weird. He was the one I gave lunch to some weeks ago. I may have told you. But even weirder, I saw this really extraordinary guy, all lumps and wounds. Just rotting where he stood. Gave me this crazy wave.'

'More denizens of squattertown.' Vic was clearly preoccupied. 'Who was that you were talking with just now?'

'That,' said Vic, 'was Inspector Dingca, a colleague of your friend and mine, Sergeant Cruz. You remember Sergeant Cruz? Well, they're both on at Station 14 and this is in their patch.' As they passed the guard standing by the barrier at the entrance to the cemetery he gave the man some coins. 'Old Hershey's still there, see? Even kept its hubcaps. You bothered? Priests and derelicts ganging up on you and now here's a mean-looking bastard who's a colleague of the man we filmed tipping bodies out of barrels? That makes you some sort of accessory. Getting a bit near the edge for an academic anthro?'

'It's *not understanding* that's the hard part.'

'So relax. Dingca's okay. He and I may have a deal going.'

'About Cruz?'

'He doesn't know I'm interested in Cruz. Forget Cruz. He's unfinished business. He'll keep. . . How about that buffoon, then, what's his name? Tugos. The vampire man who drove into the wall before tossing his cookies? There's your ghost story. What a waste of time! In three days San Clem'll be back off the map and the story'll be dead. A veteran reporter speaks.'

Spoke, and could hardly have been more mistaken. Three days later it was not the story which was dead but Eddie Tugos.

20

I N T H E P I T of her own making Sharon had dug on for many months, for what seemed a lifetime, the shadow of San Agostin church falling across the canvas awning overhead. So often had she straightened up to blink the sweat from her eyes and stretch her neck muscles that she could now tell the time accurately by this shadow. Working inside a sundial while digging backwards through time afforded ample opportunity to relect on her own mortal progress, especially since late one afternoon she had decided there was no point in digging down further. She had reached the end. Below her feet lay nothing but alluvial gravel which the Pasig had deposited in one of its prehistoric meanderings. Beneath that was the vast compacted history of a planet without people.

The next day she had been waylaid in her office by a vacationing American and his family who had wanted a list of fieldwork projects in which his children might participate unpaid for a couple of weeks. Why? she had asked. Once all the pieties about broadening young minds had been rehearsed what remained, though largely unexpressed, was the answer to her question: getting ahead. It was all about school projects and grades and CVs. They were amazed to find a fellow-American actually working in this department (looking about them at the dust and brown paint). Only a visiting professor, Sharon had told them. 'Then you'll understand,' they said with relief. 'We've not been in the country long, but they do things sort of differently here, don't they? Relaxed, right? For people like us with only a summer vacation to spare. . .'

Later, she had thought about the effects of living abroad with a settled lover and a shared home. At some point in the last six years, though she couldn't have said exactly when, she had stopped thinking of Manila as temporary, of her presence there as a stay which could be cut short at whim for a return to the 'real' world. This must have coincided with the dilution or actual shedding of certain aspects of what it meant to be American. What she had lost was all too obvious to her once the ambitious parents and their two porky adolescents had filed out of the room clutching a sheet of her departmental writing paper ('Dear Bernie, This is to introduce Mr & Mrs'.) What had gone was all sense of a career. If coming to Manila had once been a shrewd move, staying on had been dumb. Fieldwork was essential; experience abroad looked even better. But not indefinitely. To have stayed abroad implied a paradox: fieldwork that was both obsessive and academically unserious.

From time to time she flew back to California to see her parents, stayed a few weeks, became restless after an initial three days spent in a whirl of pleasure visiting friends, revelling in half-forgotten tastes, marvelling at how clean and easy everything was. On a couple of occasions Crispa had come too, but they had not been wholly successful. To spare her Orthodox father's sensibilities they had had separate rooms and behaved with the ghastly decorum of pals. Sharon had also been obscurely ashamed that her home town was not on the fabled coast but forty miles inland on a road which ran up the valley of the Santa Clara River, heading for the Mojave Desert. There again, the area whose principal towns were Ravenna and Acton was close enough to San Fernando to make an outsider wonder whether it wouldn't have been better simply to have moved down into Los Angeles proper or out of the region entirely. L.A.'s proximity, with its huge Filipino population, had made Crispa uneasy. She hadn't wanted to be taken for a misplaced member of that community, as an economic refugee, as yet another scrambling Asian in the grip of The Dream. She was, in fact, one of that probably large (but seemingly tiny) number of her compatriots who didn't want to emigrate, not even to the States; who were never less than courteously impressed by the deal offered but who remained unenticed.

So there they were, Sharon supposed: two people who according to conventional wisdom had blown their respective career chances. She by a fatal flaw in her national character had turned down ambition and was foreseeably doomed to remain a visiting professor (some visit!) on a salary ludicrous by American standards and only made livable by the supplement she received from her university in California. Likewise Crispa had not availed herself of the opportunity offered by Sharon's nationality. This single factor had probably done more than anything else to cement their friendship by neutralising any corrosive suspicion of ulterior motives. In any case there was a price to be paid for all this wilful behaviour. *Do it. Be it. Go for it.* These were the mottoes for living, by disobeying which Sharon knew herself to be no longer as American as she had been. They were not false, precisely, nor even discredited; simply irrelevant. They presupposed a curious creature, a unique individual never to be satisfied by anything short of a determined act of self-sculpture, hacking itself free of an amorphous block of common clay until it stood perfect and realised and a little breathless with success. If this notion underwrote a Western idealism, then maybe Sharon was becoming Eastern. She knew too much about instability and contingency to believe any longer in personal destinies manifest from the egg. To hell with genes. Nothing but compromise and the awareness of compromise made anybody anything. All else was role playing, the futile trying on of masks.

Now as regards role playing: what was this Ysabella Bastiaan person up to? What image was this temporary assistant of hers hacking her way towards? Manila was changing her, too. A certain haughtiness always would remain but whole lumps of affectation had fallen away from her. To take a single example, she no longer bothered to remove the labels from the clothes she bought. 'What's the point?' she'd said, returning from a shopping trip down Rizal Avenue with stonewashed Levi's and Lacoste sports shirts for herself and a Slazenger basketball for some street kids living behind her block on Roxas. 'They're all fake anyway, the whole lot. It's a much better idea. Manila's *full* of better ideas. Nobody I know would be seen dead with anything genuinely by Pierre Cardin or Nina Ricci, so strutting around with the bogus article's actually quite chic as well as being liberating. Who cares? Down in Santa Cruz you can buy great rolls of jeans labels, have you seen? All the brands, brilliant imitations. They look absolutely genuine to me. I presume the rag trade buys them in bulk and sews them on their own stuff. Oh, and those wonderful hangdog men flashing counterfeit Rolexes at you. Everyone assumes it's a pathetic yearning on the part of poor folk dazzled by the all-important tokens of successful living. Just at the moment I'm taking it as more than fifty percent deliberate mockery. It's fabulous.'

Well, perhaps Ysabella hadn't changed that much. But in the intervals between shopping sprees and often during work her face could be glimpsed wearing the thoughtful expression of somebody forced to do serious stocktaking. 'A place like this makes you re-think home,' she said once. And it did, of course. Not only the private angle for both of them (foreign lover, assassinated father) but for Sharon especially there was also the business of being American in an ex-American protectorate, ex-colony by any other name. Impossible to see in action an entire administrative system – Flag, Constitution, Senate, Congress, judiciary, everything down to the lowest levels of grade school – without being made conscious of its model. Equally impossible to see the instances in which that model had been travestied without wondering if the original hadn't itself become something of a travesty even in the United States. What the Founding Fathers would have thought of plea-bargaining was one thing; but would they really have maintained that a people's freedom still lay in the right to fill their houses with high-powered firearms, a citizens' militia bearing Saturday night specials? And notions of democracy itself, supposedly the United States' most valuable export, had surely lost something at home when mass votes were regularly swayed by the advertising muscle of commercial and other interests. When transplanted to a former colony they lost a good deal more when citizens were as free as air to vote for the candidate who handed out the most cash from the back of a jeep and who had the most terrifying goons outside the polling booth. There was nothing exclusively Filipino in this democracy. It was merely a faithful reproduction, on a national scale, of the version once purveyed by Tammany Hall, the Democratic Party's own organisation in distant Manhattan.

Sharon supposed the final sign of her shedding crude aspects of her cradle nationality was that the instinct with which she had once risen to defend it had gone, transferred to a weary combativeness when faced with the grosser Western misreadings of the East. Had she herself once shared them? She presumed she must have, just as Ysabella still did: that amused, urbane way of making parallels, often beginning with the phrase 'What this place is, is –' and going on after thought, 'The Weimar Republic! That's it! Bit far-fetched, but you know what I mean. Wild moral laxity hand-in-hand with economic instability and political decadence. Partying on the rim of a volcano.' (Always that damned volcano.) These days this struck Sharon as the quintessential outsider's view; an exploiter's view, above all, eyes gleefully open for the main chance with zero accountability. From inside the society, though, her own view was one of codes of behaviour still surprisingly traditional, still demanding, even relentless, but which had a habit of effacing themselves when they brushed up against Western mores. A meekness, a passivity, a declining to confront, a withdrawal. She liked this now. It had come to seem like a sign of strength; but she was still perfectly American enough to know how it struck the foreigners themselves. For many of them the Philippines was simply a place where people from the developed nations came to empty out their seminal vesicles, much as their governments looked at poor countries generally as good places in which to dump their toxic wastes. Out of this grew the image of a Weimarian moral anarchy they half expected and more than half desired: of mothers implacably spreading their own children's legs that the rich might more easily enter. The needle's eye.

Early one afternoon Sharon was called to the phone, returning with a puzzled expression to where she and Ysabella were planning a permanent Intramuros exhibit for the museum.

'I'm afraid I've got to go out for an hour. It seems I have to see a cop.'

'Trouble?'

'I sure hope not. He's someone I met here about three years ago. I needed reminding but I do vaguely remember him. We had a scandal here: stuff was disappearing a bit too fast and a VIP visitor noticed. They sent some cops over and this guy was one of them. This isn't about that, though. He says he's got a pot he wants to show me.'

'Why can't he come here, then?'

'I asked him that. Says he doesn't want to make it too official.'

'Flimsy. Where are you meeting him?'

'Paco Park.'

'Why don't I come too?'

'I didn't like to ask,' Sharon admitted. 'But thanks. It'd be a lot less risky. In this city you can never tell, can you? A voice on the phone turns out to be a dingaling, a rapist or a perfectly normal cop black-marketing antiques.'

Ysabella had never visited Paco Park before and was not expecting it to be less a park than a cemetery. It was a perfect circle of high Spanish stone walls built thick enough to accommodate the long niches for coffins, each sealed with a square plaque. Together the inscriptions commemorated countless colonials who had mostly fallen victim to the various plagues and epidemics which had periodically ravaged Manila in the Eighteenth and Nineteenth centuries. At one point on the circle a small church grew out of the wall. Old trees spread their shade over stone benches on which students sat in twos and threes, doing each other's homework and flirting decorously.

'That's him,' Sharon said at once, spotting a middleaged man with greying hair sitting by himself. 'Yes, I do remember him.'

'Looks a tough customer to me.'

'I remember that look. He's okay, for a cop. Or he was then. Anything might have happened to him in three years.'

'It must be a very small pot,' Ysabella observed as they approached, for the figure was sitting empty-handed with no bag in sight. 'Be careful.'

The man stood up. 'Miss Polick?' he said, offering his hand to Sharon. 'I remember you exactly. You haven't changed at all.'

'Neither have you, er, Lieutenant.'

'Inspector. That's changed, anyway. Inspector Dingca.' Ysabella took the offered hand which felt like a piece of board. A good face, she thought; an impossible face, really, being both tough and sorrowful, depending on how one read it. 'I apologise for this, Miss Polick,' he said. 'It looks shady, I know, not coming to the Museum. But I've promised someone I'd be as discreet as possible and you know how it is. You turn up in one office and tell your tale, then they say they're not really the right people to be talking to and off you go and do it all over again further down the corridor. By the time you've finished everyone in the building knows.'

Sharon had to concede this and was reassured. 'So what's the story?'

The policeman sat down again and from his pocket pulled a small cotton bundle. Beneath the lightweight windbreaker, Ysabella noticed with a thrill, the butt of a gun showed, tucked into the waistband of his trousers. It seemed an authentic touch. The man undid the bundle which was a knotted handkerchief containing shards of pottery and a few pencil-thin fragments of bone. 'These,' he said. 'They've just been dug up. Go on,' he added as Sharon's hand went out to pick up a shard.

'Not in the city?'

'Right here in Manila. About three miles away, I'd guess. Not more. I'm sorry if you're disappointed. I should've explained the pot wasn't in one piece.'

'It doesn't matter.' Her fingers were fitting it roughly together with the practised topological skill of a jigsaw puzzle addict. 'It's all one pot, anyway.' She showed it to Ysabella, a blue and white porcelain bowl as thin as a sea urchin's shell. 'A beauty. When was this found?'

'A few days ago, a week. This person I know was having a pit dug for a CR. She tried to keep quiet about it because she was afraid of what might happen if the news was leaked to the wrong people. They've also found a skull. But it's going to get out now, anyway, hence the rush. I thought if you could tell me if this thing's interesting or just worthless rubbish we'd know how to handle it when the story breaks. It would help us a lot.'

'Is this it or are there more?'

'I think this is the only pot they've found but apparently there were more of these chicken bone things.'

'How deep's the pit?'

'Oh, three metres? Maximum. Probably less. I had a look at it.'

'That's a hell of a latrine.'

'She's a hell of a woman,' he smiled. 'She doesn't do things by halves.'

'She certainly hasn't this time. We'd have to see the site, of course; but if this pot wasn't planted deliberately and if these bits of bone really are from the same hole, then we could have a major discovery on our hands. What do you make of it, Yzzy? Any opinions?'

'You know I'm no expert on ceramics. Off the top of my head I'd say late southern Sung or maybe early Yüan.'

'So would I.'

'Doesn't mean a damn thing to me,' said the Inspector. 'Sounds Chinese. Do I take it this isn't something they broke last week in the kitchens of the Lotus karaoke on Mabini?'

'Correct,' Sharon said. 'Though unfortunately it *was* broken last week. Look at these edges: they're clean. If they'd been lying broken

207

under eight feet of earth for the last seven hundred years they'd be quite a different colour. Also, there'd be some infiltration beneath the edges of the glaze, but there's none. It's a shame. It's vital that the site's properly dug. There's probably more stuff like this waiting to be smashed.'

'Seven hundred years?' The policeman was still getting to grips with this immense slab of time. 'You mean as old as that church over there?'

'Good God,' said Sharon, 'about four times as old. I doubt if that's much older than the beginning of last century. Probably less. We're talking about a date roughly around 1280. And these bones aren't chicken, they're human. Children. These two are metatarsals or possibly phalanges. Almost certainly the foot bones of a kid, somewhere around four to six years old, I'd guess.'

'I don't do forensics,' said the Inspector with the faint belligerence of someone whose expertise has been trumped.

'Now's your chance to learn,' Sharon told him briskly. She looked him full in the face. 'Level up, okay? This isn't a scam someone's pulling?'

'I can't swear to it,' the man admitted, 'because I didn't see the stuff dug up. I wasn't there. But I've known the woman ever since I was posted away from this area here,' he glanced around, 'and her I trust. It was her husband who dug it up.'

'But him you don't?'

'Old Eddie? Well, now.' The Inspector smiled reflectively. 'Put it this way. Old Eddie keeps a weather eye peeled for the smart move. Only trouble is, he's too nice for that kind of smarts. Too dumb, too. Too nice, too lazy, too drunk. He might steal your pooch if it had a bit of meat on it but this sort of caper's way out of Eddie's league. Far too elaborate. No, if this was a hoax it would have to have been planned by someone with real knowledge. You're talking about salting, right? The old "My God, I've found a gold mine – look, take this bit of gold and get it analysed" trick. Sure. But not this one. I don't see it. I'm betting it's the real thing.'

'Then what we could have is another find like the one at Sta. Ana, which incidentally is just down the road from here. That would be something else. An untouched pre-Hispanic burial site in the city? That's big.'

'So what do we do?' the Inspector asked. From his expression

208

Ysabella thought he was not a man who relished finding himself out of his depth.

'Okay. First, is the site secure? I mean, is it on private land which can be locked up? Somebody's back yard?'

'No. Just the opposite. It's a squatter area.'

'Oh God. If we're not careful we'll get a free-for-all. Have you got colleagues you can trust?'

'Some,' said the policeman cautiously.

'Then in my opinion you ought to organise a guard at once. Twenty-four hour job. I'd like to come up and look at it right away to make quite sure, okay with you? If it checks out we'll have to get the help of someone big enough to give us the chance to do a proper dig, easy clearances, site security, etcetera.'

'Your director?'

'Er, no. Not him. But I think now's the time to go see your illustrious family friend, Yzzy. The one you don't have to name but whom you owe for hospitality?'

'Him?' But the more she thought about Ben Vicente the more Ysabella knew Sharon was right. A collector himself, he would have an interest in seeing the site protected from ordinary scavengers and pot-hunters, the 'vamps' as Sharon called them. As to whether some of the finer pieces they might discover would wind up on his own shelves, that was another matter and in a sense not her business. In any case it would be preferable to seeing things smashed by common looters or smuggled out of the country.

A soft, hollow moaning broke all their trains of thought at this moment as a toddler stopped by their stone bench and stared at them solemnly. As he did so he absentmindedly conducted some inner concert with a dayglo lime-green plastic baton, a groan tube whose internal plummet slid up and down with mortal wheezings. Only then, looking up and smiling, did Sharon know how clearly she would remember this moment in Paco Park, the sunlight falling with the lavishness of benediction on this serious child and his brilliant toy, the quiet knots of students comparing notes in this old plague spot. The burst of excitement had been delayed, suppressed by her being expected to give a professional opinion, to keep a balanced and decisive head. But she had known from the instant she saw the freshly broken fragments lying in the policeman's handkerchief. She had known that this was not another of the frauds she had been invited to connive at or fall for over the last six years. Something genuine had been found and she, Sharon Polick, was about to authenticate the site. And maybe, she thought with this smile she couldn't help, those few minutes' delay proved for certain that she wasn't ambitious. To be associated with the discovery and identification of a site, let alone with its excavation, was a career opportunity granted to few archaeologists. Always assuming it was a site, of course, and not just a chance pot in a hole. But the bones. . .

'Can you get in touch with your man?' she asked Ysabella. 'Like now?'

'If he's upstairs I can pull him out of the chamber. If he's not I'll track him down.'

'I'll go with the Inspector here and have a look at this place. What's it called?'

'San Clemente.'

'Never heard of it. Remember the name, Yzzy, but don't tell your man yet. It might be premature.'

'Isn't that the place. . .? Now where have I. . .?' Ysabella the newspaper-reader began, then 'Got it. Vampires, right? Or ghosts or something.'

'Quite right,' said the Inspector, evidently surprised by a foreigner who kept up with popular local news.

'So are they connected?'

'Here, anything is possible.'

Outside Paco fire station Dingca's jeep gleamed silver. They dropped Ysabella back at the Museum before heading towards Lawton, Sta. Cruz and the drag northwards through noxious traffic.

'If you don't mind, Miss,' said the Inspector decorously, 'I'd just like to drop by the station first and pick up a guy. Don't worry, he's okay. Young, but he's got the makings of a first-rate cop. Name of Benhur.'

Two hours later Sharon climbed with some difficulty up an improvised ladder (a single pole to which Eddie had nailed slats crosswise) out of the Tugos family's new septic tank. She was smeared with mud and so elated she was trembling. In the back pocket of her jeans were the spoon and knife borrowed from Nanang Pipa with which she had just unearthed an infant's skull and a tiny greyware dish. These had preceded her out of the pit in a basket on a length of string. She ascended into a cloud of faces.

'Almost certainly a burial ground,' she told Dingca. 'That means there's probably lots more stuff. You can forget gold, I'm afraid,' she added to Pipa, returning the cutlery. 'It's not that sort of treasure. Just bones and tradeware, probably. But it's extremely important. I'm sorry to tell you your CR's going to become a national site.'

'Oh great,' said Eddie, who apart from a headache had largely recovered from his gin-sodden morning with the Press. 'First we can't sleep for vampires and now we can't shit by decree.' He had got over his initial amazement at Sharon's fluency in Tagalog. 'Who do we pay if we want to fart?'

'Eddie!' said Pipa scoldingly. '*Bastos!*' There was laughter.

'I'd just like to remind you yet again that none of this would have happened if it hadn't been for you,' retorted her husband. 'Only a week ago we were quite happily crapping as we'd always crapped. Then suddenly it wasn't good enough. Suddenly this was no longer San Clemente, it was Forbes Park. Next week it'll be sauna baths and tennis courts –' he swept his hand around to encompass the shack walls which hemmed them all in, standing in the slimy and malodorous gully strewn with green slugs of duckshit. 'My wife has plans for a two-car garage,' he confided mendaciously. 'While I'm out perfecting my driving technique who's going to volunteer to help build it? Only *bayanihan*, I'm afraid, but she'll supply *merienda*. As many arrowroot biscuits as you can eat.'

He does love his audience, thought Dingca to himself. This man's one of nature's performers. The laughter which his extravagance earned seemed to expand but not to swell him, while even his wife couldn't be really angry in the face of such spirited fantasy. 'There we are,' said Dingca in his best policeman's pacific manner. 'I'm afraid it can't be helped. It's been found and that's that. I'm placing this pit off-limits as of now and Officer Daldal will stand here and guard it until I get back.'

But Eddie still hadn't quite finished. He looked haggard and dishevelled after gin and sleep and his voice was aggrieved. Yet the tone of heavy irony which he'd adopted was too powerful and too popular to allow him a change of mood into genuine anger. He only bellowed 'Is this justice?' with a wild upwards appeal to the nearby palm tree which hung its unmoving fronds, burnished with evening light, like rooster feathers. 'Down here, some poor sod finds a skull and that's it: all further bowel movements forbidden by law. Up there,' he swung an arm to indicate the Chinese cemetery, 'the place is asshole deep in skulls and what do they have? Flushing toilets! And, of course, telephones. Call your ancestors collect! Another Philtel miracle!'

And so on. That was how Rio was destined to recall him when Eddie, too, joined the ghosts: a man on a hill at sundown delivering a stream of ebullient words in a voice with a dark edge running through it. At that moment the sense of community was very solid: village elders gathered beneath a palm tree's ordinary splendour to examine an ominous pit from which a common threat boiled up in invisible vapour. From nearby and afar came muffled waves of children's voices soaring in excitement and sagging in groans, interspersed with vigorous clapping. All over San Clemente, as all over the city and the nation, the latest TV soap was playing to barefoot audiences crammed around flickering screens at the day's end. *Mga Yagit ng Lansangan*, 'Street Trash', revolved around a squatter family's life and tribulations, and an entranced urban poor could at last watch their own counterparts saying their daily lines for them. *Dallas* had been about men from Mars growling in Martian; *Mga Yagit* was about kids from the barrios speaking street argot.

The sound of this devoted participation rose and fell on the drowsy air. Dingca assumed that the skulls buried eight feet below where he was standing had also once met to gossip at sundown while children had sung and played in groups on the grassy hillside. And one day, presumably, other feet would walk and talk and laugh a couple of oblivious metres above his own emptied head (he glanced involuntarily upwards). There was no making sense of *that*. Just layers covering and being covered in their turn, sinking forever further from the light of day. Well, it was getting to be time to quit, that was for sure. Policemen couldn't afford such thoughts. It was strange how in middle age a new meaning for death crept up on one like lengthening eyesight, changing the focus of everything. Somehow death on the streets, death as duty – which any cop was familiar with and even ruefully prepared for – had a completely different flavour from this inexorable obliteration. Death in the line of duty positively glowed, was masked in pageantry. All those rites and taps and rolls of honour and posthumous medals made it seem less than final. While he'd still been at Station 5 he'd often been struck, even puzzled, by the verse which was the first thing anybody saw when coming down the steps of WPDC Headquarters on United Nations Avenue, engraved in cement capitals:

GO SPREAD THE WORD
TELL THE PASSERS-BY
THAT IN THIS LITTLE WORLD
MEN KNEW HOW TO DIE.

Ever the civilian at heart, Rio thought the sentiment more appropriate for soldiers. It was like admitting that the city's streets were killing fields and always would be, which struck him as defeatist and wrong. But it was noble stuff all the same, a lot nobler than the thoughts which came from watching skulls dug from so far underground in San Clemente. He had never seen anything as thoroughly forgotten.

On the walk down Sharon said, 'Now I'm afraid it's your turn to do some quick digging.'

'How so?'

'Because the vital question which has to be answered is, Who owns this land?'

'You're right.' But even his cop's certainty had become clouded by his reflections, for the idea that anyone could own land, even in San Pedro, Laguna, struck him suddenly as absurd. How could layers be owned? Time to quit, all right.

21

'MINIMALISM', wrote Ruth, 'is a bit of a bore, don't you think?' Many thousand miles away her father slanted her letter to the light by the window. Outside, the traffic roared and honked and smoked. 'We've been doing Steve Reich's *Six Pianos* & for the first three minutes you think Golly, how pretty, how complex. Then you begin to wonder if Bach didn't say it all a lot more tersely in the C minor prelude of WTC Bk 1. After ten minutes you want to scream *Where's the beef!!?* Plenty of sensibility, interesting sonority, ingenious cross-rhythm etc, but it's all just language without substance, I swear it is. It's the development I miss, real musical thinking which drags you along & makes you go Yes, that's a new thought, rather than Yes, that's a new effect. Oh, did you know? They want Jess to go to New York for a year. I don't suppose she's told you. I'm betting she won't come back, what do you think? Poor Mum. Underneath all that conferencing & power dressing they're restless & uneasy, these TV execs. I think they're frightened everyone's suddenly going to decide it's a nice sunny day and stop watching. It isn't a nice sunny day here in Durham. The rain falls & falls & everything's chill & skiddy & old people break their hips on the pavement outside Tesco's & I know why you're in the tropics.'

Lately Prideaux was wondering whether after all he'd been such a failure as a father. Weren't Ruth and he in regular touch, writing each other affectionate, easy, amused letters? Other parents he knew received nothing from their children away at university but occasional poisonous telephoned demands for funds. Imperious or wheedling, these were not always telephoned, either, but might be voicelessly faxed or E-mailed. The cry in the night which had once brought parents stumbling sleep-drugged from bed for months on end had finally congealed into sentences of ghostly green letters on a screen. He didn't love his ex-wife and now knew he never really had, though the ungentlemanliness of admitting so still bothered him. It had been one of those media marriages where glamour, loot and career advancement are the dark smear on Cupid's arrow, the curare which partially paralyses judgement and taste.

Jessie had gone, but it now seemed that Ruth had never entirely left. About his love for her Prideaux had no doubts whatever. On almost any day, listening to the news or looking around him, his eyes could fill with tears at the sight of someone of Ruth's age, her life or body or spirit shattered by cruelty or mischance. 'That could be her,' he'd think. Or, seeing a picture of a hollowed-out, anonymous refugee wandering a pitiless badland (it might be Zagreb railway station) carrying a sheet of the cardboard she or he slept on, 'That's somebody's Ruth.' Late, late, late – disgustingly, shamefully late – the discovery that no-one was anonymous: that stick figures panned in a bald African landscape had uncles and aunts and playmates, people who might say of them 'Remember the time he –?' or 'She used to make us laugh.' This secret action of bestowing a name on the nameless always brought pity in an uprush so that wherever he was he wanted to phone Ruth at once and hear her voice. This he could never tell anyone, her least of all. So to that extent, yes, a failure as a father, her fellow-mortal.

A marriage on the rocks had led to this: a survivor standing, letter from another survivor in hand, by an open window in a distant city. A survivor with a new sense of urgency, at least. He must finish up here, somehow bring to conclusion a project whose inconclusiveness he now understood as intimately bound up with everything he had ever done or been. A vague project in a vague course undertaken for motives which might, after all, have been no more than a roundabout way of discovering that he most deeply loved his own daughter. How could it ever have been unclear? Because in the night when things founder all is spray and flying rope-ends and the doomed, shouting to make themselves heard. Later, when offshore a shattered mast and davits jut peaceably from a glassy sea, objects may be found wearing their intactness like surprise, a precious chest unscratched and wedged between tufts of marram grass.

'Finishing up', though, was easily said. He was not working to an obvious clock. He was no youngster on a grant. An open return air ticket, extensible visa and a bank balance that wouldn't miss the odd thousand pounds: these were not necessarily an advantage to the middleaged student-by-default. Recently, however, as Prideaux began to organise his notes (and with them his thoughts) certain strands of interest were starting to emerge. He hesitated to dignify them as themes, still less as theories. There was, for instance, a strand which was interested in hysteria, another in the relationship between internal and external varieties of stress. Somewhere in his sleep these elements felt as though they jelled into an updated theory of *amok*. They certainly didn't on paper. Hysteria happened to be top of the list that particular morning because when Ruth's letter had arrived he'd been in the middle of laboriously translating the popular press's versions of an outbreak at a school in – of all unlikely places – the Armed Forces' HQ at Camp Crame. The reports differed somewhat, according to which of the twenty victims was being interviewed, but generally agreed that a huge red man with horns and tail had suddenly appeared. 'He tried to take us,' said one 12-year-old girl. 'His eyes were all red and glaring.' Or, in another's testimony, he said in a terrible loud voice: 'I'm going to pay you back for what you did to me. I'm going to eat up the whole of Grade 6 in this school! One by one I shall possess you all!' Most of the pupils affected were girls who fell into faints or had screaming fits when presented with a crucifix. The Camp Crame priest was called. He said Mass and burned incense, accompanied by a policeman who now and then performed exorcisms to order with a rosary given him by Pope John Paul II during his papal visit in 1981. The exact nature of the crime for which the children were to be 'paid back' was a puzzle until they remembered having set fire to some rubbish against the trunk of an ancient tamarind tree which 'old-timers' at the camp said was 'home to supernatural creatures known to have lived there since the Spanish regime'. Still another pupil claimed to be possessed by an evil spirit, having seen a woman dressed in black standing by the tamarind. A police chaplain held her head and said a prayer to drive away the demon. It was all in a day's work. Meanwhile, religious groups such as El Shaddai and the Charismatic Foundation insisted that the tamarind tree be exorcised.

A lone voice of reason suddenly spoke up in its defence, a Grade 3 teacher. 'There's nothing whatever the matter with that tree,' she said briskly. 'My classroom's right next to it and in all my years of teaching I've never seen anything strange about it. On the contrary, as a source of medicine, food and shelter it's God-given.' She then went on to observe that the first girl to become 'possessed' had recently been caught shoplifting in one of the camp's mini-groceries. She was 'an imaginative child, psychologically restless. She keeps on drawing things on the blackboard in front of her classmates. Once she started her hysterical fit the others simply took their cue from her.' This redoubtable lady added that in her view it was silly to blame evil spirits for the children's behaviour when there were far more obvious factors like drugs, emotional or family problems. 'You must now excuse me, my pupils are waiting,' she said and stumped off to teach.

'That's the sort of person for me,' thought Prideaux. 'That's who I should have married. Quezon City's Miss Jean Brodie.' The story itself was ordinary enough, but it had been given an interesting gloss by another just reported from Egypt. This was of a full-blown epidemic of schoolgirl fainting which was spreading rapidly through entire provinces. A hundred and fifty girls had succumbed at a single railway station, leading to a local medical crisis since the hospital was far too small to deal with them all. Egypt, too, had its Miss Jean Brodie, a psychiatrist who said that the first thing to do was stop all media coverage of the story at once since hysteria fed on itself. He went on to comment that this was a condition which typically affected the developing world. In wealthier countries there were many ways open to adolescents to express themselves, to be diverted and to discharge their stress. In the developing world, though, and especially in the provinces, there was very little opportunity for self-expression in the face of stultifying social conventions and official indifference. Thus worries were bottled up. Many of these worries were entirely reasonable and concerned things reported in the news such as endemic unemployment and environmental pollution. In these circumstances hysterical outbreaks were hardly to be wondered at.

Prideaux found this interesting because it was the first time he had seen mass hysteria accounted for as a by-product of socioeconomic conditions. The vast majority of documented cases (excluding things like Orson Welles's Martian invasion scare) took place in more or less enclosed communities – typically schools, nunneries, prisons, reformatories and sects living in isolation. If whole nations could fall prey to it as a response to anxiety partly generated by a constant stream of ominous news, would this make a predisposition to breakdown, to full-blown *amok*, less or more likely? Less, presumably, since a hysterical attack was a way of discharging intolerable tension. But maybe it was more open to women to seek this refuge, leaving the men to go doggedly on until they broke and went ape in a McDonald's with an Uzi?

This tied in with another of his strands: that of the way a general external threat could exacerbate purely private stress. The hollow left in him by the decamping of his own wife and daughter had been filled by a dread which had rushed in from all sides. He remembered the sensation clearly. It was as if the rituals of domesticity, no matter how time-serving, had held at bay the general alp of disaster which nowadays towered on everybody's doorstep. It was an unstable mountain, the upright equivalent of the San Andreas Fault. Everyone agreed that disaster was inevitable sooner or later but nobody, not even the insurance companies' actuaries, could put a date on it. The alp was added to daily, its details meticulously and even lovingly described by an army of newscasters and journalists. Beneath a cancer-inducing hole in the ozone layer its crags were variously labelled nuclear holocaust and overpopulation. Its vast screes were environmental collapse. Violence and extremism rumbled around its shoulders while close-up shots of its bare and forbidding faces showed the steady erosion of what little forest remained and the remorseless extinction of beautiful plants and creatures. The alp was in all weathers and from all angles so menacing that even the most optimistic measures which human ingenuity could propose were merely holding operations, remedial forays undertaken by men armed with shovels. Indeed it was so overwhelming that certain people were driven to a kind of desperate revelry. They positively cavorted on its lower slopes in a strange world where advanced technology mediated primitive behaviour. Theirs was a wilderness of futuristic atavism, of neo-Nazi rock groups and parties where parents watched violent videos before buggering each other's children and leaving the victims with a lifetime's guilt for not having been more lovable. There was a steady stream of refugees back from these regions, hollow-eyed, many with puncture marks in their arms and in the throes of terminal disease.

Thus the alp which had shouldered in after Jessie had taken Ruth away with her. It was still there, just as it was everywhere, ever more threatening and lurid and apocalyptic but none the less effectual for that, heaping up anxiety which contaminated even the most private forms of worry. There was no getting away from it, no ignoring it; and in deference to it the art of modern living had largely shrunk to concentrating on how to get away from it or ignore it. That *was* wisdom, and only that. Respectable ways had to be found to deal with the global alp so that the one and only life could be lived out in whatever light its bulk didn't block off. This was not easy. Prideaux increasingly wondered whether it was better to say To hell with respectability and simply stop reading newspapers and watching television. Something terrible was going to happen; we felt it in our bones. Desperate times required desperate measures. And mixed into it all was pity. He had had rather a nice life, all things considered, starting with the inestimable and wholly unearned advantage of having been born among the liberal and well-heeled. But what would it be to grow up in a shanty town, to be a twelve-year-old Egyptian schoolgirl all too conscious of the alp being added to everything she already didn't have, when what there was to tell of grief and dread could be expressed only by epidemic bouts of unconsciousness? And how naturally this pity led to a fear for Ruth's own future, a fear which entailed its own gloomy mathematics. *I might make it through to my threescore years and ten before the alp goes critical, but will she?*

Prideaux shuffled his notes, came upon Ruth's letter again, smelled it tenderly. Even thinking about stress made him anxious. Time to be a bit brisk; time to be worthy of the woman he hadn't married who had withstood the cultural deadweight of policemen brandishing rosaries. If he had chosen this fatuous topic in order to appease an unconscious John Prideaux who was trying to warn him he was headed for breakdown, then that was just the sort of vulgar banality one might expect of one's unconscious. In the meantime it was possible to identify an immediate source of anxiety, if less easy to face it. This was The Rotting Man, whose figure in the intervening few days had haunted him in sleeping as well as waking hours. At first he thought the power came from disgusting physical detail, the distorted head and leprous skin. He kept seeing the head like a battered sponge nodding significantly beneath wild tatters of camouflage and it filled him with its own particular dread. But beyond that lay something else, an entire landscape of unease summoned into being by that right hand's emblematic gesture. Converge On Me. Follow Me. The arm's peculiar sweep was seared forever against blue sky, calling up ghost platoons of elsewhere and elsewhen. Prideaux ran from him in his sleep, or else stood bolted to the ground, but The Rotting Man came no closer. He simply kept turning on the skyline, over and over again throwing up his right arm, locking gazes with the same electric jolt.

Melchior. One of the Three Wise Men whose name to Prideaux as a child had a sad ring to it. Probably a harmless lunatic or a man made eccentric by suffering, for all that Herrera claimed he was not mad. But then the young priest had himself been acting strangely, with his unstoppable open-air sermons. What on earth was going on in that shanty town? It seemed most likely that San Clemente was not at all untypical: that any other barrio could produce its drunks and cranks and occasional vampire. Yet there was something about its position, shallowly rooted on a hillside with the huge Chinese cemetery poised above it, which gave it and its people their own peculiar definition. It reeked of strain. In any case he knew he would have to return. He was going to have to find The Rotting Man again and confront him because there was something between them which would not let him be. He would force himself to perform this act because he was more scared of shirking it, of being thrown back yet again into sick reflection on his own timidity. Time was getting on; ghosts had to be laid. Missing Vietnam was one thing, missing the point far worse.

He thought he wouldn't ring Vic Agusan. Much as he would have preferred company he didn't wish to be dragged down into any more drinking sessions, discussions of vampires and talk about police. These days San Clemente was even more in the news. Apparently a body had been found, so had a skeleton. The two stories had become conflated in Prideaux's mind, not least because he had spent the last few days largely out of town. On impulse he had begun making early morning bus journeys to nearby provinces, escaping the city. In relief he had lain on deserted beaches and wandered around the markets of small towns which took him back to Indochina. These, too, had their slummy side; but the traffic's roar was less and fresh breezes blew in from canefields and pineapple plantations, and he had seen fish offal swept off a market's swilling cement floor into a ravine overhung by heavy vines and feathery stands of bamboo. He had wandered like a freed prisoner, blinking in the sun and gazing into people's faces as if to catch up on something he had missed. Escaping Manila, certainly; but these day trips were also efforts to escape The Rotting Man, as he could now acknowledge. In any case he had not been at home and hadn't called Vic. A part of him was beginning to insist there was little more to learn from a further piling-up of bodies. Each day a dozen men like Sgt. Cruz dumped their victims. The foulness of foul play merely repeated itself without further edification. The corpses were dumb. It was what the pre-corpses could say for themselves which might be interesting. In his mind's eye he had an impression of San Clemente divided into two. The lower part was where all the attention was concentrated (though today's tabloids gave off that exhausted reticence which implied there was currently a lull between the dramatic events of some days ago and expected future developments). The upper part of the barrio seemed to him altogether more mysterious, leaked into by the silence of the strange miniature streets and even stranger mausoleums among which The Rotting Man, that ultimate pre-corpse, flitted and gestured.

So on a sultry morning he took the LRT and walked up past where Vic and he had parked the Hersheymobile to the cemetery's perimeter street. He would simply wander down through the barrio and ask around for 'Melchior'. Soon he had left the Tan family's extravaganza behind and reached the point where the tip of San Clemente's triangle met the wall. A lone tomb stood close to it, one of those seldom visited and even more seldom maintained, to judge from its condition. With its metal window frames, stuccoed curves and flat roof it reminded him of a 1930s cinema, an Odeon among tombs, rusty, flaking, and with bushes growing over the shallow pediment. And like the Odeon (or Regal, or Roxy) there were shattered light fitments across its face, now nameless. Wondering what it looked like from behind, Prideaux discovered something not visible from the street. The tomb was connected with the top of the wall by skeins of wiring which bridged the gap like the brittle flying buttresses of mud termites build so that not even space can hold up their depredations. It was satisfactory the way the liminal held such power in this place. All boundaries had their own potency; and juxtapositions of wealth with squalor such as one could see anywhere downtown were always ironic, if a little too photogenic. Here, though, a subtle unease was added by the wealthy all being dead. They exercised their tyranny over the living on the other side of the wall, while the living retaliated by draining them of unused volts. It was this economy which gave San Clemente its uniqueness, he decided, moving around to the front of the tomb again. Tombs and shanties, liers and squatters, each needed the other in order to retain a full identity. Some way off along the deserted street with its silent, uninhabitable houses, a tall bush glided out of shadow and flung up a limb with a wild fandango gesture. Prideaux felt his blood halt. As from afar he heard his own voice call: 'Hey, I want to talk to you!' and beneath him his feet began to move.

But The Rotting Man only repeated his gay military wave and moved off among the tombs, olive drab rags and camouflage net bobbing in and out of visibility, traversing light and shade and then remaining fixed until Prideaux caught up and found only a shrub with tiny scarlet flowers like wounds. Then, looking about him in frustration and dread he would see again the distant club of a hand in its private semaphore. As they progressed he was aware of two things. The first was that if the streets they crossed were vaguely concentric then they were headed deep into the cemetery. The other, that this was no chase. He realised he could easily catch the hobbling figure ahead. Despite its visual elusiveness and spritelike gestures it was, in fact, moving quite slowly, even painfully. He found himself hanging back, almost out of respect, as if acknowledging that something which had eluded him for so long had always been within easy grasp, a seizable moment.

Through the trees to the right was some sort of church. On its porch steps four men were sitting around a trestle table playing cards. A bottle winked in the sun. Prideaux remembered Vic Agusan having said something about a detachment of cemetery police. Well, detached they certainly were, as unseen through the bushes nearby a middleaged foreigner pursued at walking pace a decaying fugitive from the armed forces. Beside the church a few huts stood beneath acacia trees, selling refreshments to those visitors who came to tend the plots and tombs. A boy lay asleep along a bench in a puddle of shade, hat over eyes, a kitten dozing on his stomach.

If this was the centre, the cemetery couldn't be anything like circular. Not much further on the tombs' condition worsened considerably and, emerging between walls set with niches for coffins, Prideaux came on what was clearly a boundary. There were gaps, as over on the San Clemente side; but instead of a view of shanty roofs here was only a wasteland of tall grasses and low trees. However improbable it seemed in the middle of Manila, his ravaged Pied Piper had led him to the threshold of a savannah. He assumed they must be somewhere near the point where La Loma, North and Chinese cemeteries all touched, the point furthest from the roads which served them, most distant from the expensive and fashionable plots. Here, in the tangle of undergrowth, graves lay opened and empty, their inscriptions leached off by tropical rains. Of their occupants there was no trace. The dead had been raised by robbers, ghouls, dogs. There were the remains of small bonfires, charred patches littered with heat-shrivelled lengths of puce and lime ribbon, a wired bundle of twigs that had been a sheaf of flowers, black meshes into which wreaths had been woven. The sun was strong, the light rebounded from cracked cement surfaces, burned against a forehead already pink from his recent trips into the provinces.

As his eyes adjusted to a nearby patch of shade they resolved a mossy reclining angel into a recumbent figure with its spongy head resting between the pages of an open marble book.

'Five minutes,' said the figure. 'You've never been a soldier.'

'What?'

'It took you five minutes to see me. You died four minutes fifty-nine seconds ago. You were point man. You led your whole platoon into the killing box. Give the man a medal.'

Absurd though it was, Prideaux felt shame rise to his face.

'Okay,' said the figure. 'You were looking for me and I found you. Big deal. I'm Captain Melchior. You're John Something.'

'Father Herrera told you.'.

'Father's good.'

'Yes, he is.'

'Not what I meant,' said Melchior, 'but what the hell. You want to know about stress in this country?'

'It sounds stupider put like that.'

'Yeah. Why don't you move out of the sun? Us baldies gotta watch the sun. You think I might know something?'

'Maybe. It's up to you. Perhaps another piece of the puzzle. I don't expect a definitive revelation as the reward for having pursued the extremest person to the extremest place.'

'Excuse me? You're British, right? The accent. Makes it harder.'

Prideaux, nettled by disadvantages he hadn't considered, asked bluntly, 'What are you wanted for?'

'Murder. Theft. Desertion. Things like that. Why, you scared?'

'No,' he said, surprised to find it true. 'The worst you can do is kill me, steal my money and abandon my corpse.'

'No it's not,' said Captain Melchior. 'Not by a long way. But I'm sick of dying and I'm sick of death.'

'Funny place to choose if you're sick of death,' Prideaux said with an attempt at flippancy. 'A graveyard.'

'Wrong. It's the only place left in this city a guy can hear himself think. Gotta hear yourself think when you're dying. Might overhear something useful.'

Now that he was standing by him, Prideaux found himself able to look down at The Rotting Man without dread and with very little disgust. It helped knowing his name and rank. Now he was Captain Melchior, clearly waiting for the celestial medevac chopper and the Great Corpsman. 'You're a mess,' he said.

'Affirmative.'

Prideaux judged that the worst of his cranial distortion was hidden by the camouflage netting, for the lumps and bulges visible beside his eyes seemed to be part of a mass which had its roots elsewhere. The unnatural width thus given his face made the eyes too close and concentrated their force. All the fingers were missing from his right hand, which ended in a flap of skin like a pasty's crimped edge. The thumb was intact, as was his left hand. Both wrists were covered with open sores which also blotched the long sleeves of the army shirt he wore. The rest of his body gave the impression of being similarly afflicted. Phrases like 'neurofibromatosis' and 'Elephant Man's Disease' went through Prideaux's mind as he confronted this suffering creature, who exuded a bitter pollen smell like pear blossom.

The Captain watched this pitying inventory and clearly hoped to forestall further conversation on the subject by saying 'Incurable.'

'What, all of it?'

'Everything.'

'I'm sure somewhere like Makati Medical Center –'

'*Ay!*' came the interruption. 'The *Kano*'s going to throw money at me! I'm not a squatter, John Something. I'm an ex-Ranger on the run. There's a difference. I'd get to spend a morning in my two-hundred-bucks-a-day bed covered in electrodes before I had a foul dream, woke up in Camp Crame stockade medical centre and found the electrodes now clipped to my balls.'

'Ah, you mean incurable in that sense, then. Daren't be cured rather than can't?'

'No. Either way I'm a dead man. I prefer to do my dying here.'

'Why can't they find you here?'

'Have you any idea how many AFP men are on the run with prices on their heads for bank robberies, kidnappings and God knows what? Thousands. Half the country's gangs are AWOL military and police. There aren't the men available to comb acres of cemeteries just for one miserable Ranger who isn't even armed and who only arranged the death of a commanding officer that deserved far worse. If I'm going to talk,' the swollen head sunk in the Book of Job eased itself tenderly, 'I need something to drink.' Passages of chiselled Latin could be seen surrounding the halo of camouflage netting. 'Soft drinks.'

'I'll get some. What about food?'

'No food. Just Coke.'

Prideaux woke the boy with the kitten on his stomach and thirstily drank two bottles of Sprite. Then he bought a family size Coke, overpaying the boy who was already a little petulant at being woken and now was inclined to be querulous about the deposit and his own lack of change. The bottle emerged from a chest of watery ice and sawdust like a log from a swamp.

'Good and cold,' said Captain Melchior when he took it from Prideaux. He tucked it beneath his right arm, screwed off the cap and drank deeply. 'Oh wow.' He belched. 'You've drunk, haven't you? John Something did some thinking as well as drinking.'

'It would have looked odd, wouldn't it, a foreigner coming out of nowhere and disappearing into the bushes with more than one drink? It's not an obvious place for a picnic.'

'Sure. Wise precaution. Wouldn't have mattered, though. They all know I'm around. How else can I eat? I get my food from them.'

'What about the police in the church?'

'They're okay. They're Catholics. Also they're Chinese. And they're not military. They're not about to help the AFP clean up its shit. I know them all. We've done a lot of talking, specially at night. Don't sleep much nowadays, so we talk. Stories. Politics. The time passes. What they call the graveyard shift, right?'

'And they keep you.'

'Negative. Nobody keeps Captain Melchior. Captain Melchior tells stories and eats rice. We're all Christians, aren't we? Who's counting? They want to hear. They're just city kids, mostly. Never been out of Manila, let alone Luzon. But I was down south for years, all the Visayas but specially Mindanao. Fighting the Moslems. They love to hear about fighting the Moslems in Mindanao.'

'Why that, particularly?'

'Why not? Moslems everywhere are news these days. Here we've got this little old war been going on for years and years, not over in Saudi or somewhere but right here in-country. These kids know nothing. They're boys. Boys like war stories.'

'Men like telling them.'

Captain Melchior focused a brief glare on Prideaux seated on an adjacent grave. Then he uncapped the Coke and took another pull at it. Tawny suds bustled behind the glass. 'Do you enjoy going to confession?' he asked with another belch.

'I don't go.'

'Your funeral. But if you did you wouldn't enjoy it. You're not meant to. When I talk about my life in the Rangers it's confession, gotta be said before it's too late. Not what I did, except a few things, but what we saw, what we knew, how things are. We're weird creatures, know that? Truly weird. One moment dead normal, the next completely out of our gourds. Then back again. Flick-flick. Over and over.'

'Ah. You're going to tell me the story of the good doctor. He's the rock-solid family man who leaves his suburban home at eight every morning, drives to a clinic behind high walls, changes out of his suit, puts on a long white rubber apron and spends the day skilfully eliciting just the right quality of scream for the men with the tape recorder.

There's a sound system in this surgery of his which plays Mozart continuously. The good doctor hums along, occasionally stopping what he's doing to point out the beauty of a particular passage and asking the patient's own opinion. Then back to work. At five o'clock the surgery is sluiced down, the good doctor showers, changes back into his suit and drives home in his unassuming little car. He greets the family, helps the kids with their homework, walks the dog, watches a bit of TV and so to bed. I've heard that story, Captain, don't worry. We've been telling it in Europe for most of this century.'

'Sure you have. I didn't exactly mean that. Now your guy, your doctor, he's pretty much split clean down the middle. Day and night, on duty and off duty, black and white. Compartments, right? I'm talking about the whole time, flick-flick, never one thing or the other. Know anything about electricity? Like AC current, always changing direction. But it happens so fast the light looks steady to us. Normal. Whatever we do kind of smooths out so we think it all hangs together. If you ever stopped, though, bang, right there in the middle of something and looked again you wouldn't hardly believe what you were doing. Me? I'm just sitting here round the fire eating with my good buddies. *Tsibog-tsibog*, chow down. I'm a *what*? I'm a *cannibal*? Don't give me that shit, man. Cannibals are African, right? Big-game hunters tied up in an iron pot, guys in grass skirts dancing around waving spears. Hell, this ain't but ordinary Moslem stew.'

'Moslem stew.'

'Right, right. Not the whole kit, usually. Just bits. Specially ears. You mix 'em in with pork and whatever else. It's the insult. Pork and Islam don't mix, right? They do in Mindanao, though. Point is, it's no grand occasion. Nobody giggles and whispers. Into the pot they go with the chopped onions. Know why?'

'Comradeship.'

For the first time Melchior looked up at Prideaux with something like serious consideration. 'Yeah,' he agreed. 'Epoxy. Sticks us together so's nothing can get us apart. Nothing. All for one, one for all, like the fella said.'

'*The Three Musketeers.*'

'Right. Great movie. You ever had that? The buddy system where you'd do anything, and I mean anything, for the guys you're with because you know they'd do the same for you?'

'I can imagine it,' Prideaux said cautiously. 'I've always been able to imagine it.' He could feel himself physically skirt a pit of longing.

'Ah, man, this isn't imagination. You're out there in the boonies with those guys, I mean sleeping rough, eating rough, that's one hundred percent enemy terrain. Punji stakes smeared with shit, ambush, all that. You never know when. Bad enough dealing with the raggies and the locals betraying your ass but you've got your own side to watch out for, too. You've got commanding officers selling off your equipment to the black market and cutting themselves illegal logging deals in the areas you've bust your balls to win. You've got air-support snafus because the fly-boys are all grounded suddenly. Shortage of fuel. Turns out it's been sold, to hell and gone in unmarked drums. And you've got the pols. New initiatives, light at the end of the tunnel, hearts and minds. Suddenly you discover you're no longer in the Philippines, you're stranded in some chunk of territory they've signed away behind your back called ARMM. Autonomous Region of Moslem Mindanao. Jesus Christ, what's this shit? Retreat! Retreat! And watch your ass before some raggie sticks a Kalashnikov up it and our President tells him no sweat, pull the trigger, that Ranger's got no business in your homeland. So yeah, in those circumstances the world kinda shrinks down to you and your buddies.'

'And Moslem stew.'

'Sure.'

'It's like cops and salvage, isn't it? There's Us and there's Them.'

Captain Melchior was not paying attention. 'Sometimes you get a laugh out of it, though. A while back we had these journalists down, choppered in, coupla guys from Manila and a coupla foreign correspondents. Italians? French? Can't remember. They wanted the whole thing, burnt villages, atrocities, you name it. What they got was hearts and minds from the brass and not much action, just a lot of bumping along lousy trails in jeeps. We could see they were disappointed. What were they going to tell the folks back home? We tried to say it wasn't all settled, not by a long way, they'd just hit a flat spot. What the hell, it wasn't a stage show they'd paid to see, some nonstop performance they could drop in on when they fancied and quit when they got bored. So we gave them an evening of jungle living. We made arrangements and served up this ace dinner, not just ears but an entire guy. Butcher it Chinese-style and you can't tell. We had ourselves a real cook-out, villagers, sing-song, the works. The journalists loved it. Wild deer and *baboy damu*, boar we'd shot on patrol, we said. How do you like it? Swell, great. Next morning they all choppered out again. No-one ever told them. To this day they don't know they ate an MNLF rebel. Laugh? We couldn't stop for days.'

'And that wasn't cannibalism?'

'Hell no. Like I said, that's what Africans do. You're a cannibal if you don't know any better. This was eating a man. You eat a man when you've got good reason. Remember Manero? Don't tell me he wasn't making a point, even if the guy was a missionary.'

It was in connection with this celebrated case not long after Prideaux's arrival that someone had coined the phrase about the notorious porosity of Muntinlupa State Penitentiary. Norberto Manero had been sentenced to life imprisonment for killing an Italian priest, Tullio Favali, in April 1985. Immediately after committing the crime he was witnessed by passers-by laughing uproariously with his fellow-assassins before scooping out the missionary's brains and eating them raw in handfuls. This had made a national impression. It emerged that he had accused the priest of being a communist sympathiser, but in the Cotabato region of Mindanao where he came from it meant he considered Favali had sided with the Moslem Moros. Manero himself was a Christian who had long been engaged in local militia activities against Islamic radicals who wanted independence. Back in the Sixties he had been a member of a dreaded vigilante group called the Ilaga whose vicious skirmishing with the Moslem Blackshirts had directly led to the Moro secessionist war which was declared in earnest in 1973 and still rumbled on. Manero was also an active member of a Christian cult called Tadtad, whose name meant something like 'The Choppers', which specialised in hacking their victims with bolos and quickly eating their entrails in front of their eyes before they could die as an act of ultimate dishonouring. One way and another he was better behind bars. After serving a mere two years in Muntinlupa Manero was transferred without proper authorisation back down to Mindanao, to a small penal colony in Davao from which, averaged out, there had been a jailbreak every thirty-eight hours over the last five years. In his turn Manero duly absented himself, a fact which only came to official notice when he was seen standing a few feet from President Ramos himself at a welcome rally in

Cotabato City. The ensuing outcry provoked reluctant enquiries which exposed an entire chain of complicities and negligence. Police and military involvement in Manero's escape was assumed from the start, and was scarcely at odds with the discovery that in the months before being recaptured he had been working in Central Mindanao as a police 'asset' while being groomed by the military to hunt down the elusive Pimpernel himself, Commander Mubarak, the man with the foetal talisman. Manero had recently been returned, laden with irons and smiling broadly, to Muntinlupa where he was placed under a twenty-four-hour armed guard, less to prevent his re-escaping than to protect him from the senior PNP and military officials he might decide to bear witness against should they ever come to trial for having facilitated his lengthy holiday from jail. This last part of the Manero story was where everybody felt they'd come in. It was the warm, slithery handfuls of brains they remembered.

'You said you fragged your CO?' Prideaux prompted.

There was a pause. Captain Melchior was draining the last of the Coke. He shuddered. 'My taste's all screwed up, you know. This stuff's sweet, right? But just recently it's been getting bitter. It's not the Coke, it's the disease, the nervous system. I smell disgusting smells that aren't there. Herrera comes up, hears my confession, says it isn't nerves, it's conscience. Makes everything bitter and foul. He's just the sort of guy to have around when you're dying. Be right back.'

He swung himself off the tombstone with slow-motion urgency and moved like a scarecrow behind the wall which hid the improbable savannah. Faint sounds of retching reached Prideaux. It was getting on for noon. The sunlight beyond the shade in which he sat was a drench of energy so rich that things no longer looked as clear as they had, blurred by thermals and his own wincing retinas. When he returned, Melchior was moving more easily. He was carrying a green rag which, as he folded and bunched it to cover the Book of Job, was revealed as a military T-shirt. 'Damn marble,' he said as he stretched out and gingerly lowered his puffy head.

'You don't mind talking?'

'Got nothing else to do. You reckon I'm the sort of person does things he doesn't want? Where was I? Yeah. Colonel Half. Colonel Saturnino Calajate. And I never said I fragged him. I said I arranged for him to die. Doesn't matter how. What matters is why. He was the one had the logging deal going. Once for forty-eight hours we couldn't stop rebels consolidating an area we weren't defending because our vehicles couldn't get out on patrol. The whole base was out of gas. How come, since we remembered seeing the Petron truck come in from Cotabato City? The SAO had signed for it and certified it only contained 500 litres. That took care of the Colonel's jeeps okay. The truck turned around and went off and sold the rest of the 30,000 litres cut price to a private gas station. After the driver had got his percentage the Colonel and the Supply Accounting Officer split the rest. Took us some time to work it out but before we lowered his flag for him the Colonel confirmed it. Cost us eleven men to re-take that territory. That kinda thing pisses you off.

'But it wasn't that. He acted improperly towards our dead, and let me tell you no-one, *no-one* messes with any man of mine killed in action. We do it by the book, down to the last comma and period. SOP – and this is the Army minimum – specifies that everyone gets a standard coffin and a fifteen day embalming, right? The body's properly washed, completely dipped in formalin, and the veinous system's infiltrated with formalin. Then you open it up and remove the guts, because that's your prime source of decomposition. You pack it with offcuts of sewing material and *bunot*. You know *bunot*?'

'No.'

'Coconut fibre. The husk, right? But very refined and combed out till it's fluffy like brown wool. Okay. That two weeks gives time for the deceased's relatives to get to the funeral, do the whole thing with decorum. Now, if the relatives are abroad, in the States, wherever, they get a thirty day embalming. Automatic. It's right there in the regulations. That's a more thorough job, more soaking in formalin plus the main veins and arteries are stripped out. You better believe all this costs: refrigeration, mortician's fees, enbalming fluid. The Colonel couldn't figure a way to work a scam, not with me standing there over my men making sure it all went by the book, so he'd say "Get him into the ground, Captain, that's an order. That guy's a GI sheet job. This is a fighting unit. We've got a war on. There isn't time to putz around. We'll tell his relatives, sorry, we had to get him into the ground." Shit.'

Looking up at Melchior's change of tone Prideaux saw he was wiping bright blood from his upper lip.

'Nosebleed again,' said the Captain, holding the T-shirt to his face. 'Happens all the time these days. Don't know why. It's all packing up.'

'Shall I get you some ice?'

'I could handle another Coke.'

This time the boy was eating a plate of rice, the kitten on the plastic tablecloth beside him chewing fishbones with its head on one side. He must have had other customers in the interim since he now had some change and the second bottle cost Prideaux rather less than the first. His teeth were as white as the cat's.

'You won't see this story I'm telling you,' the Captain said when he'd drunk. He dabbed gently at his crusted nose. 'If you've never been in the Army you won't understand. That guy on the table having his intestines taken out's your buddy. There's just nobody in the world, I don't care if it's the President himself, comes telling you What the hell, it's too much trouble, get him into the ground. Sure, sometimes you have to. If you can't retrieve a KIA for a couple of days decomposition's well set in and there's nothing to do. Embalming's useless. The blood's clotted so you can't pump the formalin through the veins. The whole system's solid. You can push it in, but it all seeps back out again and the coffin drips. You gotta seal 'em in GI sheet and that's it. Yeah.' The bottle tilted once more. 'Colonel Saturnino Calajate. Colonel Half.' A smile crossed his face which seemed so ridiculously small, as if the tumours were slowly squeezing his features together at the centre. 'Nobody ever stood around *his* coffin, that's for sure.'

And it was all he would say on the subject, leaving Prideaux to wonder for long afterwards whether by a brilliant sleight some ignorant gathering had wound up tucking into roast colonel, down there in the dark jungles of Mindanao. When it was clear Melchior had lost interest in the topic he asked: 'What happened to them? Your buddies? The unit?'

'Ah.' A long sigh. 'Broken up. Gone. Dispersed. Some dead, some re-assigned, some plain vanished. Back to their families, AWOL, unemployed. I tried to keep in touch with a couple but then this –' the stump of his right hand made a blunt gesture which might have been referring to itself or the body it was attached to. 'Know what? I found it doesn't really matter. They're still there inside, *sa loob*, where the debt is. It'll be the same for all of us. Somewhere all the old teams are still together. You think this is crap? Sentimentality?' This time the

Captain's right hand went up behind the Book of Job where it sketched a limp circling motion in air. 'Before I die they'll be here. Converge On Me. They'll come.'

For the first time in this recital the literal had failed. The ruined man and his discourse fell out of the suspended noonday heat into somewhere more shadowed. Prideaux recognised the moment; it occasionally happened during interviews for documentaries. Just when you'd convinced yourself that the whole of life was nothing but hearsay, wandering narratives of what happened to whom, you discovered that a complete dream was walking about inside. Did they know it was there? he always wondered. Beneath what they thought was a plain account of events another text showed through in an entirely different register. It was like suddenly recognising that lines of vernacular hid a poem.

'They may come. But will they recognise you?'

This time the smile stayed a little. 'Well, good for you, John Something. You're older than me, I was forgetting. Yeah, perhaps they won't.'

'Did you ever think of killing yourself?' Prideaux was astounded by his own ruthlessness. It was an art he thought he'd forgotten.

'Sure I did. Tried it. Didn't work.' Once again he held up the maimed club of hand. 'That's like asking why I didn't go amok. I've known several amoks. The military's a good place to see them, what with all that stress and weaponry and all. I watched them very carefully, how they'd go quiet before. It's a special way of going quiet, not like a guy who just wants to be let alone because he's got one of those letters from his chick. More broody, heavy, like he was hearing all his life come clumping down the stairs. Then suddenly he gets this look, his hair starts to come up and he goes for a gun, knife, whatever's handy. But he's not setting out to kill people, that's the point. Not like some crazy bastard planning a series of murders in cold blood. The amok's enemies are all inside. All he knows is it's his last chance to go in there and rescue his soul. It's been tortured and squeezed every which way and it's the only thing left on earth which is his, and he's gotta hack it *free*. He's running inwards, right? That's why he doesn't see the guys he's chopping and shooting, his own friends, his buddies even. They're not real. They're just part of the dream. Only the soul is real.' He paused. 'Do you believe that?'

'About the soul?'

'Only the soul is real. That's why I don't kill myself. Like going amok with myself as victim? This –' his left hand pointed the Coke bottle's empty muzzle from swollen legs to upper chest, leaving a dark line of spots on the filthy fatigues, 'this is a dream. We're religious people, us Filipinos, know that? Don't let anyone tell you different. You shouldn't take your own life. You should find a way of walking out on it, carrying your soul. To die not in possession of your own soul is the worst damn thing there is.'

'*La vida es sueño*? Life is a dream?'

'Castilian, right?'

'Title of a play. In one place it says "Now I'm asleep I can see that when I'm awake I'm dreaming".'

'Yeah? That's good. That's it. You look at people in the street, people everywhere, any of us. Know what? We're all out on patrol. The whole world's out on patrol. We've been given this mission, right? Target briefing. One: Get to the end of life richer than you started. Two: Have a good time along the way. Three: Breed up a family to carry it all on. Everything we do to carry out our orders is okay, sensible, rational, sane, purposeful, whatever. Then flick-flick, you're cursing a stranger for driving funny, shouting at the wife, hitting the kids, kicking the pooch. Flick-flick we wake up and find we're hunkered down around a camp fire eating some sorry bastard. People commit murder all the time but they don't know it. Specially those crazy politicians. Just that their victims are a long way away. Look at San Clemente. Look at this country. Look at the world. Is this a sane way to run things? That's how it is. Nothing people do is strange. Flick-flick.'

Far from having wearied himself with talking Captain Melchior now seemed more animated, if a little hectic about the eyes. A lizard croaked and rattled nearby and then fell silent, leaving a hush in which the faint hiss of intense sunlight on stone was clearly audible. Far away behind it lay directionless urban sound like a steady ocean gnawing at a coastline.

'Know what a gook is?' the Captain asked unexpectedly.

'Well, in Vietnam –' Prideaux began.

'Fuck Vietnam. Forget Vietnam. The original gooks were us Filipinos. It was what the Americans called our nationalist guerrillas

234

who fought them for independence at the end of last century. They say it comes from Bicolano or something, *gugurang* or *gugu*. I don't speak the damn language. What it means is a kind of spirit. You know, like you have a guardian angel? This is a guardian demon. Hell, John Something, you're in a land of spirits, didn't you know? Every last snot-nosed kid of us. You expect spirits to behave like everyone else? Like the British, maybe? Forget it. Never happen.'

Certainly the diseased Captain refused Prideaux's offers of further refreshment, food, clothing, money and medicine with all the detachment of a spirit. He seemed happy to lie on his tombstone and talk. He spoke of the time he'd first met the cemetery police when they passed on patrol, stumbling through the weeds with a weak flashlight, all four of them 'bunched together like schoolgirls'. He was lying up in one of the disused niches in the wall, a long cool pigeonhole, and gave a stage groan, followed by ghoulish laughter which pursued their panicky retreat. He'd gone and found them huddled in the church, their card game abandoned. He managed to convince them he wasn't a ghost, that the apparently un-Filipino habit of sleeping in a graveyard was explained by having been a Ranger in Mindanao. After that, there was nothing left to be scared of.

'What's going on in San Clemente?' Prideaux asked as he was about to leave. It was early afternoon and Melchior suddenly wanted to sleep. He himself was dazed with words and the stench of pear pollen. 'Vampires and stuff?'

'You don't believe that kidshit? It's a Chinese offensive.'

'I don't follow you.'

But the Captain slithered flippantly away. 'You did this morning. Couldn't stop yourself. It's the stories.' He sounded content and once again sketched his melancholy gesture in the air summoning ghosts, buddies, Chinese policemen, British anthropologists or anyone else who would listen. 'Gets 'em every time.'

22

THE INSTANT they carried Eddie's body in at five-thirty one morning Nanang Pipa experienced the effect that a sudden lightning flash has on a nightbound traveller. It was a shock too quick for detail but it left her with the general revelation of a large and menacing landscape stretching to all horizons in which her own figure was tiny and without the slightest significance. They laid him on the table and she lit a candle with shaking hands and had somebody go and fetch Fr. Bernabe. It was so brutal and unexpected that at first she was beyond emotion and could only stand, stroking his forehead and saying, 'Oh Eddie. My poor Eddie. What have they done to you?' where 'they' meant nothing more than life itself personified by its faceless agents who were never in short supply. Whatever they had done had left his face caked with blood around the mouth and with all his front teeth knocked out. He had been found up the hill, just inside the wall by the shanties as if tossed over already dead like a piece of refuse, falling in an attitude no natural death could assume. While her eldest daughter Gaylin and the youngest Jinky hurriedly rolled up their sleeping mats on the floor she fetched a bowl of water and sponged Eddie's face clean, dried it and laid a crucifix on his chest. He suddenly looked shrunken and depleted as if what had filled him in life had been the largesse of his gestures, the weight of his passion, the force of his laughter. Only when she realised that never as long as she lived would she hear that laugh again did Pipa begin her weeping, a desolate crying that penetrated the nearby shanties' slat walls.

The family rallied around. Fr. Bernabe arrived still sleepy and they held a vigil around the body for an hour or so before the first neighbours came to pay their respects. Most of the members of the sewing cooperative came, as of course did all the old friends: Bats, Judge, Billy and Petring. From all over San Clemente they came, many in tears, to see the body. The barangay captain, Monching Jandusay, arrived smelling of yesterday's drink and urine. With that divorced observation which often strikes people who ought to be otherwise preoccupied Nanang Pipa noticed that in the morning light his skin was papery and translucent, as if the more he poured gin into his body the more he was turning into a mere container, a fragile and unsteady kind of bottle. Still, what mattered was that he had come and been seen to come, as duty and etiquette required. Yet although this was all proper and consoling, it was as if Pipa were still waiting for someone secure and fatherly into whose hands she could yield the whole sorry mess. And at nine o'clock Rio Dingca appeared in the doorway smelling of Dial soap, having been alerted on arrival by PO1 Benhur Daldal who had deserted his post by the priceless pit outside in order to leave the message at Station 14. After the body had been taken away for the cause of death to be ascertained Pipa tearfully confided to Dingca that Eddie had made a confession only yesterday.

'It was all his own idea,' she said. 'The vampire. That's what he told me. I'm so ashamed.'

'But he was drunk all the same?'

'Oh, he was drunk all right. He really did think he'd seen something, too, except it was probably the moon or a cloud, you know. But he said he'd had it at the back of his mind to invent a story which would frighten people off investigating our hole too closely. He'd already found the skull, you see, and those bits of china, and we'd decided to keep it a secret. Then Ming Piedragoso told us about the spirit guardians Chinese pirates used to put over hidden treasure and Eddie said that gave him the idea. But it backfired, like so many of his brilliant ideas, and now he's *dead*,' she ended in disbelief that something as trivial as one of Eddie's stories, no more substantial than a fume of gin, could have had such a lethal outcome.

Rio Dingca took her hand. 'That didn't kill him,' he told her. 'We don't know what did, yet, but it wasn't that.' For it was as if the news of Eddie's death had made Dingca privy also to Nanang Pipa's lightning flash, leaving him with a cop's conviction that a complicated hinterland lay beyond these rickety houses, a hinterland in which powerful forces were moving with cold deliberation under cover of darkness. 'Where did he go last night? When did you last see him?'

'I don't know. He was around for supper and went off at about eight or nine. I don't know where or with whom. Out with his *barkadas* as usual, I thought. You'd better ask Bats and Judge and that lot.'

'Was he drunk?'

'No. Not at supper, anyway. Actually, he said after that day you were here with those newspaper people he wasn't ever going to drink again.' Her eyes filled at the thought of his good intentions and their unexpected fulfilment.

'Anything odd or strange you've noticed recently?' It was a dumb policeman's question ineptly put and as soon as it flew out of his mouth Dingca wished he could retrieve it, cancel it, try another tack.

'Odd? Strange?' She looked straight at him with brimming eyes. '*Diosko.* Everything's a disaster, Rio. Don't you see he was right? He said it was all my fault. If I hadn't made him dig that hole none of this would ever have happened. From the moment I opened my stupid mouth it all began going wrong. Oh, if only I could go back –' and she wept again in earnest for a while, finally shuddering and dabbing at her eyes. 'Strange?' she said at last with a deep sigh. 'Have you ever taken out a St. Jude?'

'A novena? No, can't say I have.'

'I did some months ago. I asked for several things including that Eddie would get out of jail and he did. It was you who got him out.'

'I didn't know you'd made a special novena, though.'

'I never told anyone except my friend Doding Perez. She said St. Jude was the best and she was right. But there was one thing I didn't ask for. Someone I know stole one of our edging machines. Brand new, it was. Just walked off with it and disappeared. I tried asking Mama Mary but that didn't work and I thought no, it's too mercenary to ask St. Jude to bring a sewing machine back, and I saved my special requests for Eddie and Gaylin and Boyong. Here's the strange part, though. A week ago this woman turns up again, bold as brass, says she's sorry she took the machine but it was a family crisis, she just had to have the money, the usual. Lots of tears and begging my forgiveness. "Oh yes?" I says. "Brought it back, then, have you?" I mean, she'd been gone months. Well, no, she hadn't brought it back but she wanted me to have ₱ 350 which was all she could afford right now. "Three hundred and fifty?" I says. "Have you any idea how much that machine cost?" "I ought to," she says, "I'm a member of the cooperative that bought it." "Not now, you're not," I told her. "Passed unanimously, don't you worry. It's there in the minutes, *nem. con.*" So she starts crying again and I tell her to get out and take her money with her. "*Walang hiya talaga,*" I told her. Shameless bitch. You'd think she wouldn't have the nerve to come back to a place like this where everybody knows her, wouldn't you? But she's around, all right. The strange thing I wanted to tell you is that it's her been going about this last week spreading rumours about dogs giving birth to cockroaches and how there's a curse on San Clemente and that the dead I've disturbed are going to rise and take a terrible revenge on us all. She's got a lot of people scared, too. Some are even talking of moving out, apparently. She tells them the end has started and right now,' Nanang Pipa said bleakly, 'I'm beginning to wonder myself.'

'You never told me about this theft,' said Dingca.

'You're right, I never did,' agreed Pipa, and in her answer could be read an entire history of the relationship between squatters and police irrespective of trusted individuals.

'But you're going to tell me now who she is,' he said persuasively. 'Somewhere there's a connection, Pipa. Don't ask me how I know, but I do.'

'What, you mean she. . . *she* killed Eddie?'

'No, no, no, not that direct a connection. But she's part of it.'

Nanang Pipa only shook her head and squeezed her handkerchief tighter. 'I start shopping people to the police and I'm done for in San Clemente,' she said simply. 'I'm probably done for anyway. It was our hole. They'll probably force us out for bringing ruin. It won't be enough that my husband's dead, it'll just be proof of how evil I am.' Tears ran down her cheeks.

'Listen, Pipa, I'm not just the police, I'm someone you've known for two years. We're friends. At least I hope we are because you're shortly going to need all the friends you can get. Have you any idea what's going to happen when the newspapers get hold of poor Eddie's death? They'll be back here before the morning's out. Plus we've now got a real live senator taking a personal interest in your comfort room that was. Listen,' he said earnestly, reaching forward and taking her hand again, 'if it turns out Eddie was murdered, and it certainly looks that way, you're going to be involved with the police whether you like it or not. I can pull enough strings to make sure I get assigned the case but I can't do a thing unless you help me. There's something going on here that's much bigger than a hole in the ground with seven-hundred-year-old bones at the bottom, and I'm going to dig it out. Trust me, Pipa. Who is she?'

'Ligaya Rosales,' came the small reply at length. Looking up at the way he repeated the name she saw him staring with a faraway expression at the tapestry of the dogs playing cards. She'd never liked that thing, she realised irrelevantly. Eddie had arrived home with it one day saying it had fallen off a stall in Divisoria. True, it covered the stencils which betrayed the plywood behind it as having come from dismantled tea chests, but still she'd never liked it. Everyone said it was cute, but bulldogs in eyeshades didn't look cute to her. Oh Eddie, she thought, her eyes filling once more, what *was* it all for? All of it? She tried to imagine him now, sitting for ever in glory, happy that it was over, happy to be happy. Could he see her now? she wondered. Fr. Bernabe had said that he could, but she wasn't sure.

'That name, Rosales, I know it. Yes, got it. By God, Pipa, I think that's it.'

'What?' she asked again, but he wouldn't say.

He'd been right about the newspapers coming back, which the same old tabloids did well before lunch. And when the terrible news leaked out about the cause of Eddie's death they all came, worse than ghouls themselves, to ask her what it felt like to be the wife of a man who'd been well and truly vampirised. For according to Rio Dingca when they'd opened the body at the autopsy they'd found precisely nothing. Nothing whatever. Eddie's entire internal organs were missing from tongue to rectum. Nobody had ever seen anything like it.

'How. . .?' she had begun, faltering. 'Who. . .?'

'I don't know, but I shall,' Dingca had promised her, and added a merciful fiction of his own. 'The surgeon said death was instantaneous. He couldn't have suffered.'

'Oh my God, how can he know?'

'Haemorrhage patterns,' Dingca improvised sagely. 'There's not so much blood lost if the heart stops at once.' Eddie's heart, of course, had vanished entirely. The truth was, Rio wanted to believe it as much as he wanted her to believe it, as much as he himself had once chosen to believe the surgeon who said Babs was dead before his body was mutilated. In fact Edsel Tugos's remains had been exhaustively autopsied and photographed while his case was being written up for the annals. From the direction of the tears and ruptures in the remaining tatters of his diaphragm, taken in conjunction with the severe damage to the oral cavity, the experts determined he had been put to death in an entirely novel way. Some sort of high power vacuum pump, such as might normally be used for aspirating sewage out of a blocked drain, had been employed to suck the innards from his body. It had been done with disgusting cold science as well as with the brute force needed to ram an overlarge metal nozzle into his mouth hard enough to have dislocated the jaw.

Nanang Pipa valiantly contrived to block out these details even though they were soon retailed in large print by all the tabloids. Meanwhile something like a genuine hysteria was beginning to build up in the barrio. *People said. . .* People said no human agent could have done such a thing. Who'd ever heard of an entire body being sucked hollow before? People said it was unquestionably a *manananggal.* They said poor Eddie hadn't been seeing things after all. They said they'd heard of cases like this before in Iloilo, in Bohol, in Camarines, in Negros. . . People said it was a demon the Chinese had placed to stand guard over the dead in their cemetery, come to take revenge on Eddie and anyone else in San Clemente who'd messed with the tombs and stolen water and electricity. People said Eddie's accomplices, especially Bats and Judge, would be the next to go. And indeed Bats and Judge were nowadays seldom seen outside their houses where they were holed up, white-faced and clinking with crucifixes. People said.

And the more people said, the more Nanang Pipa managed somehow to keep a clear head, asking them where they'd first heard it. In a few days her suspicions were confirmed and she had passed them on to Rio Dingca. The grossest rumours, the direst predictions eagerly taken up by the tabloid reporters had come from Ligaya Rosales. Dingca kept missing this woman whom he was now very anxious to interview and suspected she was lying low somewhere outside the barrio. Then one day he and Benhur Daldal caught her in a *sari-sari* store down by the Kapilang, thanks to an informer. He recognised her at once, arrested her on the spot, took her down to Station 14 handcuffed to the grab handle of his jeep, booked her and threw her into a cell. Later, he went back up and told Nanang Pipa that Ligaya was already wanted for jumping a ₱ 5,000 bail some months back while awaiting trial for trying to abduct a child in Harrison Plaza.

'Five *thousand*?' Pipa said. 'Who on this earth would spend five thousand pesos on Ligaya Rosales?'

'When we know that I expect we'll know a lot more,' Dingca told her cagily. She thought he probably already knew but her interest in such technicalities was fast diminishing. Her life was gripped by a sense of radical destruction and finality. With the help of Fr. Herrera they'd managed to find a plot for Eddie way up behind the Chinese cemetery in what looked to her like a derelict no-man's-land, and there they'd buried him. Fr. Herrera had told her not to worry, this part of the cemetery was shortly due for rehabilitation and Eddie's grave would soon find itself in much-improved surroundings. In any case the ground was still consecrated and the space offered too valuable to be ignored. 'It's the right moment,' he said. 'In five years' time they'll probably make cremation compulsory.' To her this prospect of terrifying impiety simply added its tithe to the rest of the menace massing all around. At night now she thought of Eddie lying up there under his simple cement inscription in a tamarind's shade. Not far away, she had noticed, was a rather grand grave which had a huge open marble book at its head as well as a marble cross and she was aware that Eddie's unpretentious resting place could hardly compete with that sort of thing. On the other hand there were also several graves in the vicinity which were empty, their slabs skewed to one side or missing entirely. Everything was insecure; not even the ground in which the dead were laid was safe. 'My poor Eddie,' she said softly in the dark. 'My poor, poor man.' She cried herself to sleep.

And now her perception of insecurity infected everything she looked at: house, family, business, future. Apart from her own children, who were being as supportive as they knew how (Boyong in particular making touching efforts to justify inheriting his father's title of family head), there were two people to whom Nanang Pipa felt especial gratitude. One was Rio Dingca, who came daily with little pieces of information which went a long way to counteract the wild rumours of supernatural vengeance which had broken out on all sides. The other was, of all people, Gringo Lapad. Pipa never considered that she'd known him particularly well, certainly nothing like as well as she knew his indolent brother Bats. To her he was just one of Eddie's wilder *barkadas* who drove the taxi in which so many of their no doubt apocryphal adventures had taken place. Yet one evening Gringo had turned up, very sober, his eyes flashing with hurt and anger and tears, and had given her an envelope containing two thousand pesos.

'But Gringo,' she'd begun.

'Expenses,' he interrupted dismissively. 'Contributions from my passengers. I've got Eddie's photo right up there on the dashboard with a rosary around it and *sampagita* flowers and they all ask me "Who's that?" and I tell them it's my best friend they've been reading about in the newspapers. They make contributions. A few pesos here, a few there. It mounts up, you know.'

'Yes, but two *thousand*.'

'Well, some of them give a lot. I had a *Kano* yesterday, a tourist, who just handed over his watch.'

Nanang Pipa didn't want to know the precise circumstances in which a tourist had parted with his no doubt expensive watch and didn't press the point. It was the thought that counted, and Gringo's practical steps to alleviate hers and his own distress touched her deeply. The money would indeed come in useful. The funeral expenses had been high, and while Rio Dingca had insisted that she start charging the newspapers for interviews they were remarkably stingy. The reporters were fine at buying drinks for their male informants because they promptly helped to drink them. Handing over hard cash to women went against the grain, however, and in any case there were plenty of Clementeños only too happy to give sensational and lying interviews for free just to see their names in print. A particularly loathsome young man called Mozart Narciso had as good as told her she was yesterday's widow, played out in terms of newsworthiness.

'Let me just quote you something someone just told me,' he'd said, flipping over the pages of his notebook. 'Here we are. Get this: "A spirit messenger came to me last night to give me a warning. He was right there, standing by that door as we were eating, not six feet away. He had these big white wings and a long robe and his eyes were like hot coals. You can ask anyone in the family. We knew at once he was a messenger from God because he had a fiery cross on his chest and there was this bluish light around his head. He said: 'Beware, beware, my children. This barrio has fallen on evil times. There are among you thieves who rob the dead and disturb the rest of souls who are in Paradise with me. By their acts they have called forth demons from the Great Pit. We are sending the Archangel Michael to deal with them but before Good can triumph the evil generation will be swept away. On this very ground the spirit armies are drawn up. Woe unto them whose shadow falls on this land when the day of battle dawns".' The reporter closed his book with a snap.

'What sacrilegious nonsense!' Nanang Pipa had exclaimed stoutly. ' "We're sending the Archangel Michael" – do you really think that's how a messenger from God would speak, you halfwit? Like the Department of Health? "We're sending rodent operatives". Terrible rubbish! And I can make a pretty fair guess where you got it from, what's more.'

'Oh yes?' prompted the journalist sarcastically, evidently stung by being dismissed as a credulous ninny when he no more believed a word of it than she did.

'The actual individual I couldn't say, but I imagine the family name's Rosales.'

'Well, you imagine wrong, Mrs,' he said; and both knew he lied.

'Some people will say anything if you pay them enough,' she pursued angrily.

'Like that they've seen a vampire, for instance?' said Narciso brutally, leaving her in tears of rage and misery.

If the tabloids now did their best to ignore her, it seemed out of petty revenge for her refusing to take them seriously or finally to see them at all, she felt herself becoming more and more the object of local attention, the butt of gossip and whispers. Her one real refuge was the sewing cooperative. That at least was a solid business concern providing an income and what little hope she might retain in the future. Yet even here fractures were beginning to be discernible of the kind which her authority now seemed powerless to mend as it once had. It was not that she was openly challenged – how could she be since the group was democratic and she held no post which couldn't be rescinded by a simple majority vote? But there were faint hints of new alliances, suggestions that unofficial meetings were being held without her in other homes. She had no proof but would have betted that all sorts of plotting and scheming were going on in the house of Danny's mother, for instance. Danny, that smarmy little call-boy who instead of sitting on his bum in school and getting an honest education went around waggling it at tourists and came prancing home in trainers which cost more than the dress Pipa was married in.

She hated herself for her bitterness; but it was as if all the apprehensions she'd always had and which nobody else ever seemed to share were remorselessly being proved valid. Everything stemmed from that one accursed moment a mere handful of weeks ago when she'd opened a new bolt of cloth and done what she always did, which was to smell it appreciatively. She not only liked the smell of new cloth, she could tell a lot about its quality from the scent it gave off, especially whether the wholesaler was trying to pull a fast one by lying about the percentage of acrylic in it. Acrylic had its own faint but unmistakable smell. That morning she'd been unable to smell it accurately because of the stench drifting in from the CR and was suddenly overcome with irritation. Business was being compromised by sanitation, so sanitation had to be improved at once. From that instant's annoyance everything had followed: vampires, horrid publicity, husband's death, social ostracism, everything. She was aghast at the unfairness of being punished so severely for what seemed such a trivial crime, if digging a new comfort room was a crime.

You didn't win in this world, she told herself as she gazed out of an upstairs window while listlessly making a work-shirt for Boyong. From down below outside came the sound of quiet English conversation as two foreign girls slowly laid bare the full extent of Eddie's discovery. You didn't win because a bit of time would go by in which it appeared you *were* winning and you would forget what you'd known all along, which was that ultimately things were stacked against you. You just chose to pretend they weren't, to live in a dreamworld normally inhabited by just the sort of idiots you had no time for, the cockfighting bettors and the *jueteng* gamblers and the lottery addicts and the rest who blew good money in pursuit of bad. Underneath, things remained exactly as they'd always been: clear, mortal, un-pitying. Her eyes unseeingly followed two kittens wrestling inside a motor tyre on the slope of a neighbour's roof. How shallowly rooted things were! It was so easy to blink and imagine everything one thought of as permanent brushed away. From one day to the next people were swept off their feet and into their graves and that was that. All these houses here, what did they mean? They weren't solid at all. There was just the sky and the earth, and between them a dreamworld in which flimsy dramas were acted out, of no more consequence than the clouds which came and went, shifted and re-formed, leaked rain and dissolved. What did it really matter who had killed Eddie? Eddie was dead of Fate; the identity of its agent was neither here nor there. Someone should be made to pay for the vile way in which he'd been done to death, certainly; but nobody would be, she knew. Well, and now what? They couldn't stay here in San Clemente, not now. She and the family would have to move. Even those friendships and alliances which so recently had seemed solid were revealed as temporary after all, no proof against unChristian superstition and malicious gossip. All those true-to-death friends of Eddie's, those Batses and Judges and Petrings and Billys – where were they now? Skulking at home in terror of supernatural vengeance and no doubt telling everyone they'd never really been close to Edsel Tugos, just occasional drinking companions. Judases, every last one of them, she thought, even as she knew she was judging them without any real evidence. Still, none of them had done what Gringo had, coming to see her and bringing a gift whose generosity spoke of real affection for Eddie. The thought filled her eyes once more.

On and on went the grunted remarks down below. Even though they were in English she could understand little. One of the girls spoke excellent Tagalog but her companion none at all. There was a foreign man, too, much older, who occasionally dropped by and asked peculiar questions. John something-or-other. He was courteous and touched her by once bringing her a bunch of flowers, but because he was foreign she couldn't tell what they meant. They weren't to do with Eddie because they were the wrong kind for death, and they weren't for her because it wasn't her birthday, and they weren't for either of her daughters because they were the wrong flowers for courting, too. She remained baffled and slightly uneasy, though a little more gossip among the neighbours could hardly make much difference now. In any case he seemed well-meaning and just for a moment she wondered if he mightn't take an interest in Gaylin now that her little problem had been solved. A rich foreign husband . . . But no; no more dreams, no more self-deception. Time to begin winding up her part in the cooperative, sell up and go, though she had no idea where. And who would want to buy a house in San Clemente now it was widely known that the landlord was the Prince of Darkness himself?

It was on one of these sad reflective mornings that Nanang Pipa remembered an additional source of help which she had been overlooking. She thought very carefully before making her second novena to St. Jude and decided not to dilute the fervour of her appeal by making requests for material things. Instead she asked most humbly for one thing and one thing only, seeing that the Saint would have known her original crime had not been committed out of greed or ill-will. She asked for Justice, and waited for the eighth day.

23

THE DIG HAD PROGRESSED slowly at first. It had proved difficult to recruit local labour to remove the first few feet of topsoil, an unexpected result of the fear gripping San Clemente. Perfectly able-bodied young men had smiled politely and nodded and taken a step backwards when Philippine Heritage Museum staff had offered them spades.

'There's an excellent English word which the Victorians used a good deal about people like these,' Ysabella observed to Sharon in frustration. 'Unfortunately it's rather out of fashion nowadays. The word is "feckless". These guys show a distinct lack of feck. Don't tell me they don't need the work.'

'They're scared,' Sharon said. 'Crispa came up after you left yesterday and it took her about five minutes to suss it out. She's from Marinduque and so are half these people here. They opened up to a fellow-Marinduqueña. They don't like burial sites being excavated right in the middle of where they're living. Plus there's all sorts of other things brewing beneath the surface.'

Ysabella looked around at the huts and the slime and the toddlers dressed in rice sacking who stood solemnly watching at a safe distance. There was a smell of fresh shit. It was hard to see what surface could possibly exist for things to brew under. It seemed less like a community than an encampment. The Museum had been obliged to hire its own labourers and between them they had now cleared a patch of ground maybe a quarter the size of a tennis court.

Little as this was, it still brought them hard up against the surrounding shanties' walls.

'We'll get rid of these,' said Senator Vicente with a wave of his hand. With the publicity accorded his presence he had become the site's de facto champion, protector and spokesman.

'Early days yet, Senator,' Sharon said restrainingly. 'We don't yet know how big it is. No point in moving people unnecessarily.'

'I'm convinced it's extensive,' he replied. 'It's going to be bigger than Sta. Ana.'

In his mind's eye, Ysabella thought, he was seeing an excavation the size of Pompeii. So far they had uncovered six little skeletons and forty-three articles of porcelain and stoneware, only five of which were broken. This corner of the site appeared to be a burial ground used exclusively for children. They had been tucked into the salient beneath the grasses and the wild deers' hooves with what must have been a pretty view of the bay and the trading settlement to the south-west. She found it easy to understand his excitement and impatience to lay bare whatever was there to be laid bare. She was equally gripped by the fascination which had infected everyone in the Museum's team. What did it mean that they had so far found only infants' and children's graves? She knew that although it wasn't common practice in these islands to bury children separately it was certainly not unknown. Indeed, she gathered that some of the mountain peoples in the interior of Panay still did so. The most celebrated previous example was at Sta. Ana itself, and it was this which brought them eagerly to San Clemente day after day, from dawn to dusk, in acute anticipation. For at Sta. Ana the children's graveyard had been attached to one for adults, and the whole area had at length been revealed as a settlement. Expectations were running high that any day now San Clemente, too, would be found to have been the site of a pre-Hispanic village. Here and there makeshift awnings had been rigged, plastic sheeting strung between nearby hovels and a single palm tree which functioned as a support for a basketball ring as well as for several TV aerials. In this vinyl-scented shade Ysabella worked away with her trowel, hoping with each peck at the earth that she would be the one to find the first fragment of charcoal, an oyster shell, a cooked deer's bone or other signs of a midden.

'We'll get rid of these,' Ben Vicente kept repeating to Sharon. 'Don't worry.' He thumped the wooden wall on the other side of which the cigar-chomping bulldogs played their endless game of cards. He spoke to the Museum staff who said, 'Yes, sir' softly, '*Opo.*' He came back and added, 'Really, it's a godsend. If we're to make any social progress at all here in Manila we've simply got to redevelop slum areas like these. Apart from the fact that it's an eyesore and a health hazard this place is a prime piece of real estate. A major discovery like ours is a perfect reason for clearing and redeveloping the area once and for all.' He caught Sharon's unenchanted eye. 'You surely can't tell me you think people should live like this in a late Twentieth-century capital city?' His gesture encompassed the little pairs of bare feet standing in the slime, the patchwork shanties, the pools of raw sewage crossed by duckboards. At her back she could feel the barrio's flimsy, creaking weight heaped on the hillside as if it only needed someone to knock a few wedges and props loose for the whole thing to collapse into noisome scree and glissade down into the culvert below.

'He's right, you know,' Ysabella said after he'd glanced at his watch, motioned to his driver and gone. 'It's no way to live.'

'Fine,' said Sharon.

'You don't agree.'

'I said "Fine". That's what I'm saying, right? Fine. Can you imagine how many times over the last six years I've been through these sorts of argument? Like daily? Us rich folks are compromised the moment we land in these countries. There's no high moral ground, Yzzy, believe me. Just unending lists of pros and cons. They want to trash San Clemente, they'll trash it. Fine.'

'Surely they'll at least have to give people notice to quit and settle them somewhere better?'

'Squatters? Sure, as there are reporters and foreigners around they'll maybe give them a statutory month or so and talk about a rehousing scheme way out in Marikina. If it wasn't for us they'd have them out this morning if they felt like it.'

' "They" being us, too, ultimately?'

'Only indirectly. As your Senator says, it's a godsend. There'll be all sorts of land deals and crap going on behind the scenes. There always are. It's someone's luck that an archaeological find's the perfect excuse to evict. If they want to back it up they'll get a tame heavy from the Department of Health to declare the place a major sanitation hazard.

Or someone from the police will say the barrio's a notorious hotbed of crime.'

'*Shabu* addicts and that sort of thing?' Ysabella had at last begun to feel her daily dose of the newspapers was giving her a certain familiarity with the domestic scene. This confidence was soon dashed.

'You've got to be kidding,' said Sharon. '*Shabu*? For chrissake, what do you think all those movieland stars are high on? It's the preferred drug of the leisure set. The Triads used to import it direct from Hong Kong and they've now got local labs producing it but even so it's way beyond the means of people like these. Corex cough syrup with beer chaser's about the level of San Clemente. The kids'll be sniffing Rugby rubber cement. *Shabu*? Oh boy.'

'Whatever the hell,' said Ysabella crossly, 'crime, sanitation, the nation's heritage – in whatever name it's done they're still only words, aren't they? The bottom line's eviction. People being moved away and dumped somewhere out of the public eye. It's a kind of airline-speak to lull fare-paying citizens.'

'The Yzzy Bastiaan theory of social infantilism.'

Ysabella hacked away at San Clemente's foundations with her trowel. I notice these things – she thought – but I'm damned if I'm going to take them to heart. Nobody at the age of twenty-nine wanted to be revealed as naive, especially when they were notoriously sophisticated. That was what happened when one came to a godawful place like Manila in defiance of friends and common sense. One could only survive with equanimity so long as social derelicts remained faceless. They belonged to a very alien culture and assuredly had their own ways of dealing with whatever injustices that culture meted out. What was the point of investing them with the sensibility of a Briton? Different strokes for different folks, and all that. The trip she and Hugh had made last year to India had proved her point to the hilt. People there blinded their own children with red-hot needles, smashed their infants' limbs, rubbed filth into their sores. When children were as much a beggar's tools as spanners were a mechanic's why bother to give them names at all? Well, it hadn't been a happy trip for all sorts of reasons, including Hugh and the ashrams. She had left India with an acute attack of xenophobia. Something white and blue was glittering from a crumble of soil by her trowel's point. Very carefully she began brushing the earth away. People grew out of each other, she thought in the moment's abandon, her excitement increasing as she made out the lines of a *ching pai* boat. And if they didn't, they ought to. She had its full length revealed now, the starboard side still embedded, the pillars of its little cabin gleaming white. Working with the camel hair brush she exposed more and more. The spots of cobalt blue had the brilliance of gems. For a moment everything in the world seemed to concentrate itself in that fragile six-inch sliver of porcelain at the bottom of a hole in the tropics. She wished only that the unknown Chinese who had wielded his brush at a kiln a thousand miles away and seven centuries ago could have known the intensity of pleasure he would one day give as his colour blazed out in the light of an alien day. That was the great attraction of this sort of dig, without a doubt. It all came down to aesthetic pleasure and neutral information. The archaeology of preliterate societies was necessarily value-free. Without written records there were no injustices, no villains, no heroes. Only skeletons, the nameless dead. No moral judgements could be made, only estimates of mortality rates, trading links, the incidence of dental caries, customs of skull- and foot-binding. Whatever appalling wrongs might have accompanied these children to their graves had long been swallowed up by the mass forgiveness of extinction.

Senator Ben Vicente came nearly every day to view progress for himself. Sometimes he brought Liezel and Woopsy, on one occasion turning up with hayseed brother Doy, Magubat's Governor, keeper of its relics and its developmental conscience. The two men ambled about, one or other throwing out a proprietor's hand over San Clemente's sagging tin and leaning doorframes. To Ysabella's slight unease Ben had intensified his mode with her. He was as proper and respectful as ever, but now assumed her agreement with all his views and even her inclusion in any schemes he might dream up. She was an honorary member of his family, he suggested, and she felt herself swept along in the opulence of his self-assurance. It didn't at all hurt to have powerful friends, she thought. When in Rome, as Sharon had once not quite said, it helped to have an introduction to Caesar. Yet the memory of her visit to Caesar's private island had about it a nimbus of disquiet as if by recalling only an atmosphere she were evading a piece of knowledge. It was contained in the hulking Boyboy's piteous internment, perhaps, or in his local jailer's polished calves with the curling fish-scales stuck to them as he went about his duties in the long shadow of his landlord's ruthless graciousness. And, to however small a degree, the extreme edge of that shadow fell across herself, too, even as it made her own father's shade still duskier, to say nothing of her mother's past. The feeling was of having unwittingly been compromised well before she ever set foot on his domain and heard forlorn crying in the night. However (as she told herself briskly) she had her own life to be getting on with and couldn't afford to waste time dwelling on things she could do nothing about. Ben remained the sort of ally one badly needed in a place like this and there was no question that from an archaeological point of view his patronage of the site had already proved invaluable. Security was good; nobody had looted anything or damaged the record by cowboy attempts at pot-hunting. The value of that sort of intercession could hardly be overestimated, and the Philippine Heritage Museum was counting itself unusually lucky.

Amongst all the city dignitaries, local bigwigs and curious rubber-neckers who kept dropping by to see what was happening in Manila's most newsworthy slum was a strange Englishman to whom Ysabella had instinctively not warmed. Tallish, baldish, forty-fiveish, he looked to her what she would imagine a Graham Greene character would look like: troubled, leached-out, pretty much on autopilot from now until the Great Touchdown.

'I do believe that's a countryman of yours,' Sharon observed mischievously after hearing him trying to question Mrs Tugos as she stood by her back door sadly watching the dig. To Sharon's great delight Ysabella had reacted exactly as she thought she might.

'Wouldn't surprise me,' she'd said gruffly without looking up from her work. 'We get all sorts here.'

So Sharon had climbed out and introduced herself and pointed out the top of Ysabella's sunhat as concealing a compatriot. He, too, hadn't let her down.

'Ah,' he said incuriously before wandering off, not without some obscure flash as of annoyance.

Sharon had never worked out why certain Britons so hated recognising each other abroad. Was it all part of their baffling class thing? It almost seemed as if they were threatened with unmasking or else losing an imagined exclusiveness. She even wondered whether they had left Britain in the first place simply to get away from each other. Still, this one had come back after a day or two, asking all sorts of questions about the barrio while expressing remarkably little interest in archaeology. At first Sharon had taken him for a journalist but he claimed to be working on some sort of thesis. He had been in the country about nine months or so and seemed to know quite a few people.

'Huh,' Ysabella said one day, 'I know that type. Not socially,' she added hastily, causing Sharon more private amusement, 'but that sort of decayed child-of-the-Sixties. Ex-TV? John Prideaux? Very vaguely; it's just a name. Famous once, you know? All those questions he was asking this morning about what you thought the locals understood by "corruption" and "fatalism" and stuff: he's so rotted with *understanding* he can't even call somebody corrupt and have done with it. My mother knows people like that. They can't speak plain English. Everything's so tentative. It's all hedged about with endless problems of definition. I mean, who's got the time? It's very elderly of him. I can't say it more charitably than that.'

'He's doing a thesis, Yzzy. He's an anthro. He wants to know how this place works. He asked Crispa the same things the other day. I told him if ever he gets any answers please to let me know. Don't think I don't ask myself these questions too, I said.'

'What, about corruption and fatalism?' But Ysabella sounded spikier than she can have felt, for eventually she introduced Prideaux to Ben, who loved nothing better than expounding on his countrymen's character. It would all have been fine had the man been twenty-five. Or perhaps not fine but explicable. What was a person like him doing still wandering the world in middle age asking dim, sophomoronic questions? At least (thought Ysabella, noting the precise position of a greyware dish on her plan and re-checking it with the tape measure) her sort of work was practical, tangible, and brought to light things which nobody even knew were hidden. At the end of the day one could point to a row of pots on a shelf, to skeletons and flints and coins and shards and glass beads. It was so much easier to ask questions of the dead. They were somewhat tight-lipped but what little they gave away one could put under a microscope or fluoroscope, test its thermoluminescence and subject tiny samples to gas chromatography and carbon dating. But the living were all motives and lacked anything concrete. They lied and deceived themselves. They lived in private dreams and pursued their own ends even as they made deals and public declarations they promptly welshed on and forgot. She had exposed Hugh's protestations, for instance, as pure blarney. Now that she came to think about it there was something about this Prideaux fellow that reminded her slightly of Hugh: a certain absence, as though a part of him were always standing a little to one side facing another direction and thinking about something quite else. Well, look where it led. This Prideaux was a horrid object lesson Hugh really ought to see before it was too late. It was true that part of Hugh's problem was that he had too much money, but a far bigger part was that he had not enough ambition. His particular brand of selective intelligence and sensibility was easily subverted into moans about mortality which produced its own hopeless inertia. In her view, after due thought in a harsh exile, it wasn't thoughtfulness at all. It was altogether less admirable, more like indecisiveness, a radical inability to make decisions and stick to them. They were both rather timorous men, she considered; and if she were to see much more of this lost old has-been, Prideaux, she would probably tell him so sooner or later. Sharon might mock her, but infantile did seem the only possible description of a middle-aged student.

And the sun roared down and drummed on the taut plastic as she squatted there day after day in her fake Levi's and Chinese Cartier watch, assiduous, intent. When ducks waddled up to the edge of the trench and roosters crowed and sparrows twittered in the lone palm's dusty fronds it was easy to imagine herself out in the coutryside. Only when she cocked an ear beyond the immediate sounds did the city's encircling drone seep in like the rising groundwater which heralds an incoming tide. From nearby shanties came a cacophony of radios and TVs: bursts of machine-gunning and women's crying or else polyglot soap powder and fast food ads. The sounds of an alien culture energetically lived. How alien it was could be judged by the people who came to squat on the edge of the trench for hours on end, just watching her and her colleagues at work as if ordinary concepts like time and boredom had no meaning. Most alien of all was a hideously disfigured creature dressed in ragged army surplus gear who was once suddenly there when she raised her head. He had watched in silence, swaying slightly with illness, before saying in shockingly clear

American English: 'I guess you've reached the future' before drifting unsteadily away, leaving her speechless with horror and pity and surprise with a little ochre skull between her hands. It was all a lot more interesting than South Kensington, as she put it in a letter to her mother. She still couldn't quite believe that her father had actually died here, breathing this air, beneath this sun, surrounded by these people.

24

IMMEDIATELY AFTER his first visit to San Clemente Vic Agusan had written a think-piece calculated to induce an unwise editor to reconsider before ever again sending a crack crime reporter out on a wild goose chase. Entitled 'Ghosts and Gunsmoke', it pointed out that these vampire stories so beloved by the popular press always had a function and were always timely. Apparitions were actually smoking guns, but when fired in squatter areas seething with secret politics only the locals knew for certain who had pulled the trigger and where the bullet had gone. Now and again (as in the case of Tondo's Miriam Defensor *manananggal* in the run-up to the 1992 election) it might be supposed there was more at stake than purely local politics. That had surely been an instance of a well-established popular genre being used as a tactic in an adroit strategy of character assassination. Miriam was dead; long live Brenda. . . This current vampire in San Clemente (Vic's column concluded) will be just as deliberate an invention but it is most unlikely that we, the general public, will ever discover its true purpose. Irreducible and ubiquitous though they are, squatter areas exist in a social limbo, drifting in and out of visibility according to the kind of scrutiny they are subjected to. Town planners and visiting popes can't see them at all, while the police can often see nothing else. It is hardly surprising that most readers will be entirely ignorant of a subculture and its currents in a festering barrio hidden behind cement block walls.

This article was favourably received as a departure from his usual chronicle of police misdoings and Vic had enjoyed a day of praise which even included an editorial mention in the *Philippine Daily Inquirer* referring to his column as 'a welcome breath of Agusanity'. If he had allowed a certain lordliness to creep into his style it was no doubt just a way of publicly chiding his editor, Bong. Since the story was so obviously a three-day wonder, he implied, just one more *ningas kugon* in a regular yearly tally, let's all hurry up and get back to the nits and the grits of serious investigative reporting.

His repentance started immediately. As if part of a shrewd plot to ruin his reputation the news of San Clemente's archaeological find had broken almost at once, followed not long afterwards by that of Eddie Tugos's horrid and sensational end. Vic did not enjoy being chastened by events and set about trying to repair the damage. Bong, meanwhile, lost no opportunity to point out to *Chronicle* staffers how necessary it was for an editor to have a 'nose' for the right story. Had he not been convinced all along that there was something in San Clemente's vampire worthy of Vic Agusan's talents even when both had seemed proved wrong? However, Vic still held a trump card, as he well knew. The case had now turned into a homicide investigation and he had just formed a working alliance with the Inspector in charge.

'If it wasn't personal before, it damn well is now,' Dingca said. 'I knew poor old Eddie and he surely didn't deserve an end like that.'

They were standing at the spot where the body had been found. Someone had planted a tiny rough cross in white wood at the foot of the wall. On it was written in pencil 'Edsel Tugos' and the date.

'Let's keep moving,' Vic urged. 'I don't want to be seen with you too much. The other reporters'll think we've got an exclusive deal going.'

Accordingly they moved through the gap in the wall and walked up to the railings at the rear of the Tan mausoleum.

'Yeah, and I've got some NBI plodder from Homicide due any moment now with more autopsy details. I'm against giving those guys the slightest chance to horn in. This is my case and my patch. If they find me goofing off with the Press instead of going around San Clemente with a magnifying glass and clue bag they'll start leaning on my OIC.'

'What details?'

'He didn't say much on the phone. Something about fragments of phosphor bronze in Eddie's mouth. Off the nozzle of that damn machine, I suppose. So okay, the NBI can sleuth that one if it likes:

they've got the lab. facilities. But I'm after the person who gave the order to suck Eddie's guts out,' he glanced up at the funerary blockhouse, 'and I don't care if she is listening.'

'You're still convinced, then?'

'Any money you like, son.'

'Cop's nose? I've already had my journalist's nose put out of joint over this slum.'

'Don't worry, it'll set straight before this is finished. You getting anywhere with the real estate angle?'

'I've run the usual checks. Town Hall, municipal offices. It's a shitheap, this whole area. As far as I can see it's a mass of tiny plots and holding companies right out to Kalookan. You'd need months to sort it out, go through the records, track it all down. There was an outfit called Trax Tracts holding this land in escrow in the middle of 1989. That's the date it was filed. The directors all sound like Pinoys and they all give business addresses in Oceanside, California. I don't know if they're still the nominal holders because those particular files are being quote *updated*, close quote.'

'I'm not too hot on this legal stuff, conveyancing or whatever the hell it is,' admitted Dingca.

'Escrow's just a third party deal, right? A third party holds the deeds of the land until certain conditions are met and it's transferred to the grantee.'

'So what's the name on the deeds?'

'Something called Varvispo.'

'Sounds like it's got to do with bishops,' said Dingca intelligently. 'It's probably run by the Vatican.'

'Just don't let your conspiracy theories run away with you, that's all. The dread hand of the Vatican's one of my colleagues' favourite explanations for just about everything from leaking condoms to the election results. As of this moment Varvispo's about number four hundred and eighteen on the list of companies being investigated as probable beneficiaries of Marcos behest loans. It's alleged to have got two hundred and seven million unsecured pesos of the taxpayer's money. Since the committee's reached company number forty-six after five weeks' beavering through the evidence and the amnesty deadline's about three weeks away, I'd say Varvispo's home and dry. Our problem is that the committee has subpoenaed all the files. I'm working on a way of getting some leverage on a couple of guys but it'll take time. There's still an alternative route. I've got a *pipit* in the BIR who usually sings if I give his balls a good squeeze. He might be able to get us a list of Varvispo's directors though I doubt if he'll give us any financial details.'

Dingca shot Vic an appreciative glance for a co-conspirator who has access to a completely new range of informants. 'The Bureau of Internal Revenue's a good source,' he said. 'They wouldn't let a cop like me in to buy a Coke in the commissary. We really need that link.'

'Don't worry. One way or another we'll get it.'

This turned out to be true, but in so painless a fashion it was anticlimactic. About ten days after Eddie's burial when the first San Clementeños, their nerves shaken, were dismantling their shacks and moving elsewhere of their own accord, an urbane lawyer named Melvin Go-Bustamante emerged from nowhere and made a statement. He was doing so, he said, to clear up any doubts about the Philippine Heritage Museum's legal right to declare its dig a National Site. Speaking for the land's future titleholders, Tango Muniplex Corporation, he said there was absolutely no conflict of interest and no question of the Museum's right to excavate.

'I can say that TMC actively welcomes this wonderful discovery,' said Melvin Go-Bustamante, his rimless spectacles flashing. The lights behind him rendered his filmy white *barong Tagalog* transparent, revealing a trim athletic figure which suggested a Harvard Law School Class-of-'Seventy-nine hardness. 'In the past such finds have often been unpopular with landowners, who saw them as infringing their right to exploit their property's potential to the full. TMC dissociates itself completely from this attitude, believing that an archaeological site of this significance and rarity is an asset in its own right as well as a priceless part of the nation's history. As of this moment the Corporation is applying for planning permits to develop historic San Clemente as a Heritage Mall with a complex of stores and offices landscaped around the dig itself, which will be permanently protected by an air-conditioned atrium. TMC believes that people in this part of the city will welcome such a development. It will, of course, attract tourism with all the spin-off benefits to the local economy and employment, thus opening up to greater prosperity an area which is sorely in need of redevelopment. Once completed, such a project can only have a long overdue beneficial effect on the locality's health standards. And finally, it will help restore peace and tranquillity to the adjacent cemeteries which at present are subject to constant vandalism, theft, and impropriety of every kind.'

'Unbelievable,' said Dingca to Vic that evening. They had arranged a meeting on neutral territory, a dimly-lit bar off Pedro Gil where neither had been before.

'Or not.'

'I meant unbelievable the amount of trouble he's saved us. Tango, eh? Tan-Go. Go-Bustamante.'

'Oh, all that,' agreed Vic dismissively. 'Sure. But you've still got a murder to pin on old Lettie and I don't think we're very much closer. If by any chance you find the murder weapon I presume you don't imagine her prints'll be conveniently on the button? You don't think they held Eddie down and shoved the nozzle in his mouth and then the Queen of Shabu clicked the switch and watched his lights and tripes go flashing up the tube in a red froth? I'm worrying about you, Rio. It's beginning to smell of a one-man vendetta. At some point it's going to stop being another job and turn into Dingca's Last Case, isn't it?'

The policeman drank some beer in silence, then poked a thick forefinger into the bowl of salted peanuts and stirred them vacantly. 'I guess it might,' he said at last. 'No point in going on until I have a heart attack. I've earned a few years of not having to wade through it all day, every day. Do a little business, maybe, practise my bowling, talk to my family.'

'You don't talk to them now?'

'Only out of the side of my mouth, my old lady says. That's no way to live, is it? How much longer has any of us got?'

'In your case not long at all if you're staking everything on tangling with the Tans. Why don't you let it go, Rio? She's just one. Think how many more there are out there.'

'I want her,' he only murmured. 'I want her for Babs and I want her for Eddie and I want her for being the Queen of Shabu and very soon I shall want her for what she's about to do to eight or nine hundred people up there in the barrio, good people like Eddie's wife and kids.'

'Who's Babs?' asked Vic acutely.

'Just someone. Seeing you're so full of good advice, what are *you* planning to do? I guess it's just another Vic Agusan story, right?'

'More or less. Generally speaking, I don't go gunning for people because I haven't got a gun and I'm not in this business to work off grudges. My job's to dig up the evidence, present it and say "There you are, guys. Go gettem." I'm not paid to make citizen's arrests. In this game you've got to keep a sense of proportion. Some of your cop colleagues have got real nasty habits, Rio, but we know the tone's always set from above, right? It's the fat cats and the pols who're ultimately to blame for the system, not a police force grotesquely underpaid and mismanaged. Look closely and you'll see my tears. Now, in this particular case I'll tell you the line I'm going to take. I shall exploit the whole business of squatters being evicted because it raises basic human rights issues. That sort of thing's increasingly effective. Good tearjerking stuff. Nobody feels comfortable with pictures of wretched people being chivvied around a city's waste lots with crying kiddies and pathetic bundles of belongings. Second, if we can dig out a piece of evidence that finally and definitely links Lettie Tan with this TMC outfit, that's about the best we can hope for. At which point I can turn around and write furious columns saying "How the hell's the so-called Queen of Shabu being allowed to redevelop San Clemente in the name of the national heritage and general moral uplift? What kind of crooked deal is this? Is a woman of her reputation to be allowed to push eight hundred and umpty-seven of our most defenceless citizens out onto the streets without anyone in authority raising a squeak in their defence?" Blah, blah. Then we can hint darkly that there's already been a murder which looks as though it was committed deliberately to play on people's fears and encourage them to leave before it came to eviction orders and bailiffs. Really, that was quite subtle. If you were a squatter you could treat it either as a crude worldly threat or as a nasty message from the powers of darkness. How do you resist all that if you're dirt-poor and have no legal right to the land you're squatting on? I think whatever happens we can at least make the whole thing a major story. The San Clem Affair. Plenty of human interest, follow-ups with people like your friend Mrs Tugos once they're thrown out on the streets, all that good stuff. Don't forget we've also got a tame Senator on the scene displaying the wiliness of his species. He's just waiting to see which way the wind blows before taking sides. I've got his number. I think I'll start pushing him tomorrow on the human rights angle. We can make Vicente look pretty sleazy if he comes down on the side of antique pots and business deals while standing right there in the middle of a lot of evicted families. Yeah, I like that,' Vic said as to himself and jotted a few words on a paper napkin. 'Plus have you noticed he seems to have something going with one of those American girls? British, American, whatever the hell she is? Hot little chick, I'd say, that one.' He made another note. 'Vicente might be vulnerable there. . . All this we can do, Rio. But to tie up the whole bag of tricks good and tight, to make it a real winner, we still need to show the merciless hand of our Lettie personally pulling the levers in the background.'

Two weeks later that hand was revealed, but by an agency bizarre beyond anyone's imagining. It was certainly not the result of sleuthing by either Dingca or Agusan, although once again Vic had spent whole days going through company files, running checks, leaning on his sources, calling loans. By the end he knew beyond doubt that the San Clemente project was another part of Lettie Tan's empire-building but he couldn't have proved it on paper. Dingca was equally getting nowhere with the murder. He wasn't surprised. This was definitely one of those cases which broke downwards if at all. Eddie's killers would be shopped as bargaining chips if ever a big name got its ass in a crack. Certainly nobody in the barrio was talking. San Clemente was sullen, the people closed and resentful. There were already gaps among the houses where families had left, taking with them whatever parts of their shanties were worth salvaging. The little heaps of rusty sheeting and crumbling cement blocks which remained had scarcely been pawed over. Scrap timber was taken for firewood but little else. No-one in San Clemente was in the mood for building.

At Rio's own urging Nanang Pipa had been one of those to leave. She and the family were squeezing in temporarily with distant relatives in Baclaran. He was both sorry and relieved to see them go and arranged for Benhur Daldal to guard the house while they made several trips to fetch away their possessions, including two sewing machines and many bolts of material which didn't belong to the co-operative. Boyong and some friends had already begun to dismantle the house as Pipa left it for the last time and stood for a moment outside, looking bleakly around her.

Why was it we never remembered how near at hand endings always were? she wondered yet again. Squatters in particular knew better than anyone that everything was temporary; yet in settled intervals came these cruel delusions of stability, of an orderly life that might have amounted to something, to a family raised above rathood. Hardly more than a month ago business was going well, Eddie was still Eddie, they were surrounded by friends and neighbours. And now. . . She looked at the plastic awnings billowing gently in the light breeze, at the strangers digging earnestly away in what had recently been a communal latrine. Well, St. Jude, she thought.

Dingca came over and produced a card which he handed her awkwardly. It had the station's address on one side and his home address on the other.

'It's not much, Pipa,' he said. 'But if ever, you know.'

'You're a man, Rio Dingca,' she told him. 'Which is more than can be said for some of the people in this barrio.' A tear fell from one lash onto her thumb. She tucked the card away. Both knew she would never use it but they also knew the offer was completely sincere at that moment. Alliances, too, were temporary.

'Don't just disappear, Pipa,' he urged her. 'We can't stop you going but there's a homicide case outstanding. As if you could forget.' He thought she looked beaten. It was hard to believe that this was the woman who'd so recently held a flourishing sewing business together and on sundry occasions had bossed her husband and his gang of layabouts into making themselves useful. 'We'll make somebody pay,' he said, nodding once.

'Don't throw your life away, Rio. It isn't worth it.' She walked away with Jinky beside her carrying a little pink suitcase on her head. Behind them came the screech of her son pulling nails.

Late that afternoon a bulldozer ground its way slowly up the cemetery approach road leaving two sets of parallel whitish scars in the tarmac. Its deep engine note faded somewhere up in the cemetery and presently the driver came walking back down, whistling. Bats Lapad, who was losing his terror of the supernatural and had ventured out with Judge and Billy as bodyguards to buy some gin, stopped him. The driver, a cheerful fellow, was from Maypajo, Navotas.

'Never mind where you live,' Bats told him sternly. 'What are you doing with that machine?'

'Just leaving it,' said the driver. 'We'll be starting work after the weekend. Redace Construction. They've got the contract to redevelop the back of the cemetery. Rough up there, isn't it? This the famous San Clemente, then? Got me crucifix,' he said with a grin, hauling a collection of amulets and a cross out of the neck of his T-shirt and jingling them under Bats's nose. 'How're the vampires these days? Still flapping, are they?'

'You don't believe in that crap, do you?' Bats asked him scornfully. 'Listen, are you sure it's the cemetery you're working on?'

'Course I'm sure. There's four hectares up there need grading, starting Monday. Why, what else would I be doing?'

'Oh, nothing,' said Bats, and he and the others turned away. 'Just wondered.' The gin was to celebrate tonight's surprise visit from brother Gringo, who had taken an unofficial break in his Melody cab to see Nanang Pipa and was upset to find her already gone, her house partially dismantled.

The cemetery police confirmed the driver's account. Yet the yellow bulldozer parked innocently up there on the hill radiated a threat which suddenly permeated the barrio. It was as if the Clementeños sniffed on the strengthening breeze its diesel and hydraulic scents, just as an old buffalo trucked into town from the paddies first gets wind of the slaughterer's yard behind the marketplace. For days now Vic Agusan and Rio Dingca had both felt a rising tension. Small, vicious fights broke out from time to time which could be heard but not witnessed. Raised voices came from somewhere in the warren of huts and there would be fresh blood soaking into a path's dried, sculpted mud. Both Vic and Rio had called respectively for reinforcements, convinced it would be a professional mistake to leave San Clemente uncovered and neither wishing to spend the whole of every day in such meagre surroundings, still less do overtime there. On this evening of the bulldozer's arrival they both chanced to be present, having dropped in separately before calling it a day and going home to their families. Just as they were leaving, fire broke out high up in the barrio. It was already nearly dark and the flames could be seen leaping above the rooftops, fanned by the east wind blowing down from the cemetery. Screams and shouts brought people running out of their homes beating saucepan lids. Dingca hurried over the Kapilang to call the fire brigade from one of the shops with a phone. Vic, who had been walking to collect the Hersheymobile, grabbed a camera as he passed it and trotted up into the cemetery and around to the Tan mausoleum to the point nearest the outbreak.

The fire spread with great speed among the closely packed and mainly wooden buildings. The gap in the boundary wall already showed as a ragged V of brilliant orange when he reached it, while the nearest flames were high enough to scorch the fringes of the overhanging trees. As Vic stood, panting, a swag of greenery above him burst into fire with a sound of Chinese crackers and drops of gum began falling around him sputtering tiny blue flames. He retreated, but the rest of the tree seemed reluctant to burn and once the leaves on that side were gone the fire in it went out. San Clemente, by contrast, might have been purposely designed for rapid combustion. From his vantage point he could see dark areas of the upper barrio still untouched by fire, but even as he watched isolated tufts of flame sprang up there as well, as if working their way along zigzag powder trails at ground level.

The leaping glow now lit the underside of a thickening cloud of smoke rolling away above the barrio, carrying with it whirligigs of sparks. The noise was a roar of blazing gases mixed with sharp detonations as metal sheeting warped and sprang from its nails. Now and then came a loud thump as though a bottle of kerosene had exploded and for an instant a tighter crimson bud opened its individual blossom above the general rags and tatters of incandescence. The noise masked the approach of half a dozen men who suddenly appeared near Vic at a staggering trot, carrying between them an assortment of containers slopping water. They were shirtless, and as they approached the gap in the wall to unsling their yokes and hurl their few gallons into the inferno inside, their chests and stomachs glinted with sweat as if oiled for desperate hand-to-hand combat. Then, exhausted by despair as much as by their long uphill run, they dropped their containers and fell back to where Vic stood.

'It's gone,' one said, his eyes glittering with reflected orange.

'Is everyone out?'

'Who knows? You just make sure your own family's out and hope everyone else has done the same.'

'Time was,' said another, 'when there was water right here. We had a standpipe before that *intsik* vampire took it away, curse her.'

Above the noise came the faint sound of a fire truck's siren. The nearest shanties had begun to collapse, leaning silhouettes which gave a sudden lurch and fell leaving an arbitrary post or two still upright and twirling flame.

'Anyone know how it started?'

'Enemy action,' said a voice. They turned to see a fantastical figure propped like a crazed saint on a tall stick. The firelit face was monstrous, a splitting melon glistening beneath a thatch of string and leaves. 'It's always enemy action. Specially when it's on your own side.' Vic would have pursued this theory with a reporter's zeal but at that moment there came from far behind them an unexpected sound. Somewhere up in the black depths of the cemetery a heavy engine had started up. 'Oy, *pare!*' said the figure as to himself in much satisfaction. 'I was just giving a lesson to young Gringo up there. How to hot-wire a bulldozer. There's nothing useful a Ranger doesn't know.'

From the sound's direction lights appeared intermittently in the darkness, the headlamps of a vehicle moving ponderously through trees and behind tombs, shining and vanishing and growing steadily brighter. The engine note had climbed to a screaming roar as though driven to the limit. It drew closer, and it was soon apparent that it was not keeping strictly to the roadway but cutting erratic corners and taking short cuts between the dainty sepulchres, ploughing through undergrowth and clipping plinths as it came.

'He'll be fine with a bit of practice,' observed the melon-headed man as a small tree toppled and smashed a tomb's coping. There was a distant shower of bricks. 'Help if he lowered the scoop, though. He could see where he was going.'

As if the bulldozer's driver had heard him and had at last hit on the right lever to pull, the huge shovel dropped with a crash and the engine snorted as it began to heap a breaker of soil and brushwood which curved up the blade, its crest crumbling and piling. Then the shovel lifted a fraction, the earth fell back, the machine bumped over the wave it had raised and swung to face the watchers. Even now Vic had no idea what its arrival meant. It was only twenty yards away when he made out the driver for the first time. Perched on top of the lumbering tons of metal the wiry figure was tiny and its antics were in strange contrast to the vehicle's impassive progress. A victim of some demonic possession, maybe, it kept leaping up and taking both hands off the levers to wave them as fists above its head. Even above the bellowing of the twelve massive cylinders the sound reached Vic of wild laughter and shouted words, exultant, wilful, even merry. And thus for a total of only about thirty seconds Gringo's path crossed that of Vic Agusan, memorably, lit face-on by the flames of San Clemente's destruction which the concave steel mirror of the bulldozer's blade flashed defiantly back. And Vic with a reporter's instinct shot Gringo *flack-flack-flack* for a series of pictures destined to immortalise them both. Only when the towering machine had drawn almost level did he at last recognise a cold intention behind this joyride. He saw the standing Gringo utter a great whoop and drop both fists to the right-hand brake for a final course correction. The bulldozer twitched its rump and slewed obediently. Vic believed he caught the shouted words 'Okay, Eddie-boy! Death to the Chinese!' as it ran the last few downhill metres and ploughed full-tilt into the ornate façade of the Tan mausoleum.

Beneath the wedding cake stucco there was evidently concrete and steel, for the impact flung the driver forward, hands grasping at the cab stays. The protesting engine was slowed almost to stalling point, an exclamation of black fumes jetting from the exhaust stack, until something in the building gave. In the lurid glow Vic saw the whole tomb shiver and suddenly craze all over before bursting to pieces, a cascade of pale masonry pouring down over the machine's cage-work and momentarily hiding it from view. An immense cloud of dust puffed out and whirled up among the still-glowing twigs of the tree overhead. From deep inside the ruin there was muffled growling and movement and then the bulldozer came wallowing out on the other side, canted steeply over. It gave a lurch and righted itself, chunks of mortar pouring off its flanks. Somehow Gringo was still on his feet at the controls but had fallen silent. Thick dust covered him from head to foot so that he had turned white. Like a plaster ghost, making no effort to save himself, he rode the machine down the slope, through the cement block wall and on into the blazing heart of San Clemente. The watchers saw him outlined against the fire, a suddenly black figure atop a black machine, heroic and transfigured at the instant of his immolation. Then he writhed briefly and sank. The bulldozer's shovel fell as the hydraulic pipes burnt through and the machine swerved a little before stalling at last. Soon afterwards the fuel tanks split and gallons of blazing diesel inflated a gorgeous canopy of gold and crimson and silver, a billowing caparison of great splendour which finally settled as a shimmering tapestry spread at the feet of an undecipherable icon.

'Way to go, Gringo,' said the figure softly in English from the shadows. 'Way to go, boy.'

Turning again, Vic saw the man sketch a salute with the stump of his right hand. 'Who the hell are you?' he asked. 'And who the hell was *that*?'

'Me?' said the figure, still in English. 'God knows. What I am, man, is *short*.'

'Short.'

'Damn short, now. You a journalist? Yeah, well, if you want a scoop you'll take an old eavesdropper's advice and have a good look at that mess there. I'm betting the late Gringo's left you a present.' The stump indicated the heap of rubble that had been the Tan family's pride. 'You might even find the Queen's crown jewels.'

Vic moved forward curiously to peer at it. Slabs of collapsed wall were slanted precariously around a central hole of unknown depth, evidently some kind of cellar into which one of the bulldozer's tracks had broken. Steps could be seen leading down, their topmost edges pulverised and scored. Had it not been for them, he realised, the machine would have dropped straight through the floor. He stared down but nothing was visible; the dying fires of San Clemente as well as this Gringo's leaping pyre shed too much ambient light. He glanced around for the crazy melon-head leaning on his staff but he had gone, swallowed up among the dark trees beyond the glare. Slightly shocked, Vic walked back along the road. His face felt baked and brickish after staring for so long into the fire; the night air was almost cold on his cheeks. Reaching his car he took a flashlight from beneath the driver's seat. At the bottom of the road a small group of police was gathered near a fire truck. At their feet a canvas hose snaked into the burning barrio from a hydrant across the Kapilang. Even at this distance he recognised Dingca's tall figure and walked on down. Rio was filthy, his face and arms streaked with charcoal. A handkerchief was wrapped around one hand.

'Do we have a casualty toll?' Vic asked him.

'Not so far. Not high, though. Too early for folks to be asleep. Herrera's a definite *dedbol*, though.'

'Who's Herrera?'

'Sort of a parish priest. One brave man. He went in to get some kids out of a house and it collapsed on him. Turned out the kids were safe all along. Who in hell was that on the 'dozer? Did he get off?'

'Didn't even try. I was watching. He rode it the whole way.'

'Who was it?'

'Someone up there called him Gringo.'

'*Susmaryosep*. Bats Lapad's brother,' Dingca explained to his colleagues. 'Yeah, that stunt had old Gringo written all over it. What was the big idea?'

'Let's go and see,' said Vic. 'He's trashed Lettie's tomb. I've got a flashlight here and my journalist's nose is twitching.'

Dingca and a couple of other officers began walking up with him, implying there wasn't much they could do down there among the pitiful knots of people who stood in silence watching their homes burn. When Vic glanced back he had a brief view, possible only because the intervening shanties had already collapsed, of the palm tree still standing there, its tall crown intact above the flames. He was just in time to see the first holes melt in the plastic awnings tethered to it. Slowly they tore like sheets of dough and fell in drooping strands into the excavation below.

When they reached the mausoleum Dingca shook his head. 'Old Gringo did this?' There was real affection and admiration in his voice.

'He sure did. Laughing like a crazy.' Vic shone the flashlight into the depths. The plumbing had burst and a split pipe was gushing. An inch or two of black water already danced on the cellar floor, but it was not that which held the men's attention. Among the objects their curious gaze began to separate from the general rubble was an industrial vacuum pump on wheels suitable for sucking blockages out of drains, and stacks of cartons through whose torn sides innumerable plastic packs of what might have been sugar were slowly slipping into the water. There was a long silence and then Dingca turned and held out a boardlike palm which the journalist took. Rio's eyes glistened in the firelight. His expression was that of a man who can at last say goodbye to a career.

'In short, bingo,' said Vic. *Flack-flack-flack.*

25

WHEN WRITTEN UP later, polished into readability and coherence, fieldwork often takes on the broad outlines of a narrative. It is a strange kind of narrative, though: one in which the story-line is little more than the setting itself, with all the interest centred in closely studied details. In this it somewhat resembles pornography. Its protagonists have no character but stand as representatives of their species and gender and age-group. It is a view of things which tends naturally towards the freeze-frame. In the resultant thesis the thick listing of social customs, habits and beliefs gives a curious impression. Nobody could say it was wrong, precisely, but neither is it right. It excludes all possibility of the insignificant, of thin, listless days which pass unrecordably and without revelation of any sort. On days like that people simply come and go under fierce blue skies, doing the acts of the basic human animal with a remarkable lack of ethnicity. They carry things, prod pigs with sticks, laugh, snooze in the shade, gather firewood. In the tropic light it is not obvious to what extent custom might underlie such immemorial activities. It can feel a gratuitous Western contrivance to draw up lists of who may carry what, note that some peoples are vehemently pigless, theorise about humour, correlate the siesta with latitude, consider the effects of deforestation. To be sceptical about such procedures won't do at all for academic purposes, of course. Home is where activities are neutral; abroad is where they are full of significance and hidden meaning. Days of fieldwork when nothing much seems to happen and one might just as well be at home are not permitted to surface in the written version. They are simply boiled away as the stew of information simmers and grows ever more concentrated. In this way the conscientious anthropologist may aspire to produce a society's stock cube version.

Well before San Clemente's destruction Prideaux knew he was not a conscientious anthropologist. Over the months his conviction had grown that it was impossible to say anything very useful about another society or, indeed, about anybody at all. He remembered the awful rows with Jessie which had so often pretended to centre around some semantic nicety. He remembered also the bleak insight that even as he searched scrupulously for the right nuance he was actually taking pains to conceal what he meant, though he didn't necessarily know what that was. We were dreamers, blanks to ourselves. And if we were blanks to ourselves how could another person be any clearer? If it became impossible to understand one's own wife, what serious chance was there of understanding a culture whose cradle tongue one didn't speak? It was beyond absurdity. In a moment of nearly exuberant glumness Prideaux toyed once more with the notion of changing the subject of his thesis. A new title suggested itself: *Determined Mistranslation. The Myth of Intercultural Understanding and the Fiction of Interpersonal Communication*. In this mood he warmed to the whole idea of communication as radically undesirable. The daily tons of newsprint, the torrent of words broadcast into the ether and down telephone lines, the yak and bluster of it all: finally it lost meaning and became mere noise. Of what use were endless documentaries when what was really needed was *silence*? International silence, that was the ideal. And he thought he might have glimpsed his private future, wandering restlessly in search of the last place on earth without television reception.

When not quite in this mood he thought it worthwhile to go about asking people what they understood by words like 'corruption' and 'nepotism' which were used by Filipinos themselves about their society but not always with the same import. That young English archaeologist, Ysabella, had clearly not taken this seriously at all, but on his slight acquaintance with her Prideaux was not much surprised. She had struck him as a sort of upper-class airhead, a dilettante prepared to poke around at bits of skull and porcelain for as long as was diverting. (' "Corruption"?' she said. 'Here? Define it? I give up'.) He wished she wasn't British. In any case she didn't seem theoretically inclined and evidently felt no necessity to be thoughtful about a word like 'corruption'. Yet the issue remained. It was, he saw, all part of the problem anthropology had with vocabulary: the use of one culture's words to describe another. All the resonances were wrong. To take a single example, he couldn't see how it was possible to address Filipino social dynamics in either large or small matters without an understanding of the *padrino* system, of the *amo*s who commanded loyalties and respect often seemingly beyond any personal qualities of leadership or patronage. It could be enough merely to have the right surname, the right historical links with sources of influence. In this way distant power rang faintly on in otherwise hollow people.

Such things could easily transcend, or at least muddy, the law itself, especially in complex transactions which a Westerner might crudely sum up as 'bribery'. Senator Vicente had leaned against the palm tree by the dig and given the example of a motorist running over and killing a child. If the driver behaved properly he would apologise profoundly and come to an agreement, usually financial, with the family who would acknowledge that nothing he or anyone else could do would bring their child back. The money was an assurance that the words were not empty gesturing. If it was all done in the correct spirit the idea of further criminal prosecution became almost improper because the grievance between the parties was already settled as well as could ever be. The payment was thus an earnest of contrition and not a bribe to stop a prosecution, as it would be seen in the West.

Now Prideaux recalled something that Fr. Herrera had said over lunch in the New Era restaurant some months ago, for it also concerned matters of terminology.

'We Filipinos listen respectfully when Westerners speak,' he had said in between sucking noisily at the stony flutes of crab's legs. 'That's what we've been brought up to do. But the educated among us ought to become damned impatient when we hear that cliché about "Eastern fatalism" used to describe our passivity, our apparent high tolerance of injustice and pain. It's as much a failure of English vocabulary as it is of perception. You use the same word "fatalism" to describe the pious Arab's *inshallah* approach to life as you do our own completely different attitude. If people here strike you as passive it's not because they think they're seeing the inevitability of God's handiwork but

273

because they know they're enmeshed in a social system they dare not fight. They don't believe their goat dies because God directly wills it but because the médicine they need is away in town, costs money they can't spare and comes with instructions they can't read. They're frightened to spend cash on the fare, to borrow from friends and risk being hoodwinked into buying the wrong expensive drug by an unscrupulous shopkeeper, and of being humiliated into the bargain. Better to keep one's head down and try a folk remedy. If that doesn't work, write the animal off and hope it won't happen again. That's not fatalism, that's common sense. Even more so if your problem's with injustice of any kind: a dispute with a *padrino*, a quarrel with a landlord, discovering your daughter failed her exam because she didn't slip the teacher enough money. Mess about with stuff like that and all the world's grief'll drop on your head. What has that to do with fatalism? Anybody can deal with Fate; it's the hand of man which beats you to a pulp.'

This line, Prideaux thought, would have made for an interesting luncheon had Fr. Herrera sat down with Thomas Hardy. Now poor Herrera was dead and who could tell to what extent he would have seen his own demise as fated by his principles or decreed by the hand of man? The precise cause of the fire would never be known but no-one doubted it had been deliberately started. Lettie Tan's interests had been too perfectly served for her not to be suspected. All further shilly-shallying and delay had been neatly cut short. San Clemente's shanties were destroyed and would not be rebuilt; the problem was solved in an hour. Aside from the bodies of Herrera and Gringo a third corpse had been found, its charred wrists and ankles loosely circled with wire. It was female and a steel tooth identified it as having been Ligaya Rosales. Revenge? Justice? Or Lettie Tan ridding herself of a stooge who no longer had any function? It was opaque, and would no doubt remain so. Herrera's death, by contrast, was transparently heroic, ironic and revelatory. The man's heroism had been exemplary and therein lay the irony for Prideaux. He could vividly recall Herrera lecturing him and saying that living well was the best revenge. Dying well was no doubt better still, and a priest could hardly have died better than in trying to rescue his lambs, even if the lambs turned out to have been saved already. And the revelation was the news that they hadn't been his lambs after all, it wasn't his flock, Herrera was not even a qualified shepherd. 'Father' Herrera was not even ordained, wasn't a priest at all, had been Fr. Bernabe's long-term companion and lover. Stranger still, everybody but Prideaux himself had known.

Once again this society had undermined a definition until it collapsed. In a land of fake policemen, bogus officials and impostors of every kind, a false priest had been revealed by an act of sacrifice as a true Christian. The social complexities were boundless; anthropology was like trying to dig mist with a spade. The subtexts of human behaviour were unfathomable and always would be: strange loves and compassions lost in the cracks, messages which disaster sometimes brought to light but which otherwise remained forever concealed. The ashes of San Clemente gave nothing back. To stand at the bottom of the hill and look up to the singed trees marking the boundary of the Chinese cemetery was to see the charred stubble of a battlefield, something erased for whose erasure conflicting reasons might be advanced (including race war) but whose actual agency could be left simply as *flames*. Prideaux had wandered the crunchy ruins. The souks and alleys were no more. Sheets of corrugated iron lay bent and pinkened by fire among pegs of charcoal which broke and tinkled like a soft black allotrope of ice. A community was demolished, its roots torn up, the bonds broken, members scattered.

'It won't be forgotten, though, will it?' he wanted to ask Crispa who was helping Sharon and her colleagues pull long strands of partly-burnt plastic sheeting out of the hole where they had fallen like melted cheese. 'It's all filed away? It wasn't casual to them just because they were squatters? They'll remember it, surely?'

Such stupid questions could hardly be asked. A far better question to pose himself as he walked the ruins of the wasted ville was how it was he had managed yet again to miss the war, to be forced to reconstruct it and its rich stew of nostalgias from the later accounts of eyewitnesses. John Prideaux, the man with the gift of absence, the man on whose headstone might be carved the epitaph '*In Absentia*'. This unfailing instinct – or unconscious determination – to be consistently in the wrong place at the right time was the one attribute which disqualified him from ever making a success of journalism, anthropology or, for all he knew, marriage. Was it Fate which had inexorably led him to try all three? Or only passivity? He had no idea.

He spent a further month in Manila tracking down the story which had already tracked him down. He talked to Rio Dingca at his home in San Pedro, Laguna, and spent a beery evening with him and his *barkadas* at the Bowl-o-Rama, even briefly meeting the Big Girl herself, Patti Gonzales. Patti, who struck him as dull and demure, had evidently changed her mind about a career in the police. She was working as a checkout girl in the local Mercury drugstore. Dingca drove him back to the city next morning, sedately and rather silently, keeping to the middle lane all the way. When they arrived he confessed to having been nervous about highway holduppers since he felt acutely responsible for his foreign guest. One of their techniques, he explained, was to lurk on the shoulder and pounce on likely targets in the slow lane. Prideaux thought he was also regretting having been rather too frank and unbuttoned the night before.

From him Prideaux obtained Mrs Tugos's address. He went looking for her and found her, to her evident amazement, embarrassment, and probably distress. She was living in a room the size of a large cupboard in Baclaran where the whole family slept on cartons of their own belongings. He went twice and had gone away with at least one of his questions answered. She, at any rate, would never forget San Clemente. Her husband's death would have been reason enough; but she spoke of the barrio's destruction as if it had marked the beginning of her own, the end of her resilience. Already she looked older. She seemed not to notice the stench of sewage brewing up somewhere nearby. The electric fan tied to a nail on the low ceiling only intensified it since there was no window anywhere in the plywood box which marked Nanang Pipa's new horizons.

He saw little more of Vic Agusan since the journalist had asked to be sent for a month to Davao to follow up some incredible police racket or other. His breaking of the Lettie Tan story, complete with dramatic pictures, had been masterly. She, of course, was no nearer arrest than she had ever been despite the discovery of the best part of eighty kilos of *shabu* in her family's mausoleum as well as a murder weapon, to wit, one pump. Her lawyer described the evidence as 'flimsy and inferential'. His defence was to maintain that the Tans were victims of vandals, San Clementeños with a grudge who had broken into the tomb and planted the evidence just as they had once broken in and stolen the water. This was brazen enough to content the already satisfied. Vic's pertinent question – as to how squatters too poor even to buy the rice they needed had come by eighty kilos of an upmarket illegal drug – was unanswerable and so went unanswered. One day after a long, long delay it would doubtless all come to court and be thrown out for lack of evidence. Where was the case now that San Clemente's inhabitants had vanished? On the other hand Vic's own advocacy in a week's worth of vividly sarcastic columns had queered Lettie's pitch to the extent that nobody in government was prepared to risk public crucifixion by allowing Tango Muniplex Corp. to go through with its project. The matter was put on hold until some other, less tainted, corporation came forward to do the right thing by the nation's heritage. The latest news was that Senator Benigno Vicente was forming a consortium.

Prideaux heard this from Ysabella Bastiaan, with whom in his last month a certain familiarity did develop, if not quite actual friendship. She turned out to be considerably less defensive than he, not to say merrily indiscreet.

'I don't care,' she told him. 'Go and write it all up, I should. Even the stuff about my father. What are you waiting for?'

It is take-off that Prideaux, finally embarked, is waiting for, leafing through a scrawled notebook, restless with departure. He finds something he hardly remembers having jotted down after an evening with the Agusans. When Imelda Marcos first returned from US exile in November 1991 (he reads) she stayed in a $2000-a-day suite in one of her own 'edifices', the Philippine Plaza Hotel. It stands by the sea on the same spit of reclaimed land as another of her projects, the infamous Manila Film Center. Like that building, and for the same reasons of over-rapid construction skimped to meet a whimsical deadline, the Plaza was born amid a rubble of collapsed scaffolding and a half-dry ballroom ceiling which fell on sleeping workmen. As with the Film Center a strict security blackout was imposed so that even today it remains unknown how many died there. As they go about their daily tasks, it is said, the hotel's electricians and maintenance men are always finding inside mouldings and ductings, behind panels and false ceilings, little pencilled crosses, a name and a date written by workmen to commemorate a lost friend.

The aircraft shudders as it trundles backwards across the concrete apron.

Before his death the fake priest Herrera had lamented the demise of Judgement Day when (in the John Prideaux version) everyone who had ever lived would be forcibly shown the definitive documentary which God had shot of their lives. 'Here,' the divine Five-in-One (researcher, scriptwriter, producer, director and cameraman) would say, 'these are my allegations, this the evidence. Your confession? Thank you.' Another cell door slams. But because it was all so unerring, so predictable and repetitive, such justice was tainted by the stench of a show trial. What, the whole of humanity, every last one of us? Until guilt loses all moral meaning and becomes simply another attribute like warm-blooded, mammalian, air-breathing, bipedal?

The aircraft turns heavily at the runway's end. It is carrying Prideaux and Prideaux's fieldwork notes to see his daughter in a grey climate half the earth away. A tornado of burnt kerosene roars off across the scorched perimeter, over huts and smallholdings and plots where people raise ducks, dismantle batteries and bodies. Soon he is able to look down and see the plane's scudding ghost beneath, diminishing by the second, its flaps withdrawing and profile tilting.

Somewhere on the long journey westwards as they flee the dawn he ignores the imperious stewardess who insists the window blind be pulled down for the comfort and convenience of passengers who may wish to watch the in-flight movie. He opens it surreptitiously. The cold silver wing is polished by the moon and he is drawn into the invisible planet's majestic emptiness, into lame thoughts confronting stars and the calm rush of altitude. Time is erased until he becomes aware that hours have passed and the moon has gone and a wing as dark as Ulysses' sail is afloat on a milky bath. From the window's extreme rearward edge he sees the first pale strip of day fall across earth's sill as if a vast door were slowly opening in Asia. The planet is round, there is no day or night; we cannot say where we have been or when.

It should break open, he thinks. On the day when the sun is peremptorily stopped and the clouds freeze where they stand and the winds hold their breath and the great voice or trumpet or whatever it is rings around the troposphere, it should all break open. Down to the last bank vault of armoured steel buried in the heart of a Swiss mountain it should break open, and what would be listed with especial care would be the millions upon millions of secret inscriptions everywhere brought to light, fallen down the cracks and scribbled behind the world's wainscoting: the hurried memorials of those given names by anonymous friends. And then the sun should be released and the clouds given a push and the winds told to blow again among the silent ruins. These inscriptions would join the rest already incised in bronze and marble and cement. Beneath this weather they would stand for a while: the scattered fragments of an immense collective love which once sparkled and gleamed and never quite focused itself.